THE BODY IN THE CASTLE WELL

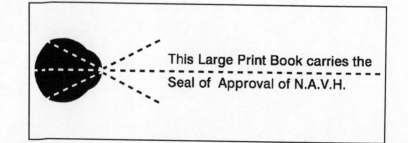

This Large Print Book carries the
Seal of Approval of N.A.V.H.

A BRUNO, CHIEF OF POLICE NOVEL

THE BODY IN THE CASTLE WELL

MARTIN WALKER

THORNDIKE PRESS
A part of Gale, a Cengage Company

Farmington Hills, Mich • San Francisco • New York • Waterville, Maine
Meriden, Conn • Mason, Ohio • Chicago

**LIBRARY OF CONGRESS CIP DATA ON FILE.
CATALOGUING IN PUBLICATION FOR THIS BOOK
IS AVAILABLE FROM THE LIBRARY OF CONGRESS**

ISBN-13: 978-1-4328-6658-7 (hardcover alk. paper)

Published in 2019 by arrangement with Alfred A. Knopf, an imprint of The Knopf Doubleday Publishing Group, a division of Penguin Random House LLC

Printed in Mexico
1 2 3 4 5 6 7 23 22 21 20 19

In memory of Josephine Baker,
the Black Pearl and Resistance heroine

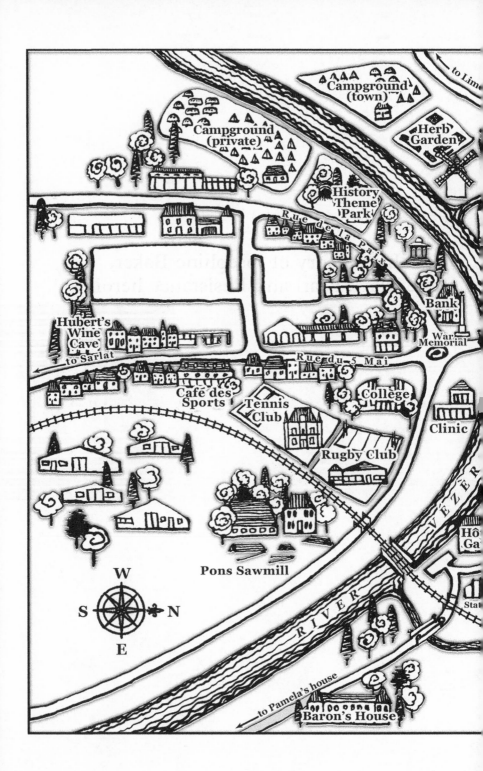

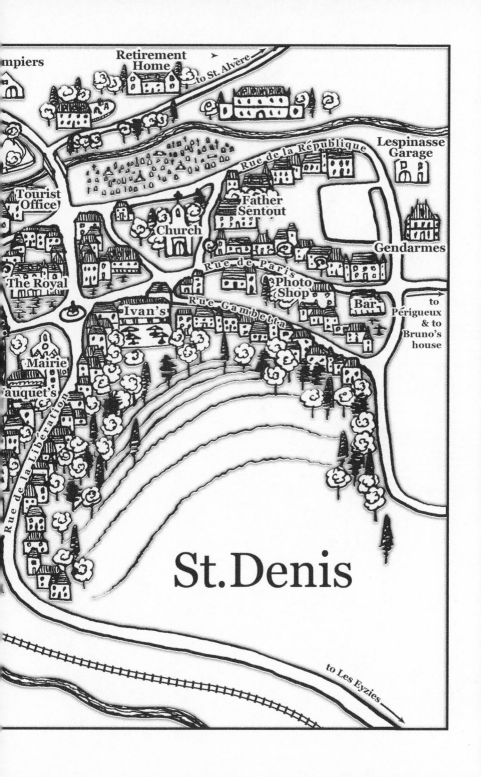

CHAPTER 1

Bruno was still glowing from his morning canter at Pamela's riding school as he sipped his first coffee of the day at Fauquet's café and scanned the headlines of *Sud Ouest*. Balzac, his basset hound, was waiting patiently at Bruno's feet for his customary portion of croissant when the dog felt rather than heard the vibration of the phone at his master's belt. Balzac slumped glumly onto his belly and lowered his head onto his paws, knowing that this meant his morning treat was likely to be delayed.

"Bonjour, Florence," said Bruno after checking the caller's number on the screen. "This is an early call. Everything okay with the children?"

"We're fine, Bruno, but I'm worried about Claudia. She was really sick last night at a lecture in the castle in Limeuil, but there was no answer when I called just now to see how she was. And her landlady says she never came home."

Along with several of his friends, Bruno had instantly liked and befriended Claudia, an American student from Yale University working on her doctorate in art history and studying with an eminent local scholar. "Maybe she met a boyfriend," he suggested.

"I don't think there is one, at least not in France. Bruno, she really wasn't in good shape last night, dizzy and white as a sheet. I wanted to walk her home, but she said she'd be fine, just needed to lie down and rest."

"Did you check with the *urgences*?"

"No, I have to get the kids to the *maternelle*."

"Okay, I'll take care of it."

Bruno ended the call, knowing instantly that he wouldn't be able to perform his usual morning role, managing the traffic at the town's nursery school. He called the local fire station — the *pompiers* also served as the local emergency medical service — to learn that they had not been called out the previous evening. Then he phoned the town medical clinic. They also reported nothing unusual. He paid for his coffee and croissant and climbed the steps to the *mairie* to tell the mayor's secretary he would be

10

going to Limeuil. Back downstairs, he installed Balzac in the passenger seat of his van and set off past the fire station, past the town vineyard and up the long sloping hill that led to the top of one of the prettiest villages in France, and one of the oldest.

Bruno knew there had been an Iron Age hill fort on this site before Julius Caesar's Roman legions stormed it. They then built their own fortification to command the strategic hilltop that overlooked the point at which the River Vézère flowed into the larger Dordogne. What Florence had called the castle was a modern addition, little more than a century old and erected by a former doctor of the sultan of Morocco who had retired to his native Périgord. He bought the hilltop, ruins of the old medieval fortress and all, and commissioned a new house designed, Bruno assumed, to look like one of the French Foreign Legion forts in the Moroccan desert. The original white stucco of the walls and battlements was now gray, and the building held the gift shop, café and offices of the team of young gardeners who tended the sprawling hilltop for the town and had turned it into a popular tourist attraction. The castle's large rooms with their view over the two river valleys were now the local cultural center, hosting lectures, liter-

11

ary events and occasional art exhibitions.

The previous evening there had been a lecture by a local historian on the archaeology of Limeuil, which Bruno would normally have attended but for the weekly meeting of St. Denis's town council. It had been a routine session, and Bruno's only role had been to report on the progress of the plans he'd drafted for the free concerts, night markets and fireworks displays that were mounted for the summer tourist season. This role as impresario for civic entertainments gave Bruno huge pleasure. The session had ended early, and after a brief *vin d'honneur* for a veteran council member who was retiring, Bruno and the mayor had taken him for a convivial dinner at Ivan's bistro. Bruno had been home and in bed with the latest issue of *Archéologie* magazine soon after ten and asleep by ten-thirty, and looking forward to riding his horse, Hector, at seven the next morning.

Limeuil's hilltop parking lot was already full, the cars bearing license plates from Holland, England and Germany, although it was April, still early in the season for tourists. Bruno left his van outside the nearby restaurant and followed Balzac up the twisting path into the gardens, not yet open to the public, and asked for David, the bearded young man who ran the place. Bruno found him weeding in an area called the apothecary's garden, full of medicinal plants and herbs. As always, whatever the weather, David was wearing ancient leather shorts and several layers of T-shirts, and he and Balzac greeted each other like old friends.

"I haven't seen anything unusual this morning, but I'll ask the others," David said when Bruno explained the reason for his visit. "Do you want us to organize a search for her?"

Bruno nodded. "I'm told she was feeling dizzy, so she may have fainted. Were any of the staff at the lecture, someone who saw her leave?"

"I'll call a staff meeting, organize a search," David said, pulling out the kind of whistle used by sports referees. "We've got a school group coming in forty minutes, but we should have enough time."

He blew three quick blasts, and from various spreads of foliage, past the giant sequoia tree and water garden and around the heap of stones that were all that remained of the medieval tower, two young men and two young women emerged with pruning shears or spades in their hands. Each put out a forearm for Bruno to shake rather than offer a muddied hand and then bent down to

13

greet Balzac as David explained the reason for his visit.

"I was at the lecture," said Félicité, whom Bruno remembered from his tennis class when she'd been a schoolgirl. "I know Claudia and I remember she got up, said something to Florence and left very discreetly not long after the speaker dimmed the lights to start screening slides. Florence said later that Claudia wasn't feeling well."

"What time would that have been?" Bruno asked.

"We were all there by seven, and I think the lecture started by seven-fifteen. The part with the slides came a few minutes later," Félicité said. "There was fruit punch before the talk began. Maybe it disagreed with her."

The search began while Bruno, Balzac at his heels, went down the hill to Madame Darrail's house, where Claudia had rented a room. Built on a slope so that the entrance from the street seemed to lead into a small, single-story building, the house once entered revealed a much larger home. Stairs led to a second, lower floor down the slope of the hill, with the rooftop of another house below. The widow of a man who had run the local canoe-rental center, Madame Darrail was a dour woman of about sixty with a trim build, dark brown eyes, a sallow skin and iron-gray hair. She spent her summers in the kiosk by the river, taking bookings and money and handing out life jackets while her son, Dominic, ran the canoe business. A native of Limeuil, she was accustomed to walking up and down the steep slopes three or four times a day at a pace that left Bruno breathless. This morning, he felt himself lucky to find her at home.

"Ah, Bruno, you must have got my message," she began, a worried expression on her face that eased into a faint smile as she noticed Balzac and bent down to pet him. "About the American girl."

"There was no message on my mobile," he replied. "If you called the landline, I'll get it later when I get back to the office. But that's why I'm here. Florence from the *collège* was worried about Claudia and called my mobile. She said she'd spoken to you."

"I last saw Claudia around six yesterday when she got back from work. She'd said she was going out to a lecture, so I'd made some soup and put out some cheese for her, but she said she couldn't eat a thing. She had cramps, you know, so I made her some thyme tea and she took a pill and felt well enough to go to the lecture. I had an early night and didn't realize until this morning

15

when Florence called that Claudia hadn't been back. Her bed wasn't slept in."

"Can I see her room?" Bruno asked. "Was it unusual for her not to come back? Did she have a boyfriend?"

"First time I've known her not to have slept here, not that she's been with me long. She never spoke of any boyfriend here. But I think there was somebody in America. She used to have his photo sitting next to her bed, but I don't see it now."

"And do you know what pills she was taking?"

Madame Darrail shrugged. "There are some medications in her room."

Madame Darrail lived on the top floor of the house, with a kitchen and dining room to one side of the entrance hall and a living room and her bedroom on the other. Along the hall was a series of framed photographs, one that seemed to be of her wedding, another of an attractive city of white buildings climbing a hillside from a port, which Bruno thought might be Algiers. The next two were of military men, both in parachutists' uniforms and wearing red berets. One was a stranger, but the other was the unmistakable General Jacques Massu, his tough features slashed by a brisk mustache. He had been a loyal Gaullist from 1940 until

16

his death.

"Massu," Bruno said, pausing and looking at the photo.

"A great soldier," she said. Bruno nodded, although he thought Massu's temporary victory in suppressing the Algerian independence fighters had been a classic example of a military victory that was also a strategic defeat. Massu's use of torture had hardened Algerian resistance while at the same time eroding support in France for the war.

"And the other soldier?" he asked.

"My late father. I left Algeria as a baby with our whole family."

Bruno nodded again. Something like a million French settlers had left around the time that de Gaulle had negotiated Algerian independence. Madame Darrail moved on to a staircase at the far end of the hall. It led to a lower floor that contained two bedrooms and a separate bathroom. Each bedroom had its own sink.

Claudia's room had a magnificent view over the Dordogne Valley, and a narrow balcony with just enough room for two folding chairs. The room held a double bed that was neatly made, a wardrobe, a chest of drawers, a mirror and a small table and chair. A backpack was under the table, which was piled high with books on art. A smaller pile of paperbacks stood on a bedside table. Postcards of what looked like paintings by old masters were scotch-taped to every wall.

Tucked into the gap between the mirror and its wooden frame were family photos. Two of them featured a young girl of about nine or ten years old standing between two people, probably her parents. The man was tall, bald and had his hands on the little girl's shoulders. The woman was plump with fine eyes and a cheerful expression, as if she smiled a lot. Behind them was a large garden with steps leading to an imposing terrace and mansion. Despite its old-fashioned style, the building looked new. Another photo, which seemed to have been taken five or six years later, showed the same girl with the same tall man with a third person clearly cut out of the photo.

On a glass shelf above the sink a cosmetics case was open, and Bruno saw two pharmacist's containers of orange plastic and an opened packet of an extra-strength painkiller, an ibuprofen. One container came from a pharmacy in New York City, another from a store in New Haven, Connecticut. Bruno did not recognize the names of the drugs but scribbled down the details.

In the wastepaper basket beneath the sink were some used paper tissues and a photo that had been torn in half. Bruno donned a pair of evidence gloves and put the two halves of the photo together. It showed the head and shoulders of a handsome young man holding a tennis racket, with a handwritten note in English that said, "All my love to darling Claudia. Ever yours, Jack."

"All her clothes are here as you can see. Lovely dresses, Armani and Chanel, but most of the time she seemed to wear jeans and sweatshirts," said Madame Darrail, opening the wardrobe. "And her lovely silk nightie is under the pillow. It's a Lanvin. When she's not out at work she's working in here on that little computer of hers." She looked around quickly and then said in a tone of surprise, "Funny, she must have taken it with her."

Bruno was leafing through the papers on the desk, mostly printouts or photocopies of what seemed like articles in various learned journals in French, English and Italian about the French Renaissance and the art and sculpture of the period. There were piles of handwritten notes on similar topics, each headed by the name of a specific museum or château. A sketch pad contained a series of pencil drawings of Limeuil and its two bridges over the rivers, of the castle and its gardens and several quick sketches of the market in St. Denis. They were so good that Bruno recognized two of the people. Claudia was a talented artist. Alongside all the papers was an iPhone, still plugged into its charger, lying on top of a blue American passport.

Bruno picked up the passport and read that Claudia Ursula Muller had been born in Philadelphia and had a French student visa that was valid for two more years. She was twenty-five years old. Her passport showed she had visited Thailand, Singapore and Britain during the past year. In the phone's case was a small flap that opened to reveal two credit cards. One was a platinum Visa card and the other a black card issued by Muller Investment Trust, of which Bruno had never heard. As Bruno touched the phone screen it came alive with the photo of a white cat staring impassively at the camera. Below it a keyboard of numbers seemed to require him to enter an access code to open the phone, so he put it back down.

"Did she have a handbag or a purse?" he asked.

"I never saw a handbag; she always had that computer case. When she paid the rent, it came from a man's wallet that she kept in her back pocket. She paid me with a check on a French bank account, but I forget which one. Claudia kept some other papers in the wallet, like her driver's license and student card, that sort of thing, but there's no sign of it here."

"Who's staying in the second bedroom?" Bruno asked, wondering if the landlady had made a point of prying into her lodgers' affairs.

"One of the girls who works in the gardens up the hill, Félicité. She and Claudia are friendly. What do you think has happened to the girl?"

"She may have been more ill than you thought and collapsed somewhere. The gardeners are looking. But if you'll let Balzac sniff her nightie, he might be able to track her down."

CHAPTER 2

Bruno and his dog went back up the hill, Balzac trotting ahead and sniffing with that purposeful air he had when on a scent. He went straight up the winding track and into the lecture room at the castle, still full of chairs from the previous evening. He sniffed around the room and then went out again through a French window and up the slope past a giant sequoia tree to the waist-high stone wall that circled the hilltop. Farther along the wall Bruno saw that two of the gardeners were already leaning perilously over it, scanning the steep slope below.

Bruno looked over the edge to the long drop, maybe five or six meters to the first of the houses, a little more than that to the eighteenth-century building the locals called the new château. There were fissures in the rock, and Bruno thought he'd have little difficulty in climbing it and imagined most of the young boys in the village would have done so. To the right there was a long terrace of grass and another stone wall beneath it. Bruno saw no sign of Claudia, and now Balzac was moving on. The hound trotted along the wall to the viewing point that looked down over the two valleys and then along the avenue of chestnut trees and up to the stone well that had for centuries guaranteed the castle's water supply.

On Bruno's previous visits the well had been sealed and covered, with a stout chain and padlock securing the wooden lid. Now the well was a work site, flimsily roped off with a single strand of red-and-white tape and a warning sign but with no lid to seal it. Bruno knew that was a serious safety violation. Scaffolding had been erected around and above the well, a cement mixer stood alongside, and a rope ladder hung from the scaffold. David was perched on a couple of wooden planks that spanned the scaffold, gripping the rope ladder and peering down into the depths.

"Was this well left like this overnight, or are the workmen here somewhere already?" Bruno asked, pulling out his phone to take a photo to record the scene. It would be time-dated automatically.

"The workmen didn't show up today so far," David replied. "We're having to repoint the joints in the wall because it hasn't been done for decades, maybe for a century. I can't see anything much. Do you have a flashlight?"

"Just a little one, a key light," Bruno said, handing over a bunch of keys. "Don't drop it, or I'll never get back into my van or my house. Have you got a better one here somewhere?"

"Yours is no good, too feeble," said David, tossing back Bruno's keys. He swung down onto the stone wall and vaulted down to the ground, then darted off, shouting over his shoulder that he had a powerful spotlight back in the castle.

Bruno climbed up and looked into the well. He saw nothing except some ropes and the descending rope ladder. He could just about imagine that a disoriented young woman, feeling dizzy, might stumble through the red-and-white tape. But the wall was well over a meter in height. She would have had to climb it, which seemed unlikely.

Then he heard a faint catlike sound, and at once Balzac barked in the way he did to draw Bruno's attention. Bruno peered down and then heard it again, a meowing. It sounded far away. Bruno clambered onto the rope ladder and went down a few steps to escape the glare and let his eyes adjust to the well's darkness. Then he heard the cat again, sounding very weak.

Bruno climbed back up the rope ladder. The workmen had used a flimsy platform, just three stout planks screwed together with a bolt at each corner through which ropes coming down from the scaffolding had been secured. A pulley system with a brake allowed it to be raised and lowered. The platform was covered in small lumps of dried cement, and it did not look very stable. When David returned, Bruno asked him to keep a tight grip on the ropes while Bruno found out how to lower the thing.

He went down as far as the rope ladder reached, perhaps five or six meters. With one hand gripping the rope ladder and the other holding one of the platform supports, he peered over the edge, seeing only a deep blackness below. He was suddenly aware that it was markedly colder inside the well. A strange smell seemed to seep from the depths, something he recognized from far inside the very deepest caves. It was not unpleasant but somehow alien and lifeless, as though the damp limestone was so ancient it was expressing something of the fossils of which it had been formed.

A shout came from above, and then something was coming down slowly toward him, a beam of light that was swinging one way and then another, and then dazzling him when it flashed across his face. David was lowering a large spotlight on yet another rope. Bruno let go of the rope ladder, grabbed the light and shone the beam below. But as he shifted his weight, the platform began to swing, and he felt even less confident of his hold. He told himself to pause and think this through. Finally he took in his teeth the rope that held the spotlight, transferred his grip to the rope ladder and waited for the platform to stabilize. Bruno wondered how the workmen had ever managed in such perilous conditions to cement the joints between the stones of the well.

He managed to hook one leg around the rope ladder, and that seemed to keep the platform in place. Gingerly, trying to shift his weight as little as possible, he peered over the edge and shone the light down, hearing yet more meowing as he did so. At once he saw that the stone walls of the well went down only another two or three meters, below which it seemed to have been carved out of solid rock, or perhaps widened from some natural seam. The sides of the well narrowed unevenly, or perhaps that was just the perspective. Shining the light straight down was a mistake, sending up a shimmering, uneven reflection from the water far below.

Bruno pointed the light at the wall just above the waterline, and this allowed him a fleeting glimpse of a small cat, apparently sitting on the water. He adjusted the light and saw the animal was clinging desperately to something he could not identify. It was rounded, perhaps a log. He knew that people put logs in their swimming pools in winter to prevent them from freezing over. Maybe they used the same method in wells.

Bruno heard a shout and looked up at the narrow circle of sky, suddenly dazzled by the change in light and the way movement sent the platform twisting again. It took him a moment to make out the silhouette of a head and shoulders looking over the well's rim. The head seemed much farther away, although it could hardly be more than ten meters.

"Are you okay?" David called. "Do you see anything?"

"Will the rope ladder take your weight as well?" Bruno called up.

"There are usually two guys down there, one working on the platform, the other on the ladder," David shouted back, his voice strangely distorted. "Do you want me to come down?"

"I can see a trapped cat," Bruno called back. "Wait and I'll look again."

He looked down, less troubled by the swinging of the platform now that he had the rope ladder wrapped around his left arm. Then he felt a sudden shoot of pain in one knee as he shifted his weight onto one of the small lumps of dried cement the workmen had left on the platform. He put the rope with the light back between his teeth, used his free hand to remove the lump, and then thinking it might give him a sense of depth he dropped it into the well. Mentally he counted, a-thousand-and-one, a-thousand-and-two, and he was about to begin a-thousand-and-three when he heard a faint splash.

He remembered from grade school that an object dropping in gravity fell at just over nine meters per second. That meant nine meters in the first second and then eighteen in the next one and twenty-seven in the third. *Mon Dieu,* he thought, this could go down thirty meters.

He took the rope from his teeth and shone the light down the walls. Keeping the beam above the water, he aimed all around the rough sides of the rock. It gave just enough light for him to see the cat moving, backward and forward and now circling. Whatever surface the cat stood on, it seemed unstable, bobbing in the water as the cat moved. It was certainly no log. As that thought penetrated, Bruno felt a sudden foreboding of what else it might be.

He moved the light's beam a little and told himself to look for certain predictable shapes. What he'd thought was a log could be a leg. Perhaps there was the curve of a rump and a bobbing head. It was hard to be sure. Was he being carried away by his own imagination? He should try to get lower to be sure. He tried adjusting the pulley, but it refused to allow the platform to descend farther.

"How far down does this rope ladder go?" he called up.

"It's only fifteen meters, but I have a second one. I could attach it. What can you see?"

"I'm coming up," said Bruno, deciding that it would be foolish to try going down farther with a makeshift rope ladder. This was a job for professionals with the proper equipment.

Bruno put the rope holding the light back between his teeth and began to climb the rope ladder, his legs feeling strained from kneeling and his hands almost numb from gripping the various ropes. The rope ladder began twisting and swaying as he climbed, bouncing against one wall and then swinging back against the ropes holding the work platform below. Bruno paused, catching his breath and taking one leg at a time from the ladder to ease the strain in his thigh muscles. He gritted his teeth and climbed again, one step at a time. Maybe three steps to a meter, he told himself, only thirty steps at most, and he must already have done more than half that.

He began to make out individual stones from the light coming in from above. He must be almost there. Five, four, three more steps and he saw that David was standing on the rim of the well, steadying the rope ladder with one hand while gripping the scaffolding with another.

"*Putain*, I don't want to do that again." Bruno panted as David helped him off the ladder and onto the stone rim. Bruno heard a whimpering sound from below and looked down to see Balzac wagging his tail at seeing his master reemerge from the depths. "But someone has to go down properly; I mean all the way," Bruno said, taking a deep breath of fresh air. "I think the cat may be standing on a body."

"A body?" David's voice rose an octave as he said the words. He looked aghast. "Christ, you don't think . . ."

Bruno was already calling the *pompiers* in St. Denis. Ahmed answered. He was one of the two professional firemen who managed the score or so of volunteers in the town's fire brigade. He was also qualified as a paramedic. Bruno explained that there might be a body as much as thirty meters down the well at Limeuil, over which scaffolding had already been erected. Could they help?

"Thirty meters?" exclaimed Ahmed. "We'll have to get one of the trucks up there with a winch, but, yes, if the truck can get there we can do it."

"You'll need four-wheel drive," said Bruno.

"No problem. Limeuil, you say. Give us fifteen minutes, maybe twenty. Any chance the body may be alive?"

"I doubt it, and I'm not even certain that it is a body, but a young woman has been missing since last night . . ." Bruno's voice trailed off.

"We're on our way," Ahmed said. The confidence in his voice was reassuring. "Do you want me to call the medical center?"

"I'll do that," said Bruno. "Even if she's

dead, we'll need a doctor here for the death certificate. One more thing: there's a cat down there, Ahmed, and it's definitely alive."

He ended the call and hit the speed-dial for Fabiola, his good friend and the doctor he most trusted. He got her voice mail, left a message asking for an urgent callback and then dialed the medical-center receptionist to find out if Fabiola was on call that day. She was with a walk-in patient, he was told. The receptionist promised to get Fabiola to call Bruno as soon as she was free. He turned back to David.

"The first thing you have to do is close the garden. I'm sorry about the school trip, but this now looks like the scene of a death that needs to be investigated. It might even turn out to be suspicious."

David's eyes widened, and he opened his mouth to protest, but Bruno simply ignored him and kept talking.

"Then I want you to make as complete a list as you can of everyone who was at the lecture last night and which staff you had here, particularly whoever locked up. I need to talk to all of them right away."

David nodded and pulled out a mobile phone.

Bruno then pondered whether he should

add that there could be serious ramifications for the town and its hilltop gardens if his suspicions turned out to be correct. He decided they deserved the warning. And he felt angry at the irresponsibility of the builders working on the well.

"You also might want to inform your mayor that the town could face legal proceedings for failing to secure a dangerous construction site."

Bruno held up a hand as David tried to interrupt and raised his voice to talk over his protests.

"I can't believe you were prepared to let schoolkids walk around these gardens with the well left wide open and scaffolding that made it easy to clamber up. The whole site was protected by nothing more than a flimsy bit of red-and-white tape." The more Bruno thought about it, the angrier he felt.

"I suppose the builders thought it was too much bother to dismantle the scaffolding every evening and replace the locked cover. I'd like their names and contract details and a copy of the estimate they must have given you before the work started. I want to see if they included a charge for securing the site."

"I'm not sure we have much paperwork," David replied. "The guy who's doing the job is a member of the town council. You know how it is in a village like this. It was pretty informal."

Bruno looked back at him impassively. "Then you'd better tell your mayor to take a very careful look at the town's insurance policy about injuries to third parties."

"*Merde,* Bruno, the outer gates were locked last night."

Bruno shook his head firmly. "Not while the lecture was taking place, they weren't. And if that's who I think it is down there, your builders and the town could be facing a charge of negligent homicide."

CHAPTER 3

As he waited for the *pompiers* to arrive,
Bruno thought back to his first meeting with
Claudia. It had been one of the days gov-
erned by the *cahier de surveillance,* the
logbook on suspect persons and activities
that was kept in every police station in
France. It was marked in the *cahier* as the
day of the expected return of one of the few
notorious citizens of St. Denis, a young man
who was being released that day from prison
after serving a ten-year sentence, with
another year added for taking part in a
prison riot.

The arrest and trial had taken place
sometime before Bruno had arrived in St.
Denis to take up the job as town policeman, but he knew about it. The case had
been all over the French media. Laurent
Darrignac had been a bright and enthusiastic youngster, son of a local farmer, who
had just graduated from a respected agricul-

tural college in Lorraine before returning to help his father and eventually take over the prosperous family farm. It was a fine property, some fifty hectares, which was big for the Périgord. They raised dairy cattle and veal on the slopes and had corn and sunflowers growing on a wide stretch of fertile and lucrative valley land, attracting generous subsidies from the European agricultural authorities.

On graduation day, Laurent and his classmates had gone out for a celebratory lunch, and since he had drunk the least he was asked by the others to drive back from the hilltop restaurant. It was late in the afternoon, the sun low enough to dazzle a driver. Rounding a bend while trying not to be distracted by his boisterous classmates who were passing around a bottle of cognac, Laurent had run into a group of Boy Scouts who were hiking up the side of the road. Three died from the impact, including the scoutmaster who led the way, and four were injured. One would never walk again.

The accident occurred at a time when the French National Assembly was debating a toughening of the laws against drunk driving to bring the legal limits for alcohol into line with those of other European countries. Opposition to the new law, which had come mainly from deputies elected by regions producing wine and spirits, melted away with the news of the disaster. But that did not deter the various pressure groups from intensifying their campaign. Laurent was in their sights as a symbol of the damage drunk drivers could do.

He had a fraction over 0.8 milligrams of alcohol in his blood, which at the time was the legal limit. The campaigners were trying to lower the limit to 0.5 milligrams, and Laurent became the focus of the crusade led by a pressure group called Mothers Against Drunk Drivers, which also brought a civil lawsuit against Laurent demanding compensation for the victims' families.

Under the law as it stood at the time, the deaths of the Boy Scouts meant that Laurent should have lost his license for five years, paid a heavy fine and faced a short prison sentence, most of it probably suspended while he remained on probation for two or three years. But public opinion being what it is, and politicians being who they are, and the opinion polls and the media being so overwhelmingly against the young man, the court had thrown the book at him. Laurent was given three sentences for manslaughter and four for grievous injury, all to run consecutively. Already facing the loss of the family farm from the private lawsuits, his parents decided they could not afford an appeal.

The farm was indeed lost soon afterward. Laurent's father shot himself. His mother died of breast cancer soon after the prison riot that saw Laurent's sentence extended. He was escorted to her funeral under police guard and in handcuffs, still so famous that the scene attracted TV cameras and a scrum of press. But by now, the public mood had shifted, and the media, ever capricious in their judgments and always looking for a new angle to revive an old story, claimed that the law had gone too far and that Laurent was as much a victim as a villain.

So on the day Bruno first met Claudia, Laurent was coming back to St. Denis, where Bernard Marty, one of the fellow students who had been in the car on the day of the fatal accident, had agreed to give Laurent a room at his own farm while Laurent tried to rebuild something of his life. Bernard was also the only one in the car who had regularly visited Laurent in prison.

Bruno wondered how rough a time Laurent had known in prison and how much resentment he might feel about the draconian nature of his punishment. He did not relish the prospect of an embittered and probably unemployable ex-convict in his village, but Bruno felt there might be some grounds for hope. The *cahier de surveillance* had noted that Laurent had been moved to an open prison in the Jura Mountains for his last three years, where he was allowed out to work each day on a nearby farm, returning to the prison each evening.

Bruno knew that Laurent had merely been given a rail warrant for a one-way ticket to the train station of St. Denis. Afraid of press coverage, Bernard Marty had told Bruno he thought he'd better not meet Laurent at the station. Bruno had understood. So it was Bruno who waited, in his own elderly Land Rover rather than his police van, for Laurent's train. He had arrived a few minutes early to see if any media had got wind of Laurent's return. He told himself that if Philippe Delaron, the local correspondent for *Sud Ouest,* was waiting with a camera, he'd have to think of a way to dissuade him. Laurent deserved a new start without the press dogging his footsteps. But the platform had been empty when the train pulled in.

The first person to descend had been a stranger, an attractive young woman in jeans and a leather jacket with a long scarf wound several times around her neck, making her ponytail of light brown hair jut out almost horizontally. She was carrying a rucksack and a crammed and evidently heavy laptop bag. She looked around the deserted station in bewilderment, noticed the sign for the local taxi service and pulled out a phone. At the last moment before the doors closed, a burly man in his thirties with thinning fair hair stepped down from the train and placed an old-fashioned suitcase without wheels on the platform. He looked around. Laurent had aged a bit, but Bruno recognized his face from the prison photo.

He had powerful shoulders and the thick wrists of a farmer, and he stood with his feet planted squarely on the ground as if he'd be hard to shift. On a rugby field, he'd be an opponent to take seriously or a team-mate one could count on. In the army, Bruno thought, he'd have been a natural sergeant.

A wintry sun was taking some of the chill from the January day, and Bruno was wearing a red jacket over his uniform shirt and trousers. He climbed out of his car with Balzac at his heels, approached Laurent, stretched out his hand to welcome him home and offered to drive him to the farm where he was expected.

"Thank you, but who are you?" Laurent asked as they shook hands, looking surprised but then giving a hesitant smile and looking down at Balzac. Bruno saw that Laurent was fit and in blooming health, his face weather beaten rather than suntanned, and his hand roughened by work.

"I'm Bruno Courrèges, the municipal policeman for St. Denis. I replaced Joe when he retired. I thought you might have seen enough of police vehicles and uniforms lately, so I came in my own car." He picked up Laurent's suitcase and turned to head for the Land Rover.

"Your dog? Does he hunt?" Laurent had crouched down, and Bruno saw with approval that he waited for Balzac to come to him.

"He comes along when I go hunting *bécasses* and he's usually helpful unless some other interesting scent captures his interest. That's the way with basset hounds."

"You know where we're going?" Laurent asked, still crouched down and now scratching Balzac's chest in that special place between the two front legs, one of the few spots the dog could not reach. Balzac looked ecstatic.

"Yes. I'll take you to Bernard Marty's farm."

"I thought Bernard would be here."

"Bernard and I discussed it and agreed

41

that it might be better for me to pick you up in case the media showed up."

Laurent gave a curt nod, rose and followed Bruno, glancing curiously at the young woman with the rucksack who had been the only other descending passenger. She was standing by the taxi sign, her phone to her ear, but looking disconsolate.

"Bonjour, mademoiselle," Bruno said, opening his jacket so she could see the police insignia above his shirt pocket. "I'm the town policeman, Bruno Courrèges. We only have one taxi here, and this is usually the day he takes people from the retirement home to the hospital in Périgueux for their treatments. He won't be back for a while. Can I help?"

"Bonjour, monsieur, and thank you," she said in good French but with a strong American accent. "I have an appointment with a Monsieur de Bourdeille at the Chartreuse de Miremont and don't know how else to get there."

"Then let me give you a lift; it's on my way. And please call me Bruno." He put out his hand for her to shake, and she took it, looking surprised when Bruno helped her out of her rucksack and installed it in the back alongside Laurent's suitcase. Bruno introduced her to Laurent, describing him as a local farmer, held the rear door open for her and gestured Laurent to sit in front.

She gave him a friendly grin as she settled into the back seat, the look of a young woman who expected events to turn out to her satisfaction. There was a self-assurance and an easiness of manner about her that reminded him of other American women he had met.

"I'm Claudia Muller, and thanks, this is really nice of you. Do you know the way to the *chartreuse*?"

"Of course, Monsieur de Bourdeille is well known in these parts. We don't have many eminent art historians and collectors like him."

"And a war hero, I was told," she said.

"He was shot and arrested for Resistance activities as a schoolboy," Bruno replied. "He's in a wheelchair but otherwise in good health for his age. What brings you to visit him?"

"I'm a graduate student in art history, working on the French Renaissance, and he's the expert, a legend in the field. My supervisor in Paris arranged for me to spend some time studying with him."

"Your French is excellent, but I thought I detected an American accent," said Bruno.

"Right you are. I'm at Yale University, in

the States, but right now I'm attached to the Sorbonne, and my French supervisor is one of the curators at the Louvre." She had leaned over the rear seat to reply. Then she shifted her gaze to ask Laurent what kind of farming he did.

"Mostly dairy cattle," he said, turning around in his seat to address her.

Bruno was struck by the thought that this was a man who would have had little contact with women for many years. Yet he seemed at ease in the presence of an attractive and friendly young woman and not overawed by her evident intelligence and qualifications.

"I'm also interested in falconry and I'm hoping to do more of that," Laurent added.

"That sounds interesting," she replied. "Have you flown birds yourself?"

"Yes, two of them," Laurent replied to Bruno's surprise. There had been nothing about that in the *cahier de surveillance*. "I flew a red-tailed hawk and a peregrine falcon, beautiful birds. That was at a specialist farm in the Jura."

"Did they only come back to you?"

"No, they were training birds, raised to be accustomed to different people, so long as they had food to offer. I got pretty close with the hawk and I'll miss him. I'm hoping to raise a bird of my own now if I can."

44

"I'd love to see that, if you'd let me," she said, and again Bruno noted her natural friendliness and ready enthusiasm. He wondered if he should warn her that it might be misinterpreted, especially by someone like Laurent, fresh out of prison. Bruno glanced at Laurent and noted a solidity about him, a man of self-control. And Laurent answered Claudia with cool courtesy.

"That would depend on how long you are here. It takes a lot of time, and I have to find a very young hawk and get the bird used to me."

"Let's stay in touch," Claudia said eagerly. "Here's my card with my French mobile number and here's one for you, too, Bruno."

She chatted on, about falconry, about farming, asking about the cattle in the fields they passed until she could tell the difference between a Blonde d'Aquitaine and a Limousin. She asked Bruno if he also came from a farming background.

"No, I was raised in Bergerac, which counts as a big city around here. But I keep some geese and chickens," he said.

"What about horses?" she asked. "Is there someplace around here I can go riding, like rent-a-horse?"

"There's a good local riding school, and

you can join the morning or evening exercise rides. It's not expensive." He rattled off Pamela's number from memory, and she put it into her mobile phone. "I go myself whenever I can."

"How far is it?" she asked. "I'm not planning on getting a car here."

"It's a ten-minute drive from St. Denis. Let me know when you want to try it, and I could pick you up." Bruno turned to Laurent and asked if he'd ever tried riding.

"I did a bit lately at the farm in the Jura, and I'd like to do more, but I'll have to see if I can afford it."

Bruno took the long hill up to Limeuil, slowing where he had to creep through the narrow stone archway at the top of the village. He then drove along the wooded ridge that led to the *chartreuse.* Occasional breaks in the trees offered magnificent views over the valley, and then he reached the stone gateway that opened to a wooded avenue of plane trees and a gravel drive that led as straight as an arrow to the *chartreuse.*

A long, low house of pillared stone, built in the early eighteenth century, it was only one story high except for a handsome square tower with a domed roof above the pillared entrance. French windows led from the tower room to a balcony on which someone was sitting. As he parked, Bruno saw it was an old man in a wheelchair, enjoying the sunshine of the late afternoon and apparently unaware of their approach. He might have been asleep. The sun glinted on a bottle of wine that stood on a table at his side.

"Why, it's beautiful, like a small château!" Claudia exclaimed. "And what a great garden. It must take a lot of work. And that looks like a vineyard over there. Do you think they make their own wine?"

"Indeed they do, and it's very drinkable," said Bruno, taking her rucksack and leading the way to the main entrance. Laurent clambered down from the Land Rover to shake her hand in farewell, and he wished her good luck with her research.

Madame Bonnet, the housekeeper for Monsieur de Bourdeille, opened the door with a welcoming smile as they approached. Bruno explained that there had been no taxi at the station, so he had given Claudia a lift.

"Let the young woman come up, Madame Bonnet," came an imperious voice from the balcony above. It did not sound like the voice of an old man, but Bruno knew that de Bourdeille had to be at least ninety. "Let's see what my colleagues at the Louvre have sent us."

"Don't worry about him, dear," said Madame Bonnet, ushering Claudia inside and shrugging apologetically at Bruno as she closed the door. "He likes to sound like an old bear, but deep inside he can be a kindly old soul."

"Bonjour, monsieur," Bruno called up to the balcony as he waved farewell to Claudia and returned to the car. The old man waved airily in return.

Bruno had then driven Laurent to Marty's farm and on the way learned that Laurent had become friendly with his prison governor after volunteering to work in the library and had been assigned to day release at a place where the farmer kept raptors as a hobby. Bruno had wanted to ask if it felt odd being a prisoner and letting the birds fly free only to return to the falconer's hand. It seemed uncomfortably close to Laurent's own situation, so Bruno held his tongue and listened to Laurent talk about the difference between various species and the way the females were usually larger than the males.

"Did you know that there's a château here in the Périgord where they practice falconry?" Bruno asked him.

"Château des Milandes," Laurent replied. "I know, I've got the chance of a job there.

The falconer is an old friend of the farmer who trained me, and he's offered to give me a trial. He's getting on in years and is looking for someone to work with him and maybe take over one day. I'd like that."

"How do you plan to get there?" Bruno asked. Laurent had no driving permit, which would take several weeks to obtain even if he passed the test, and no money for a car.

"My friend is lending me his little scooter," Laurent replied. "It's only fifty cc, so I won't need a permit. I won't go much above fifty kilometers an hour, but at least I'll be mobile. In the meantime, I can practice driving Bernard's car on the farm and then take the test."

When they arrived at Marty's farm, Bruno was asked to stay for a glass of wine. Thinking it might help ease the reunion of the two men, he accepted. But first Marty showed them around, proud of his herd of Blondes d'Aquitaine, and assuring Laurent that although originally prized for the quality of their beef and the ease the cows had in calving, which meant lower vet bills, they were now becoming much better at milk production than in the days when the two had been at agricultural college.

"The Blondes have been a godsend,"

Marty said, leaning on a gate that overlooked a field filled with grazing cattle. "Things have changed since we were studying. The big supermarkets have forced down the price of milk until you can barely cover the costs of production. But I'm getting nearly seven thousand kilos of milk per cow, and the beef I sell is where I get my profit. People like your dad who stuck with the Limousins have been in real trouble. Even the ones who invested in Holsteins have been squeezed by the vet bills."

Bruno enjoyed hearing farmers talk, even though more and more these days they spoke as if they farmed Brussels for the European subsidies rather than farmed the land.

"What's your percentage of calving problems?" Laurent asked.

"About two percent," said Marty. "They've got a high pelvis and the calves are slim in the shoulder, which helps explain it. I used to reckon on six or even eight percent with the Limousins, which is how the vets got so rich."

"Two percent?" Laurent shook his head in near disbelief, but he was smiling at his old friend. "Things have certainly changed since my day, but it's good to see you doing well, Bernard. And the cattle look in fine shape; you can be proud of them."

They were getting on easily, Bruno saw, so there was no need for him to stay, but Marty insisted and they walked back to the farmhouse. At their approach Marty's wife came out of the kitchen with a toddler in one hand and a baby in her arms. Another shock for Laurent, Bruno thought, a little nervous at the way the ex-prisoner would react at this new reminder of what his jail time had cost him. But apparently he knew all about Bernard's family, greeting the wife by name and taking the baby boy in his arms saying, "So this is little Laurent." And at that, Bruno knew it would be all right.

"I know it's been rough on you, these last few years," Bernard said as they sat around the kitchen table with a glass of his own wine in hand. "But you've taken good care of yourself, kept fit, stayed in touch with farming."

"It was a lot tougher on the parents of those boys who were killed than it ever was on me," Laurent said. "They lost everything, and I just lost a few years, but I learned a lot when I was inside, about life, about people. Convicts are much like everyone else. I even made a few friends."

"It reminds me a bit of my time in the army," said Bruno. "Your time was never your own and someone else was always in charge, but there were compensations, comradeship. It must have been much, much harder in prison, but I have to say I admire your attitude, Laurent. I'd better be going, and thanks for the wine, Bernard."

As Bruno rose to go, Laurent put a hand on his arm. "Thanks for picking me up, Bruno. You should know that I'm not bitter about what happened. I deserved it. But there was one thing that kept me going while I was in there. That new law on drunk driving they passed after I killed those kids, you know it worked? Deaths are down forty percent since then. That's over five thousand lives. That's how I can sleep at night. So don't worry about me."

"Good for you," Bruno said, leaving most of his wine undrunk as he left.

CHAPTER 4

French driving lessons were expensive, usually around twelve hundred euros for the minimum twenty hours of instruction required, and Laurent had almost no money. He opted for the cheap alternative: registering Bernard Marty as his supervising driver and undertaking to do a thousand kilometers driving with him within the next couple of months before taking his test. And his work on Bernard's farm in the mornings and evenings prevented him from joining the riding-school exercises. Claudia, however, became a frequent rider, getting her mother to FedEx her riding boots and clothes overnight from New York. She paid Madame Bonnet to borrow her car to get to and from the riding school.

It was clear from her first session that she was a fine horsewoman, and Bruno had no qualms in letting Claudia ride his own horse, Hector, when he was too busy. Félix, the stableboy, fell instantly in love with her, and Bruno noted how well she managed his teenage crush with a blend of kindness and courtesy. Pamela was cool with her at first, critical — in private — of someone who paid two thousand dollars for handmade Tucci riding boots from Italy. But Pamela warmed to Claudia when she saw how readily the American girl joined in with the rubbing down of the horses and helped muck out the stables.

Claudia soon struck up a friendship with Miranda, Pamela's partner in the riding school, who invited her to one of the Monday evening dinners that had become a regular event for Bruno's friends. Claudia volunteered to cook one evening and persuaded the local butcher to furnish her with a dozen enormous T-bone steaks, a cut little known in France. It was to be, she announced, an all-American meal, with fish chowder to begin, the steak and French fries, and chocolate brownies with ice cream for dessert. She even ordered a case of Stag's Leap, a California wine, from Hubert at the wine cave. Florence quickly established a bond when Claudia volunteered to give a talk on art history at the *collège* where Florence taught.

"She's obviously wealthy, but she certainly

makes every effort to be friendly," Pamela agreed one Monday evening when Claudia had made one of her regular trips back to Paris to see her supervisor at the Louvre. "I hope our local young men don't misinterpret her openness."

"Not once they've seen her playing tennis, they won't," Bruno had replied, recounting his own defeat at her hands.

Claudia seemed careful to avoid any local romantic entanglements, referring occasionally to her American boyfriend of long standing. She made a trip to see him in London, where he was working at a law firm, and there were weekends together in Paris, where she kept an apartment. Bruno knew she saw Laurent from time to time, visiting him and his hawks at Château des Milandes and at Marty's farm. She had them rocking with laughter one Monday evening when she recounted how Laurent had tried to teach her how to milk a cow.

Bruno invited them both to join him and the mayor one afternoon at SHAP, the Périgord history and archaeological society, for a lecture on medieval falconry in the region, which he thought would interest Laurent. He and Claudia had been impressed by the SHAP building, an imposing seventeenth-century *hôtel* that had belonged to a noble family, and even more by the lecture. It was given by one of the society's members, an antiquarian bookseller and amateur historian who showed a series of slides of medieval paintings and miniatures on the theme.

Bruno was fascinated to learn that falconry was introduced to Europe by the Huns after the fall of Rome and that it had spread quickly. The first slide the lecturer showed was an image from the Bayeux Tapestry showing King Harold of England hawking. The Arabs were the real masters of the sport, he explained, noting that the Koran states that meat caught by a trained hawk is considered clean for Muslims to eat. Scientific hawking began in Europe in the thirteenth century when King Frederick II of Hohenstaufen learned the sport when on Crusade and had the classic Arabic text on falconry by Moamyn translated into Latin. He then wrote his own version, *De Arte Venandi cum Avibus* — *The Art of Hunting with Birds* — which swiftly became popular in France. It was, claimed the lecturer, the first serious work of ornithology to appear in Europe since classical times, and even had the temerity to challenge some of Aristotle's writings on nature.

Bruno had always assumed it was a sport

for the aristocracy and was surprised to learn from the lecture that each social class had its own proper bird: an eagle for an emperor, a gyrfalcon for a king. Earls and bishops had the right to fly peregrine falcons, and knights and abbots had sakers. A lady would train a merlin, and a yeoman would fly a goshawk, while the humble parish priest had to make do with a sparrow hawk.

When the lecture ended, Claudia signed up on the spot to join the society and began poring over the index of its bulletins and publications. The mayor went off chatting with old friends while Bruno and Laurent joined the lecturer in the garden, where wine was being offered.

Bruno listened, fascinated, as the two men began discussing whether the bell should be attached to the two center tail feathers, as Laurent argued, or to the leg, as the lecturer preferred. The bell, Bruno learned, was to help locate the hawk in the field and also back at the farm to alert the falconer if his hawk was nervous or unsettled. The lecturer went on to claim that a peregrine-saker hybrid was his preferred bird, while Laurent defended his own redtail. In any event the two men soon agreed to go hawking together. Their conversation quickly became too technical for Bruno to follow, so he began chatting to other members he knew until people began to leave and it was time to prize Claudia away from the library.

"I can't tell you how pleased I am that you brought me here, Bruno," she said as they drove back to St. Denis in the mayor's car. She tried to invite them all to a local restaurant for dinner, but the mayor had a meeting, Laurent had to help Marty to bring in and milk the cows, and Bruno wanted to give Hector his evening ride. They all agreed to meet and dine another evening. Then she insisted that Laurent teach her how to tie a falconer's knot as they sat in the back of the car.

A few days later, he had seen Claudia shopping with Madame Bonnet in the market in St. Denis, greeted her and asked how her research was going. She said she was pleased and would be heading back to Paris the next day to see her supervisor and then hoped to return, since Monsieur de Bourdeille was being very helpful.

"He's taking his life in his hands and so is Madame Bonnet," Claudia said, laughing. "They've accepted my offer to cook them a farewell dinner tonight, since they've been so hospitable to me."

"What are you planning to cook?" Bruno

asked her.

"A little smoked trout to begin, then some calf liver in sage and butter with potatoes dauphinoise, because Madame Bonnet says that's Monsieur de Bourdeille's favorite. And then for dessert I'm making a *tarte Tatin.*"

"It sounds wonderful. I wish I were coming," he said, enjoying her enthusiasm. It was a quality so many Americans displayed, Bruno had found, a confidence that the world was essentially a welcoming place. Most French people thought of life as a challenge, only to be enjoyed with serious application.

"What about the wine?" he asked.

"Monsieur de Bourdeille says he wants to take care of that. You know he installed a private elevator so he can get down to his cellar? His doctor has told him to drink only one glass a day, so he insists he's delighted to have my company to help him enjoy it. I just wish I knew more about wine, but everything we've drunk has been heavenly. He made me take note of each bottle."

"Which was your favorite?"

"A 2005 Château Margaux from the Médoc."

"*Mon Dieu,* that's a wonderful wine, but it's way beyond my price range. You're very lucky." Bruno smiled at her. "When you get back here, we'll have to teach you about the more affordable wines from the Bergerac. That's something else for you to look forward to. And I recommend the croissants at Fauquet's café here, just behind the *mairie,* so let me invite you both to have some coffee and try one."

Claudia gave Bruno a wide smile, revealing her perfect American teeth, and said, "I'd love to, but we have to get the shopping done."

Madame Bonnet shook her head and gave Claudia an indulgent look. "I'm very partial to Fauquet's croissants, but I had a good breakfast, so off you go. I'll do the shopping and join you both at the café later."

Once they were installed on the terrace, Claudia said Bruno I should let her treat him, since he'd acted as her unpaid taxi when she arrived. Then before he could reply, she said, "Where's that lovely dog of yours?"

"He's in the stables with my horse, Hector. They've been friends since Balzac was a puppy. I suspect they assume each is a differently sized version of the other. I have a long drive today to see a colleague in Montignac, so I've left him there. Have you had a chance to see Lascaux yet or any of our other painted caves?"

"Yes, Monsieur de Bourdeille insisted that I should, and Madame Bonnet lets me use her car, so I was able to see Lascaux, Font de Gaume and Cap Blanc. It reminded me of what Picasso said, that in all these thousands of years we've learned nothing new about art beyond what they achieved. It's very humbling. The real surprise was Cap Blanc. I'd read about Lascaux, so I knew about the cave paintings, but those sculptures of the animals coming out of the rock were a real surprise."

The croissants came, and Claudia pronounced them far better than anything she'd had in Paris. Then she shifted the subject. "You mentioned that Monsieur de Bourdeille was in the Resistance as a schoolboy, but he didn't want to talk about it when I asked him, saying the memories were too painful. What did he do exactly?"

"He was arrested for painting Resistance symbols on a wall. But it's more a matter of when than of what he did," Bruno replied. "Bear in mind that when France fell in 1940, de Gaulle was widely seen as a madman for asking France to fight on. And don't forget that one and a half million French soldiers were in prisoner-of-war camps in Germany, hostages for French good behavior."

"That explains a lot about Vichy France," Claudia replied.

"Yes and no," said Bruno. "It's significant that when the British pulled out at Dunkerque, they took a hundred thousand French soldiers with them, but almost all of them chose to return to occupied France. Like most French people, they were convinced that Germany would win the war. Only about three thousand stayed with de Gaulle to fight on. But by 1945, almost everyone claimed to have been in the Resistance all along, a myth de Gaulle encouraged to try and heal the rifts in French society."

There was little resistance until June 1941, when Hitler invaded the Soviet Union, and France's Communist Party started to organize a clumsy underground. They began sabotage operations and occasional shootings of German officers, swiftly countered by the arrest and shooting of French hostages. Resistance gathered pace in 1943, when heavy German defeats at Stalingrad and in North Africa suggested they would lose the war. Fearing an Anglo-American invasion across the Mediterranean, Hitler dropped the pretense of a self-governing Vichy state and sent troops to occupy all of

France. He also ordered young Frenchmen to go and work in German factories. That was when the Maquis was born, as young men fled to the countryside to avoid the STO, the obligatory work service.

"The important thing about Bourdeille was that he was arrested as a schoolboy in May of 1942, when resistance was relatively rare and most people still thought Germany would win," Bruno went on. "There weren't even any German troops in Périgueux at the time. He was arrested by Vichy police and it's ironic that being in a French prison may have saved his life. Once German troops arrived here in the Périgord, newly captured *résistants* were sent to concentration camps, and few of them ever returned. Bourdeille was shot when he was arrested and never walked properly afterward. He used to get around on crutches, but he's been confined to a wheelchair for years."

Claudia nodded slowly. "So most French people just put up with the occupation and got on with their lives?"

"Yes. And the Germans looted the country as they occupied it, imposing food rationing on France to feed Germany, making our factories work for the German war effort. Many of those one and a half million French POWs had wives and children back in

France, who needed ration books to get food. Vichy had a special police force, the *milice,* a very nasty bunch who often demanded sexual favors in return for those books. It was a grim time. There's a village near here where the women kicked two *milice* men to death after the Liberation."

Madame Bonnet came into view, heading for the café until she was stopped by a friend and paused for a chat. Claudia leaned forward and spoke in a low voice. "Before she arrives, have you heard anything of how Bourdeille made his money? Was his family rich?"

"I don't know. Why do you ask?" Bruno replied. "I assumed he made it from dealing in paintings."

"He did, later, once he'd become rich. It's how he got started that interests me."

"Maybe he had family money," Bruno said. "Or perhaps he had a wealthy partner who invested with him."

"In a book the Louvre published of his collected attributions of paintings that had never before been identified, I found a sheet of paper inside the back flap that listed different sums of money beside each of the numbered paintings. Some of the numbers were huge, in the millions. He called them commissions."

"Was there a date on that sheet of paper?" Bruno asked. "We went from old francs to new francs in about 1960, and a hundred old francs were worth just one new one. But for years people spoke in old francs, and a lot of older people still do."

"The book came out in the 1970s, but the paper wasn't dated. I suppose the amounts could have been in old francs. But here, I took a photocopy." She slipped a piece of paper to him beneath the table. "That's why I think I should consult my supervisor in Paris."

"You think his attributions of these paintings are suspect?" Bruno asked, putting the photocopy away.

"I don't know, but in the United States these days there's a mandatory course on ethics for art historians. Identifying or attributing paintings can involve big money, and there are still huge controversies over artworks that were confiscated in World War Two, not just from museums in occupied countries but from private collectors, particularly Jewish ones. And Bourdeille has been one of the most important experts on attribution in postwar France."

"Have you raised this with him?"

"He says he's so old he can't remember and I have to go by what's in the archives, but he won't let me see his private papers."

"Did he say why?"

"He gave different reasons at different times: that they are personal, that they've never been properly filed and organized, that there are tax issues." She paused. "I thought he was being evasive."

"Are you staying at his house?"

"No. They found me a room at a guesthouse in Limeuil. But Madame Bonnet gives me lunch every day, and at five in the evening I'm invited to join Monsieur Bourdeille for a glass of wine before I leave."

"He's certainly treating you to excellent wine. I'm envious," Bruno said as Madame Bonnet ended her conversation in the market square and began heading their way. "Let's talk again after you get back from seeing your supervisor in Paris. Who is he, by the way?"

"It's a she, Mademoiselle Massenet, a real scholar. She even learned to be a restorer in her spare time so she would have a better sense of the way individual artists prepared their canvases, the paints they used and the way they applied their brushstrokes. I've learned so much from her, but she can be kind of intimidating."

Madame Bonnet sat down at their table, put a full shopping bag onto the wooden floor of the terrace and asked Claudia, "How were the croissants?"

"Wonderful, I don't know how you could resist one. And the coffee was just as good. You're lucky to have a place like this in St. Denis."

"I think we all know that," Madame Bonnet said. "On Sunday mornings, I drive down here to get a croissant for monsieur's breakfast and one of their cakes for his dessert. One week, he'll want a *tarte au citron,* the next a black chocolate cake with Armagnac, and in summer he'll have a strawberry tart."

"Can I get you a coffee, madame?" Bruno asked. "Perhaps some cake or a *galette?*"

"No, thank you, just coffee. I need to watch my weight. What have you two been talking about all this time?"

"The Resistance and Vichy," said Bruno, signaling to the waitress with a mime of drinking from a cup, and he held up three fingers.

Madame Bonnet grimaced. "Thank heavens I was born after the war."

CHAPTER 5

Bruno reflected mournfully on his encounters with the young American woman as the *pompiers* hauled up the flimsy platform on which he'd crouched in the well. What a waste of a promising young life it would be if her days had ended down there. He watched as they attached a special cradle to the steel hawser on the winch of their vehicle. It was like a cage, a circular metal platform with three metal poles forming a man-sized space before they curved in to meet above where the man's head would be. Two of the vertical poles were joined by a horizontal bar at waist height, and the remaining gap could be sealed by a strap and metal catch that looked as if it had been adapted from a car's safety belt.

Now they were fixing the steel hawser and a heavy-duty pulley to the scaffolding. Bruno helped Ahmed carry the cage to the well, where Ahmed attached the hawser, signaled to the winchman and tested that it rose and fell easily. Ahmed then put on a hard hat, strapped something that looked like a boat hook onto one of the bars of the cage and a heavy-duty flashlight onto the other and draped a coil of rope around his neck. He fashioned the end of the rope into a noose with a slipknot, climbed inside the cage and closed the safety belt. He then tested that the walkie-talkie around his neck was working.

"Have you ever done this before?" Bruno asked him.

"No, but I've practiced it a few times."

"You won't have much room to work. Your cage is nearly as wide as the well. It narrows as it gets deeper," Bruno said.

"We'll try it this way first. If it doesn't work, I'll rig a sling for myself below the cage and do it that way."

Ahmed nodded to the winchman, turned on the powerful light and began his descent, leaving Bruno standing on the rim of the well, one hand clenched to the now familiar scaffolding. Watching Ahmed descend, he heard footsteps heralding a new arrival, the mayor of Limeuil. He was followed by Fabiola, who had gotten Bruno's message at the medical center.

"Are you sure there's a body down there?"

the mayor asked, sounding as much worried as aggressive.

"Bonjour, Monsieur le Maire. I'm not entirely sure," Bruno replied politely. "But I couldn't see what else it might be, and a young American woman was reported missing. With tourism so important to Limeuil, you understand that we have to take every precaution."

Ahmed was going down slowly, and Bruno could follow his progress by the powerful lamp. He heard Ahmed's voice, tinny over the walkie-talkie, as he told the winchman to keep going, to stop, to go down slowly and then to stop again.

"Damn cat," said Ahmed with a muffled curse. And then, "It's a body. Lock the winch and keep it there."

The mayor looked aghast. Under Bruno's hand, the steel hawser was trembling and swaying as Ahmed worked below.

"How far down is he?" Bruno asked the winchman.

"Thirty-two meters."

They waited for what seemed a long time, but Bruno checked his watch and saw that Ahmed took less than three minutes before he reported the body was secure and asked to be raised back up again. Bruno realized he was close when Ahmed turned off his

70

light. Soon his head emerged, then his waist and almost at once a small white cat with light brown patches, perhaps a kitten, jumped onto the rim of the well and stood there, blinking at the daylight. Then its back arched and the cat began baring its little teeth and spitting as it saw Balzac waiting below.

Ahmed, whose overalls were sopping wet, released the safety catch on the cage, stepped out and told the winchman to raise the cage as high as he could. Bruno saw long, bare legs that looked female and some sodden clothing around the neck. He and Bruno then hauled the body from beneath the cage and onto the ledge of the well. The loop of Ahmed's rope was beneath the body's shoulders, and he'd fixed a second rope between its legs and attached it to the first.

"Damn these knots, they're wet and tightened," said Ahmed, and called for a knife from the winchman. Bruno took his own knife from his belt and began cutting at the nylon. As they turned the body over, Bruno recognized that it was Claudia, wearing black panties and a bra, her blouse ripped open by her fall and with only one sleeve still attached. They handed her down to Fabiola, who had a tarpaulin ready to

71

receive the body.

Fabiola turned Claudia onto her back, pressed firmly three, four times on her chest, and water spouted out.

"Try giving her mouth-to-mouth while I look for vital signs," Fabiola told Bruno, and he did as he had been taught while the doctor listened to her stethoscope and then pulled down Claudia's panties to insert a thermometer to measure the internal temperature.

"I think she's been dead for hours," said Fabiola. "But to be sure, we'll just check for any internal temperature. Keep on with the mouth-to-mouth."

Bruno complied. Claudia felt as cold as ice, but her body was supple rather than stiff, although Bruno had no idea what immersion in the well would do to rigor mortis.

"There are scrapes on her limbs and back consistent with hitting the side of the well as she fell," Fabiola said, speaking into a tiny tape recorder. "There are no visible signs of any blow or violence around the arms and shoulders, but her fingers and nails are badly scraped and broken. She may have been trying to break her fall against the wall or maybe even trying to climb out when she was in the water. I'll bag her hands for later analysis."

She withdrew the thermometer and put her hand on Bruno's shoulder. "You can stop now. There's no sign of life." Bruno sat up and looked down at the body while Fabiola was tying plastic bags around each of Claudia's hands. Her immersion in the water had washed away any signs of blood, but there were scrapes along her arms, shoulders and the front of both thighs. Could someone have lifted her by the legs and heaved her into the well? It looked possible. Then Fabiola bent to the face and lifted each eyelid, shining a tiny flashlight.

"*Mon Dieu,* look at those pupils," she said. "They're pinpoints. We'll need a full toxicology report. She must have been heavily drugged, almost unconscious, but there are no signs of needle marks."

"So it was a tragic accident, fueled by drugs," the mayor said.

"I can't say at this stage," said Fabiola. "When I fill out the death certificate, I'll have to say the circumstances are unclear, possibly even suspicious." She pulled out her mobile phone to take a series of photos of the dead girl before placing a blanket over the body. "We'll have to take her to the pathology lab in Bergerac. I'll let them know."

Bruno was already calling J-J, chief of detectives for the *département*. Jean-Jacques was an experienced policeman and a good friend. Beyond the *pompiers'* vehicle, Bruno saw Ahmed stripping off his wet clothes and briskly toweling himself dry.

"Was there any sign of other clothing?" he called across to Ahmed.

"A shoe — looked like a ballet shoe. I left it on the floor of the cage. I didn't see a skirt or anything else," he replied, putting on some dry clothes he'd taken from the vehicle. Then he and the winchman began to detach the cage, pausing to allow Bruno to recover the sodden ballet shoe.

"I'll do the preliminary interviews here and get her room sealed off by the time you arrive," Bruno told J-J. "She's an American art history student, so we'll have to inform their embassy, and I'll try to reach her academic supervisor at the Louvre."

J-J said he'd come down right away and ended the call. Fabiola then signaled Bruno to join her at some distance from the others.

"You may have noticed that she'd been menstruating," Fabiola began. "You should know that she came to see me a few days ago, saying that she suffered severe period pains and was often almost immobilized by the cramps. She asked me for fentanyl, saying this was what had been prescribed for her back in the States. You've heard of the drug?"

"No, but there are two empty pharmacist's containers in her toiletry bag, and I made a note of everything on the labels." He pulled out his notebook and checked. "Yes, one was fentanyl, and the other was oxycodone."

"*Mon Dieu,* those American doctors." Fabiola groaned. "Those are man-made opioids. They killed something like sixty thousand Americans last year. It's an epidemic. And fentanyl is one of the most dangerous, at least fifty times stronger than morphine and very easy to overdose. You say both her containers were empty?"

"There were no pills in them, just two little sticks like the ones you use to clean your ears."

"These are the lollipops Americans sometimes use to deliver fentanyl. It's easily absorbed through the skin inside the mouth."

"Did you give her anything for her pain?"

"An extra-strength ibuprofen," said Fabiola. "That should have been enough. There was nothing fundamentally wrong when I examined her. In fact, she was a healthy young woman, very fit with good muscle tone. That may have come from her horse-back riding. And didn't I hear that her tennis game was good enough to beat you?"

"She was a good player. Do you think she climbed up onto the well herself and then fell in?"

"I suppose it's possible, but I'd have to see how much of the stuff she'd had, and that means waiting for the toxicology report. I'd say it was unlikely, but I saw no real evidence that she was pushed or heaved in. She might have been looking for that damned cat."

"She seems to have had a liking for them — she has a cat as the screen saver on her phone," Bruno said, leaving Fabiola shaking her head at the oddities of human behavior.

David had assembled the gardeners, and between them they had drawn up a list of everyone they could remember who had been at the previous evening's lecture. Bruno asked if any of them had seen Claudia after she left the lecture, and none of them had. He had a few more questions. Did Claudia know the gardens? Yes, she had taken a tour. Did she know about the work being done on the well? Yes, the builders were working on it when she visited. Did she have any special friends they knew of?

"I knew her pretty well. We both had

rooms at the same place," Félicité said, her face pale and a grimy handkerchief pressed to her cheek.

"What about boyfriends?" Bruno asked.

Félicité shrugged, and the others looked pointedly at David, who shuffled his feet and said that they had shared a pizza at Le Chai down by the Limeuil waterfront one evening.

"I'd like to have known her better, but that was all," he said shyly. "She spent most of the time working."

Bruno asked them to keep the main gate closed until further notice and to stay away from the area around the well until the detectives arrived, and then he went to tell Madame Darrail the grim news.

"Detectives are coming because her death could be a police matter, so I want to see if I can get into her room through the balcony," he explained to her. "That may have been the way her laptop disappeared."

"Oh, my heavens," exclaimed Madame Darrail, putting her hand to her mouth. "And she was looking forward to dinner this evening. Dominic was coming, that's my son, and she was hoping to get him to give her a guided trip down the river. Have her parents been told?"

"That's being taken care of," Bruno

replied, asking her to ensure that Claudia's room was sealed off until the detectives arrived. Then he went outside to the narrow, sloping street and turned into the first narrow alley between the houses. Such gaps were a tradition in French towns to prevent fires from spreading but essential in Limeuil as runoffs for rainwater to escape down the hill.

When he reached the house immediately below that of Madame Darrail, Bruno donned a pair of evidence gloves, put one foot on a slightly projecting stone in its wall and then scrambled up to get a grip on the drainpipe of the Darrail house, and with a quick heave he was able to clamber onto the balcony outside Claudia's room. He opened the balcony door, still unlocked, and entered. Somebody could have got in that way and taken her laptop. But no casual thief would have left her iPhone.

Still with his gloves on, Bruno pressed the button that launched the phone and held the screen horizontally so he could squint against the light and see which numbers had signs of wear on the glass. It was a trick J-J had taught him. Three and five and seven and nine seemed the most likely. He checked the passport for her birth date, May 7, 1992. He tried seven and five, nine and two, knowing most people used some variation of their birth date. That failed. He tried five and seven, putting the month first, and then nine and two, and the phone opened.

He scanned the e-mails, seeing several to and from Madame Massenet, her academic supervisor in Paris, and more from someone with an address at Yale.edu who was probably also linked to her studies. There were others to and from various people with the name Muller in the electronic addresses, probably family. He opened the phone log and saw that most of the calls in and out were identified by name, which meant they were in the contacts section of her phone. He scribbled down the numbers that had no name attached. He'd check those later. Then he looked in her picture gallery to find a lot of photos of cats. Perhaps Fabiola was right, and Claudia had fallen in while trying to save the kitten in the well.

But then Bruno stopped, surprised to see a photo of Laurent, the ex-prisoner, and then another. He recognized the place where it had been taken, the entrance to the bookshop at Lascaux, site of the cave that contained the greatest of all the works of art of prehistoric peoples. There was another photo of the two of them sitting on a riverbank, with the remains of a picnic beside them. They were close together, arms around each other and smiling for the camera phone. There was another selfie of them together, and from the background Bruno was pretty sure it was at the covered gallery where visitors waited to go into Lascaux II, a duplicate created by artists over the course of a decade after the original cave paintings began to be obscured by a white film, a kind of fungus that came from the breath of tens of thousands of visitors into an environment that had been sealed for more than seven thousand years.

Most of the rest of the photos seemed to be of paintings, but there were some pages of documents, one of which he recognized as the photocopy Claudia had given him in Fauquet's café. He scrolled on, seeing several more selfies of her and friends in front of various Parisian monuments, in street scenes with the Eiffel Tower in the background, at Versailles and outside the better-known Loire châteaux. He went back to the log, saw a number for Madame Darrail and called it on his own phone, asking her to come downstairs and let him out of Claudia's locked door. When she did, he asked her to witness him putting Claudia's toiletry case with its two pharmacy containers into an evidence bag.

CHAPTER 6

Rather than interrupt Florence with the bad news while she was teaching, Bruno texted a message for her to call him and then climbed back up the hilltop to check with the restaurant whether any of the staff had seen Claudia the previous evening. He was about to show them the selfie on her phone, but it turned out that Claudia was known. The restaurant was within walking distance of Bourdeille's house and from the room she rented, and she'd eaten there twice. Nobody had seen her the previous day, and they were appalled to hear of her death.

He came out of the restaurant to see J-J parking his car, his assistant Josette on the pavement, guiding him into a very cramped space. A big man with a paunch that paid tribute to his love of good food, J-J had trouble easing himself out of the driver's seat. A local newspaper cartoonist had done a caricature of J-J and himself as the two comic-book heroes of ancient Gaul, Astérix and his fat friend, Obélix. Ever since it had appeared, Bruno could not rid himself of the image. J-J even had something of the look of Gérard Depardieu, the rotund French actor who played the Obélix role in the movie.

"What have we got here, Bruno, an accident or something worse?" J-J asked by way of greeting.

"It looks like an accident, but there may be complications," Bruno replied. "Claudia Muller was here last night for a public lecture. She was drugged with an opioid that had been prescribed by an American doctor. She loved cats, and there was a cat at the bottom of the well with her, so she may have fallen in while trying to rescue it and feeling dizzy. You'll probably want to interview the builders who were working on the well and failed to secure it overnight in violation of the construction code. I'll send you my photo of what it looked like when I arrived."

"Do we have a preliminary death certificate?" J-J asked.

"Yes, from Fabiola, who says that while there's no immediate sign on the body that the girl was pushed or manhandled, she's worried about the drugs. So she wants a toxicology report before she'll sign off on the death."

Bruno handed over Claudia's passport, sealed inside an evidence bag. "The details of her next of kin are inside. I found it in a room she rented here in the village."

"Since the woman's a foreigner, I suppose I'd better order an autopsy," J-J said, taking the bag and handing it to Josette, who pulled on a pair of latex gloves before opening it. "Do we have a full list of everyone who attended the lecture?"

"I'm working on that. Claudia was a graduate student in art history doing a research year in France, attached to the Louvre. She made a lot of friends around here, spoke good French, cooked well and made a point of integrating. She was here only a couple of months, but she'd come riding with us at Pamela's and played tennis well enough to beat me. She might have had a local boyfriend, and she seems to have broken up with her American one. There was a torn-up photo of the guy, very affectionately inscribed, in her wastepaper basket."

J-J nodded. "I'll have to contact Hodge at the American embassy, the legal attaché we worked with during that IRA business," J-J went on. "They'll have to be officially notified, and we'll let them worry about informing the girl's next of kin. Anything else, Bruno?"

"There are a couple of odd things you might want to check," Bruno went on. "Laurent, the local guy in that famous drunk-driving case who was released from prison in January, met Claudia by chance when I picked them both up at the station on his return. They became friendly, and I took them both to a lecture on falconry in Périgueux. He appears in selfies on her phone, and it looks like they went to Lascaux together, so you'll probably want to talk to him. I can give you the number of the farm where he was staying, but he's now working with the hawks at Château des Milandes.

"Then there may be some funny business with Monsieur de Bourdeille, a rich old art dealer who won the Resistance medal. Claudia had been at his place interviewing him and researching in his library for her own art history doctorate. She told me the other day when I ran into her in the market that she was concerned that he might have been profiting from attributions he made on what she thought were suspect paintings. She wasn't very specific, but I thought I'd follow up with her supervisor at the

Louvre. I know Claudia went to see her about it."

"Bourdeille is the one in the wheelchair, about ninety years old?" J-J asked, looking skeptical. "I don't see him pushing a healthy adult down a well. That's all you have so far?"

"Her laptop and case seem to have disappeared from her room, according to the landlady. I checked and it's easy to get into her room via the balcony. And here's her phone, which was left in her room." Bruno handed it over, still inside an evidence bag, and gave J-J the code.

"I used the system you taught me to get into it," he added. "And in the other bag is the stuff from the American pharmacy. Be careful with those two little white sticks; Fabiola told me that's how the drug is delivered. Maybe Hodge can check with the American pharmacy and her doctor. I never saw any of the usual signs that she was on drugs."

"So you think it might not have been an accident because her laptop is missing, which suggests someone might have a motive to stop or at least learn about her research," said J-J, looking doubtful. "She might just have left it at Bourdeille's place if she was working there."

"Her falling down the well and the laptop's disappearance may not be connected," Bruno conceded. "But it would be quite a coincidence."

"Who was the last person to see her alive that you know of? And when was that?"

"Florence, the science teacher at the *collège* in St. Denis. She was the one who told me that Claudia was missing after leaving the lecture early, feeling ill. When Florence called her this morning, there was no sign of her, and her bed had not been slept in."

"The sooner you can get that list of everyone who was at the lecture, the better. This place used to be a fortress," J-J said, looking around at the stone walls. "Could anyone have got into these gardens when the gates were locked?"

"Probably. At a glance I'd say there are several places where an active person could climb in. I asked the staff to close the gardens to the public for the rest of today, and the four gardeners are all here. David is in charge, and they all knew Claudia. David tells me he had a pizza with her one evening."

"Right, I'll talk to him first," said J-J. "I presume he can call the builders in, since we need statements from them. If they left the well unsealed like this overnight, they're in trouble. Then give me a number for this ex-convict. He sounds interesting. I'll get hold of him, and you go and have a polite chat with Monsieur Bourdeille. I'm not sure how we can make much progress before we get the toxicology report."

"If you want this well sealed off as a possible crime scene, we'd better arrange for a gendarme to stand watch until your forensics team can look at it. Right now, it's a public hazard. I can call Yveline at the gendarmerie to see if she can spare someone."

"Good idea," said J-J. "Forensics should be here by lunch-time, maybe a bit later."

"I'll also talk to the American girl's supervisor in Paris, a Madame Massenet at the Louvre."

Each man turned away to dial, and Bruno heard J-J say, "*Attaché judiciaire 'Odge, s'il vous plaît.* This is a police matter, an American citizen found dead. I'm Commissaire Jalipeau from Périgueux, and he's worked with me before."

Bruno called Yveline first, and she promised to send a gendarme, then he called the number for Claudia's supervisor at the Louvre.

"Massenet," came a voice so quiet that he had to strain to hear. He explained the reason for his call and said he was notifying

87

her as Claudia's academic supervisor.

"*Mon Dieu,* this is terrible news," she responded, sounding stunned. "How did it happen? Poor Claudia, she was such a gifted student and I had great hopes for her. Was it an accident?"

"We think so but can't be sure at this stage. I understand Claudia had recently come up to Paris to consult you on an ethical question, concerning Monsieur de Bourdeille."

"Did she tell you that?"

"Yes, just over a week ago, the day before she went up to Paris to see you."

"I told her that Monsieur de Bourdeille was held in the highest esteem here at the Louvre, and I was proud to have been one of his pupils."

"Did she show you a photocopy of what seemed to be commissions involving several paintings?"

"Yes, and I told her that such honoraria were not uncommon in the art world when it comes to making an expert attribution for an important painting. A great deal of scholarship and research are usually involved."

"Did she seem troubled by the matter?"

Massenet paused a long moment before replying, "No, I'd say she was curious rather than troubled. I had explained to her that Monsieur de Bourdeille had been a pioneer in his research methods. It was one of the main ways that he built his reputation."

"How do you mean?"

"He delved far beyond the usual family letters and ledgers or church archives and had learned to explore regional tax records and the accounts kept by *notaires* of wills and bequests, as well as police records of thefts or confiscations during the Revolution."

"Can you give me an example?"

"Certainly. He found a treasure trove of historic customs records in Bordeaux, where many of the wealthy French sugar planters in the eighteenth century listed the paintings and furniture they had bought to ship out to their plantations and to bring them back. He also learned to use the archives in Venice and Florence to see from artists' taxes and guild records what French customers had bought. He opened whole new fields of research and did so despite his handicap. He'd been shot during the war while being arrested and lost the use of one leg. When I was his pupil, he had to wear a stiff brace and use crutches, but soon after that he was confined to a wheelchair."

"I meant a specific example, madame."

"I see. Well, there is the diptych of Nicolas of Ypres, and then Caron's *Surrender of Milan,* some of the etchings of Jean Cousin. He wrote a famous monograph on the illustrators of Protestant Bibles that were printed in French in Geneva when they were banned in France."

"And this was the period Claudia was studying?"

"Yes, her thesis was on the artists of the French Renaissance who were not painting for the royal courts. The Netherlands fashion of prosperous merchants commissioning works for their local churches and for their homes was just starting to come into France. It's a very promising field."

"How much of her thesis was written? I ask because her laptop seems to have disappeared."

"Well, she'd just begun her research here in France, so not very much. She sent me a couple of draft chapters, an introduction on the period and the research methods she intended, focusing on French artists who went to Italy to study and French people, mostly soldiers and mercenaries, who brought artworks back as loot from the Italian wars. They were usually intended as a gift to their local church in return for masses to be said for their souls, but some artworks were kept to decorate their homes and display their wealth."

"And you think she'd have earned her doctorate from what you've already seen of her work?"

"Oh, certainly. She worked hard and had a good eye, and she is, I mean, she was very enthusiastic about her research. She was a gifted and delightful young woman and I was convinced she would go far. I'm going to miss Claudia. Would you know her next of kin, monsieur? I feel that I should write to them with my condolences."

"We're checking that with the American embassy. As soon as I know, I will e-mail you with their full names and addresses."

Bruno set out for Bourdeille's *chartreuse,* pulling in when his phone vibrated, and he took the call from Florence. He passed on the bad news, explaining what little he knew and emphasizing the possible role of the cat.

"*Mon Dieu,* this is dreadful, her poor parents — dying so young and so far from home," Florence exclaimed. "I feel like this is my fault, Bruno. I should have seen her safely back to her room."

Bruno tried to reassure her, with limited success. But Florence was not a woman to take up unnecessary time. She said she was about to be late for a class, thanked him for letting her know, said they should talk later and ended the call.

CHAPTER 7

Resuming the drive to Bourdeille's home, Bruno smiled recalling his first meeting with the old man. It had been in Périgueux the previous November at one of those public culinary events the French do so well, the kind of meeting which for Bruno embodied the concept of *fraternité* that has defined the grand experiment of the French Republic since the Revolution of 1789.

Bruno recalled the way the grand master had carefully tucked the napkin into his collar over the flowing robes, raised his forearms to let the full sleeves fall back and only then picked up the dish of pâté with both hands, brought it to his nose and sniffed deeply. He put the plate down and beamed at his fellows around the long table. Most of them were wearing the same medieval robes of green and red and the floppy green beret that distinguished them as members of the Confrérie du Pâté de Périgueux.

Bruno did not have the thousand or so euros to spare that the formal robes would cost. He had borrowed a set for his inauguration the previous year, and so now wore only the pewter medal of office on its green velvet ribbon around his neck. On the medal were carved a small flock of ducks and geese and the seal of the ancient town of Périgueux, which dated back before Roman times.

"That is what I call a real *pâté de Périgueux,*" said the grand master, setting down the plate.

It carried one small cylinder of pork pâté, about six centimeters high and ten in diameter, covered with thin slices of black Périgord truffle. A similar cylinder had been carefully sliced into eight triangular portions by one of the *confrères* who sat opposite the grand master. These slices revealed that the pork pâté was only a thin shell that covered the luscious foie gras inside. This unique combination of pâté, black truffles and foie gras was the celebrated *pâté de Périgueux,* the gastronomic pride of the city and of its specialist chefs. This day's annual concours, held in the place St. Louis in the heart of the old town, which had been stoutly defended against the English invaders in the fourteenth century, was to establish which of the pâtés to be tasted was worthy of the seal of recognition by the *confrérie.*

Twenty men and three women, most of them in the formal robes of the *confrérie,* sat around the long table, score sheets and pencils lined up before them. Each of the pâtés to be tasted would be scored out of a hundred: thirty for appearance, fifty for taste and twenty for seasoning. Any pâté that failed to win at least an average score of fifty would not qualify for the *confrérie*'s approval. The winner was then privileged to proclaim his or her triumph at each point of sale for the forthcoming year.

Each member of the *confrérie* had to be inducted formally at a public ceremony in the place St. Louis, in which the merits of the new candidate were extolled by an existing member. The oath of fidelity was then sworn to the *confrérie,* at which point the new member was tapped on each shoulder with the beak of a duck, and the mayor of Périgueux hung the medal of office around the new member's neck and embraced him or her with a *bise* on both cheeks.

Bruno knew that he owed his own induction, and his presence at that day's table, to his investigation and exposure of a lucrative fraud involving the substitution of cheap

Chinese truffles for the genuine black diamonds of the Périgord. He had been formally nominated by an elderly war hero known as the Patriarch, a former fighter pilot with the French Normandie-Niemen squadron that served on the Eastern Front with the Soviet air force during World War II. Only weeks earlier, Bruno had attended the funeral of the old man, who had died in his sleep at the age of ninety. In recognition of another case in which Bruno had saved his family from scandal, the Patriarch had bequeathed to Bruno in his will a valuable Purdey shotgun and a case each year for the rest of his life of the Patriarch's Reserve wine from the family vineyard.

As Bruno tasted the third of the pâtés being offered, he looked down the long table at the other members of the *confrérie* and smiled to himself in affection for this classically French tradition of the brotherhoods. Each of them appealed to local pride, to the distinction of French wines and cuisine and to the French love of ceremony and dressing up. They had each devised or inherited robes of varying colors and designs that were said to follow ancient tradition, and each one gathered formally once a year to honor their devotion to the particular wines or foodstuffs celebrated by their *confrérie*.

The Périgord being the gastronomic heartland of France, it was host to eleven, more *confréries* than any other region. Bruno knew of the Consulat de la Vinée de Bergerac with red-and-gold robes; of the brotherhood of the wines of Domme and another of the golden grapes of Saussignac; of the truffles of Thiviers in northern Périgord and of the truffles of Sarlat and Ste. Alvère in Bruno's own region of the Périgord Noir; of the brotherhood of the region's famous strawberries; of its walnuts; of its chestnuts; of its mushrooms; of its honey and, last, of the fine hand-crafted knives of Nontron. Each of Bruno's companions was using just such a knife to cut open and examine his slice of pâté and to smear it onto a hunk of fresh bread, still warm from the bakery.

This being France, although it was just past nine in the morning, the table also carried several bottles of red Bergerac wine and whites from Montravel, the region of Bergerac that adjoined the vineyards of Bordeaux. One bottle of the sweet and golden wine of Monbazillac that Bruno thought went best with foie gras stood before the grand master's place in the center and another at each end of the long table. Bruno, who sat between the formidable and cheerful woman who ran the Auberge de la Truffe at Sorge and a charcutier from Thiviers, offered a glass to his neighbors before pouring one for himself.

"And one for me, if you please, *cher confrère,*" growled the voice of an elderly man three seats away from Bruno. Although he had gone along the table shaking hands with everyone present when he'd first arrived, Bruno had not noticed until now that the speaker was in a wheelchair. A heavy greatcoat had been slung over the back of the wheelchair, disguising its shape, and the speaker was decked out in a set of formal robes that looked almost as old as their owner.

"With pleasure," said Bruno, rising and taking the bottle across. The old man seized it and examined the label.

"Clos l'Envège." He grunted. "That will do. Young Julien makes a good wine, and the 2010 was a fine year." He poured out a glass and sipped, keeping the bottle close, sighed with pleasure and then lit a cigarette in defiance of the rules against smoking in enclosed places.

"I'm Pierre de Bourdeille and I know who you are, Bruno. Going to arrest me?" the old man asked with a sly grin.

"It would be a bad precedent for one

member of the *confrérie* to arrest another at our concours," Bruno replied politely, shaking hands again. "And the man who had my job before me always said that the art of police work was knowing what and when one should avoid noticing."

De Bourdeille laughed, a harsh cackle. "I wish some of your predecessors had learned that aspect of the art of policing. I might not be in this thing." He slapped the arm of the wheelchair, which did not distract Bruno from noticing that he had been addressed in the intimate form as *tu,* as was customary for members of a brotherhood.

At that point Bruno knew why the name was familiar and realized that the man before him was one of the most respected figures in the region. After the war in which his father had been shot as a hostage, Bourdeille had then been named *une pupille de la République.* An institution for which Bruno had deep respect, the *pupilles* were orphans of men and women in the police and military who had been killed in the line of duty. Their care, health and education became the responsibility of the state. More recently, the status had been extended to the children of those killed by acts of terrorism. Although the system of *pupil-lages* had almost died out, successive terrorist attacks meant that there were now more than three hundred such *pupilles*. Bourdeille, Bruno recalled, had gone to one of the Grandes Écoles in Paris and then to the Louvre, where he had become a leading art historian and was reputed to be a wealthy man. He was now something of a recluse, and Bruno had not heard of his appearing in public before today.

"I'm the oldest man here today and the longest-serving member of the *confrérie,* and you are one of the most recent," Bourdeille went on. "What do you make of this year's efforts at *pâté de Périgueux?*"

"I'm enjoying the one we're tasting now."

"What score are you giving it?"

"Twenty-five for appearance, forty for taste, fifteen for seasoning, eighty in total," said Bruno.

"You're a generous marker," said the old man. "I agree it's the best, but I'm giving it sixty-five. The first two just made fifty. But then I judge these things severely, since I can remember the magnificent ones made by *le père* Dubreuil, long before your time. He used to have a stall in the market near here on place du Coderc, God rest his soul. I'm sure *le bon Dieu* will comply, so long as Dubreuil continues to pursue his trade in heaven. I don't know about you, Bruno, but

I find it impossible to imagine an afterlife without food and wine."

"I agree, *cher confrère,* and I'm not sure if I'd enjoy an eternity without dogs and horses," said Bruno.

"Remember what Mark Twain said," Bourdeille added. " 'Heaven for the climate, but hell for the company.' "

Bruno smiled, resigning himself to the fact that the bottle of Monbazillac was not going to be shifted from the protection of Bourdeille's arm. He returned to his seat and to the next plates of *pâté de Périgueux,* this time accompanied by the Montravel. It was very good, but it was not Monbazillac.

By the time the tasting was finished, the scores added up, the winners awarded their medals by the mayor of Périgueux, and the assembled members of the *confrérie* began their annual parade through the old town before sitting down to the ritual lunch, Bourdeille had disappeared.

"He never stays beyond the tasting and goes straight home," replied the grand master when Bruno asked if Bourdeille had been taken ill. "I'm just grateful that he managed to attend at all at his age. The only other event that draws him out is the annual commemoration on June the thirteenth of the shooting of the hostages in Périgueux.

His father was one of those killed. I'm sure you'll have heard the story and the fuss when he changed his name."

"It must have been before my time," said Bruno. "I didn't know he'd done that."

"His father's name was Descaux or Descour, something like that. His mother was a Bourdeille, but without the particule that would have made her a member of the de Bourdeille family," the grand master explained. "Our *cher confrère* conducted a long search of archives and baptismal records and established to his own satisfaction that his mother descended from a remote branch of the family or from the wrong side of the blanket, I forget which. There were some testy negotiations, but finally the family dropped their objections to his changing his name to de Bourdeille, so long as he abandoned any claim on the family estate or inheritance. He agreed, so long as they dropped any claim to inheriting *his* estate with its art collection. It made quite a stir at the time, but the joke was on them because his art dealings made him as rich as Croesus while the old family fell on hard times."

And now as Bruno reached Bourdeille's *chartreuse,* smaller than a château but grander than a manor house, he wondered how rich the old man was. His home nestled among the smaller farmhouses where the tenants had lived when the place was the heart of a thriving farm. These days, the fields were mainly rented to a local veal-and-dairy farmer. Two of the farmhouses were holiday homes, bought by foreigners. Two more were for Bourdeille's staff: one for his gardener and the man's family; the other for the widow who was his house-keeper, Madame Bonnet.

Madame Bonnet was dabbing at her eyes with a lace-trimmed handkerchief that looked inadequate for the task when she opened the door. "We heard the news," she said. "Madame Darrail called me. It's such a tragedy, she was so young and so gifted. I liked her a lot and so did monsieur."

"When did you last see Claudia?" Bruno asked, stepping into a hall that seemed the grander for its very simplicity. Old tiles of large black and white squares covered the floor, and a handsome staircase curved its way up the rear wall, to the side of a large, slightly faded tapestry of a biblical scene Bruno could not quite identify. Tall double doors on each side opened into the wings of the *chartreuse,* and a full-sized classical statue in white marble of Pan with his pipes stood on a plinth in the center of the hall beneath a crystal chandelier.

"Yesterday afternoon. She'd been working in the library all morning, and she and I had lunch together. She hardly ate a thing, which wasn't like her. Then she went back to the library until monsieur had woken up from his nap, and they spent about an hour together before she came down to say goodbye to me. She said she would go back to Madame Darrail's house before going on to some archaeological lecture at the castle. She was looking forward to it because it was about art."

Madame Bonnet gave a wistful smile. "She was such a one for knowledge. Even with her work here she was reading all the time about Lascaux and prehistoric art. She knew so much about it, even monsieur told me he was impressed. Did you know about the site they found in a cliff near here, twelve thousand years old, hundreds of shards of limestone, each one engraved with very similar animal shapes, mainly deer and horses, some retouched and corrected? It must have been an art school, the archaeologists say, where people learned to draw and then practiced to improve their skills. Claudia told me that. I'll miss her and so will monsieur. Such a waste of a young life."

"You have my sympathies, madame,"

Bruno said. "I only met her a few times, but I liked her and thought she was very impressive. And how did that farewell dinner go that she cooked before going to Paris?"

"It was excellent. Monsieur was very pleased and ate more than he usually does. He normally eats like a bird, poor man. Of course, in that wheelchair, he doesn't get much exercise."

"What was her mood when she left here yesterday?"

"She wasn't her usual self, not eating much, as I said. She told me it was her time of the month. I remember her wincing and clutching at her stomach as she got up from lunch. I sympathized, since I used to get terrible cramps when I was younger. She left early, disappointing monsieur, who was looking forward to his glass of wine with her."

"What time did she leave?" said Bruno, remembering that Madame Darrail had said she had arrived at her house around six.

"About three, maybe a little before. She'd worked awhile in the library after lunch before seeing monsieur, but she said she thought she'd go back and lie down. She sometimes walked here and back, said it did her good to get some exercise."

That meant there were three missing hours to account for, Bruno noted to himself. He then asked if monsieur knew of Claudia's death.

"I was about to go up and tell him when you came."

"In that case I'll break the bad news myself." He headed for the staircase.

"I'd better show you up, and then I'll bring you some coffee, or would you like something stronger?"

"Just some mineral water, please, unless you're already making coffee."

"I will be. Monsieur lives on the stuff." She led the way past the tapestry and toward a handsome curving staircase, and Bruno realized that the front of the *chartreuse* had concealed its real size. An extension had been attached to the rear of the hall. Through an open door Bruno saw a large kitchen with a dining area and other doors beyond, one of them looking like an elevator.

"Is that where you live?" he asked.

"No, just where I cook and where Claudia and I would have our little lunches. I have a cottage just a few steps away in the hamlet. It's one of several houses that come with the *chartreuse,* where the farmworkers used to live in the old days."

"Was that an elevator I saw?"

"It goes up to his floor and down to the cellar and makes it easier for me to take him his meals. Monsieur planned it very carefully. The extension has two stories, so on his floor you have his study, the library and his bedroom and bathroom, all designed for his wheelchair."

"So what are the other rooms of the *chartreuse* used for? They look pretty big from the entrance drive."

"They are big, with lovely high ceilings. There are three rooms on each side of the entrance, and monsieur has made them into galleries for his private art collection. He comes down every morning after his breakfast and wheels himself all the way around looking at them, and then again last thing at night. I'm sure he'll be happy to let you see his collection before you go."

"Doesn't he open it to the public?"

"No. He sometimes says he would like to do so, but it would be a big problem for his insurance and *le bon Dieu* knows that costs enough already."

"Has the collection been valued?" he asked.

"Not that I know of, but after Claudia had taken note of the contents, she told me that she was sure it was worth millions."

CHAPTER 8

Bruno walked through the open door to the balcony where monsieur sat waiting in his wheelchair, a plaid rug tucked around his legs. A flimsy chair of wood and metal, like the ones at outdoor cafés, awaited Bruno. To the side of the wheelchair stood a small table with two glasses, a decanter of wine and a large ashtray half filled with cigarette butts. The old man was staring out over the valley, a filtered cigarette smoldering in fingers that were brown with nicotine. As Bruno stepped in to take the spare chair, he saw that while the old man's dense and spade-shaped beard was white, his mustache had been stained to a youthful russet by his smoking.

"I bring bad news," said Bruno.

"I know. Claudia is dead, drowned." The old man held up a modern smartphone. "It's on the *Sud Ouest* website. I hope you don't share their foolish belief that it was an accident involving some damn cat. The Claudia I knew was far too shrewd for that."

"You think it was no accident?"

"I don't know, of course, but I very much doubt it. My former colleagues at the Louvre don't send me many aspiring young art historians, but when they do, they're usually impressive. Claudia was the best of the lot. And she was by far the richest. Do you know of her background?"

"We only just found her body. There hasn't been time. From her credit cards I gather she's connected to a financial trust that carries her family's name, but that's all I know. What else can you tell me?"

"You'll find it all on the Internet," Bourdeille said, dropping the still-lit cigarette into the ashtray and at once lighting another from a pack of Royale filters he took from the pocket of his jacket. Quilted velvet, in a bold burgundy with silk lapels, it was a garment Bruno had seen only in ancient photographs or historical films.

"Her father is chairman, founder and chief shareholder of a financial firm in New York," Bourdeille went on. "If he's not a billionaire, he must be close to it. He's also politically active, a member of the finance committee for the campaign of that man who sits in the White House, so I imagine we'll all be overrun by agents of the FBI."

"Do you always check out art students on the Internet?"

"Yes, when they interest me. When her adviser wrote suggesting I see her, she sent along a copy of Claudia's master's thesis on Clouet. Nothing original, of course, you don't expect that for a master's degree. But it was very well informed and thoughtful. She'd done a lot of research into the allegories he used and knew the difference between the religious ones and folktales. I certainly didn't expect that from an American."

"I see you respected her. Did you also like her?"

"At my age, respect and liking tend to be synonymous. But I have never been able to take much interest in women since I had my encounter with the *milice*. Our young American knew something about that, enough to ask me about it, which suggested she had researched me just as I had her. That impressed me. And she had certainly read all my books, which I don't expect you to do. From what I read in our local newspaper, *mon cher confrère,* you are far too busy. Or should I call you Lieutenant these days? I gather you've been promoted."

"Bruno will do."

"Good, and in that case why don't you pour us each a glass of that Château Ausone 2000, the wine I was going to offer Claudia yesterday evening if she hadn't left early. We can drink it in her honor."

"She told me you had taken her wine education in hand. I gather you had shared a bottle of Château Margaux."

"It was a pleasure for me to meet a young woman, particularly a young American, who appreciates good wine enough for me to enjoy sharing it."

"I'm honored to be included. Even on duty, I couldn't possibly refuse such a wine," Bruno said, lifting the decanter and pouring two glasses. He swirled the wine and sniffed, deeply and with appreciation, before taking a long sip. He let the wine rest in his mouth to reach the less-used taste buds near the rear of his tongue and then swallowed.

"That's a wonderful wine," he said. "Is the vineyard really on the site of the villa of Ausonius?"

"Who knows?" Bourdeille said, dabbing at his lip with a white silk handkerchief from another pocket of the garment Bruno suddenly recalled had been called a smoking jacket in its day. "But it makes a damn good story, a Roman governor who was also a notable poet as the first recorded connoisseur of the wines of our region. And a very fine wine it is."

"Did Claudia know much about wine?"

"A great deal, although naturally she knew more about American wines. On her return from Paris she brought me a bottle of an extremely luscious Napa Valley Cabernet called Screaming Eagle. She claimed to have acquired it from the American ambassador's own cellar but didn't say whether she'd been invited to do so or just made off with the bottle. She told me that the ambassador's an old and close friend of her father."

"Did you always see eye to eye with her, or did you ever argue about anything — art, for example?"

"We had some delightful arguments. That's why I enjoyed her company so much. She disputed two of my lesser-known attributions, then retracted handsomely when I made my case. And then she gave me something which she'd been sketching as we argued back and forth, hammer and tongs. I could never do two things at once, but Claudia certainly could." He gestured to the magazine rack beside his wheelchair. "Take a look inside that leather folder."

Bruno opened it to see a pencil sketch of

the old man, wearing his smoking jacket and holding a glass of wine in one hand, a cigarette in the other, a roguish glint in his eye. A background of hills and trees had been artfully captured with a few almost careless lines. Bourdeille's face had been portrayed in a level of detail that seemed to convey the depth of each individual wrinkle around the eyes.

Bruno nodded. "That's very impressive."

"I always told my pupils that they'll never understand a painting until they learn how to draw. How else can one understand why an artist should compose his work as he did or appreciate the brushwork until he can at least command a pencil? And Claudia was a real artist as well as a scholar. You can see that at a glance."

Bruno leafed through some other sketches, evidently by the same hand, of Madame Bonnet; of Bourdeille's *chartreuse;* of the old man dozing in his library, the books on the shelves below him seeming to hold him up even as those above threatened to tumble down and overwhelm him. A sketch of the meeting of the two rivers at Limeuil was enchanting, ripples on the water coming together in a way that made the confluence almost lascivious.

"Did she ever paint?" Bruno asked.

"Not that I know of. She said she had done some watercolors in Paris and promised to send me one. I suppose I'll never get it now. Will they send her body back to America?"

"If that's what her family wants to do," Bruno replied. "All that remains to be decided, and I'm not even sure the next of kin have been informed yet."

"Has anyone told that young man of hers? Jack, I think his name is. I know they met once in Paris and another time in London. She took a flight from Bergerac. I think she was something of a romantic at heart."

Bruno's thoughts drifted back to the torn-up photo of a man signing himself Jack. "I don't know anything about him," Bruno said. "Is he American? English?"

Bourdeille lit another cigarette, shrugging. "He's American, a lawyer, based in London with some international law firm. I got the impression that the two families had known each other for years, and she and Jack had played together as children on summer vacations at some place where I read in the papers that American presidents like to go for their holidays, somebody's vineyard — was it Mary's vineyard? No, it was Martha's. Then they met again at Yale."

"You don't know his surname?"

"No, she never said, and I didn't ask. It depressed me, the thought that she might marry and start having children, interrupting what would otherwise have been a brilliant career, some of which I might have had the pleasure of watching from afar. My last pupil, and probably my best." Bourdeille asked Bruno to refill their wineglasses, and he complied but left his own glass almost empty.

"And you don't think her death was an accident?"

"How would I know? But I don't think she fell into a well while trying to rescue a cat, and I'm sure it wasn't suicide. I suppose we can't rule out murder. But that's far too melodramatic, even if she'd been here long enough to make enemies. So I suppose some kind of accident is possible."

"Why do you rule out suicide?"

"Because she had plans, goals to live for and the means to carry them out."

"You mean getting her doctorate?"

"Not only that. She was confident of getting her way in a current negotiation." He gave Bruno a teasing grin, enjoying the knowledge that he knew something that Bruno did not. "She was too confident, perhaps."

"And what was this negotiation?"

"She was planning to buy my *chartreuse,* along with my library and my art collection, while offering to let me remain here rent-free for the rest of my life."

"You were going to sell everything?" Bruno was more than surprised.

"Why the devil would I do that? What use would I have for money at my age? But every time I said so, she seemed to think it was a negotiating ploy to drive up the price. It became almost a game between us. She was sure she'd win."

"Did she have money of her own, as well as her father's?" Bruno knew that wealth would always be a plausible motive if an autopsy found Claudia's death was suspected murder.

"She said she had her own funds."

"How much was she offering?"

"None of your business, Bruno. But her initial estimate of the value of my collection was more than four million."

"*Mon Dieu,* was that in euros?"

"Dollars. Would you like to see my collection?"

"Very much."

"Take the stairs down to the hall and I'll come in the elevator." Bourdeille turned his wheelchair with the ease of long practice and rolled to the discreet wooden door where the elevator button was the navel of a small plaster cherub on the wall.

"We'll start with the oldest works, early fifteenth century, mainly Burgundian, although in those days that meant Flemish." Bourdeille led the way to the last of three rooms and then turned, gesturing at the wooden panels that had been fixed to the plain white wall and protected with thick glass screens. In the center of the room was a wooden Madonna with a lusty child on her lap, clutching at her breast and looking more like a cheeky cherub than an Infant Jesus.

"This was when wealthy merchants, usually from the cloth trade, began requesting that their faces be included in the religious scenes that custom required. I began acquiring them in the 1950s when they were quite cheap. Ten years later, I couldn't have afforded them. Then these next two rooms are of sentimental value, works by young French painters who were working in the studios of Italian masters, late fifteenth century and early sixteenth. Again, they were cheap in the fifties when I found them, mainly in Italy and Germany. Then I published my book on the roots of the French Renaissance, and their value soared.

"This is my glory room," Bourdeille said

as he led the way across the hall, taking out a very advanced-looking key and, from a separate pocket, a small fob, which seemed to undo a separate electronic lock. "My insurance company requires these precautions for this room. There are only four works of art, but these are the ones that modern fashion deems the most valuable. I almost agree, but not quite. Money and art have always seemed to me such unhappy bedfellows.

"But here they are." He opened the door with a flourish and then touched a small light switch, and three gentle spotlights lit one painting and three sketches that left Bruno feeling awed, less because of his artistic knowledge than because of the drama Bourdeille had infused into their presentation.

"Antoine Caron, François Quesnel and Valentin de Bourgogne, known as the French Caravaggio," he said. "One came to me as a gift from a grateful client some forty years ago. Another was a bequest from a dear and lamented friend. The third I got cheaply because its provenance and authorship were both disputed. But I was certain and wrote an essay to explain why and gave a lecture on it at the Louvre. Not everyone was convinced, but most of those I respect were persuaded.

"I found the Valentin through pure luck at a flea market in Brussels in 1960," Bourdeille said, and Bruno could hear both pride and glee in the old man's voice. From an ornate table in the center of the room he pointed to a folder of soft dove-gray leather. "In there you will see a photograph of how it looked when I first saw it."

Bruno took out a photo, the same size as the painting, and saw a drab and clumsy painting in the cubist style. The colors were lifeless, dirty yellows and dull browns with a small black oblong off-center. Bruno had never warmed to cubism as a style of painting.

"It belonged to a Jewish dealer who had covered it with this daub when the German army was at the gates of Brussels. He knew what was coming and entrusted this and some other paintings to his gardener, who later died in a bombing raid. Heaven knows what happened to the other paintings, but the moment I looked at this squalid little work in the flea market I felt an urge to turn it around and saw that the wood of the frame was hundreds of years older than it should have been. I got it for the equivalent of less than fifty euros, took it back to my workshop and cleaned it, and you now see what I found underneath."

"Did the Jewish dealer have an heir?" Bruno asked.

"Not one. The dealer was originally from Vienna. He and all of his family were sent to Auschwitz. I advertised, of course, and contacted the office for the restitution of artworks in Paris and tried the Israeli embassy. There were no claimants and no evidence of the painting's existence, so I could establish my own claim to ownership. Then I began my own research into its provenance. I'd like to bequeath this to the art museum in Tel Aviv in the names of the dealer and his family, but I doubt whether France would grant an export license."

Bourdeille looked up. "Am I boring you?"

"Quite the reverse," said Bruno, fascinated as much by the old man's excitement as by the painting itself.

"I found it had belonged to Talleyrand, Napoléon's foreign minister, and it was listed in the archives of his château at Valençay. But when Napoléon installed his brother Joseph as king of Spain, the real king was housed at Valençay. Doubtless in retaliation for the French looting of Spain, the Spaniards made off with several of Talleyrand's treasures and sold them off in Austria to defray expenses during the

Congress of Vienna that ended the Napoleonic Wars. Metternich, the Austrian foreign minister, bought it, but it disappeared when his home was looted during the revolution of 1848, and it hung in a Viennese café until the Hapsburg Empire collapsed. Vienna was in chaos, and the father of the art dealer who later fled to Brussels became the owner."

"What a strange journey it took," said Bruno, peering closely at the painting. "You must have enjoyed the hunt almost as much as the painting."

"Indeed I did. But there are so many wonderful stories and so many strokes of luck. I only knew about the Valençay archives because of another strange tale of the Congress of Vienna. Having betrayed Napoléon and maneuvered to restore the Bourbon monarchy, Talleyrand was France's representative at the Congress of Vienna. In return for his services the Prussian king made him a duke of a minor German principality called Sagan. So when France was defeated in 1940, and Göring's little band of art thieves in Luftwaffe uniforms came looking for loot, Talleyrand's descendant was able to claim that because he was the Herzog of Sagan, the château of Valençay was German property and could not be touched. Disciplined as they were, the Germans accepted this, and the Louvre then sent some treasures, including the Venus de Milo and the Winged Victory of Samothrace, there for safekeeping throughout the war. I was part of the team the Louvre then sent to Valençay to check that everything had been accounted for, which is how I knew Talleyrand's archives."

Infected by the almost boyish delight of Bourdeille as he recounted this story, Bruno was grinning as he said, "It would have been a loss to art, but you're also a loss to my own profession. You'd have made quite a detective."

The expression on the face of Bourdeille darkened suddenly into an angry glare, but then he shook his head, his features relaxed, and he said, "I'm sure you mean that as a compliment. Forgive me, I did not mean to be rude. But it was a policeman who put me into this wheelchair when I was just a boy."

"Not a policeman, a Fascist thug from the *milice,*" Bruno replied. "But I understand. And I did mean it as a compliment."

"Thank you, but the policeman was a Frenchman, nonetheless, acting under the authority of a French government with a claim to legitimacy." Bourdeille took a deep breath and collected himself. "I'm tired and need to rest, but I hope to see you before long and show you the rest of the collection. Madame Bonnet will call you to arrange a suitable time. I enjoyed your visit, despite the sad death of Claudia which prompted it. *À bientôt*, Bruno."

CHAPTER 9

Back at the castle in Limeuil, Bruno scanned the list David had assembled of those who'd attended the previous evening's lecture. Not greatly to Bruno's surprise, several of his friends were among them. He could have predicted that Horst and Clothilde from the prehistory museum at Les Eyzies would have attended, but the baron had joined them with Pamela. Joe, his predecessor as the St. Denis policeman, had also attended with his wife. Micheline from the St. Denis tourism office had been in the audience with her husband, the local taxi driver, along with Julien from the town's vineyard. There was a retired English couple whom Bruno knew slightly from the tennis club and a group from Montignac, friends of the speaker, who was one of the curators at the new Lascaux center for cave art.

He saw Florence's name listed, along with three of her pupils from the *collège,* and

Bruno's English friend Jack Crimson. The surprise was to see Laurent's name on the list, along with two friends he had brought along, their names unknown. There were more than twenty people to be interviewed, including some from Limeuil whom Bruno did not know. But Bruno knew he'd be seeing his friends in a few hours at the usual Monday evening supper at Pamela's riding school. He took a snapshot of the list on his mobile phone.

Bruno began by phoning Joe to ask him to put together a list of the attendees he recalled. Then he phoned Juliette, the policewoman in Les Eyzies, to ask her to check with Horst and Clothilde if they could remember any others at the lecture. He e-mailed her the list from his phone. Then he called Louis, the policeman at Montignac, and asked him to do the same with the speaker and his guests. He called at the various addresses in Limeuil, trying to assemble a full list for the town. But only two of them had noticed Claudia leaving early, and nobody had seen any others leaving before the end of the lecture.

Back in St. Denis, he checked his list with Micheline and then went to his office to log on to the police computer and download the list onto the case file J-J had opened.

J-J's visit to Laurent had established that Laurent had been at the lecture with two friends, the falconer and his wife, who each said the three of them had stayed until the end and then dropped Laurent at Marty's farm on their way home. J-J had added that a toxicology report was expected the next day, and a full autopsy would follow later. As he was dealing with other e-mails, Bruno's desk phone rang, and he recognized the American accent of Hodge, the FBI agent who was legal attaché at the American embassy in Paris.

"Thought I'd better warn you that this news has gone right to the top," Hodge began. "The girl's father is a close friend of the ambassador, a big player on Wall Street and a major donor to the president's election campaign, so the ambassador let the White House know about her death. Now he wants me to come down to help with your investigation. I'll try not to get in your way."

"You're always welcome," said Bruno, who had got on well with Hodge on a previous case. "Would you like me to book you a room at a hotel in St. Denis?"

"Sure, get me a nice one. But the girl's father, Abraham J. Muller III, is going to want his own investigation. Since he's in finance, he won't be going to a detective agency but to the people he uses on financial inquiries. You know these specialist firms, they charge like lawyers, a thousand bucks an hour. And for that kind of money, Muller will want results. And he'll get them, right or wrong. If these financial gumshoes can't find anything you guys have missed, they'll start looking at you and J-J so they can write a report that blames it all on the incompetent French police."

"Right now, it looks like a tragic accident while the girl was using powerful medication," said Bruno. "She had fentanyl and oxycodone in her room, prescribed by an American doctor and issued by an American pharmacy. She tried to get some more here from a doctor who refused, saying it was too dangerous. You met Fabiola when you were here. She prescribed ibuprofen instead."

"Jesus, fentanyl and oxy, that's all we need," said Hodge. "J-J only told me that he was waiting for a toxicology report. Can you give me the details?"

Bruno read out from his notebook the name and address of the New Haven pharmacy, the prescribing doctor and the other details he'd taken from the medicine containers.

"I'll check those out. When will you get the toxicology report?"

"It's due tomorrow," said Bruno. "Two more things you should know: she seems to have had an American boyfriend named Jack, but his photo was torn up and tossed in the wastepaper basket. I'm told he's a lawyer, based in London, and they were childhood playmates. And she had a couple of family photos pinned onto her mirror. There's one that looks like her as a young girl with her parents, and another shows the same guy a few years on, but the photo is truncated as though the second person had been cut out. Do you know if her parents were divorced?"

"I'll find out. I'll come down from Paris tomorrow morning, ambassador's orders. I imagine her father might want to fly in, and they'll certainly want the body."

"Under French law, they can't have it until our investigation is complete. You know that. And whatever the report, after what you've said about this girl's political connections, J-J will want an autopsy."

There was a long pause followed by a heavy sigh from Hodge. "I understand, but the ambassador won't. He's already called your foreign minister, and I've been asked to use all my French police connections."

"That's what you're doing," Bruno said.

"They'll want an American autopsy, if there's to be an autopsy at all."

"The best you'll get is for an American doctor to attend our autopsy, and even then you'll need to pull a lot of strings. Do you want me to call Prunier?" Bruno asked, referring to the police commissioner for the *département*.

"No, I'd better do that myself. I'll get the early morning fast train to Bordeaux and then rent a car and drive to see Prunier and J-J. I'll try to be with you in the afternoon. Just make sure that everything you do is by the book and logged. Like I said, Muller's private investigators will be looking for someone to blame for this, and sure as hell it won't be Muller's daughter, whatever drugs she was on. Throw in the ambassador and the White House and this could finish your and J-J's careers and maybe Prunier's, too. I'm serious, Bruno. This is going to get rough."

"If her father wants someone to blame, you should know that we'll probably be taking action against the builders who failed to secure the well properly."

"I don't think you understand, Bruno," Hodge said patiently. "The guys who'll be coming down on your neck will want some real heads to roll. Builders are little people, so they don't count."

"This is France," said Bruno, bridling despite his respect for Hodge. "They will get French justice under French law."

"I hear you, Bruno, but good luck with that when our president calls your president and makes it personal. I'm just trying to warn you of what you'll probably be dealing with here, and I count on you to let J-J and Prunier know just how heavy this could get. I'll see you tomorrow. By the way, I saw Isabelle the other day at one of the antiterrorism coordination meetings. She's looking well, put some weight on, which she needed to do. She asked if I'd heard from you, and said to send you her love if we spoke."

"Give her my love when you next see her," said Bruno, an automatic response. He didn't want to think about Isabelle just now. Their occasional reunions, snatched weekends between Isabelle's high-powered job on the antiterrorism task force, were no way to conduct an affair even if there had been the prospect of a steady relationship, even a family, at the end of it. And with Isabelle, that was never going to happen.

Hodge hung up, and Bruno sat back, thinking, not greatly surprised by Hodge's warning. Policing and high politics were always a difficult mix, and the police usually ended up taking the blame. He logged back in to the computer to add to the case file Muller's name, his wealth and his connections to the American ambassador and to the White House, but without any reference to Hodge as his source. He'd pass on Hodge's warnings privately to J-J and Prunier. Then he went in to relate it all to the mayor of St. Denis, a man with his own political connections at the Élysée Palace. If there was to be a diplomatic fuss over this, the sooner the staff of the president of France knew about it, the better.

An hour later, after a phone call that persuaded J-J to ask the pathologist to perform the autopsy on Claudia first thing the next morning, Bruno was mounted on his horse, Hector. As he waited for his basset hound to catch up, he watched the majestic sweep of the clouds drifting toward him. Their edges were gilded by the slanting rays of the sun sinking in the west, somewhere far out over the Atlantic. Man, horse and dog, all three of them were catching their breath after a gallop along the ridge overlooking the twin bridges where the River Vézère flowed into the wider Dordogne. The village of Limeuil climbed sinuously up the hill to the new château and then to the stone walls and the neo-Moorish castle on the summit, itself dwarfed by the height of the sequoia tree.

Someone at this spot the previous evening, he mused, would have had no knowledge of the drama being played out in the castle gardens, Claudia tumbling down the well to fall into the water below, past the kitten whose cries, Bruno assumed, had attracted her. Suddenly he stopped his train of thought. Where had the kitten been when it had started the plaintive meowing that had caught Claudia's attention? It could not have been on the workmen's platform. That had been hauled up high when Bruno had first arrived at the well. He had noticed no ledge or projecting stone on which the kitten might have sat. Could it have been on the lip of the well? In that case, Claudia might have clambered up, reached for the kitten and, with her sense of balance blurred by the medicine she had taken, fallen into the well.

But if it had been an accident, what had happened to Claudia's bag and the laptop it contained? Might someone have had a motive to help her on her way? There were questions to be asked about that lawyer boyfriend, Jack, and whether she had broken off their relationship. And perhaps Bourdeille had been more troubled than he had admitted about her questioning of his attributions. And what of Claudia's family? Presumably she had made a will of her own, despite her youth. With a fortune at her disposal, sufficient to think of buying Bourdeille's estate, that might provide a motive for someone to have killed her. He'd have to ask Hodge about the fate of Claudia's estate.

Perhaps he should ask her adviser in Paris again about Claudia's life in the capital, about any friends or connections she might have made, someone who could help Bruno learn more about her. And there was her professor back at Yale, with whom she had exchanged regular e-mails about her research. He might know more about Claudia's private life.

Bruno pulled out his notebook to check for the professor's e-mail address and thought about the way he should phrase his questions to an English speaker. He shrugged and used his phone to send an e-mail that read simply: *I have sad news about your pupil, Claudia Muller. She died yesterday after falling in a well at Limeuil, where she lived while studying with art historian Monsieur de Bourdeille. Please call or e-mail me to arrange a time to talk. Chief of*

Police, Vézère Valley, Benoît Courrèges.

He added his phone numbers and hit Send. It would be early afternoon in the United States, so he might get a reply that evening. Pamela might be able to help when his English failed him. He nudged Hector with his heels and turned to canter back to the riding school, Balzac racing along behind with his short legs and flapping ears, doing his best to keep pace. After he dropped onto the hunters' trail and turned back toward Pamela's place, Bruno saw the rest of his friends trotting in line along the valley floor. They had already left for their evening ride when Bruno arrived, but he'd called to say he'd catch up with them.

Pamela was in the lead, Fabiola and Gilles behind her and Félix the stableboy bringing up the rear. The baron and Jack Crimson would be back at the big house behind the riding school, opening bottles of wine while Florence and Miranda, Jack's daughter, tried to prevent their four children from swamping Pamela's bathroom as the kids enjoyed their communal bath time. They'd probably be trying to stand on the side of the bath to see if they could spot the return of the riders, although it was usually Balzac rather than the adults that they raced downstairs to greet. Bruno smiled at the thought and increased his pace to catch up with Félix, who seemed to have no trouble controlling the big warmblood he rode.

"Bonjour, Bruno, terrible news about Claudia," Félix said.

"Really sad," Bruno replied, nodding at the youth whose life had been transformed by working at Pamela's stables. Son of an unemployed drunk of a father and a hard-working mother from the French islands of the Caribbean, Félix had been a truant and heading for a juvenile detention center until Bruno had realized he loved horses. At his urging, Pamela had given the boy a chance. Now Félix had caught up at school, and Florence reckoned he had a good chance of passing his *baccalauréat* and going on to veterinary school. For the moment, Félix insisted, he wanted to stay as a stableboy. But now that his father had a job as handy-man at the riding school, Félix's family was equally determined that he should get a proper education.

"How's the lycée going?" Bruno asked. Félix had now started his two years at the upper school in Périgueux. Like most of the rural pupils, he stayed in a dormitory from Monday until Friday. He could hardly wait to get back to the riding school on Friday evenings.

"It's tough, and even when I get back here on weekends, Florence comes to check I'm doing my homework," Félix replied glumly. "I barely have time to do my real work, even now during school vacation."

"Félix, for the moment, school is your real work," said Bruno as they rode into the stable yard. "You can't stay a stableboy forever."

"You sound like my father. And my mother. And Pamela. And Florence."

Bruno grinned at Félix as he dismounted. "It looks to me like you're outnumbered," he said before embracing Pamela.

"So young, so sad," Pamela murmured. "Fabiola already told me about Claudia."

They took the horses into the stables, rubbed them down and checked their hooves before feeding them their evening bran and fresh water. It had been a long day, thought Bruno, and took off his shirt and T-shirt to rinse himself down in the stable sink. As he dried himself off, he saw Balzac playing with Félix before the basset hound trotted into Hector's familiar stall and began making a nest for himself in the hay. It wouldn't be long, Bruno thought, before the children came down from their bath to greet the dog who now seemed to be part of everyone's extended family.

CHAPTER 10

"Who's cooking tonight?" Bruno asked, and Pamela rolled her eyes as she replied, "It's Jack's turn. The usual stewpot special."

"I like it when he cooks," said Fabiola. "It always tastes a bit different even though it looks the same."

Jack Crimson was officially a retired British diplomat, but with a knighthood he never used, which testified to a distinguished if discreet career in intelligence. Cooking, however, was one of the few skills he had never acquired. And since each of the members of the Monday evening dinners, except the two mothers, had to take turns in providing the meal, Jack was learning as he went.

Now that he had understood the importance of beginning with a good stock, Jack had started by boiling down the carcass of a duck to create a good bouillon before adding smoked duck sausages to chopped-up carrots, leeks, potatoes and then a large can of peeled tomatoes and a smaller can of the petits pois that he thought essential to every dish. Then Jack always added a random collection of dried herbs and a great deal of chopped garlic to the giant stewpot that had been simmering away on his woodstove for the past two days, a half bottle of red wine being added each day. Finally, in tribute to the culinary idiosyncrasies of his homeland and despite all the hints from his daughter, Jack liked to add a few splashes of Worcestershire sauce to his concoctions.

For a final touch, shortly before serving, Jack fried a generous handful of *lardons* of pork with chopped onions and mushrooms and added them to his stew. Bruno and the baron had privately agreed that Jack's dishes reminded them of meals they had been fed in the army. Since Jack invariably brought some excellent wines and cheeses to accompany and follow his dinners, along with apple pies from Fauquet and a giant container of vanilla ice cream, none of the adults complained.

Jack's daughter, Miranda, rolled her eyes at the sight of the stewpot and took only a token portion of her father's food. But since her children and Florence's always anticipated Jack's turn to cook with great excitement and devoured second helpings, even Miranda smiled indulgently at the chorus of praise that followed Jack's latest offering. As Fabiola had said, it tasted a little different every time, even though it always looked the same, a brown and glutinous mass embellished with the odd flash of red tomato, a glint of orange carrot and the occasional green pea.

"Chicken," said Gilles as they all sat around the huge table in Pamela's kitchen and dug in. "You've added some chicken breasts. That's new."

"One each, the children like them," said Jack. "And I sautéed them in duck fat, in Périgord style."

"The aroma goes very well with the delightful bath-time scents of the children," suggested Fabiola, straight-faced. "But should we take red wine for the duck or white wine for the chicken?"

"I'm having a glass of each," replied Jack, cheerfully. "The white is a Verdot from David Fourtout, and the red is something a bit special from Château Tour des Gendres. There's a corner of their vineyard with old vines of Cabernet Franc, which is new to me. They call this one Les Anciens Francs, and I think it's excellent."

It was a pleasure, Bruno and the baron

had told each other, to share in Jack's self-taught education in the wines of Bergerac. Guided only by a map of the vineyards from the tourist office, he went on weekly forays, half pilgrimage and half exploration, among the eleven hundred winemakers of the region. Bruno had to admit that Jack was introducing him to good wines he had never known before.

"What I like is that I never know what my *fourchette* will pick up next," said Félix, examining the almost black lump on his fork with interest.

"That's smoked duck sausage," Jack explained. "It's the only sausage I know that doesn't fall apart in cooking. If you find something white, that's the chicken."

Bruno and the baron exchanged glances, and then each filled his glass with the Verdot. In fact, this particular stew was a success, thought Bruno. The textures were varied, although the tastes had merged together, but the duck sausage remained true to its origins, and the chicken had been added late enough to retain its flavor. The sauce itself was rich and nourishing, the potatoes so overcooked that they fell apart under his fork to soak up the juices. The children, he noticed, had already finished their second helpings and were clamoring for their ice cream and apple pie.

"Any developments on Claudia?" Fabiola asked, once the meal was over, the coffee served and the children put to bed.

"Not really, because we're still waiting for the toxicology report on that painkiller she was taking."

"Fentanyl is more than a painkiller, Bruno," she said. "It's an opioid, dangerous as hell and addictive. We've had our own problems in France with it, but in the United States it's almost out of control. Oxycodone, fentanyl, doctors are giving out over two hundred million prescriptions a year, and then there's the black market."

"Why aren't they banned?" the baron asked.

"Its skin-patch delivery system is on the World Health Organization's list of essential medicines because properly used it's a terrific anesthetic. It's also lucrative. The commercial name is OxyContin, and the company that produces it has made over thirty billion dollars from it. People in pain want painkillers, instant relief, but it comes at a high price," Fabiola replied. "We tried using it in France during the AIDS epidemic to stop heroin addicts from infecting themselves with dirty needles, but then we found we had a whole new problem on our hands."

141

"How did it start?" Florence asked.

"German scientists developed it during the First World War, thinking it would be less dangerous than heroin. They were wrong, but it was certainly an effective painkiller. Adolf Hitler used to get injections of it."

"And Claudia was taking it?" Pamela asked.

"She'd been prescribed it for menstrual pains by an American doctor," Fabiola said and tossed up her hands in despair. "She even asked me for a new prescription."

"So it's an open-and-shut case," said Jack. "Why are you still working on it?"

"Her computer and her purse are missing, so that raises questions, and the American ambassador is getting involved," Bruno replied. "It seems he's a friend of her father, so J-J has ordered the autopsy for tomorrow morning to speed things up. But I need to ask those of you who were at the lecture in Limeuil to check whether my list of attendees is complete, and whether you saw anyone leave the event early or arrive late."

"The only person I saw leaving was you, Florence, with Claudia, but then after a minute or two you came back," said Pamela, turning toward her friend.

"When I came back inside the lecture hall,

I took a seat near the door rather than disturb people. I'd certainly have seen if anyone else left, but nobody did," Florence said firmly. "Do you have a final list of those who were there, Bruno?"

Bruno took out the list he had printed in his office and passed it around.

"There was a young man who ran the slide machine," said the baron, looking at Bruno over his spectacles. "Have you included him?"

"He was one of those who came from Montignac with the speaker."

"Then your list may be complete," the baron replied. "Do you know how many chairs were put out before the lecture?"

"Yes, twenty-eight, which is all the chairs they had."

"There were four vacant seats; I remember counting them because for a moment I thought we might run out of chairs, and I'd spotted a window ledge that I could sit on if necessary. And you have twenty-four people on this list, so I'd say it's complete."

Bruno nodded before speaking. "Yes, but wouldn't that depend on when you did your count, after or before Claudia left with Florence?"

"It was before, when we'd all taken our seats and the mayor's wife was introducing the speaker," the baron replied. "I was wondering if there might be any late arrivals."

"And the young man in charge of the slides? Was he sitting in the audience or standing by the slide projector?"

"Standing," interrupted Pamela before the baron could reply. "I remember because he dropped some slides, and I turned around to see what the noise was."

"That means your list can't be right, Bruno," said Florence. "Twenty-eight seats, four of them vacant, and one man standing at the slide projector. That means twenty-five people were there. And I remember there were only two chairs behind the table at the front, one for the speaker and one for the mayor's wife."

"That's right," said Gilles, looking up from his notebook where he'd been scribbling down figures. "Your list has one person missing."

"What about the girl from the garden staff who was serving the fruit punch, Félicité?" Bruno asked. "Could it be her?"

"No, when I came back into the room I sat near the door and she was beside me," said Florence. "I remember that because I was wondering whether there might have been something in the punch that made

144

Claudia feel odd. I asked Félicité later, and she said it was just white wine, fruit juice and sparkling water."

Gilles started sketching a diagram in his notebook. "Here is the lecture hall, here at the front is the table with the speaker and the mayor's wife, the slide projector man at the back and three rows of chairs. I'll make the rows A, B and C, and then I'll number each chair. Where were you, Pamela?"

"I was here, in the second row with Jack and the baron," said Pamela, reaching across to put her finger on Gilles's notebook. "That's B-two, -three and -four, and that English couple from the tennis club was in B-five and -six. When the lecture started, Claudia was in our row, in B-one."

"I started in the front row with my students, and I was at the side, so that's row A, one to four," said Florence. "Joe and his wife were next, in A-five and -six, and then some friends of the speaker in seven and eight."

"There were three Périgord people sitting just behind me in row C," said the baron. "The accents were unmistakable, a couple in their sixties and a younger man of solid build. And Horst and Clothilde were also behind us."

Bruno nodded, thinking of Laurent and

his friends. "I have a good idea who the Périgord people must be."

"When I came back, I sat in the first seat in row C, and Félicité was beside me in C-two," said Florence.

"So if there were eight chairs in each of the three rows, that makes twenty-four. There were two chairs at the front table, twenty-six, and twenty-eight chairs in total," said Gilles. "Where were the other two chairs? Was one of the rows longer than the others?"

"The front and second rows were longer," the baron said. "I remember from when we helped clear them away at the end."

"That means we have A-nine, B-seven, -eight and -nine and C-eight to account for, plus one that Florence vacated," said Gilles. "That makes six empty seats."

Bruno pulled out his phone and called Clothilde, explaining that he was trying to account for everyone at the lecture. She said she and Horst had come alone, but they had sat beside a middle-aged woman from Limeuil named Marie-Claire, who had come with the mayor's wife. Bruno nodded, having called at Marie-Claire's house earlier in the day. He thanked Clothilde and hung up. Jack Crimson was on his own phone, speaking English and thanking someone before he ended the call.

"That was the Sharps, the couple from the tennis club," Jack said. "There was one young man they'd never seen before beside them and then two empty seats. They didn't speak to the young man and couldn't say if he was French or English."

"We have a mystery man," said Gilles, his eyes lighting up. "This is turning into a good story."

Bruno's heart sank. Gilles might now make his living writing books, but the news instincts honed by his years in journalism with *Libération* and *Paris Match* remained strong. "Please don't use what I said about the American ambassador," Bruno told him. "I'd be in real trouble."

Once the dishwasher was filled and people began to take their leave, Bruno was startled when Pamela murmured to him, "Don't go just yet." She then discreetly stroked the palm of his hand with a finger, which surprised him even more. This had always been her private signal that she would welcome Bruno to her bed that night. Pamela had ended their affair several months ago, so Bruno was intrigued and more than a little excited. He bent down to rearrange some of the dishes that had been clumsily stacked on the shelves beneath the kitchen counter as Gilles and Fabiola left, and he and Pamela were alone.

He rose to his feet, feeling uncertain both about his own feelings and about Pamela's motives. Did she want to relaunch their affair or simply have Bruno spend the night? Despite the familiar tingle of anticipation he felt at the prospect, did he really want to resume a relationship that was delightful but that seemed to exist always in the present tense, without a future?

Intensely aware of the tension between his conscious thoughts and the urgings of his body, Bruno gazed at her standing at the sink with her back to him, the slim waist and the flare of her hips reminding him of the lithe horsewoman's body beneath the jeans and sweater. Pamela emptied the carafe, pouring each of them a last half glass of red wine, and then carefully rinsed the heavy crystal decanter at the sink and turned to look at him with that curious half smile and dancing eyes that he knew so well.

"Surprised?" she asked, her tone playful.

He nodded, smiling at her. "And intrigued. I remember that speech of yours on horseback when you said our affair should come to an end."

"Do you recall what I said about how I'd reached that decision?"

"Very clearly. You said while I was involved with you, I would not be free to find the woman I should marry to have a family and raise children."

"And you haven't done that, even though you always said that's what you wanted to do," she said. "I'm not suggesting that it's for want of trying, but that's the way it is. And I miss you and there's no other man I want in my bed." She paused and took a sip of wine, her eyes on his before she spoke quickly. "And sometimes when I'm there alone I find myself wanting you very much."

"And I you," he said, taking her glass from her, putting it on the counter and taking her in his arms.

CHAPTER 11

This was Bruno's second visit to the Château des Milandes in a week. The first had been six days before, when he'd been completing his plans for the free concerts that St. Denis would stage in July and August, the peak tourist season. His promotion to chief of police not only for St. Denis but of its neighboring communes along the River Vézère had not precluded Bruno's other role as the impresario of local entertainments. He relished the annual haggling with the fireworks company for the cost of the *feu de joie* each year on Bastille Day and on the Feast of Saint Louis. He enjoyed arranging the annual vintage-car parade, the anglers' competition, the literary day with local authors, the tennis tournament and all the other events that delighted the tourists and animated the town's calendar. But most of all Bruno enjoyed arranging the free concerts that took place on summer evenings along the riverbank of St. Denis.

Most of the musicians were regulars. He could never fail to invite the town's own rock group, which included Lespinasse from the garage on drums, the church organist on the keyboards and Denis from the newspaper shop on lead guitar. Robert, the architect who sang as well in English as in French, played bass. And the massed elders from the local retirement home would hang Bruno from the town bridge if he ever failed to provide the accordion group that played the old bal musette numbers that got them on their feet and dancing with the enthusiasm if not quite the energy of their youth. The church choir always gave one lively concert of nonreligious songs, and the mayor insisted on at least one string quartet to play chamber music.

Other than those essential events, Bruno had a free hand. And this year he was very proud indeed that his friend Amélie Duplessis, a young magistrate working at the justice ministry, would be singing. She had made a couple of jazz albums and had agreed to spend a week of her vacation in St. Denis to give two riverbank concerts. He allowed himself a smile of satisfaction knowing that Amélie would now be able to return to Paris eleven hundred euros better off. Bruno's own budget for the concerts was limited. He could pay her two hundred euros and provide her with room and board and train fare. But he had managed to negotiate another two hundred for her to give a concert at Montignac, and two hundred more from Les Eyzies. He had previously secured a contract for five hundred euros at Château des Milandes, a special concert of the songs of the legendary American jazz singer Josephine Baker, whose home the château had once been.

This was likely to be a less agreeable meeting, despite the pleasure Bruno always took in the château and its setting on a low ridge above the River Dordogne. It had been built at the end of the fifteenth century by the seigneur of the imposing fortress of Castelnaud at the behest of his young and famously beautiful bride. She had persuaded him to build a new château, in the fashionable style from Italy that was becoming known. The young countess wanted a pleasurable home rather than a bastion of war, a dwelling that would be lighter, more airy and stylish, with windows rather than arrow slits and balconies rather than battlements. And he had built her a jewel, overlooking one of the loveliest stretches of the Dordogne Valley.

Warned that their investigation into Claudia's death was likely to be double-checked and questioned, J-J had asked Bruno to take formal statements from the three people at Milandes. Suspicion was bound to fall on Laurent as an ex-convict who had been in touch with the dead woman, and J-J had asked Bruno to nail down Laurent's alibi for the evening. The task proved simple enough. He started with the chief falconer, Arnaud, a man in his early sixties who had taken up the art after retiring from the army after thirty years in the signal corps. Bruno's own military career provided an instant bond when he spotted the ribbon of the Croix de Guerre on Bruno's uniform.

Arnaud gave Bruno a statement, wrote *lu et approuvé,* read and approved, on the bottom and then signed and dated it before taking Bruno home for a coffee, where his wife gave her own statement. Laurent had been with them throughout the evening since they had left Milandes soon after six until they had dropped him off at Marty's farm at about ten-thirty.

"I gave him a chance on the recommendation of the man who taught me falconry," Arnaud said over the coffee. "I'm glad I did. He's a natural with the hawks, patient but firm. I'll be happy for Laurent to take over the flying displays for the tourists next summer. I know about his past, but he more than paid for his mistake. Ten years was a ridiculous sentence for what was a tragic accident. Anyway, he's in the clear on this latest business about this poor girl. Laurent was stunned when he heard the news from that colleague of yours, the detective who came by yesterday. Not that he showed his grief — he's got a lot of self-control. But I could tell he was badly shaken. Laurent went off to his hawks, sat quietly for a while with the redtail he trained and then cleaned out all the mews."

"The mews?" Bruno asked.

"That's what we call the cages. They have to be big, the size of a bedroom, so the birds can more than spread their wings. They need to do that. And I always like to have a safety chamber, a kind of vestibule where I can go in and close the outer door before going into the mews."

"How did he get the hawk?"

"It's his own bird, a redtail he trained in the Jura. People usually start off with a smaller hawk. I started with a Harris hawk, like most people in France. The red-tailed hawks came from America originally, but they've become very popular recently. They're a good hawk to start with. The falconer who trained me and then Laurent arranged for someone to bring his redtail down here when I told him I was happy to take Laurent on. You should have seen his face when they were reunited. And the hawk seemed just as pleased to be with him again."

"Laurent's a decent man, always helpful and polite," said Arnaud's wife, Myrtille, whose Périgord accent was even more marked than her husband's. "We think we've found a place for him to stay here, a cottage on the estate that's been used just for storage, but the roof and walls are good and there's an old woodstove for heating and cooking. We're giving him a hand in fixing it up."

Arnaud took Bruno to the row of mews, where seventy different owls, eagles and several kinds of hawks were housed, and each of them stared impassively at Bruno as he watched. Arnaud pointed out his own pride and joy, two peregrine falcons he'd raised and trained.

"What are those cords on their legs?" Bruno asked.

"We call them jesses, and we use them to tether the hawk to the falconer's glove and in training. That's probably what Laurent is doing now. You'll find him beyond the steps

155

somewhere."

Laurent was in the garden beyond the mews, a falconer's bag slung crosswise over his left shoulder and hanging down at his right side. He wore a heavy gauntlet on his left hand and forearm, but there was no hawk in sight.

"Hi, Bruno, good to see you, but don't come too close and don't talk yet," Laurent said, speaking softly and barely turning his head to look at his visitor. "Strangers make him nervous, and I'm trying to get him accustomed to his new neighborhood. He's up in that pine tree, looking for squirrels."

Bruno wondered if there would be any squirrels left, this close to the raptors of Milandes. He knew little of falconry and the various sizes of game they would hunt. He knew there had been some concern among farmers about their newborn lambs when Milandes had brought in the first eagles, but there had been no reports of their being taken. There had been claims of some free-range chickens being lost, but since the avian-flu warnings all chicken coops now had to be covered in netting.

Suddenly Bruno caught a flash of movement high up in the pine, and then the hawk swooped, not down to the ground but into the open air above the garden. He climbed and then circled, once, twice, and Bruno heard the rasping *kree-ee-ya* screech that seemed to go on forever until the tone dropped and the noise died. The wings were now outstretched in a glide so perfect and graceful that Bruno caught his breath before the hawk swept effortlessly overhead and beyond the château roof before wheeling back to Laurent and seeming to hang motionless in the air for a long moment before settling onto the glove. Laurent gave his bird some morsel to eat, fastened the jess to a small ring on his gauntlet, tying the falconer's knot with one practiced hand, and then told Bruno he could approach.

As he came closer and could judge its size against Laurent, Bruno saw that the hawk was almost the same height as Laurent's arm, close to half a meter tall. And its wingspan when it had hovered before perching was at least a meter wide, making the bird much bigger than Bruno had expected. Its folded wings were dark brown, its belly white and its chest feathers mottled, brown and light gray. The feathers continued well down the bird's legs, almost as though it wore trousers, and Bruno was surprised by the size and evident strength of the talons. The red tail feathers that gave the breed its name spread out over Laurent's gauntlet, descending a good ten centimeters below what Bruno thought of as its rump. There would probably be some falconry term for it. Bruno's eye returned to the beak, which looked suitably lethal, curving down like a scimitar before ending in a pronounced hook that seemed perfectly adapted to catching and fixing its prey.

"Does your hawk have a name?" he asked, seeing a flash of yellow in the hawk's eyes before Laurent slipped a leather hood over its head. Taking one end in his teeth and the other in his right hand, he tightened the two straps that secured the hood, and the bird seemed to relax, almost as if it were dozing.

"I just call him Hawk. They aren't remotely human, so I never saw a point in giving him a human name."

"How old is he?"

"Nearly two years old, almost ready to start breeding. I've had him since he was a chick. Arnaud wants to breed him to one of his Harris hawks. He reckons it will make a good hybrid. I'm not so sure. Redtails often like to hunt in pairs and then tend to stay loyal to their mate, so I might try to find him a female."

"How do they hunt in pairs?"

"When they're after squirrels, they each

take one side of a tree. One swoops in to drive the squirrel to the other side or down, and then its mate takes the kill."

"What were you feeding him when he landed?"

"A bit of raw beef. Mainly he catches mice and voles, sometimes a rabbit."

"I know rabbits breed fast, but I'm surprised there are any left around here, with all these hungry raptors at the château."

Laurent smiled. "Hawks are carnivores, so they'll eat any meat, even worms and beetles if they're hungry. There's no shortage of food for them around here, although you can get some competition at twilight when the owls come out. And they can range a long way, maybe not as far as St. Denis but certainly beyond Beynac Castle."

"Those talons look very strong."

"For their weight, hawks are by far the strongest living creatures as well as the fastest. Those talons can exert five hundred kilos of pressure per square centimeter," Laurent replied. "But that's not what you came here to talk about. Let's walk back to the mews, but there's nothing I can add to what I told that detective yesterday."

"That was just preliminary questioning when we were trying to understand what happened to Claudia. I'm here to take a formal statement. I just took ones from Arnaud and his wife, so your movements are accounted for. It will be a formality."

"I've heard that from cops before," Laurent said stiffly, looking straight ahead as he plodded up the stone steps. "I thought from what the detective said that it was an accident."

"Probably — she was taking some strong medication that could have made her dizzy. And there was a kitten somewhere on or in the well, and it looks like she tried to help the cat and fell in, but you'll understand that we have to rule out the other possibilities, and you were one of the few people she knew around here."

"I met her a few times. You were there the first time at the station and again when we went to that lecture at the history society, and then she got in touch through the château here and asked me if I wanted to join her on a visit to Lascaux. She came here to pick me up, and I showed her the raptors and my hawk, and then we drove to Montignac. And I saw her Sunday night at Limeuil."

"Did you like her?" Bruno asked. "Were you attracted to her? She was a lovely young woman, it would be natural enough."

Laurent paused as he came to his hawk's

mews and turned to face Bruno. "It was a very good day we had together; perhaps the best I've had since I got out of prison. She was friendly and open and more than just intelligent. Claudia has, or rather she had, a very lively mind. She was genuinely interested in all sorts of things from my hawk to the château to the cave paintings."

Laurent paused again, then looked away across the valley as if searching for words and phrases he barely knew. When he spoke, it was haltingly, coming in bursts.

"Claudia was eager about life, confident about everything, infectious in the way she spread her own happiness. I'd never known anyone like her before. So yes, I was attracted, but not in the way you think. She was too young, too innocent, almost childlike in a way. She seemed to have no idea that the world could be a hurtful place, and I'd have hated to see that realization come to her."

"When you went to Lascaux, did you spend the whole day together?"

"We spent the morning here with the birds, and I showed her around the château and the Josephine Baker exhibition, then we left in a car she'd borrowed. She'd brought a picnic, so we stopped by the river at La Madeleine and ate bread and cheese, some salami and apples and drank cans of Orangina like a couple of kids." He smiled at the memory.

"Then we went to Lascaux and walked around St. Léon Vézère on the way back. It was perfect, two youngsters on a day out without the grown-ups. I hadn't felt like that for a long time, and it was great. When she dropped me off, we hugged each other goodbye like brother and sister."

"What about Sunday night at the lecture in Limeuil? You must have seen her again then."

"Yes, but she looked tired, with dark shadows under her eyes, as though she wasn't feeling well. And she was quieter, distracted. I thought she had something on her mind. And I was with Arnaud and Myrtille, and there were other people that Arnaud wanted me to meet, so we only exchanged a few words over a glass of punch, and then she hurried out soon after the lecture started. I never saw her again."

He opened the outer door of the mews, took his hawk inside through the inner door, checked its water and then returned.

"Let's go and write down my statement but only the facts, Bruno. I don't want to include all that flowery stuff I told you."

He led Bruno to a hut that seemed to be

an office for the falconers, with a small bookshelf, a table made of plywood atop two waist-high filing cabinets and two hard-backed chairs. A bare bulb hung from the ceiling, and an electric kettle and some mugs stood on a shelf above the books, all of them about birds and falconry.

"I've got instant coffee or tea," he said.

Bruno accepted tea, took out a statement form, filled in the details and began to take down Laurent's slow, deliberate dictation. Laurent read it over, approved and signed it. Then Bruno took Laurent, Arnaud and Myrtille to the château office, where a woman in jeans and a sweater who looked overworked agreed to witness the three statements. Bruno was surprised but impressed that she read them aloud to each of the three before appending her own signature.

"Are you the policeman from St. Denis who arranged the Josephine Baker concert?" she asked when the paperwork was complete. Bruno said that he was, and the woman told Laurent and his friends that she would like to talk with Bruno, since she had some queries about the playlist and the concert.

Bruno sat in a stiff-backed chair, studying the woman on the other side of the desk as he shifted mental gears and tried to recall the discussions about the performance. Her dark hair was tied up in a loose bun, and she wore no makeup, no rings and no jewelry. She had good cheekbones and brown eyes and looked to be in her forties, maybe a little more. Her figure was hidden by the baggy woolen sweater she wore. Even with the sleeves rolled up to her elbows, it was far too big for her, and Bruno suspected it had belonged to a man. Maybe it still did.

A large computer screen took up part of her desk. She pulled a wireless keyboard toward her, and her fingers danced over it with easy familiarity to call up something on the screen, presumably the contract.

"I didn't come prepared for this, so I don't have the contract with me, and I'm working from memory," Bruno began. "I negotiated the contract for the concert with a Monsieur Varin at the château here, and there was an appendix to the contract. It included the playlist, about twenty songs, along with a verbal tribute to Baker and her career. We agreed on a total performance time of ninety minutes with a half-hour break."

"That's all fine, but we'd like to add a song, 'C'est un Nid Charmant,' before the finale of 'J'ai Deux Amours.' It's a favorite of one of the important guests who'll be attending from the *conseil régional.* I have a CD here for you that includes the song so your singer can be familiar with it, and then there's the question of costumes. I think there was some discussion of her wearing one of the original costumes from our collection, but I'm afraid that the insurance costs rule that out. Still, I'm sure we can arrange for a copy or two."

"Monsieur Varin said that a decision on costumes could wait until Amélie, the singer, arrives in the Périgord," said Bruno. "She already has a white satin dress and fur cape. But I made it clear that she would definitely not be wearing the banana skirt that Baker made famous at the Folies Bergère. Nor will Amélie perform topless. That's already in the contract."

"Of course, that wouldn't be appropriate, but we were hoping that for the last song of the first act, 'Aux Îles Hawaii,' Amélie might agree to wear a lei, a Hawaiian necklace of flowers, which would completely cover her breasts."

"Monsieur Varin and I discussed that and agreed that it would mean the distraction and interruption of a costume change."

"Yes, but now we have a short newsreel film of Mademoiselle Baker that we could screen while your singer changes."

"I'll put it to her," Bruno said, thinking Amélie would probably jump at the chance. He recalled the deep, admiring chuckle that had come from her when they had visited the château on her last trip to the Périgord. She'd been fascinated by the display of La Baker's costumes and suggested she'd be happy to perform in any one of them, even the famous skirt made only of bananas. It was Bruno who thought that it might not help her career in the justice ministry, nor Amélie's political ambitions, to be known as a topless dancer.

"Just goes to show you know a lot less about politics in France than I do," Amélie had replied with that enormous grin that Bruno found so infectious. He hauled his attention back to the discussion and the woman who was gazing at him quizzically, as if uncertain of his attention.

"Do I come back with her reply to Monsieur Varin or to you?" he asked her.

"It's probably better to talk to me, since I have some legal training and I deal with contracts. My name is Jeannette Neyrac, and I'm the new treasurer here. Monsieur Varin is with the entertainment team, but the project has grown quite a bit since he got the ball rolling. Perhaps we hadn't realized at first just what a marketing opportunity we could make of all this."

"I'll get back to you as soon as I can, madame," Bruno said.

"It's mademoiselle," she replied at once. "I know that you're Chief of Police Courrèges."

"Excuse me, Mademoiselle Neyrac. Were there any other questions about the show or the costumes?"

"No, but I'd like to emphasize that this is an important event for us, a celebration of the seventy years since La Baker bought the château."

"I thought she'd been here throughout the war," Bruno said.

"Yes, but La Baker was only renting it during the war, and she bought it later. Her work with the Resistance will be part of the show. The second act opens with the wartime songs 'J'Attendrai' and 'Le Chant des Partisans,' and we'll have the Anciens Combattants marching down through the hall to the front of the stage with their banners to reopen the show after the break. And we also thought we might reenact her being awarded the Légion d'Honneur by Général de Gaulle."

"I hope you get someone tall enough to play his part," said Bruno, smiling. "This show seems to have become a lot more ambitious since I signed the contract with Monsieur Varin."

"It's turned out to be very popular, already overbooked, so we're having to change the seating and get rid of the tables to pack more people in. There'll be another newsclip interlude, of La Baker with Martin Luther King Jr. at the March on Washington in 1963. We'll play part of his 'I Have a Dream' speech, and then she sings 'We Shall Overcome.' That was already on the playlist, but not many people know how important she was to the civil rights movement, so we thought we might make something special of that."

"I know she refused to sing before segregated audiences in the United States," Bruno replied.

"It went much further than that," Mademoiselle Neyrac said briskly. "When Martin Luther King Jr. was shot, his widow asked La Baker to take over the leadership of the movement, but she declined because of the needs of her twelve children, the multiracial family she adopted from all over the world."

"Perhaps you could send me the revised details of the show, with a list of the various newsclips and inserts you're planning,"

Bruno said. "Are there any other special moments that you have in mind?"

"We're getting a choir of a dozen children to sing when we commemorate the multiracial family she raised. That's when Amélie will sing 'Dans Mon Village' and 'Donnez-Moi la Main' before she leads them offstage with 'La Conga.' "

"I suspect we'll be needing some more rehearsal time for all this."

"I thought you might say that," said Neyrac, with an almost-cheeky smile that made her look younger and a great deal less serious. Bruno got the impression that she was enjoying this exchange, in which she held all the cards and had all the information, while he was left flailing in her wake.

"I fully understand your concern for your artist," she said, that smile playing again around her lips, as if to say she knew he was just a country policeman who arranged a few amateur concerts. "We can add something to the fee to account for that. By the way, did you know the show is going to be televised?"

"Televised? By whom?" Bruno almost jumped out of his chair, and that half smile of hers had become a broad grin. She was evidently enjoying his confusion. He thought of the contract that he'd signed so casually on Amélie's behalf. He'd used a standard artist's contract form that he'd found on the Internet and dimly recalled it had a clause about audiovisual representations and recordings, but he'd need to reread it closely.

"The ARTE channel said they'll screen it simultaneously in France and in Germany, and we're hoping for an American screening on their Black Entertainment Network."

"This comes out of the blue, but I'm happy to hear it."

"We only had it confirmed late yesterday. There's a letter on its way to you. And, of course, we're planning to make our own video of the event that we can sell here at the château, and there will also be a CD of the show. You allowed for that in the contract."

Bruno nodded, feeling out of his depth. This went far beyond his usual role as an amateur impresario of summer entertainment.

"But I'm being thoughtless," Neyrac said. She tapped a few letters on her keyboard, and a modern printer on a side table purred out a printed copy of the contract without any of the mechanical clatter of Bruno's ancient printer and in a fraction of the time. She leaned across to grab the printout,

170

stapled the sheets together and handed them to him, saying, "Maybe you'd like to refresh your memory."

"Thanks. But I'd better consult with Amélie, and I have to get back anyway. I just came here to get those formal statements you witnessed."

She nodded. "That tragic business with the American girl in the well at Limeuil. It's in today's *Sud Ouest.* Don't let me keep you, but get back to me as soon as you can, please. We don't have a lot of time."

CHAPTER 12

Bruno returned to his office and logged on to his computer to find that the toxicology report had already been posted on the case file. Claudia's blood showed a high level of oxycodone, enough that the lab technicians had thought she might easily have gone into a coma. But the report also showed the presence of strong caffeine and some methamphetamine, a combination usually found in a recreational drug widespread in Southeast Asia where it is known as *yaba,* the Burmese phrase for "mad drug." Burmese gangs were reported to be making a billion pills a year for export to Thailand, Bangladesh, China and India. Bruno remembered the Thai stamp in Claudia's passport.

The combination of the opioid, which would induce sleep, with the *yaba,* which would sharply increase energy and wakefulness, was particularly dangerous, the report stressed. It would severely impair the sub-

172

ject's motor skills and slow her reaction time. The interaction of the two drugs was likely also to provoke hyperconfidence verging on a sense of invulnerability.

The preliminary findings of the autopsy showed death by drowning, since water had been found in her lungs along with tiny granules of stone dust consistent with her drowning in a well. Overall she had been a healthy young woman. Her body showed no signs of struggle apart from some recent parallel scratches on her right hand and forearm that had probably been made by a cat.

There were scrapes on her hands and back that were consistent with falling down a stone well. Some grazes and bruising on her legs had probably been caused by bumping into obstacles when drugged, but the pathologist could not rule out the possibility that an assailant had gripped her legs to boost her into the well. Traces of stone and cement dust had been found under the fingernails, two of which had been badly broken, probably in her fall, but there was no sign of human flesh or hair, which suggested there had not been a struggle.

Another casualty of humanity's appetite for drugs, thought Bruno. The Périgord was not free of them. He knew that cannabis was common among young people in St. Denis, and he'd taken part in the arrest of one pupil at the *collège* who had been dealing in locally grown marijuana. He'd also come across some Ecstasy when a Dutch gang had been caught distributing it along with amphetamines from a camping site. Doubtless there would be a handful of cocaine users. Normally drug offenses accounted for around five or six hundred arrests a year in the *département,* on average around 5 percent of all arrests. But in St. Denis the proportion of drug arrests was much smaller. This was the first case that Bruno had come across involving fentanyl, oxycodone or the *yaba* cocktail the report had mentioned. He added a note to the case file about Claudia's passport showing a visit to Thailand and then pulled out Amélie's contract and began to read.

He had on Amélie's advice downloaded a sample contract issued by UNESCO, which made it clear that any recording for sale of her performance or any broadcast would incur extra fees to be negotiated at a rate not less than the initial performance fee. Amélie would also get royalties of 10 percent on the sale price of all recordings. And the Josephine Baker estate would waive for Amélie any license fees for the use of copyrighted music and songs during the performance. That seemed clear enough. Bruno e-mailed Amélie, asking her to call him urgently about some new issues on her contract.

Since Bruno knew that Amélie lived with and by her mobile phone, he didn't expect to wait long, and she called him within a minute of his sending the e-mail.

"Hi, Bruno, it's good to hear your voice. What's up?"

"I have some interesting news. It looks like you'll be earning more than we thought from the Josephine Baker gig at Milandes, though you might want to handle these negotiations yourself, since I'm now well out of my league. They want to record it and sell CDs of your performance, and your show is going to be televised by ARTE."

"Wow! That's great, Bruno. Is there already a provision for that in the contract?"

"It says the fees are to be negotiated but in each case not less than the performance fee and they were paying you five hundred. So that's at least another five hundred for the broadcast and five hundred for the recording, but you might want to discuss that with them yourself and see if you can get more. Maybe you ought to think about getting a proper agent."

"If they are doing a sound recording and a video recording, that's two recordings, so that's a thousand extra, minimum," she said. "And since ARTE broadcasts in Germany as well as France, that's two broadcasts, so another thousand at least."

"That's why I think you ought to negotiate this one yourself or get an agent," he said. "With a televised concert in the works, one ought to snap you up." He gave her Mademoiselle Neyrac's name and phone number and was about to end the call when she spoke again.

"Since you're on the phone, you know I have a Google alert about anything in the media about St. Denis, so I saw that item in *Sud Ouest* about the American girl falling down the well. It turns out that a friend of mine knows her — Chantal, a law school classmate who works for the Louvre. We're together now, having an early lunch where Chantal and the American girl ate together last week. Isn't that weird? Apparently the girl was well liked at the Louvre, and Chantal was really upset. Do you want to talk to her? Here, I'll put her on. I told her all about you, so you don't need to explain that you're a cop."

"Monsieur Bruno? Bonjour," came a quiet voice, a Parisian accent.

"Bonjour, Chantal. This is quite a co-incidence. When did you last see Claudia, and what was her mood?"

"I saw her last week, and she was fine, except that she'd just broken up with her boyfriend."

"Would that be Jack, the lawyer in London?"

"Yes, that's right. He'd come to Paris, and things didn't work out, so Claudia broke it off. She said it was quite a wrench, since they'd known each other since they were five years old."

"Childhood sweethearts," said Bruno. "Was she depressed about it?"

"No, she was relieved and said it had gone on too long. She'd tried to end the relationship before, but Jack had talked her out of it. What happened to her? How did she fall down the well?"

"We're still trying to understand what happened, but she'd been taking some powerful painkillers, and she may have been trying to rescue a cat that had got trapped in the well."

"That sounds like Claudia, she was a real cat person. But why was she on the painkillers?"

"She had a doctor's prescription. Did she ever mention taking them to you?"

"I know she was a martyr to cramps. She used to dread that time of the month, but she said she had some medicine that really helped. *Mon Dieu,* I wonder if Jack knows she's dead. He'll be devastated."

"Did you meet him?"

"Yes, several of us had dinner together the evening he arrived in Paris. She said she'd rather not start with a romantic evening, just the two of them. I think she'd already decided to end their relationship."

"Did she ever say why?"

"Not exactly, but when she came back from seeing him in London not long ago she'd been depressed over some row, and he'd lost his temper . . ." Her voice trailed off, and Bruno felt now she was talking to Amélie, not to him.

"You mean he hit her?" Bruno heard Amélie say. He could hear the shock in her voice.

"That's what I asked," Chantal said. "She didn't say so, not exactly, but . . . you know how you can read these things."

"Excuse me, but this could be serious," Bruno interrupted. "Do you have Jack's full name and where he works in London?"

"Jack Morgan. Claudia called him JP, like the bank. I don't know where he works but he went to Yale Law School, if that helps."

178

"How long was Jack in Paris?"

"He came over Friday evening on the Eurostar, and we went right out to dinner because Claudia had asked me to make sure they didn't spend too much time alone. So with my boyfriend we met again the next afternoon at the Marmottan Monet Museum, walked back along the quayside to have a drink at the Café Flore, then dinner somewhere she knew off rue Jacob. Later we went to a place called the Caveau in rue de la Huchette to listen to jazz, and we left around midnight. We met again for a brunch party at Claudia's apartment on Sunday, and Jack was going back on the Eurostar to London later that day."

"Claudia knew Paris well?"

"Pretty well. Her father bought her an apartment on rue Jacob for her year in Paris, and she liked to throw brunch parties on weekends."

"Did she have other friends in Paris?"

"A girl called Marge she'd been at school with who was studying at Sciences Po, a couple from the American embassy and a British girl, Judy, a photographer who did some work for one of the London papers. They were usually at her brunches, and I think she was seeing a French guy she met at one of Jim's Sunday dinners."

"Jim? Who is Jim?"

"Jim Haynes. He's an institution, an American who has a terrific artist's studio in Montparnasse where for forty years he's kept open house for dinners every Sunday evening. I think he's in some record book for having more dinner guests than anyone in history. Claudia took me once — she would go along if she had nothing else to do, and you never knew who you'd meet: expats, tourists, artists, writers. Jim knows everybody. He ran the Arts Lab in London back in the sixties."

"Do you have a name for this French guy?"

"Marcel. I never met him and never learned his last name, but she liked to go dancing with him at the Batofar near the Gare d'Austerlitz and that old beatnik place near Pigalle that's become fashionable again, the Bus Palladium."

"It sounds like quite a social life," Bruno said, thinking Claudia's days in Limeuil could hardly have been more different. "Next time I'm there, I'll have to ask you and Amélie for a few tips."

Chantal laughed, and Bruno heard Amélie's voice in the background. "She says she'll bring me down when she's singing so I can taste your cooking."

"With pleasure," said Bruno, taking her name and number in case J-J needed to follow up on Claudia's life in Paris. As he ended the call, he saw two urgent messages, one from Hodge asking for a callback and the other from J-J. He called J-J first.

"You'd better get to my office right away," J-J said. "We've got Hodge and the dead girl's mother on the way here, and they're bringing Maître Duhamel from Bordeaux, who's one of the more expensive lawyers in the city. It seems the mother flew in overnight from New York as soon as she got the news. God knows what she wants, but Prunier wants us both to attend."

"Strings being pulled," said Bruno. "The dead girl's father is a friend of the ambassador."

"And of the White House. Better put your siren on, and you can be here in thirty minutes."

"Hodge asked me to call him," Bruno said. "And I haven't had lunch."

"I'll buy you a sandwich, and you'll see Hodge when you get here. Just get moving, and I'll tell the police garage you can park here."

Pausing only to tell the mayor's secretary of his movements, Bruno trotted down the spiral stone staircase, put the flashing blue light on his van and headed out of town for the forty kilometers to Périgueux. He could think of few things sadder than a mother learning of the death of a child, so he could expect the woman to be in shock and probably exhausted after a sleepless night on the plane. He wondered why she had brought the lawyer with her and hoped she might have something to say that would help him and J-J understand more about Claudia's death.

There were three items that nagged him, beyond the exotic *yaba* pills. There was her laptop and its bag, which she seemed to take everywhere with her. He'd like to find her purse, but that may have been in the laptop bag. And there was the unknown man at the lecture. He knew there were no traffic lights on the route until he reached the city, so he pulled off at a cutout, connected his earphone and called the *mairie* at Limeuil, a place small enough that the mayor's wife often came in to help.

By chance, she was there, and as he drove off, Bruno asked if she could identify the solitary man in the lecture hall. He could have kicked himself for not checking with her earlier when she answered that it had been Madame Darrail's son, Dominic, and he like everyone else at the lecture had

182

remained until the end. Bruno would have to double-check what had happened when the lecture ended and when Félicité had closed the castle and locked the main gate into the garden. Had she checked off everyone who had been present? Someone could have stayed behind.

Then Bruno recalled his climb over the roof onto the balcony that led into Claudia's room. Dominic had been raised in the house and would certainly know about that route. As a boy he'd probably have found all the ways to climb into the castle gardens. He ought to be interviewing Dominic right now rather than racing to Périgueux. Then another thought struck him, and Bruno pulled in at the next available cutout and called Bourdeille's home. Madame Bonnet answered, and Bruno, recalling that on occasion she had lent Claudia her car, asked if Claudia's missing laptop might be in the vehicle.

"I don't know," she said. "I haven't used the car since the last time I saw her. She borrowed it last week to do some shopping. It must have been Friday, maybe Saturday. She said she had to go to the pharmacy in St. Cyprien. But I can go home and check. It won't take a minute and I'll call you back."

Bruno drove on, wondering why Claudia had gone to the pharmacy in St. Cyprien when St. Denis was so much closer. He'd have to talk to the pharmacist. And if Claudia had left her laptop in the car on Saturday, why hadn't she picked it up on Sunday? She would have needed it when working in Bourdeille's library. His phone rang, and it was Madame Bonnet to say that she had found the bag with Claudia's purse and laptop tucked into the well behind the driver's seat.

"Claudia had a shopping bag when she came to give me back the keys," she said. "Perhaps she didn't want to handle that and the laptop bag on her bicycle."

Bruno thanked her and ended the call. He'd just entered the low-speed zone of the hamlet of Versannes and so put on his siren to race through. There was radar on the road here, but with his blue light flashing he ignored it and used his siren again to get through the usual lines of traffic at the roundabouts on the main road to Périgueux. He drove into the garage beneath the *commissariat de police,* took the elevator to J-J's floor and found him waiting as the doors opened.

CHAPTER 13

"You're just in time," J-J said. "We're meeting in Prunier's office, and he'll probably want to talk before the girl's mother gets here."

Bruno handed J-J the statements he'd taken at Château des Milandes and explained the two new developments about Dominic and Claudia's laptop as they rose to the top floor. In return, J-J told him they had the complete autopsy report, which had nothing new to add. But Yves, who ran J-J's forensic team, had filed his own report on the search of Claudia's room. There had been some unknown fingerprints, probably male, on the balcony rail, and inside the hollow metal tubing of her rucksack he'd found a plastic straw.

"A drinking straw?" Bruno asked.

"Yes, and it was full of little red pills, those Burmese ones. I'll let Prunier decide whether we tell the mother about that. For

185

me that about wraps this case up. She must have been drugged to the eyeballs — you read the toxicology report. Still, we'd better do it by the book, just as Hodge advised. So you'd better interview Dominic and make sure to bring that laptop in. Yves has already been working on her phone, and he's been trying to get access to her stuff on the cloud."

Prunier was on the phone when they knocked, and he called for them to enter. He gestured to the conference table, and they each took a seat as the *commissaire* ended the call with a polite, "*Bien sûr,* Madame le Préfet."

"She's a big improvement on the last prefect we had," he said, shaking hands. "She let me know she's had a call from the foreign minister's office after the American ambassador called him, but as far as she's concerned we're to treat this as a normal case. That means we handle it, and there'll be no Parisian hotshot coming down to second-guess us."

"Hodge warned me that the dead girl's father was likely to hire some private investigators," Bruno said.

"And now the mother's coming with a fancy lawyer," added J-J, his voice a resentful grumble.

"Look on the bright side," said Prunier. "If she complains about the autopsy and starts demanding the body, which is what I expect, her lawyer can explain French law to her and save us the bother. But let's be polite, professional and compassionate. This is a mother who's just lost her child."

Bruno had not known what to expect, but the idea of a wealthy divorcée from New York had triggered his subconscious to assume she would be a fashionably thin, overdressed and overstressed woman with a chip on her shoulder from the failed marriage and probably resentful of men, all men. Instead, he recognized the plump woman from Claudia's family photos as she was led into Prunier's office. Then, she had looked happy. Now she was stricken and staggered a little as she walked. She was wearing sneakers of leather and a shapeless tracksuit that looked comfortable over a cashmere turtleneck sweater. There were dark shadows beneath eyes that were red from weeping, and with an effort she squared her shoulders as if to brace herself.

"I'm very grateful that you gentlemen could spare the time to see me," she said in excellent French and then introduced the elderly lawyer who had followed her into the room. Hodge took up the rear, shook hands all around and then they all sat at the conference table.

Prunier offered his condolences and suggested they help themselves from the pot of fresh coffee and small bottles of fruit juice and mineral water.

"Maître Duhamel has explained the provisions of French law to me, so I understand that for the moment you'll have to keep Claudia's body while your investigation continues," she said with a catch in her voice. She paused to dab her eyes and apologized before she blew her nose. "I'll have to discuss this with her father, but I expect we'll have her cremated here, and then I'll take her ashes back to New York. What can you tell me about the circumstances of her death?"

Prunier gave a standard response: inquiries were at an early stage, but so far everything pointed to an accident, to which Claudia's medication may have contributed. The builders who had failed to secure the well faced charges for negligence.

"Is there any background information I might have about Claudia that could help you?" she asked. She tightened her mouth, bracing herself. Bruno saw a woman devastated by grief but determined to hold herself together.

"Let me just add that after hearing from Chief of Police Courrèges here about the medicine found in her room, I checked with the pharmacies in New York and New Haven," Hodge interrupted. "I also spoke with her doctors, one in Manhattan and the other at the medical center attached to Yale. The fentanyl and oxycodone were separately but legally prescribed, and the New Haven narcotics unit tells me her doctor has a fine reputation. He's not known for overprescribing. The doctor told me that it was an unusual case, that your daughter suffered very severely from menstrual cramps. He was not aware that she already had a prescription for oxycodone from New York. If he had, he'd never have prescribed the fentanyl."

"Do you know if your daughter ever took any recreational drugs, madame?" Prunier asked.

"I know Claudia tried marijuana because she told me so, but she said she didn't like the feeling of not being in command of her senses. She tried cocaine once at college, she told me, but I don't think she made a habit of it."

Her hands were twisting together in a way that looked painful. She coughed, or perhaps it had been a sob. "I know that she suffered from menstrual cramps, often accompanied by migraines."

"Thank you for your frankness. What about amphetamines?" Prunier asked.

"Not that I know of. Why do you ask?"

Her lawyer intervened. "I presume that by now you have the toxicology report. And I advised Madame Muller that you almost certainly arranged an autopsy. We very much would like to see copies of both reports."

"In principle, I have no objection," Prunier replied. "But I think that had better wait until our investigation is complete and one of our magistrates has had an opportunity to examine our findings and make a judgment."

"I have explained the critical role of the magistrate under French law," Duhamel said. "Is there any reason to expect anything but a verdict of accidental death?"

"Perhaps I could answer as the officer in charge of the investigation," intervened J-J. "It's too soon to tell. We have just located Claudia's laptop, which we have yet to examine, and have only just received the autopsy report. We are still interviewing the people at the lecture who seem to have been the last people to have seen your daughter alive, but since there are twenty of them it takes time. It was only yesterday morning that Chief of Police Courrèges tracked her down to the well with the help of a sniffer dog. Otherwise this might still be a missing person case."

"Thank you, monsieur," the woman said to Bruno, forcing herself to be polite. Her fingernails were digging hard into the back of her hands. "Could you tell me exactly what happened?"

Bruno explained about Florence's unanswered phone call to Claudia, the landlady finding that the bed had not been slept in, Bruno's dog tracking Claudia to the well, his own descent and the arrival of the *pompiers* and the doctor who pronounced her dead.

"We did all we could, madame," he said. "I tried giving her mouth-to-mouth resuscitation, but it was much too late. She'd been dead for several hours."

"The autopsy report is wholly consistent with her death by drowning after falling down the well, perhaps while trying to help a cat," J-J said. "Certainly her arm was marked with cat scratches."

"Claudia was a real cat person, endlessly sending me little videos she'd seen on social media," said her mother. She gulped, and for the first time since entering the room

191

she seemed on the verge of losing control. Then she looked intently at Prunier. "You didn't reply when I asked why you had that question about amphetamines. Is there any evidence she was taking them?"

Prunier nodded. "I'm afraid so, a pill called *yaba*, a mix of caffeine and amphetamine that's common in Asia. Several more of the pills were found hidden in her rucksack. They are illegal under French law. Her passport shows that she visited Thailand earlier this year."

Madame Muller had her hand to her mouth, and her eyes looked alarmed. Bruno opened a bottle of mineral water and poured her a glass.

"Shit," she said in English. "Yes, she went to Thailand with her boyfriend, a young man I've known for years." She closed her eyes, sighed and dabbed at them again with her handkerchief. "Does he know yet that she's dead?"

"I just learned about Monsieur Morgan today," Bruno said. "I was about to contact Yale Law School to get a current address for him in London when I was called to this meeting. Would you know where we could reach him?"

The woman pulled out a phone. She consulted her address list and read out some numbers and an address, which Bruno noted down.

"One of her friends in Paris told me that Claudia had broken off the relationship with Morgan after his last visit to her in Paris, just over a week ago," Bruno said.

"I didn't know that," Madame Muller said slowly, examining Bruno with new interest. "But you've obviously been working hard if you've been talking to her friends in Paris. It's interesting that you would go to such lengths if everything points to an accidental death."

"We are taking this very seriously, madame, as you can see," said Prunier, "following every possible lead. Do you have any more questions, since these officers naturally want to get back to work?"

"Can I see her? Don't you need a close family member to identify her body?"

"There is no need, madame. She was identified by several people who knew her here in France. And after an autopsy, it might be upsetting for you."

"I'd still like to see her, please." Her voice was suddenly firm, and for the first time Bruno saw fire in her eyes.

Prunier glanced at the lawyer and then back at Madame Muller. "If you insist, I'll make arrangements with the morgue in

Bergerac. The pathologist put off some other urgent cases to work on Claudia, so I think you may have to wait until the morning."

"I think she would like to see her daughter today, if that's at all possible," said Duhamel eagerly, at last finding something for which he could justify his fee.

"Leave it to me," said J-J, rising to his feet and pulling out his phone as he left the room.

"To which of her friends in Paris did you speak, monsieur?" she asked Bruno.

"I don't think we want to identify any of our witnesses at this stage," Prunier intervened.

J-J came back into the room to tell them they could see the body in the morgue at six that evening.

"I know where it is," said Hodge. "I'll go with Madame Muller."

Prunier rose. "With your permission, madame, I think it's time for these officers to return to their work. Can we help you with any arrangements for staying in the Périgord, or will you be returning to Paris?"

"I'm already booked into a hotel near Limeuil," she replied. "I expect to stay here until you or your magistrates reach a conclusion."

"Fine. If I can be of further assistance, madame, please don't hesitate to call me." He handed her a card.

"Thank you, Commissaire Prunier," she said, glancing at his card. "I'm sad to return to France under such tragic circumstances. I lived in Paris for some years when I was a young economist at the OCDE." She used the French initials for the Organisation for Economic Co-operation and Development, the body that had been founded to manage the Marshall Plan after World War II, when the Americans pumped money into rebuilding the war-torn economies of Europe.

"It was a very happy time for me, and I've always loved Paris. I suppose I should think of it as a comfort to know that Claudia loved it too." From her handbag she took out a card case and gave each of them her card. "This has my American cell phone and e-mail address if you need to reach me. And Maître Duhamel can tell you the name of my hotel."

"The Vieux Logis in Trémolat," Duhamel said.

Bruno was looking at the card she had given him. It was engraved rather than printed and revealed that she was a professor of economics with a doctorate. The card also said that she was a member of a policy advisory board of the New York Federal Reserve.

Bruno was no expert in such matters, but he seemed to recall from reports of the financial crisis in 2008 that it was a regional wing of the American central bank. Evidently she was a formidable woman in her own right. That might add some complications to her divorce from a husband who ran a large investment trust. Bruno's thoughts went back to Claudia's family photo, the one that showed just her and her father with a third person carefully scissored out of the picture.

CHAPTER 14

Yves from the forensic unit followed Bruno in a separate car to Bourdeille's home outside Limeuil, where Madame Bonnet handed over Claudia's laptop bag, and Bruno took it out to Yves, waiting in his car. Bruno slipped into the passenger seat and opened the bag.

The laptop was a slim, sleek MacBook, and the purse held eighty euros in banknotes, an American driver's license, a Louvre ID, a French student card and loyalty cards for airlines and hotels. There was a diary, a set of headphones and a small notebook along with pens, tissues, lipstick and a tube of hand cream. There was a slim book in French, *La Renaissance Française* by Thérèse Castieau, and a thicker one in English on the same theme by Henri Zerner. The two men donned evidence gloves, and Bruno examined the diary while Yves opened the laptop.

"Password protected," said Yves. He tried various combinations of Claudia's date of birth, initials, passport and cell-phone numbers, without success.

"Merde," he said. "Anything in her diary?"

Bruno skimmed the first pages in which Claudia had written her addresses and various ID and credit card numbers. None worked. He turned to the backflap and saw a Latin phrase in capital letters: VIRTVTEMFORMADECORAT. Yves typed it as Bruno spelled it out, and the screen opened. Yves opened the search function on his own phone and typed in the same phrase.

"It means 'Beauty adorns virtue' and it's painted on the back of one of Leonardo's portraits of a young woman," he said. "Interesting choice. I've never seen Latin used in a password before."

Thumbing through the diary, Bruno saw a small red cross against the dates for the latest weekend, and again for each date four weeks earlier throughout the year. He saw references to flights and train times, Jack's weekend visit to Paris, lunch with Chantal and some dates with simply a capital *M*, which could be Marcel, the dance partner from the Batofan. Birthdays were listed for her parents and friends, and he saw random shopping lists.

At the bottom of the bag he found two USB sticks, a handful of euro and American coins and various receipts for Paris restaurants, the hilltop restaurant in Limeuil and for two supermarkets, Monoprix in Paris and Carrefour in St. Cyprien, dated the previous Saturday. She'd bought soap, chocolates, a three-pack of white T-shirts and another of panties, Tampax, two pairs of black tights and a bottle of Smirnoff vodka. What had happened to the vodka?

"You ever heard of a company called Hexagon Trust?" Yves asked.

Bruno shook his head.

"They're based in New York, but their letterhead shows offices in London, Paris, Singapore and Dubai. They look like lawyers, but they seem to do something called forensic accounting and investigations. What's the name of the guy who lives at this *chartreuse*? Did you say Bourdeille? There's a long report these lawyer-accountants have done on him, but it's all in English."

He passed the laptop to Bruno, but the language was far too specialized for Bruno's limited skill. It was broken up into sections, and he understood that part of it concerned Bourdeille's career in the Resistance and his time in prison. Another was about a

Resistance colleague called Paul Juin, of whom Bruno had never heard. Yet another was about Juin's sister, and seemed to suggest Bourdeille had been married to her. The rest covered individual paintings and Bourdeille's work as an art consultant and collector. He scrolled through to the end, more than sixty pages, and found a bill for the report made out to the Muller Investment Trust, for fifty thousand dollars.

"Mon Dieu," said Bruno. "Look what they charged for this report."

"*Merde,* we're in the wrong business," Yves said as he looked at the bill. "And J-J is going to go crazy over the cost of an official translation. To get something we can use in court the translators charge eighty euros a page. That's going to cost five thousand."

"We don't need a copy for a court, at least not yet. I have English friends who can summarize it if you can print it out. Or put it on one of these USB sticks."

"I'd better look at them first," said Yves. He put the USB sticks from Claudia's bag into the slot on the computer, one after the other. The first one seemed to be all about Claudia's art research, but the second seemed to be personal — letters, bank statements and a copy of the Hexagon Trust report.

"Let's go back to your place, you download this report onto your own laptop, then I'll take all this back to Périgueux," said Yves. "If there's anything useful in her e-mails that isn't duplicated on her phone, I can let you know. Fair enough?"

Bruno agreed and went back to the house to give Madame Bonnet a receipt for the laptop bag and its contents. He brought Yves to his home, copied the USB stick and then drove to St. Cyprien as Yves left for Périgueux. The pharmacy closest to the Carrefour supermarket was busy, but the pharmacist spotted Bruno's uniform and waved him through to an office in the rear. Bruno asked if he recalled a young American woman on Saturday.

"Yes, it was unusual, so I recall it," he replied and went on to explain that one of the counter staff had called him to deal with the young woman who had an American doctor's prescription for a drug called fentanyl and asked if the pharmacy could supply it. The prescription seemed in order, and she'd presented another form about her international health insurance and her passport. The pharmacist had to explain that he couldn't honor a foreign prescription for a controlled drug. She had offered to pay cash, but he'd repeated that it wasn't possible. He'd said a French doctor might be able to prescribe it for her if Claudia's own doctor in America sent an official e-mail. Otherwise, she should try the American clinic in Paris, which might be able to help.

Outside in the parking lot, Bruno called Hodge and found him in Bergerac with Madame Muller, sitting in a café while waiting for their appointment at the morgue.

"Are you free tonight?" Hodge asked, explaining that Madame Muller was exhausted and planned to go directly to her hotel and try to sleep once she had seen her daughter's body. "My per diem doesn't run to the kind of hotel she's in, but I can certainly take you to dinner at that bistro I recall in St. Denis where we had lunch."

"You mean Ivan's place. That's fine, but it will be a working dinner," Bruno replied. "There's a long but interesting document in English I'll need you to translate, not word for word but enough for me to get the gist of it. It comes from Claudia's laptop. Have you ever heard of a firm called Hexagon Trust?"

"Yes, but we'd better discuss that this evening," Hodge replied. Bruno understood he did not want to discuss it in the hearing of Madame Muller and her lawyer.

"I've booked you into a decent place in St. Denis, the Vézère Lodge," Bruno said. "It's on the road out of town toward Les Eyzies."

"Thanks. When we get back from Bergerac, I'll go there and take a shower and meet you at Ivan's at about eight." Hodge hung up.

Bruno checked his watch. He had time to get to the *mairie,* scan his mail and e-mails, brief the mayor and still get to Pamela's riding school in time for the evening exercise. Once installed in his office, he scanned the e-mails from his colleagues Juliette in Les Eyzies and Louis in Montignac. They had each taken statements from the people at the lecture, and although he saw nothing new in their reports, he added them to the case file on Claudia's death.

"It's very sad about this young American girl," said the mayor, coming into Bruno's office and closing the door. "I got your message about her mother flying over from New York. What are her plans?"

Bruno explained that she intended to stay until the magistrate was able to determine whether the death had been accidental, and that private investigators might be hired.

"It must be very distressing for her. Jacqueline was wondering if she could help in any way. A woman of a similar age, a fellow American . . ." His voice trailed off.

Jacqueline was a historian who taught at the Sorbonne, daughter of a French mother and an American father, and she was at home in both countries. After the death of the mayor's wife, he had started an affair with her that seemed to make them both very happy. It had certainly put a new spring into the mayor's step and a gleam in his eye. There was no more talk of his retiring before the next election, rather to the discomfiture of Xavier, the deputy mayor, whose ambition for the succession had become something of a local joke. And there was nothing worse for a politician than to be thought of as a joke, Bruno knew. He got on reasonably well with Xavier and admired his confidence in running the town budget, but he had few of the mayor's political connections in Paris and Brussels and was no match for his massive experience in local and national politics.

"I'm having dinner with Hodge, the FBI man at the American embassy who came down for that IRA problem we had," Bruno said. "His ambassador has sent him down to babysit Claudia's mother. Not that she needs it — she speaks excellent French, spent some years working in Paris. She's a professor of economics and on some board of America's central bank. And as you know Claudia's father has powerful political connections, which is why Hodge has been sent down here to escort her. I'll mention Jacqueline's offer to him over dinner. It's a kind thought."

"There's another thing," the mayor said. He'd been telephoned earlier in the day by Bourdeille, who wanted to discuss something interesting for St. Denis. He had mentioned a bequest, without going into specifics. Might the mayor and Bruno find it convenient to call on him at some point in the week, his own mobility being understandably constrained.

"A bequest?" Bruno asked. "Do you think he wants to include the town in his will?"

"He didn't want to go into details on the phone."

"Maybe he's heard that rumor about Claire listening in on your calls," Bruno said with a grin. "She seems to have given up on me, but I know she's been fluttering her eyelashes at Xavier lately."

"Xavier is safely and stably married," said the mayor. "And he's a careful man, so I think we can be sure he'll stay that way."

Bruno nodded. Xavier's father owned the town's Renault agency, but there was talk of its being closed unless the family could come up with the funds to build a lavish modern showroom. The old man was close to retirement and had been heard to say that Renault wanted to close the small local agencies and focus on those in the big towns. That could blow a hole in Xavier's income, but his wife's family owned a lot of woodland as well as the town's sawmill. And Xavier was far too careful a man to risk that for Claire's blowsy charms.

"I'm surprised Bourdeille wants me to be there for the meeting," Bruno said.

"He stressed it, saying he'd enjoyed seeing you despite the sad occasion of Claudia's death. He called you his *cher confrère,* which I presume was a reference to that foie gras club you both belong to."

Bruno nodded. "That's right, but I'm intrigued by his talk of a bequest. He told me that Claudia had been trying to buy his *chartreuse,* along with all the art inside it."

"Did he? That's interesting. Did you believe it?"

"Oh, yes," Bruno replied, explaining the report that had been found on Claudia's computer. "I can let you know what's in it tomorrow, after I've gone through it with

Hodge."

The mayor left for the evening, and Bruno locked up and drove to Pamela's place, where his dog seemed to recognize the sound of the police van and raced out to greet him. The others were already in the stables, saddling up. Bruno quickly greeted them all: Pamela, Fabiola, Gilles, Félix, and for once Miranda was there too. Her father would be looking after the children. Despite their renewed status as lovers, Pamela was careful to give Bruno only the usual friendly *bise* on each cheek, the same courteous formality the other women offered. From this he assumed she wanted their relations to remain private.

Bruno put on his riding boots and cap and changed his jacket. He gave Hector his customary carrot before putting on the saddle and bridle. Hector was feeling playful and tried his little game of blowing out his stomach, and Bruno kneed him there gently so he could tighten the girth.

"Your choice of route, Miranda," called Pamela as they led the horses out of the yard and mounted.

"Let's go to that long firebreak in the woods on the way to Campagne," she answered. "I feel like a real gallop. But I don't want Hector's hooves kicking mud into my face, and you know what he's like, Bruno. He always wants to be in front. Can you hold him back for once?"

"I'll take a different route, since I can't ride for long tonight. I have to get to dinner with a visiting FBI man about the dead American girl."

"Wait," said Fabiola, signaling the others to go on ahead before addressing Bruno. "They certainly rushed through the autopsy report in record time. Somebody must have been putting the pressure on. I hear the American embassy got involved."

Bruno nodded. "They certainly did and I've seen the report. The pathologist carefully hedged his bets. He said her injuries were consistent with falling in by accident or being pushed."

"What happened to her skirt?"

"How do you mean?" Bruno asked.

"Her legs were bare. I'd be surprised if she'd been wearing trousers or jeans. They tend to stay on, so I assume she was wearing a skirt, which I'd have thought would have floated like that ballet shoe Ahmed brought up. There was no sign of it at the scene and no mention of it in the pathologist's report."

"I didn't know you'd seen it."

"Professional courtesy among the medical mafia."

"Would it tell us anything?" he asked.

"I have no idea. Do you plan to drag the well?"

"No, but it's a good point and I'll raise it with J-J."

Fabiola trotted off after the others, and Bruno turned Hector to ride up to the ridge with its familiar view over St. Denis. He stopped and called Florence at home to ask if she recalled what Claudia had been wearing at the lecture.

"Let me think. A light-colored blouse or shirt, pleated. I noticed it because it looked like an Anne Fontaine, which is way out of my price range. She was taking notes in a small notebook, and yes, she took it from a blue denim skirt that had pockets."

"Nothing else? The evenings get cool."

"I didn't notice. Maybe she hung up a jacket when she arrived."

He thanked her, ended the call and cantered on, making a mental list. He still had to check with Félicité about closing the castle. Had she locked the gates, counted everyone leaving and checked for any forgotten coats? He needed to inform Jack Morgan of the death and suggest that J-J or perhaps Prunier might ask Scotland Yard to make a discreet check on his movements. And this evening, with Hodge's help, he could look at that curious file on Bourdeille from Hexagon Trust. Bruno could understand Claudia commissioning some research into Bourdeille if she was serious about buying his home and his art collection, even more so if she was still suspicious about his attributions.

As he reached the open stretch of ridge, he checked that Balzac was still at Hector's heels and then let his horse bound forward into the gallop Hector loved as much as his rider. Everything else faded from his mind as Bruno thought only of the wind in his face, the sound of drumming hooves and the intense awareness of his horse and the speed they were making together. It felt so much faster than any journey by car or train, faster even than accelerating along a runway as an aircraft reached flying speed. And it ended all too soon as the trees and brush came close and Hector turned without any nudge from Bruno's knees and trotted back to meet Balzac, who was bounding toward them, giving a joyful bark. Hector threw back his head and whinnied in response.

CHAPTER 15

Thirty minutes later, his horse rubbed down
and his own head, chest and shoulders
rinsed off in the sink of Pamela's stables,
Bruno entered Ivan's bistro with his laptop
in hand and a copy of Yves's USB stick in
his pocket. Hodge had not yet arrived.
Bruno shook hands with Ivan and then
greeted two other tables of friends who were
dining there: Rollo, the headmaster of the
local *collège,* and his wife and Lespinasse
from the garage with two strangers, who appeared to be talking business.

Bruno chose the table farthest from the
others and booted up his computer. He
inserted the USB stick and called up the
file on Bourdeille. Ivan brought him a kir
and pointed to the blackboard on which
he'd printed in chalk the menu of the day:
split pea and ham soup to be followed by a
terrine of hare, with *rognons de veau au vin
blanc* as the main course. The desserts on

offer were a choice of crème caramel, a selection of sorbets, chocolate mousse or rhubarb and apple pie. Ivan had a special way with fruit pies.

"How are you preparing the kidneys?" Bruno asked.

"A bit of fatty ham for flavor, shallots, some old-fashioned mustard with seeds, crème fraîche and a persillade. I'd recommend a red wine with that, even though I cook it with white. For the red wine, that Montravel you like from Château Moulin Caresse would go well. I'll decant it now if you like. Who's your companion?"

"That FBI man from Paris I brought here before. We need to catch up, so maybe you could bring him a kir and give us a few minutes before you start to bring the food."

"I remember him, a tall guy, looked a bit like one of those sheriffs in a Western movie. You and he had lunch here with that other man from Scotland Yard. Will ten minutes be enough?"

"Make it twenty," Bruno replied and checked his phone. He had an e-mail from Claudia's professor at Yale, who said he was flying to France at her family's request. He'd contact Bruno on arrival. That was interesting, Bruno thought as the bistro door opened. He stood to welcome his friend.

Hodge was tall enough to duck his head as he entered. He stuck out a hand to greet Ivan and spread his arms to give Bruno a warm hug before he sat down and rolled his eyes at Bruno's laptop.

"I thought it was only us barbarians from across the seas who spoiled a good dinner by working," he said.

"I need your help with a file that's in English," Bruno said, explaining the relationship between Claudia and Bourdeille and the very expensive investigation carried out by Hexagon Trust. Not only had Hodge heard of it, he had former colleagues from the FBI who had joined the firm for much higher salaries. It was a small but very exclusive company specializing in financial investigations, often hired by banks and corporations to run due diligence checks on potential takeover targets or acquisitions. Unlike the usual private investigators who hire ex-cops, they hired accountants, computer geeks and money-laundering experts from the United States Treasury and the FBI.

"They have a reputation for being able to get through banking secrecy and into tax havens and track money and the real owners of assets," Hodge said. "I'd be surprised if that investment firm of Claudia's father didn't use them. When I warned you about the kind of overpriced private investigators Muller might hire to investigate her death, these were exactly the sort of guys I had in mind."

"Have they been going long?"

Hodge explained that Hexagon had started in the seventies when President Carter had appointed Stansfield Turner to clean out the wild boys at the CIA. Turner laid off eight hundred agents in a purge that became known as the Halloween Massacre. Many of the ex-agents took their skills into the private sector as consultants and started Hexagon. Pretty soon they realized the real money was in finance, and they began to hire lawyers and accountants. That was when they added the name "Trust."

"But they never stopped picking up good people with intelligence backgrounds: us and the Brits, Mossad and the French," Hodge went on. "I might end up with them myself, if the college fees for the kids start breaking my back. I'd be surprised if that Brit friend of yours, Jack Crimson, isn't tied in with that kind of organization."

"I know Jack does some consulting," Bruno said. "That's why I thought twice before asking him about this file. Claudia mentioned to me she thought Bourdeille might have been playing tricks with his at-tributions of paintings to make money."

"Wouldn't surprise me," said Hodge, sip-ping at the kir Ivan had brought him. "The art world can make the Wild West look like Sunday school."

Hodge put down his drink and began scrolling down the text on Bruno's laptop. "I see he wasn't called Bourdeille at this point — you might want to check into that name change. He was shot while avoiding arrest while scrawling anti-Vichy slogans," he said after a while. "What would they be?"

"Painting V FOR VICTORY signs on walls."

"This guy who got away when Bourdeille was arrested sounds interesting, Paul Juin. What do you know about him, other than that he's a Compagnon de la Résistance?"

"Nothing yet," Bruno said. "But they only made about a thousand people *compagnons,* and de Gaulle had to approve each one personally. I'd better check him out."

"The master forger of the Resistance, it says here; false papers, work documents, birth certificates, travel documents. Juin even forged some release papers to spring people out of prison and made big money after the war with a printing and engraving business. I imagine there were always lots of juicy government contracts for a loyal *résistant.*"

Hodge paused, scrolling down through the pages quickly, occasionally breaking off to speak in staccato phrases: "Bourdeille marries Juin's sister after the war. Juin buys them a château and Bourdeille inherits it when his wife dies. Wait, she committed suicide, threw herself under a train. Now we come to the fishy paintings. A couple of lawsuits settled out of court. Speculation that some of the attributions could be based on some dubious documents that may have been slipped conveniently into the archives by Juin. The plot thickens."

Hodge looked up. "I guess if Juin was good enough to fool the Gestapo, he'd have no trouble fooling people in the art world who want to believe Grandpa's ancient painting is really an old master." He plunged back into the report.

"Bourdeille turns the château into a Société Civile Immobilière after he inherits. What's that, some kind of tax dodge?"

"A lot of old families use it to protect the estate," said Bruno. "It turns a house into a company owned by shareholders. It can help avoid estate taxes, but it also means that the usual heirs do not automatically inherit."

"Usual heirs, huh? It says here that Bourdeille's wife had a daughter in 1944, but he only married in 1946. When she got pregnant, Bourdeille was still in prison. He can't have been the father, so I see why he wanted to be sure she didn't inherit. I wonder who the father was."

"That's not in the file?"

Hodge shook his head. "Ah, now we're into a new area. Bourdeille wanted to change his name, claiming to have old family documents that prove he's descended from a bastard child of someone called Pierre de Bourdeille, abbot of Brantôme. The real family objects, claims the documents are forgeries. Settled out of court — he can call himself Bourdeille, but he can't be in the line of inheritance. Nor can they inherit from him."

Hodge looked up again. "This is all very interesting about Bourdeille, Bruno, but I don't see what it has to do with Claudia. There's not enough evidence here to turn the guy into a crook. And his reputation in the art world remains strong. He's still a consultant at the Louvre."

He closed the laptop lid. "The last page is about the paintings in Bourdeille's collection. The Hexagon people reckon the current market value to be five million bucks or more, if the identification of the paintings by the client — who is Claudia — is correct."

"So there's nothing in the report that suggests Bourdeille might have had a motive to have Claudia killed?" Bruno asked, wondering whether he should tell Hodge about Claudia's interest in buying Bourdeille's estate. Recalling Bourdeille's wish to discuss a bequest with the mayor, Bruno thought it best to keep this to himself for the moment.

"Not that I can see," Hodge replied. "He's ninety years old and in a wheelchair. He couldn't have done it himself even if she was drugged to the eyeballs."

"Then there's the American boyfriend she ditched, Jack Morgan."

"He's already on my list," Hodge said. "We've got people in London who will take a good look at him, check his movements."

Ivan brought the soup, the bread and the decanter of wine. They ate in silence, and Bruno poured a splash of the red wine into the last spoonfuls of soup in his dish, swirled them together and then raised the bowl to his lips to drink it dry.

Hodge grinned. "The custom of the Périgord. I remember. What do you call it again?"

"*Chabrol.* It keeps you healthy."

Over the terrine, Bruno asked if Hodge had any other names on his list to be investigated.

"Well, so far the assumption is that she died by accident. But you know my suspicious nature. So I start with the obvious one, the family. Claudia's daddy ditched her mom and got himself a trophy wife who is said to be desperate to get pregnant and is currently going through fertility treatment. If it succeeds, she'll want her own offspring to inherit Daddy's money, not Claudia. And if the treatment doesn't work, she'll want the dough for herself. Either way, Claudia is a rival."

"How do you know this?" Bruno asked.

"There is a charming but vengeful old lady who used to be on the protocol team at the White House, so naturally she knows all the social and political gossip. She took a final job as social secretary at the embassy in Paris. The ambassador traded her in for a newer model who's very attractive but not nearly as well informed. I make a point of being very attentive and respectful to the old biddy, who would have made a wonderful spy. I take her to lunch from time to time, and she tells me things."

"You mean the second wife might have

wanted Claudia out of the way?" Bruno was thinking of that second family photo in Claudia's room, the one that had been truncated, as if a person had been cut out of the picture.

"Claudia made no secret of despising the second wife, which I imagine was mutual."

"How would a woman in New York arrange the death of a young woman five thousand kilometers away in the Périgord?"

Hodge shrugged. "She's rich. You can hire experts in damn near anything these days. I was going to ask if you'd checked the hotels for strangers."

"*Rognons de veau au vin blanc,*" announced Ivan, putting down the plates with a flourish.

"Smells wonderful," Hodge said, bending over the plate. Bruno was impressed. Not every foreigner would relish that faint hint of the urinal that wafted from kidneys in white wine, however long they were soaked.

"One more thing," Bruno said as Ivan poured them each a glass of the red Montravel. "Claudia's professor at Yale, the guy supervising her doctorate, is flying over here at the family's request. I'm not sure why. There's a lot of e-mails to and from him on Claudia's computer that I haven't had time to go through yet. I'm sure J-J will let you see them, because getting official translations would probably bust his budget. It might be useful to know what they were e-mailing about before we see this professor."

"Good idea. I'll be happy to take a look at the e-mails, and I'd appreciate a copy of this Hexagon report," Hodge said, eating. "This dish tastes wonderful. What's this professor's name?"

"Reginald Porter. Have you ever heard of him?"

Hodge had his eyes closed as he savored the latest mouthful and shook his head.

"I did a little research on the Internet," Bruno said. "Porter is in his fifties, recently divorced, an expert on the Renaissance. He spent his entire life at Yale, as a student, then to get his doctorate, then as a lecturer and now as full professor. He wrote a book on the German Renaissance and was one of the curators of an exhibition of Cranach and Dürer at the National Gallery in Washington."

"And because he's recently divorced, you want me to find out if he was enjoying a dalliance with his favorite pupil?"

"The thought had crossed my mind."

"I would hope so. Such dark suspicions lie at the very heart of good police work."

CHAPTER 16

At nine the next morning the driver of the vehicle from the mobile service for the disabled lowered its hydraulic ramp outside Bourdeille's home, wheeled him inside and secured the chair. Twenty minutes later, having already taken a morning jog through the woods with Balzac, ridden Hector and enjoyed his morning coffee and croissant at Fauquet's, Bruno met the vehicle and wheeled Bourdeille into the elevator of the *mairie* and pushed the old man to the mayor's office.

"I still don't understand why we couldn't come to you," said the mayor.

"I enjoy getting out from time to time, and this way we can be sure that we won't be overheard," said the old man, before sniffing the air and saying delightedly, "You smoke a pipe." He then lit a cigarette.

"Just to be sure we aren't overheard, perhaps we could find an errand for Claire,"

Bruno murmured. The mayor nodded, summoned his secretary, asked her for three cups of coffee from his private stock and then to visit the archives and dig out the property tax files for Bourdeille's *chartreuse* for the past six years. Bruno nodded his approval. That would keep Claire busy.

"You mentioned a bequest, monsieur," the mayor said.

"I propose to donate my home and its contents to St. Denis, along with a financial endowment that would pay for cleaning, maintenance and a qualified tour guide for the art museum that I hope will be an adornment to the region," Bourdeille began. "However, the cost of insuring the paintings would be for the commune to pay, or perhaps the *département.*"

"That's an interesting proposal," the mayor said. "What about any family relatives who might expect to inherit?"

"The building is owned by an SCI of which I hold ninety-nine of the hundred shares," Bourdeille replied. "The final share is held by my *notaire.* The paintings are owned not by me but by an art trust I founded, and as chairman of the trust I would like to appoint you two gentlemen as trustees. I own two of the small houses in the hamlet adjoining my *chartreuse,* and they will be bequeathed to the current inhabitants, one of whom is my gardener. The other is my only living heir, Madame Bonnet."

"Is Madame Bonnet aware of your plans?" the mayor asked.

"No, nor do I wish her to be informed of them. Therefore I would like you to convene a small group of a lawyer, a doctor and the chief of police here to satisfy themselves and certify that I am of sound mind and that in this decision I am acting of my own free will, in complete command of my mental faculties and that nobody has taken advantage of my advanced years. I want this bequest to be legally beyond question."

"I don't think I should be a member of that group," said Bruno, quickly. "As the policeman of St. Denis, a lawyer could say I'm not an impartial witness. I'm sure we can find another, more senior policeman."

"What is Madame Bonnet's relationship with you, exactly?" the mayor asked.

"She is the granddaughter of my late wife. Madame Bonnet's late mother was born to Rebekkah during the war while I was in prison and before our marriage. She is no blood relative of mine. Indeed, I believe that Madame Bonnet is descended from the *milice* swine who shot and tortured me."

"Under French law, your wife's daughter became your daughter on your marriage," the mayor said.

"The circumstances of her birth were unusual and most unhappy," Bourdeille said. "You are aware that I was arrested in 1942 for anti-Vichy activity and sent to prison. I was shot by the policeman who arrested me when I attacked him to enable my friend and fellow *résistant,* Paul Juin, to escape."

Because Paul was a Jew, Bourdeille went on, arrest for him would have meant death. Paul was able to disappear, but not to warn his family in time. His family was arrested, and his sister was tortured to reveal where he might be. His father was later shot as a hostage in retaliation for the deaths of some German soldiers. His mother was sent to Ravensbrück and never returned. The torture of Paul's sister, Rebekkah, took the form of repeated rape by the *milice* man who shot and arrested Bourdeille. One result was that she became pregnant and gave birth to Madame Bonnet's mother. The second was that Rebekkah lost her mind temporarily and was put into a mental institution until the war ended and Juin could take care of her.

"Why did you choose to marry her?" the

mayor asked.

"Paul asked me to do so, to give her a name, a home, some stability. And since I was impoverished and Paul had money, and because my injuries left me no prospect of a normal marriage, I agreed. The three of us lived together."

"What happened to the child?" Bruno asked.

"She was sent to a church orphanage, where Paul and I finally traced her some years after the war. By then Rebekkah seemed to have recovered after treatment by a very able young female psychologist, and we married. I had hoped that reunion with her daughter would help Rebekkah, but she refused to have anything to do with the child. In fact, it unhinged her. The week after we brought the child home, Rebekkah committed suicide by throwing herself under a train."

Bourdeille's tone was flat, formal and utterly devoid of emotion. He might have been reciting entries from a telephone directory. The effect was to make his words all the more haunting. The mayor opened his mouth as if to speak but then simply bowed his head as if in silent prayer. Bruno could think of no words that might match the situation. He simply closed his eyes and sighed.

After a long moment Bourdeille spoke again. "I have never forgotten that as far as I know I never met a single German in the whole course of the war. There might have been a plainclothes Gestapo man at one of my interrogations, but I never heard the language spoken. Everything that was done to me — and to Rebekkah — was done by fellow Frenchmen."

"You mean the police of the Vichy regime, the *milice*?" the mayor asked. "Was it them who shot you?"

"Yes, but it was what the *milice* did to my wounded leg while I was being interrogated about Paul's whereabouts that crippled me for life. Their attentions also put an end to my sexual life before it had even begun. I had no idea where Paul might have gone. We had no connections to the Resistance, no idea where to find them. We had simply decided to paint slogans. It was all we felt we could do."

"How did Paul survive?"

"He went to a Spanish family, the parents of someone we knew at school. They had been refugees from Franco and the civil war. He knew I had been arrested and as soon as the *milice* had my address from my identity card they would be at my house and then at my school to ask about my

227

friends. And Paul and I were known to be inseparable."

"Did the Spaniards help?"

"They put him in touch with the Communist underground. At the time, they were the only serious Resistance, at least around Périgueux. The Communists were very suspicious at first, even more when they found that he had two ID cards, one of which he had forged himself, and some extra ration books, again forged. They didn't believe that Paul could have made them until he showed them what he could do. Then he became a prize asset."

It was one thing, thought Bruno, to read about the Resistance in history books and memoirs, but quite another to hear the matter-of-fact words from Bourdeille's lips.

"Where were you painting the slogans?" he asked. He wanted to envision the place and keep it in his memory and visit it when he went to Périgueux.

"We had painted V signs on place du Coderc, since that was where the market was held, and then we went on to place St. Louis, and that was where the *milice* found us. A few nights earlier we had painted them on the big statue in place Bugeaud, so they had mounted special patrols to find us."

"What happened to the *milice* man who

shot you?" the mayor asked.

"His name was Michel Cagnac, and he was arrested after the Liberation, tried and imprisoned," Bourdeille said. "He was released early when he volunteered for the army — they were desperate for men for that ridiculous colonial war we fought in Vietnam."

Cagnac had remained in the army after the French defeat in 1954, he explained, and had later joined the military coup attempt in Algiers in 1961, when some elements of the army tried to reverse de Gaulle's decision to grant Algerian independence. When the coup failed, Cagnac joined the OAS, the Organisation de l'Armée Secrète, to maintain the struggle. He was named as one of those involved in car bombings and the uprising of the *pieds-noirs* in Bab el-Oued, the white quarter of Algiers. He was also accused of involvement in the attempt to assassinate de Gaulle at Petit-Clamart in 1962. Cagnac was killed in a gunfight in Madrid in December of that year by Gaullist agents.

"Poor France," said the mayor. "Such unhappy history."

"It could have been worse. If they had managed to kill de Gaulle or if the coup of '61 had succeeded . . ." Bourdeille shrugged.

"As it is, Cagnac and his friends lost both times, in 1944 and 1961. But enough of that," he went on. "Now you'll understand why I'd like to name my home the Juin Museum, for Paul and Rebekkah. I imagine you would have no objections to that."

"No, I'd support it," said the mayor. "But I'll have to put this project to the council. They may have some concerns about the insurance costs you mentioned, but they will also have some questions about Rebekkah's daughter and her inheritance."

"That's another grim story," said Bourdeille. "Paul and I did our best, we tried nannies and church schools, then a private boarding school in England, but we could never get through to her. She went wild in the sixties — Paris, then London and California. She came back to France in time for May '68. She got pregnant, but we never learned who the father was. She died of a heroin overdose, leaving a daughter whom you know as Madame Bonnet.

"I would rather no word of this emerges until it is a fait accompli, preferably after my death," he went on. "But certainly I'd like this all to be confidential until after a reputable tribunal has declared my bequest and my will to be valid and made while I am of sound mind."

"Is that because you're concerned that Madame Bonnet will contest the will?" Bruno asked.

"Yes. I have no doubt that she and her family are looking forward to inheriting it all, selling off the paintings and living on the proceeds. For some time she's been pressing me to hire a professional house-keeper rather than employ her. More recently, she suggested that I should move into a retirement home."

"I see," said the mayor, rising. "I'll consider your generous offer and consult in confidence one or two close colleagues. In the meantime, I think we can arrange for you to meet some professionals who can establish that you're in complete possession of your faculties as they witness your legacy." He shook Bourdeille's hand and asked Bruno to wheel him downstairs and out to the waiting vehicle.

"I'd rather not return home just yet, I get out so seldom," Bourdeille said when he and Bruno were in the elevator. "And Madame Bonnet is not the most agreeable of companions. Would you join me for coffee in the local café?"

"With pleasure," said Bruno, and wheeled Bourdeille into Fauquet's. The old man ordered two coffees with a glass of Calvados and a *pain au chocolat* for each of them. When they came, he put three lumps of sugar into his coffee and bit greedily into his pastry, washing it down with a swig of the apple brandy.

"This is a treat," he said, around a second mouthful.

"Tell me," said Bruno. "Your relations with Madame Bonnet don't seem to be going well. Are you being mistreated at home in any way?"

"Nothing obvious," he replied, finishing his Calvados. "She nags me and there are some petty humiliations when I ask for help in going to the toilet. I'm now required to wear a diaper, which is too infrequently changed. She seldom cooks these days, so I'm fed packaged meals like frozen pizzas, which I loathe, and quiche Lorraine that tastes like cardboard. The best meal I've had in weeks was when Claudia cooked for me before she went back to Paris."

"You could book that special taxi to take you to decent restaurants."

"There's little pleasure in dining alone, and I've outlived most of my contemporaries and those I considered friends. That's why I enjoyed Claudia's company so much. I even enjoyed our brief meeting this morning, unpleasant though the topic of our discussion turned out to be. Claudia's company reminded me how agreeable a polite conversation with an intelligent partner could be. I haven't had much of that since Paul died."

"Have you ever tried taking a holiday, a week in Paris seeing your old colleagues at the Louvre?" Bruno asked. "You could revisit your favorite paintings, go to the opera, take your old pupils to lunch. It's much easier than it used to be to get around in a wheelchair."

Bourdeille sat back, looking surprised. "That's exactly what Claudia said," he said. "I was even thinking of taking her up on the idea, but then her death intervened."

"You could still do it. You could even find a specialist guide for people who have trouble getting around on their own, and you can certainly afford it."

"That's something to consider. I'll reflect on that. Aren't you going to drink your Calvados?"

Bruno shook his head.

"In that case . . . ," Bourdeille said, taking the glass from in front of Bruno. "Am I correct in thinking that the mayor seemed rather less excited than one might have expected about my proposal?"

"He's a very cautious man, not given to

rushes of enthusiasm," Bruno replied. "And he'll need support from the town council. The important thing is that he said he will convene the meeting of lawyers and doctors to validate your will."

"Very well." Bourdeille put a twenty-euro note beneath his saucer. "Perhaps you could take me out to that ingenious vehicle that brought me."

CHAPTER 17

Bruno had been back in his office for less than ten minutes when Hodge called to say that he had just had breakfast with Claudia's mother. She wanted to know if it would be convenient for her to see the well at Limeuil where her daughter had died. Bruno said he would meet them there and called David, the chief gardener, to warn him of the visit. He then called J-J to inform him.

"It's fine with me," J-J said. "But you'd better check with the magistrate who's deciding what charge to file against the builders. It's that rally-driver friend of yours in Sarlat, Annette. She handles building-code offenses."

Annette was already at the site in Limeuil when he called her and said of course the girl's mother could come. Bruno joined her at the well with David, the mayor of Limeuil and a local insurance agent. Annette was taking pictures on her phone while the mayor and the insurance man argued in low voices. David and Félicité stood to one side in their gardening clothes, looking as if they'd rather be somewhere else. Bruno shook hands with the men and Félicité, embraced Annette and asked whether the builders would be joining them.

"No, I'm going to see them separately," Annette said. "David tells me you took photos of the well before the young woman was pulled out and you thought there might be a question of negligence. They deny that in the statement they gave to J-J, saying they understood the gardens would be locked overnight."

"They weren't locked until after the lecture ended, and when I checked the perimeter I saw several places where a youngster could climb in. They didn't even put a lid on the well, let alone lock it."

"I was just telling the magistrate that we usually keep it locked permanently," said David.

"The building code says work on a well should be cordoned off when the site is unmanned," said Annette. "Is this her?" she asked.

Bruno turned to see Hodge and Claudia's mother coming up the path. Today Madame Muller was wearing slacks, a tweed jacket and a silk head scarf. The same leather sneakers were still on her feet, but she looked better than she had the previous day, as though she had had some sleep. Bruno made the introductions, and she accepted the mayor's flowery condolences politely, her eyes flickering to the well and back.

"You must have been one of the last people to see my daughter alive," she said to David, but he blushed and said he hadn't been at the lecture.

"I was on the door for the lecture and I saw her that evening, madame," said Félicité. "I'm very sorry for your loss. She and I lived at the same house, and I liked her a lot. She was very kind and friendly and I'll miss her. At the lecture, I was told your daughter was not well and had gone home. The next day I found what we think was her jacket hanging in the coatroom."

"Thank you," said Madame Muller, giving Félicité a grimace that she probably intended to be a smile. "Perhaps at some point you might show me the room where she stayed." She stepped forward to peer over the rim of the well. "I was told there was a cat. Does it live here?"

"I haven't seen it since it was pulled from the well on Monday morning, along with Claudia," said David. "It was a kitten and there are many cats in the village. They often come up here at night."

Madame Muller turned around, addressing Annette. "Are you the magistrate who will decide when to release her body?"

"No, madame. My job is only to draft an initial report on the site of her death, and the *procureur* will make the real decision. He's my boss. But we still must wait for the police to say whether they believe it was an accidental death or if they recommend further investigation. At that point the case will probably be handed to a senior magistrate."

"You mean there's a suspicion it wasn't accidental?" she said, her voice rising sharply. "That Claudia could have been murdered?"

"No, madame, not at all. It simply means we don't know at this stage, but what we have so far seems to suggest an accident. But as you see, the well was not secured as it should have been. That could lead to charges against the builders."

"I would certainly hope so."

"I'm very sorry for your loss, madame, and we'll try to resolve this as quickly as we can and to minimize your inconvenience."

"Inconvenience is not what I'm feeling at this time, mademoiselle."

"I understand," Annette said, biting her lip and blushing with embarrassment. "Forgive my clumsy choice of words. I meant that we will do our best to resolve this as quickly as we can."

"Can I see the lecture hall, please?" she asked. Félicité stepped forward, but Bruno put a hand on her arm and asked David to escort Madame Muller. Hodge followed them, casting a curious glance at Bruno as he left.

"I need to ask you about the procedure when you closed the castle after the lecture," he said, leading Félicité off to one side, out of earshot of the others. "Did you count the people out?"

"No, I had to stay to tidy up, clear away the plastic glasses and napkins and straighten the chairs. By the time I came out of the castle, almost everyone had gone, just a few people still chatting outside. Florence and one of the English people were asking the lecturer about something, and then one of the locals came down from the bushes. I think he'd been for a quick pee — he said something about the toilet in the castle being in use."

"Are you sure this man had stayed till the end of the lecture? He didn't slip out sooner?"

"No, I was by the door, so I'd have seen him leave. And I know him, it was the guy from the canoe rentals, Dominic."

"And did anyone come out from using the toilet in the castle?"

"I don't recall, but there were one or two people coming and going, putting on their jackets, making sure they had everything. When they'd all gone, I went back to the castle and checked that the place was empty and there was nobody in the gift shop. I turned out the lights and locked the main door. Then I locked the garden gate behind me and went home."

"Did you go into the garden near the well at any point?"

"No." She shook her head firmly.

"Does that mean you didn't see that the builders had left the well unguarded?"

She shook her head again. "No, I didn't see that."

"Had the builders been working that day before the lecture?"

"It was a Sunday, so I doubt it."

Bruno let her go and then went back to ask Annette if she had a copy of the statement the builders had given to J-J. She pulled it out of her file and handed it to him. He read that the builders had worked on Saturday because they usually took

Mondays off. So the well had been un-guarded all of Sunday when the gardens were open to the public. He pointed this out to Annette, who said she'd been asking David that very question. He'd been on duty on Sunday and must have seen that the well had been left open.

"That could make him negligent, too," she said. "Look, the mother and the FBI man are coming back."

"Were you here Sunday when the gardens were open?" Annette called to David as he approached from the castle.

"I was here, yes, but down in the lower garden working with the bees, and then I cleaned the water garden."

"So you weren't guiding the visitors?" Annette went on.

"We don't usually do that, unless there's a school group and a special tour. People find their way around with the map."

"Would you know if the well was left open like this on Sunday?" Annette's voice was becoming aggressive.

"No, I had no occasion to come up here," he replied, looking bemused, as if surprised by her line of questioning. "The men may have been working. They worked on Satur-day."

"Who else was here from the garden crew

241

on Sunday?"

"Antoine, he was working in the herb garden."

"Do you make an inspection tour at the start or the end of the day, looking around the whole garden?"

"Not always. I've usually been pretty much everywhere in the course of a day. We do a check on the paths before closing and ring a bell, but you'd need several people to do a proper search every evening."

"So you aren't sure if the men were working Sunday, or if the well was left unguarded like this from Saturday when they stopped work?"

"No, I'm not sure," he retorted, his lips tight and his voice rising. "But that's not my job. I'm the gardener, not a security man. And I'm not a builder, nor do I know anything about building codes."

"Calm down, David," interrupted the mayor. "He's right, mademoiselle. I drew up David's job description. He's the chief gardener, and he acts as guide to the place on special request. And he and the other staff volunteer to be here when we have special events like the lecture."

"Did the job descriptions you drafted assign anyone to check that all the visitors had gone at the end of each day?"

"No."

"What about the *devis* your builders would have given you before they started work. Was there anything in there about security and building codes?"

"It's a standard form that says the builders undertake to carry out and complete the work according to professional norms and standards," said the insurance man, waving a copy of the contract he'd plucked from the file in his hands. "That means following the building codes."

"So they are liable," said Annette sharply. "Not the gardeners and not the town council or the *mairie*."

"I'd say so," the insurance man replied. "Not that I'm a lawyer or any kind of expert, but it seems that way."

"I think we'd better leave you to your discussion," said Madame Muller, who'd been watching this exchange from her standpoint beside the well. Hodge was standing behind her, a worried look on his face. Ignoring him, she turned to lean over the lip of the well and gaze down into the depths where her daughter had died. It was an awkward pose, her hands at her sides and her body bent, and deliberately refusing to touch any part of the stone rim. This lasted for several seconds. Then she stood up straight and stared directly at Bruno, her eyes bright. "You went down this well to look for her?"

"Only a little way, enough to be worried at what I thought I saw. That was when I called in the *pompiers.*"

"Thank you," she said. "I'm glad somebody here was behaving responsibly. I just wish you'd arrived sooner."

She turned on her heel and began to walk away. Hodge shrugged, and then mimicked to Bruno making a phone call and followed her.

"One second, madame," Bruno called and went to join her. "Claudia's teacher from Yale, Professor Porter, let me know that he's coming here at the family's request and has asked to see me. Did you ask him to do that?"

"No, it must be my ex-husband. That's interesting," she said, sounding surprised. "I know that Claudia respected Professor Porter very much, so I have no objection to your telling him what you can. Still, I'd better check with my ex's office and let you know."

CHAPTER 18

When Bruno returned to St. Denis, two people were sitting on the wooden bench inside the reception area at the *mairie*. Claire tossed her head at Bruno in a way that signaled they were waiting to see him. The man was in his fifties with thick gray hair that hung to his collar, dressed in corduroy slacks and a tweed jacket over an open-necked denim shirt. He looked tired and his clothes were crumpled as if after a long flight. Beside him was a handsome woman in her forties wearing a smart suit with a round collar. Bruno was no fashion expert but thought it might be Chanel. Her dark hair was pulled back into a severe bun and her eyes were cold. A small and boxy handbag of patent leather hung from a chain over her shoulder, and she held a briefcase against her stomach as if it required protection.

"*M'sieur-dame, bonjour.* Professor Porter?"

Bruno inquired.

"Yes, and you must be Chief of Police Courrèges." His French was good, and they shook hands. "And this is Madame de Breille, who represents the family's interests."

"Bonjour, madame," Bruno said. "You represent Claudia's mother or her father?"

"Bonjour, monsieur. I represent Monsieur Muller." Her accent was cut-glass Parisian. "I believe you are this commune's *garde champêtre* who found Claudia in the well?"

Bruno raised an eyebrow. *Garde champêtre* was a very old-fashioned and somewhat contemptuous way to describe his work. He turned to Claire. "Is the council chamber free?" She nodded.

"My office is small, so let's go in here." He pulled out a chair that faced the long window with its view over the river for Madame de Breille and went around the table to take his own seat with his back to the view and all the light on the faces of his two visitors. He pulled out his notebook and a pen and pushed two of his business cards across the council table.

Porter returned his own card emblazoned with his university's crest, and the woman presented a card that listed only her name engraved in flowing script.

"No phone number? No e-mail? No company address?" Bruno said, surprised.

"I'm particular about those with whom I share private details," she replied coolly.

"I presume you have some letter of authorization from Monsieur Muller?" he asked.

"There wasn't time. Kindly stop being so officious and just get on with your job, monsieur."

Bruno sat back in his chair, looking at her steadily. She held his gaze. "Do you have some other means of identification, madame?"

She rolled her eyes.

Bruno stood up. "Professor Porter is of course welcome to stay, but I'm afraid I don't share police details with people I can't identify."

She leaned back, looked out of the window and replied in a voice that sounded deliberately bored. "You may be a village policeman, but you are also a public official. I represent a bereaved parent who is entitled to learn at first hand the circumstances of his daughter's death. You can contact me through Mr. Abraham Muller's office at the Muller Investment Trust in New York."

"If you can show me some evidence of your role, madame, you will have my full cooperation," Bruno said politely and remained standing. "Otherwise, I'll have to refer you to the official police spokesman in Périgueux, where you will find the officer who is formally in charge of this matter, Commissaire Jalipeau. I suspect that he, too, will expect some proper identification."

She glowered at him and remained seated. Bruno began to count to five, at which point he would open the door and escort them out.

"Perhaps this will help," said Porter as he took from his wallet another business card and pushed it across to Bruno. It identified Madame de Breille as a vice president of Hexagon Trust with an address on avenue d'Iéna in Paris, with fixed and mobile-phone numbers and an e-mail. "It's the card she gave to me when she met me at Charles de Gaulle Airport this morning."

Bruno sat down and beamed at him. "If you can vouch for Madame de Breille, Professor, then of course she's welcome to stay while I answer your questions. How can I help you?"

The woman opened her bag, removed an elegant notebook in black leather and a fat Montblanc pen that Bruno suspected cost more than his weekly pay. She also pulled out a new-looking smartphone and tapped on it.

"Are you recording, madame?" Bruno asked.

"You have any objections?"

"It's not only polite to ask permission before recording, madame, it's legally required. Unauthorized recording without consent is illegal under Articles 221 and 226 of the French Penal Code and can lead to a fine of up to forty-five thousand euros or a year in prison, depending on the circumstances. I do not give my consent to be recorded. I see you have a pen and paper. You are entitled to take notes."

"This is ridiculous," she said.

"Madame, either you turn off your phone or this meeting is over. It's up to you."

She turned off the phone.

"We seem to have got off on the wrong foot," Porter said. "I'm sorry about that. Could you please tell me what happened to Claudia, step-by-step."

Bruno explained the events of the Sunday evening lecture and his search for Claudia on Monday morning, the role of the *pompiers* and the arrival of Fabiola and J-J and the passing of information to the legal attaché at the American embassy.

"Why was Monsieur Muller not informed?" the woman asked.

"The next of kin in Claudia's passport was

listed as her mother. That was the only reference we had to go on, apart from her supervisor at the Louvre, whom I also informed. Madame Muller has already been briefed by the *commissaire* for the *départe* —"

"Her father is entitled to the same briefing," Madame de Breille interrupted, speaking over Bruno.

Bruno took a deep breath and told himself to stay calm. "That's a matter for Commissaire Jalipeau."

"When will Claudia's body be released?" Porter asked.

"When the *procureur*'s office decides whether this was a tragic accident or whether others might have been responsible, possibly through negligence. When I arrived at the scene, the well had not been secured as the building regulations require."

"Will there be an autopsy?"

"An autopsy has already taken place." Bruno described the drugs found in her body. Porter shook his head sadly.

"A question for you, Professor," Bruno asked. "Did Claudia share with you any of her concerns about Monsieur de Bourdeille's attributions?"

"Yes, she did, suggesting that at least three times the attribution hinged on archive material which Claudia thought was unsafe."

"Unsafe? You mean forged?"

"No, just that a scholar would be unwise to rely on it as evidence. Claudia found three examples of copies from archives that she could not trace in the original archives. I intend to pursue this and replicate her research, as her father has asked me to do."

"Madame de Breille, since your company, Hexagon Trust, billed Claudia fifty thousand dollars for research into Monsieur Bourdeille, I trust you will be sharing this information with the professor," Bruno said.

Madame de Breille remained silent while Porter stared at her, his mouth open in surprise.

"You didn't tell me any of this," Porter exclaimed. She rolled her eyes again, ignoring him.

"Really?" asked Bruno, suppressing a smile and starting to enjoy the open hostility that had developed between his two visitors. "Didn't she tell you Claudia was negotiating to buy Bourdeille's house and his art collection?"

"This is outrageous," Porter said angrily, standing up. "I can't work under these conditions. I need to talk with Abe Muller right now. Alone."

He pushed his chair back and stomped toward the door. Before opening it, he paused and turned to thank Bruno for his time. "I hope we can arrange to meet, just the two of us."

"At your service, Professor," Bruno replied, standing as Porter disappeared. He looked down at Madame de Breille. To his surprise, for the first time she was smiling.

"That went well," she said. She leaned back in her chair and extended her arm to push the door closed and then leaned forward on the table to face him.

"He won't go far. I've got the car keys and he doesn't even know which hotel we're in. Now the amateur is out of the way and it's just us two professionals. I presume you've read the report we did on Bourdeille. I've already seen the autopsy report, don't ask how. It's ambivalent as to whether she fell while drugged or was given a little help on her way. What do you think?"

"It doesn't matter what I think," Bruno replied and remained standing. "I'm just the *garde champêtre,* remember."

"We can be very generous to our friends, Lieutenant."

Noting that she knew his official rank, Bruno walked around the table to the door. "Why don't you let yourself out while I report to the mayor what sounds to me like attempted bribery."

"That won't stick and you know it. It's not attempted bribery, but it might be recruitment. Think whether you want to stay forever in this dreary little provincial town with so many empty shops that it's visibly dying on its feet. You have the card I gave Porter, so you know where to reach me. I'll be staying at the Vieux Logis in Trémolat."

She put away her notebook, picked up her bag and walked serenely from the council chamber, pausing at the elevator to smile and flutter an eyelid in what might have been a wink. "By the way, Bruno, regards from our mutual friend in Paris, Yacov Kaufman. He tells me he'd very much look forward to working with you again."

In his office, Bruno called the law office in Paris where Yacov worked, at least nominally. The switchboard said he was out at a meeting, and his mobile phone was turned off, so Bruno texted him asking for a callback. They had become friends when Yacov was acting as a lawyer for his grandmother, who as a girl during the war had been sheltered from the Nazis by people from St. Denis. In commemoration, she had turned the remote farm where she and her brother had been hidden into a camp for Boy Scouts and Girl Guides. Yacov had made no secret of having served in the Israeli military, but it was only in the course of another operation in which Yacov had been wounded that Bruno learned that his friend worked closely with Mossad.

That made Madame de Breille all the more interesting. Since she had evidently seen the autopsy report, or at least its conclusions, she had police contacts either through her employers or of her own. Bruno had realized that she had set out to provoke a confrontation that would lead to Porter stalking out. Was that piece of theater necessary if all she wanted was a private word with Bruno? He thought not. If she knew Yacov, she might know through him that Bruno had his own contacts in the French security services.

Bruno called J-J to brief him on Professor Porter, Hexagon and de Breille and enjoyed J-J's snorts of anger and disbelief that punctuated Bruno's report. In closing, he asked if J-J could arrange for Yves to send him the e-mail exchanges between Professor Porter and Claudia that were on her computer. Then Bruno printed out the Hexagon report about Bourdeille on his own computer and went to see the mayor, suggesting that it was time to send Claire on another errand in the archives. Once she had left her desk outside the mayor's office, Bruno explained what the American professor had said about Bourdeille and suggested the mayor read the report.

"Do you think a scandal is brewing that would make it unwise for us to accept Bourdeille's bequest?" the mayor asked.

"Not necessarily, since the Louvre still holds him in great esteem. But we might want to delay reaching a deal with Bourdeille while all this plays out. And we have no idea what Professor Porter's research will reveal. I'll try to find out the details of Claudia's concerns about Bourdeille's attributions."

"I assume the implication is that Paul Juin forged some archive documents which helped make Bourdeille's career and his fortune," the mayor replied. "In that case, why would Claudia want to buy his home and his collection?"

"Maybe she just wanted to bring the price down."

The mayor shook his head. "If that were so, she'd have kept it to herself rather than alert her professor. I agree that we should go slowly, but we also need to learn as much as we can about all this before taking a decision."

"You still want to go ahead with Bourdeille's plan?"

"I'm not sure. Even without the prospect of a scandal, we're a town council, not a gallery owner. Tourism is our key industry, and properly managed it could be a valuable attraction. I'd prefer us to set up an autonomous association, Les Amis de la Renaissance or something of the kind, with its own board of local worthies and artists and maybe somebody from the Louvre and the Périgueux museum."

"Have you talked to anyone on the council about this?"

"Not yet, Bruno. Once word gets out, there'll be a price to pay if we are seen to be rejecting such a princely gift."

Bruno smiled inwardly. The mayor was a politician and was thinking of the political fallout that might affect him.

"What if Porter confirms Claudia's suspicions?"

"We'll leave that to the experts from the Louvre. But you know human nature, Bruno. The publicity that would follow such a scandal would make Bourdeille's collection a much more popular attraction. By the way, is he really a descendant of the original de Bourdeille? That alone could bring in the crowds."

Bruno shook his head. "I know he claimed to be a member of the family, and there's a town and castle named after them, but I'm not sure why the name is so important."

"Pierre de Bourdeille was one of the great men of the Périgord, Bruno," the mayor said, leaning back. Bruno smiled to himself, knowing that the mayor was seldom happier than when sharing his vast stock of historical knowledge.

"De Bourdeille was at the heart of the great drama of the sixteenth century, the civil war between Catholics and Protestants. He was the younger son of a noble family who became a soldier, perhaps a soldier of fortune," the mayor went on. "He was a courtier, the man selected to escort Mary, Queen of Scots, back to her homeland to assume the throne. And he was an inveterate gossip who scribbled down much of what we know of the court life of sixteenth-century France. He was also abbot of Brantôme, who in the religious wars persuaded his old comrades in arms who happened to be Protestants to spare the great abbey they planned to loot and destroy. On top of all that, he was a pioneering pornographer."

"*Mon Dieu,* I had no idea," said Bruno, suspecting that the mayor had barely started. Once launched on a historical lecture, he could go on for hours. At least this one sounded interesting.

"He wrote *The Gallant Ladies of the Court,* a work that took romantic indiscretion to sublime heights, describing the charms and attributes of the maids of honor around Queen Catherine de' Medici in the most intimate — I might even say gynecological — detail. And he makes it clear that he wrote from personal knowledge. The term 'hotbed' might even have been invented for life at the royal court."

"Have you read it?"

"Yes, in my youth, in the restricted section of the Bibliothèque Nationale in Paris, the old one named after Richelieu, before Mitterrand put up that monstrosity that bears his name. It was one of the books that Rousseau said should be read with one hand, which makes me think that old fraud never perused it. It's far too clinical to be exciting."

At this point, Bruno's mobile phone vibrated. He looked at the screen and saw it was Yacov. "I need to answer this. It's Yacov Kaufman from Paris."

"Give him my regards," said the mayor, waving his dismissal.

CHAPTER 19

As Bruno left, he saw that Claire had returned and was standing close to the door, one hand in the open filing cabinet as if searching for something. It was her usual eavesdropping pose. He hit his button to answer the phone.

"Yacov, thanks for returning my call. I just had a meeting with a formidable woman called Madame de Breille from Hexagon who says she knows you. Is that so?"

"Yes, and 'formidable' is the word. We often work with Hexagon in doing due diligence reports for clients, and she's the dynamo in their Paris office. She started out in the *douanes,* investigating customs fraud, and was then put on a task force the finance ministry set up to investigate the collapse of Crédit Lyonnais and the fuss over their payments to Bernard Tapie over the sale of Adidas. She was hired by Hexagon when they opened their Paris office."

"She's down here claiming to represent Abraham Muller."

"He's the head of Muller Investment Trust. We've done a lot of work with his venture capital operations in Europe and Israel. Madame de Breille told me about the death of his daughter, and since she knew I'd spent time in the Périgord, she asked for some contacts. I gave her your name. Is there a problem?"

"No, I was just checking. How's your arm?"

"I'm doing a lot of physiotherapy and it's getting better, but it will never be a hundred percent. That AK-47 bullet did a lot of damage. I'll be seeing you this summer when I bring a scout troop down to the camp."

"I'll look forward to it. And you know Amélie is coming down as well? I've lined up some concerts for her."

"That's great, but we're not seeing that much of one another these days. We're still friends but no longer lovers. I was probably too long in the hospital. *C'est la vie.*"

Bruno made a sympathetic grunt, thinking how difficult it was for male friends to talk with each other about their love affairs or their feelings, at least unless they were face-to-face with a glass in their hand and one bottle already empty on the table

261

between them. He groped for some way to change the subject.

"Another thing before you go," he asked. "Could you ask your physiotherapist if she knows of anyone who could act as a guide in Paris for someone in a wheelchair?"

"Will do, but have you tried the tourist office of Parisinfo.com? You'll probably find something helpful."

Ten minutes later, Bruno called Bourdeille to give him the name and number of a young woman who had passed the two-year course and the challenging test to be a licensed Paris guide and specialized in guiding disabled people. She could be hired by the day and had planned her own tours for people restricted to wheelchairs.

"She'll even meet your train at Montparnasse with a suitable vehicle, arrange a wheelchair-access hotel and restaurants, book opera and theater tickets," Bruno said. "It sounds perfect for you."

"This is very kind of you, Bruno. I don't know what to say, but the idea excites me a great deal. Thank you, I'll call this woman today. But I hope the mayor arranges this meeting with lawyers and doctors before I leave."

"I understand; the mayor is working on it."

"One more thing I remember. Claudia told me she had met a falconer, a young man who trained hawks. She visited Lascaux with him. I'd love to see him at work. Out here on the balcony I watch the hawks all day, the most graceful things in all creation. Do you know where he's based?"

"He's at Château des Milandes, not even thirty minutes from where you are if you take that taxi you used this morning. You may not be able to get around the château itself, but the hawks and owls are kept in the garden, and you should be able to manage that. The man's name is Laurent Darrignac. Tell him you were a friend of Claudia. He liked her a lot, and in fact he was at the lecture in Limeuil, the last night anyone saw her alive." He gave Bourdeille the phone number, ended the call and saw from his list of incoming e-mails that Yves had sent a large file.

Bruno took a deep breath and began going through the long e-mail correspondence that dated back over a year, when Porter had first begun supervising Claudia's thesis. Bruno scrolled down until Claudia had reached Paris, enthused about the Louvre and the city, and reported what she was reading. She described what she was seeing as she went around the Renaissance châteaux of the Loire and complained how much more remote and impersonal was her French supervisor, Madame Massenet, than the teachers she had known back home. There was an e-mail full of her shock at learning how many of the treasures of the Louvre came from Napoléon's looting of the churches and palaces of Europe. She quoted Napoléon's boast, " 'We will now have all that is beautiful in Italy except for a few objects in Turin and Naples.' "

Then Claudia started to write about Bourdeille and his stellar reputation at the Louvre, the new research systems he had pioneered. She cited his discovery of a long-lost Velázquez on the wall of an English stately home, a painting that had been acquired in mysterious circumstances by a Royal Navy captain during the Napoleonic Wars. Bourdeille had tracked down the ship's log and palace inventories to argue persuasively that it had been part of the treasure of the royal family of Naples when they were being evacuated from Napoléon's clutches.

Her first concern with Bourdeille's research came when she went through the local archives in Toulon, Marseille and Avignon. They listed those possessions of royalists confiscated by the revolutionaries in the summer of 1793, when much of southern France had declared for the king and welcomed the English fleet into the great naval base of Toulon. Bruno remembered reading of the Siege of Toulon in one of the biographies of Napoléon, who as a young officer had made his name by mounting the artillery batteries that destroyed the town's defenses and forced the British fleet to evacuate the port.

Bourdeille had found a reference to a religious work by one Jean Lefrinc, along with a description that the art historian cited to identify a work that currently belonged to the descendant of a French officer who had been ennobled by Napoléon. But when trying to trace the reference in the National Archives, Claudia found no sign of it. She did find, however, that the painting had been attributed by Bourdeille to Josse Lieferinxe of Cambrai, who had worked at the papal court in Avignon. Shortly after Bourdeille's attribution in 1962, the work was sold at auction in Paris for the equivalent of four hundred thousand dollars.

"Archives are never perfect, bureaucrats mislay documents or forget to copy them or use the back of the paper for a family shopping list," Professor Porter had replied to

Claudia's query.

Over the next month Claudia questioned two more of Bourdeille's attributions. The first was based on his finding a letter in the archives of a monastery that noted the gift of a painting described as "An allegory by a M. de Boijs," which Bourdeille identified as the work of Ambroise Dubois, a court painter of the day. Again, the owner sold it for a handsome sum shortly after the attribution. And Claudia had found no evidence of the letter being received in the monastery's letter book, in which all correspondence was customarily listed.

The second case hinged on Bourdeille finding a receipt from the customs office at La Rochelle of duty being paid on a hitherto unknown painting by Antoine Caron. It was being brought back among the possessions of a planter returning from Martinique. Again, she had found no matching record in the archives of the *douanes.*

This time, Porter's response was a little longer. "The Caron attribution was endorsed by the legendary Charles Sterling, of the Louvre and the Metropolitan Museum in New York. As a Jew Sterling fled there from Nazi-occupied France. Sterling is one of the great connoisseurs of the century, and his attributions are wholly reliable. But well done on your research and on your inquisitive mind."

It was shortly after that, from the dates on the bill from Hexagon, that Claudia had commissioned them to investigate Bourdeille and his background.

All this was unfamiliar terrain to Bruno. None of the names of the artists meant anything to him, but he could appreciate the work Claudia had done in the archives. It suggested a degree of commitment to art history that he found impressive. It also sat oddly with her drug use. The fentanyl was understandable, prescribed by her doctor. It was the other drug that struck him as unlikely to be taken by the young woman he'd known, however briefly. He knew young people experimented with drugs, often foolishly, but he couldn't understand those *yaba* pills. Didn't everyone know the dangers of amphetamines by now?

His phone rang as he pondered. The screen told him it was Amélie calling from Paris to say that she was taking two days off to come to the Périgord and negotiate in person with Mademoiselle Neyrac about her concert at Château des Milandes. She also wanted to see the large hall where she'd be singing and to check out the costumes and sound system. She'd get the train that left the Gare d'Austerlitz just before eight and would arrive in St. Denis at one-thirty, just in time for a late lunch at Ivan's. She'd go back to Paris Sunday afternoon.

As he put down his desk phone, happy at the prospect of seeing her, his mobile vibrated. The screen told him it was Florence, and he had a sudden premonition that this call, like the one from her that had launched his week, would lead to the discovery of another death. He shook his head and told himself not to be so foolish.

"Bruno, I need a great favor. Could you possibly take care of the children for me tonight? And as soon as possible? I have to go out, but everyone else is tied up, so you're my last hope."

"Of course," he said, instantly wondering what might have cropped up or why all her friends and her pupils at the *collège* who usually babysat were not available. He dragged his mind back to practicalities and looked at his watch. "Have the children eaten yet?"

"No, I'm afraid not. You'll need to make their dinner, bathe them, give them a story when you put them to bed. It will be all right. They know you, and they'll think it's an adventure."

"If I make them spaghetti and give them

some fruit, will that be all right?"

"Perfect. I have spaghetti and bananas in the apartment. I'm sorry, but I need to leap into the shower and change, but I'll wait for you to arrive. Soon as you can."

"It sounds like an emergency — anything I can help you with?" he asked, consumed by curiosity.

"No, no. Just come."

Bruno collected Balzac from the stables where he'd left his dog after the morning ride, explained to Pamela that he'd have to miss exercising Hector that evening, stopped at the supermarket for some chopped meat, onions, tomatoes and fruit juice and picked up a baguette at the bakery. Within less than thirty minutes after Florence's call he was knocking on the door of her maisonette, one of a row of subsidized apartments the *collège* had erected to tempt teachers to a country school.

Florence always dressed well, but he was struck when he opened the door by how good she looked, in a fitted suit of light blue, a white silk blouse and navy-blue high heels with a matching bag. Her blonde hair was piled into a loose bun, emphasizing her slim neck. She looked attractive but somehow businesslike, as though going to an interview for a job she really wanted.

"You look great," he said, and as she darted her head forward to brush his cheeks in greeting he caught a whiff of scent, something she hardly ever wore. It must be a date, he thought, wondering whether she would choose to tell him about it.

"Bonjour, Bruno," the twins chimed, darting from behind their mother's legs to embrace Balzac before raising their arms for Bruno's usual trick of lifting each of them once. Rather than disappoint them, he handed the bag with his shopping to Florence and raised the children, saying *"Bonjour, Dora, et bonjour, Daniel"* as their little arms went around his neck and Florence backed away so he could carry them into the hall, uncertain whether to take them into the kitchen or the living room.

"We have a new book for you to read us," said Daniel. "Can you tell us a story?" asked Dora at the same time.

"Thank you so much for this," Florence said, already halfway out of the door and waving goodbye. "I won't be late back, by ten-thirty or so."

"I think we'll have to have a story and read the new book," he said, walking with the children into the living room and lowering himself into an armchair as the children squabbled over which of them would have his képi and then squirmed down to the floor to play with Balzac.

"But first, which of you is going to teach me how to cook?" he asked.

"You cook all the time," they cried.

"But this is magic spaghetti, and I don't know magic. Balzac hasn't taught me yet, but he says you two know how to cook it. Should we go in the kitchen and find out? Then we can have dinner and read a story before bath time.

"I only know the simple stuff," said Bruno, washing his hands before peeling and chopping two onions and then cutting three tomatoes into rough chunks. "You two have to find the saucepan and the frying pan."

The children began to forage in cupboards.

"Now I need salt and pepper," he said, and Daniel climbed onto a stool and pointed to where they stood on the table. Bruno found duck fat in the fridge and began frying the onions and put a kettle on to boil. "Where does *Maman* keep the spaghetti?"

Dora pointed to a cupboard. "That's where she keeps the ordinary spaghetti, but we don't know where the magic one is."

"Balzac will tell us," said Bruno, tossing the meat into the softening onions, adding salt and pepper and stirring the pot. "He only eats the magic spaghetti. Now you need to break up the spaghetti sticks so the bits are each as long as your finger, otherwise Balzac won't eat them. Now can you set the table, a plate for each of us, a fork and spoon, and a plate for Balzac. If you want apple juice, you need to set a glass by each plate."

The water was boiling, so he poured the contents of the kettle into the saucepan, added salt and then the strands of spaghetti, now broken into child-sized pieces. He added the chunks of tomato to the mixture of meat and onions and began stirring, then he brought two stools close to the oven and stood a child on each stool so they could watch.

"Ladies first," he said, picking up Dora and giving her a wooden spoon and holding her so she could stir the meat. Then he picked up Daniel, gave him another wooden spoon and let him stir the spaghetti.

"Now we say together after me the magic spell." He began to chant, making up the rhyme as he spoke:

Les pâtes nous remuons
Afin que nous mangions.

La sauce deviendra magique
Sinon c'est très tragique.*

He put the children down, put a tiny portion of spaghetti with a little sauce on a plate and then put the plate in front of Balzac, who sniffed it curiously for a moment before wolfing it down. The dog ran his tongue around his teeth and looked up hopefully for more.

"It worked," cried Dora. "It's magic spaghetti. Balzac says so. Was it the magic spell?"

"I think so," said Bruno. "Now let's eat our own."

The plates were soon emptied, the apple juice drunk, the bananas eaten and the new book read as they all cuddled together in the big armchair. They read until it was time for the children's bath, with some extra bubbles so they could hide the yellow rubber ducks Bruno had given them the previous Christmas. Dried off, teeth brushed, pajamas donned, they knelt together beside their bed, closed their eyes and said their prayers for Mummy and Balzac and Bruno and all their friends. Then they clambered together into bed and sat up waiting for a

*"We stir the pasta so that we can eat and the sauce becomes magic. If not, it's very tragic."

story, which Bruno made up as he went along.

"Once upon a time there was a beautiful young princess and a brave young prince and they went for a long walk, much longer than usual, and began to worry that they might be lost. But then an enormous and friendly basset hound, bigger than Balzac, came along and said his name was Lancelot and asked if he could help. But they would have to climb up his long ears so that they could sit on his back . . ."

Their little eyes were drooping by the time he finished, so he kissed them good-night, tucked them in and left the door open so there would be a little light from the hall while he washed up. In the living room, he looked through Florence's well-stocked bookshelves, pulled out a copy of Le Roy Ladurie's *Montaillou,* which he'd always meant to read, and settled down in the armchair.

But he couldn't concentrate, wondering where Florence had gone and why she hadn't described her plans for the evening. She could have been dressed for a date, and the timing suggested she was going out to dinner. She was an adult woman, long divorced, and her life was her own, he told himself, and sternly ordered himself to drop this line of speculation and read the damn book. He managed a page or two before glancing at his watch to ponder where she might be, and with whom, before he sat up straight and returned his attention to the book.

This time he managed five pages before he began to ask himself why he should be feeling so unsettled. The image of Florence as she had opened the door to him that evening, looking so attractive, kept coming into his mind. Florence was a sensible, mature woman, he told himself. But nonetheless, she had been hurt in her marriage, abused in the dreadful job she had when he'd first met her before he'd told her about the vacancy for a science teacher that had cropped up at the local *collège.* Still, a woman alone was always vulnerable, so perhaps, just for reassurance, he should try to find out precisely who it was she was seeing this evening. He owed it to the children, Bruno said to himself.

He'd managed to get through perhaps forty pages before she returned, just a few minutes after ten-thirty, looking just as lovely as when she'd left, but with more of a sparkle in her eye, as though her evening had been a great success. She checked on the children, thanked him for cleaning up in the kitchen and saw him to the door, pressing *Montaillou* upon him when she saw he'd been reading it.

"It was so kind of you, Bruno," she said, giving him a maternal, or perhaps a sisterly, peck on the cheek, and with a final word of thanks waved him a cheerful good-night. An unusually pensive Bruno drove home, not even noticing that Balzac was eyeing him curiously from the passenger seat and not at all looking forward to reading more about the medieval village of Montaillou in the shadow of the Pyrenees and the coming of the Inquisition to stamp out the heresy of the Cathars. But it might, he thought, help put him to sleep.

CHAPTER 20

Before eight the following crisp and misty
April morning, Bruno was parked by the
canoe-rental shack on the waterfront of
Limeuil waiting for the arrival of Dominic
Darrail and listening to the local news on
France Bleu Périgord. The third item
quoted Madame Muller in that morning's
Sud Ouest saying she didn't understand
why the police would not release the body,
since she understood that her daughter had
died in a tragic accident.

"Merde," Bruno said aloud and called up
that day's paper on his phone. There was a
small headline on the front page saying "Billionaire's Daughter Death Clash" and a full-
page story inside with a photo of Claudia
and another of her father in white tie and
tails with his second wife at a White House
event. The byline was Philippe Delaron of
St. Denis. At least it was datelined Trémolat, where Claudia's mother was staying. At

277

the end of the story was a single-column photo of J-J with the caption "Police chief says, 'No comment.' "

Bruno had a good idea how Philippe had got the story. The bustling young reporter had cultivated contacts among the staff at most of the main hotels in the valley and was always happy to reward his informants. A chambermaid making ten euros an hour would be delighted to make another ten with a quick call to Philippe.

Bruno looked around impatiently for Dominic to arrive. His canoe-renting friend Antoine in St. Denis had brought out his canoes a week earlier from the garage where he stored them in winter. He'd cleaned them, checked the life jackets and waterproof containers, where clients could put their spare clothes and valuables, and spent a day paddling downstream from Montignac on his annual inspection of the river. Dominic seemed to take a more casual approach to his business, so Bruno ordered a cup of coffee at the quayside café-bar and read the rest of *Sud Ouest* while waiting.

It was close to eight-fifteen when Dominic arrived, red eyed and with a hint of last night's alcohol. A swarthy, thickset man with a taste for gold neck chains and bracelets, he was in his early thirties, divorced and starting to get fat. He no longer resembled the fit young man Bruno recalled who had played for the local rugby team. But his shoulders were broad, and he was still strong enough to have tossed a woman twice Claudia's size down the well. Eight canoes were stacked on the trailer behind his four-by-four vehicle, and it looked to Bruno as if they and the life jackets had not been cleaned before being put away for the winter.

"Bonjour, Dominic," Bruno said, shaking hands. "I need to ask you about that lecture you attended Sunday night. We're trying to find out if anyone saw Claudia after the event."

Dominic shook his head firmly. "I saw her before it when they were handing out glasses of that cat's piss they call punch. We just said hello and that we'd talk later about her doing a river trip."

"What about when the lecture finished?"

"I didn't see her, and the mayor's wife said she'd left early, not feeling well." He gave a sour grin. "Probably that damn punch."

"How was the lecture?"

Dominic shrugged. "Useful, I suppose. I learned a thing or two to tell the tourists. They like to hear some history about the place. That's why they come here, some of them."

"And after the lecture, what did you do then?"

"Went home, watched some film on TV that was already halfway over."

"Which film, do you recall?"

"I dunno, about a black guy taking his kids skiing."

"I heard you'd gone for a pee in the bushes after the lecture."

Dominic shrugged again. "I was dying for one. There's only one toilet and it was occupied. Anyway, it's good for the plants."

"Did you see anybody else in the garden when you were taking your leak?"

"No, not that I was looking out for anyone."

"Do you recall who was still there as you were leaving?"

Dominic screwed up his eyes as if to remember and then began to roll himself a cigarette as he spoke. "I'm pretty sure that Mad Englishwoman who rides horses was there and the teacher from the *collège*. I think they were chatting with that redhead from the museum. And there was the garden girl who let us in, Félicité. She saw me zipping up when I finished." He shrugged. "Nothing she hadn't seen before."

"Your mother told me she was planning to have you and the American girl to dinner. Did you like her?"

"Who wouldn't, pretty girl like that?" He winked at Bruno. "A bit intellectual for me, though. All those books."

"What books?" Bruno remembered Claudia arriving at the station with only a rucksack. She couldn't have carried many, but he recalled seeing a stack of art books on the table in her room.

"I dunno, but my mum had asked if I could knock out a bookcase for her. She said she was sick of seeing all the books and papers piled around."

Bruno nodded. "You grew up here, I bet as a kid you and your friends used to climb into the gardens."

Dominic grinned. "Of course we did, used to dare each other to do it at night. It was all more overgrown then."

"Could you show me all the places where you could climb in? I just have to finish the report on the accident, but the *procureur* wants me to see if there are any signs of some stranger getting in."

"Why would they do that when the gate was open for the lecture?"

"Ask the *proc,*" Bruno replied with a shrug. "I just follow orders."

"You want me to show you now?" Dominic looked at his watch. "I've got to get these canoes cleaned."

"It won't take long. We can go up the hill in my van, and then I'll run you back here."

They went past the commune school and turned left up the long hill to park outside the restaurant at the top. To the left of the garden gate was a footpath that led downhill, and Dominic showed Bruno a spot close to the entrance that looked feasible, particularly if one were ten years old and had no fear. Then he led the way back, through the square where the wall was high and forbidding, except for an angle where some of the cornerstones protruded. The garden of the hotel, Au Bon Accueil, also looked like a possible way in. Dominic pointed out gaps between the houses lower down on the rue du Port after a big stone archway where the wall could be reached, but it would take a skillful climber to scale it.

"Then there's this garden behind the house where my best pal lived. We used to climb up there. It was the easiest way. That's it. Can we go back now?"

Bruno made a note of the house, drove Dominic back to his canoes and then returned and knocked on the house door. A young woman answered, a baby in her arms and a toddler clutching at her skirt, looking at first surprised at the sight of his uniform and then worried as if she expected him to bring bad news. Bruno had learned to expect this with strangers and smiled reassuringly.

"There's no problem at all, madame. I'm Bruno Courrèges, chief of police for the valley, just finishing the report on the death of that young woman in the well up in the castle gardens on Sunday night. I need to check whether anyone could have climbed in. One of the locals told me he used to climb up from here when he was a kid."

"I'm Sylvie Postrelle, and I know who you are, I've seen you in the market in St. Denis. You're welcome to take a look, but my husband repointed all the cracks in that wall when we moved in, worried that our kids might break their necks trying to scale it."

She led him through the house to a kitchen where he'd interrupted her washing the breakfast dishes in the sink. The back door opened onto a narrow patch of garden, maybe three meters long or a little more and backed by a wall of old stones about four or five meters high, then a narrow terrace of grass with another, higher wall behind it. The wall facing the garden had indeed been repointed, but the stones were lumpy, and a skilled alpinist could probably have managed to scale it, but not Bruno. The garden was fenced off to waist height at each side, but there was a latched gate that led to a small alley where the family kept their garbage cans, the yellow-topped one for recyclables and the black one for organic waste.

"Is that gate kept locked?" he asked.

"My husband checks it every night, in case little Michel here gets out. He's at that age where he's exploring everything, full of mischief," she said fondly. "Can I offer you a cup of coffee?"

"Thanks, but I just had one down at the port. You moved here recently?"

"Yes, my husband works for Gaz de France in St. Cyprien, and we moved here just before Christmas from Nantes. It's a lovely area. Michel is the toddler and the baby is Jeannette."

He thanked her, chucked the baby under the chin and suggested that in a year or two Michel might want to join one of the sports clubs for *minimes*.

"We'll be joining the tennis club when the season starts," she said.

"It's already open. We have a covered court. I give weekly classes for the children, and you're more than welcome. You know where it is?"

"Yes, we've driven around a bit, and thank you, I'd like to get some more exercise. By the way, did you find anywhere else someone might have climbed in, because my husband was a bit worried about a burglar getting up onto the terrace, and there's a place farther down where it looks easier."

"Could you show me, please?"

From her doorway she pointed him to an angle in the wall a few houses down the street, and he saw that it went back about five meters, turned at a right angle and then another right angle to come back to the original line of wall, leaving a house-shaped space. Looking at the right angles, Bruno thought he'd have little trouble getting up onto the terrace if he stood on another garbage can. He strolled on and saw a narrow lane, the entrance to the new château, guarded only by an ancient iron gate. The château was still sealed and all the shutters closed until the owners returned in the summer. He climbed up to look over it and saw that once over the gate it would be easy to get up to the terrace that way. He could have climbed over the gate but thought that would not be wise while wearing his uniform

He went back to the house-shaped gap in

the wall, clambered up without tearing his uniform trousers and then strolled along the terrace, waving at Sylvie as she stood watching from her back door. The stones in the wall here were more carefully dressed, and he saw no easy way up, so he retraced his steps, and a few meters beyond the spot where he'd climbed up Bruno saw a fissure in the wall. Moments later he was on the second terrace with just one more wall to climb to get into the gardens. He walked along toward the hotel and when past it saw a triangular-shaped archway in the wall that gave him an easy scramble into the gardens. It had probably been a sally port, a way for the defenders to launch a sudden attack on any besieging force that had reached this point. He clambered up once more and found himself face-to-face with a bewildered David.

"What are you doing here, Bruno? How did you get in?"

"I wanted to see if it would be possible for someone to climb in even when the place was supposed to be locked up. There are some cracks in the wall that need repairing. By the way, have those builders of yours capped the well yet?"

"Yes, and it's padlocked. Come and see."

"Better late than never," said Bruno,

wondering why Dominic had not shown him the spot that was easiest to climb.

"Did you arrange to meet the doctor here?" David asked. "She wants me to take the lid off the well again, just for a few moments. Would that be okay?"

"That's fine with me so long as you seal it again. Did she say why?"

"No, but she asked if Claudia had ever done any rock climbing."

"Knowing Fabiola, she'll have her reasons."

CHAPTER 21

When they reached her, Fabiola was examining the stone rim of the well with a magnifying glass and then looking back at the screen of her phone.

"Bonjour, Bruno," she said, standing up and putting forward her cheek to be kissed. "Do you know if Claudia did any climbing?"

"I can find out. Why?"

She turned to David and asked him politely to remove the lid of the well. It was a heavy circle made of thick wooden beams, held down by a chain secured into brackets in the stone wall and then padlocked. Bruno nodded, and David opened the padlock. Bruno helped him remove the chain and then with difficulty lift off the heavy lid. Fabiola asked David to move away, out of earshot and out of sight, saying she needed to speak to Bruno in private. Bruno grinned, thinking of the gossip that the young man could get from this.

"Something was nagging at me," Fabiola said when David had gone. "And when I looked again at the photos I'd taken of the scrapes and bruises on her limbs, there were none on her knees. Could you just climb up onto the lip of the well, please, but from the other side, not here where I've been looking. And don't use the scaffolding."

Bruno walked around to the other side, put one foot on a small ledge formed by a bulge in a large stone, placed his hands on the lip, levered himself up until he could place one knee on the flat rim and used it to lever himself up.

"Now see me do it," she said, picking the same spot and performing the same actions except that, instead of placing her knee on the rim, she stretched her leg straight and put her foot on the rim to get her leverage.

"I'm a trained rock climber and we almost never use our knees. It's feet and hands because you have more control and more balance. Knees are clumsy things, just joints. If she was a serious climber I could understand there being no marks on her knees. But if she wasn't, it's odd. In fact, it's more than odd; it could be very significant. Now please roll up your trouser leg and show me your knee."

Bruno complied, glad that David was not seeing this latest development. Fabiola peered and pointed.

"You see that red mark where you rested your weight and pivoted on it, that's very mild bruising, even through your heavy uniform trousers. Claudia was wearing a skirt, so her knees would have been bare. She had scrapes, but there were no signs of even the faintest bruising when I first saw her body. Immersion in cold water inhibits bruising, at least at first, but the Americans have done some work on this at their National Center for Biotech Information and found that bruising inflicted before death can appear later, even after prolonged immersion. In this later photo from the autopsy there's no sign of bruising on her knee but look at her lower legs, just above the ankles. That's the kind of bruising consistent with someone holding her firmly by the legs, possibly so he could lift her, but using a cloth or mittens because there are no finger marks."

"You're saying she didn't climb up herself, but someone hoisted her up."

"Yes, almost certainly a male because of the strength required. Try it on me while I stand with my hands on the rim. Use a handkerchief on one hand but not on the other."

Bruno took out his handkerchief, relieved that it was clean, bent down from his knees and not from his waist and took a firm grip just above each slender ankle.

"Now lift me, not all the way."

He straightened his legs but did not raise his arms, realizing that doing so could catapult Fabiola into the well. He let her gently down again.

"Now look at my ankles. Your finger marks are on one but not the other, a general redness like the one in my photo. I don't know about you, but I'm now convinced she wasn't alone here, and it's possible, even likely, that she was deliberately thrown into the well by a reasonably strong man."

"You've convinced me somebody could have lifted her," he said, "but whether that was to help her onto the rim or to throw her in is another question. I can see someone lifting her so she could get to the kitten, and then she lost her balance and fell in and the guy panicked and bolted."

"I agree, that's another possible scenario."

"Let's call David back to help me replace the lid on the well, and then I'll find out if Claudia was a climber."

Rather than call Madame Muller on her

American number, Bruno dialed Hodge and found him having coffee with Claudia's mother at her hotel. Hodge passed the phone to her, and Bruno asked her about Claudia's climbing experience.

"She's a New Yorker, brought up thinking that height was something you take an elevator for. The only mountains she ever visited were those with ski lifts. Why do you ask?"

"The pathologist is investigating the bruises on Claudia's legs."

"And this helps?"

"I'm not a pathologist; I'm just passing on the question."

"I wanted to thank you anyway for putting Jacqueline in touch with me, that friend of your mayor. We had a very fine dinner here at the hotel together last night, and it turned out we had some friends in common in New York and Washington and even in Paris. Then I remembered seeing a good review of her book in the *New York Times,* so we had a pleasant evening. It was just what I needed, taking my mind off Claudia for an hour or so."

"I know she enjoyed meeting you," he replied, thinking of the way he'd seen at funerals how the social courtesies seemed to provide a respite from grief.

"Are you any closer to releasing her body?" she asked.

"That's for the *procureur* to decide, but I hope it won't be long now. Have you run into Professor Porter? He's also staying at your hotel, along with a Madame de Breille. She works for an investigation agency that's been hired by your ex-husband."

"No, I'll ask Mr. Hodge."

Hodge came back on the line to tell Bruno he'd had a call from Porter, and they had arranged to meet that morning at the Vieux Logis.

"Did the professor say what he wanted?" Bruno asked.

"No, only that he wanted a briefing and he'd be happy to tell me anything that might help."

Bruno described his own meeting the previous day with the professor and Madame de Breille and what had seemed like a rupture between them and added that he had the e-mails between Claudia and Porter if Hodge needed them.

"I'm seeing him at ten — that's in twenty minutes — and I'll let you know after that. Do you have other plans today?"

"I'm meeting a friend at the station and then having a late lunch at Ivan's. I don't know if I told you about Amélie. She's from

Guadeloupe, a jazz-singing magistrate who's coming down to perform at our summer concert. She's also doing a Josephine Baker memorial concert at Baker's old place, Château des Milandes."

"I'm a big fan of Baker. Along with Jackie Kennedy she's probably the most popular American woman we've ever sent to France," Hodge replied, adding that he'd like to come for the event. "And does the cultural attaché at the American embassy know about it?"

"I don't know, but it's going to be televised."

"Let me call our culture office at the embassy, and maybe I could drop by at Ivan's to say hello." Hodge paused, and Bruno heard faint voices before Hodge resumed. "Madame Muller has just nudged me to say she's also a Baker fan, and maybe she can come with me. Is that okay?"

"That might work. We should be there around one-thirty, but she may have to leave early for some contract negotiations," Bruno said. "I'll let you know, but if necessary we'll certainly find another opportunity. You'll like Amélie; she's bouncy, very smart, full of energy and a rising star in politics. She might even be a minister in a future left government. She was working for the justice ministry when she came down here, doing a time-and-motion study on me as a typical countryside cop."

"I've often wondered," Hodge replied, laughing. "Is that what led to your latest promotion?"

"Probably."

"I'll look forward to meeting her. Give my regards to Ivan."

Then Bruno called his friend Annette, the young magistrate in the Sarlat office of the *procureur* who was dealing with the building-code violation, to ask if a decision had been made on how to proceed. The dossier remained open, she told him, until J-J as chief detective had formally signed off on an accidental death, which looked to be the most likely outcome. The builders would then face a far more serious charge.

"Your dossier could stay open for a while," Bruno said. "Fabiola is filing an addendum to the pathologist's report arguing that the bruises on the legs suggest the dead girl may have been deliberately lifted up and possibly tossed into the well."

"*Mon Dieu,* if Fabiola says that, we'd better take it seriously. Does J-J know yet? The last I heard he was close to wrapping it all up."

"I'd better call him now. I'll ask Fabiola

to e-mail you a copy of her addendum."

J-J was not happy for a case he had thought almost concluded to remain open, but he knew Fabiola from previous cases and respected her work.

"*Putain, tu me casses les couilles,* Bruno," J-J said when Bruno explained. "The press is hounding me enough already. And the chief pathologist won't be happy to be second-guessed."

"You can tell him it's something only a skilled climber would have known," Bruno replied. "And it may not be murder. Someone may just have lifted her up to reach the kitten, she fell in, and then he ran away."

"We don't have any suspects," J-J said, sighing deeply. "There was no sign of sexual activity, so that wasn't the motive. And we heard back from Scotland Yard today about the boyfriend, Morgan. Witnesses and credit card records placed him in London all weekend, including Sunday evening. Not only does he have no record of drug use, he's an athlete, in some tennis competition where they're required to take drug tests. He's got two years of clean records and even invited the police to search his apartment. When Scotland Yard checked with his friends, they laughed at the idea that he was a user. I think we can rule him out."

"That suggests that Claudia might not have got the drugs when she was in Thailand with him," said Bruno. "So how did she get hold of them? I'd never heard of them before, have you?"

"Our drug squad had never heard of *yaba* pills. They checked and came back to tell me there's a little of the stuff around in Paris, mainly in the *treizième,* the Chinese and Asian quarter around Porte de Choisy, but there's hardly any market for it in Europe. I sent a message with her photo to the Paris narcotics guys asking if any of them recognized Claudia. No reply so far. But what about this art fraud business you were telling me about? The old art historian may not have been able to do it himself, but he could have paid someone to do it. Yves said he sent you the e-mails she exchanged with her professor — was there anything substantive in them about the fraud?"

"Yes, a few questions were raised, but her professor didn't take them seriously. Since she was trying to buy the historian's collection, she might have been trying to use the accusations as a bargaining point."

J-J grunted in reply and then sighed again before speaking. "I'd better arrange to go and see Bourdeille. I agree it's a long shot, but what other suspects have we got? I could get to see him this afternoon. If he's in a wheelchair, I don't suppose he's moving around much."

"Maybe we should check out that guy she would go dancing with in Paris. That friend of hers at the Louvre told me about him. I put a note in the case file, but I only have his first name, Marcel."

"That's not much help."

"It gets worse," Bruno said. "I was in Limeuil today, checking on the wall. I could climb up fairly easily from the village and into the gardens. That means anybody could have got in, not just the people at the lecture. You saw my note on the case file about identifying all of them, including the canoe guy, Dominic, the one who went to piss in the bushes. I still have to check his alibi."

"What is it?"

"Watching a film on TV, France Two."

"On Sunday night? I was doing that. I fell asleep during a comedy about some guy whose wife threatened to leave him unless he took the kids on a ski trip."

"That's the one he was watching."

"You'd better find me another suspect. And get a move on. The new prefect is calling me every day about this case and complains that Paris is calling her. And who the

298

hell is this Madame de Breille who claims you said I should see her?"

"She's the private eye that Hodge warned us about, hired by Claudia's father. She's a former customs inspector who now runs the French office of the Hexagon Trust, which mainly conducts financial investigations on Wall Street and in tax havens. Hodge says it's also staffed by former spooks. She seems to have a lot of heavyweight contacts in Paris."

"And why should I see her?"

"Two reasons. The first is because the *procureur* won't release the body to the family until he gets your report. So you're responsible. And second because of Hodge's warning that if Madame de Breille doesn't get what she wants, she'll make sure the blame falls on us country bumpkins in the local police."

"I can't finish the report until I've interviewed Bourdeille and you've tracked down that dancing man in Paris. *Merde,* she's sitting outside my office right now. Maybe I can off-load her onto Prunier."

"He won't thank you for that. And he'll almost certainly want you to sit in on the meeting."

"*Putain,* I'm tempted to declare this an

accidental death fueled by an overdose of drugs."

"You're too good a cop to do that, J-J," Bruno said firmly. "And that will upset Claudia's family, along with the American ambassador and the White House, and then Madame de Breille would probably declare war on you personally. What's more, this new report from Fabiola gives her all the ammunition she needs."

CHAPTER 22

Bruno went back to his office and called the Louvre to track down Claudia's friend, Chantal. When he finally reached her, he said he was trying to find some of Claudia's other friends in Paris and in particular the dancing partner, Marcel. Chantal gave him a number for Judy, the photographer, but knew nothing of Marcel beyond Claudia's occasional reference to going dancing.

"You said they might have met at a Sunday night dinner given by an American called Jim. Might he know Marcel?"

"Yes, Jim Haynes. I think he takes phone numbers when people book, but you might have to give him the date. Here's his number."

An American voice answered in heavily accented French, and Bruno switched to English, introduced himself and explained why he was calling.

"Claudia, the art student, she's dead?" the

American replied. "Yes, I remember her. Oh, that's awful. What happened? Was it a car crash?"

"We think it was probably an accident, monsieur, but we have to check, and I'm trying to find a Frenchman named Marcel. They met at one of your dinners, and she used to go dancing with him. Do you have a number for him?"

"Hold on. It may take a while, she was here three or four times. I'll miss her — she was really nice, friendly to everyone, always offering to stay and help clear up."

Bruno heard papers rustling over the background noise of what sounded like CNN and then the American came back.

"There's a Marcel Deguin. He came one evening with his daughter, but I'd say he's a bit old to take a girl dancing. And then there's Marcel Morlac, a young guy, a Breton. Here's the number he gave when he booked."

Bruno thanked him, ended the call and tried the number for Morlac. It began with 06, so it was a mobile rather than a fixed line.

"Ouay," came a brisk answer.

"Bonjour, m'sieur. Is this the Marcel Morlac who would go dancing with an American girl, Claudia Muller?"

"Who the hell are you?"

Bruno explained, and a stunned voice replied, "Claudia's dead? How did it happen?"

Bruno explained again and asked when Marcel had last seen her. It had been more than a month ago. Bruno asked if he'd been romantically involved with her.

"No, I'm gay, we just loved dancing together. She was a wonderful dancer. This is terrible news."

"May I ask where you were Sunday evening?"

"Here in Paris, at La Mano in Montmartre, an old Mexican restaurant that's pretty hot for dancing these days."

"Do you know anybody who could vouch for your being there?"

"A few hundred people. I was working behind the bar. That's what I do. Why the questions? Do you think Claudia was murdered or something? I thought you said it was an accident."

"We think so, but since she was a foreigner you'll understand why we need to double-check everything. Thank you for your help."

Bruno googled the bar, found a number, called and spoke to the deputy manager, who confirmed that Marcel had been working there Sunday evening. Bruno hung up and added another note to Claudia's case file on the Périgueux police computer. Then he called Bourdeille.

"Thank you for your advice, Bruno," the old man replied. "I'm having a wonderful time here with Laurent at the falconry."

"I'm glad to hear it, but will you be there all day? I ask because Commissaire Jalipeau wants to come and interview you about Claudia, either this afternoon or tomorrow morning."

"I'm going to be here until the special taxi picks me up at five. I believe I told you all I know, Bruno."

"Yes, but Claudia's family is insisting that we leave no avenue unexplored. And it was you who told me very firmly you didn't think Claudia died by accident."

"Very well. Tomorrow morning, anytime after nine. Will you be joining us, or is the *commissaire* coming alone?"

"I don't know. That will be up to him."

Bruno texted J-J and checked his watch. Amélie would be arriving soon. Pamela had an empty *gîte* where she would stay, but she'd be here for the weekend, so he ought to give her a dinner party. Amélie and Pamela had become friendly, so she would come. The baron loved Amélie's singing and he liked Hodge, so he could invite those two and Claudia's mother. Madame Muller liked Jacqueline, so she should come with the mayor. That made eight, but maybe he should invite Laurent, who could tell Madame Muller about his excursions with Claudia, and Florence who had also been friendly with her. That made ten, about the maximum he could fit around his table.

Bruno loved having friends to dinner, and the prospect cheered him up almost as much as planning the meal. It was springtime, so a *navarin* of spring lamb would be a good choice. He had new potatoes, peas, shallots and baby carrots in the garden, which would go splendidly with it. He could make a *tarte Tatin aux oignons rouges* for a starter, and he'd need something light for dessert, perhaps that fruity, sweet lemon syllabub that Pamela made so well. He'd always wanted to try making that.

He had a magnum of Château de Tiregand, the *grand millésime* from 2005. The wine would be at its best, and the Pécharmant had the depth and finesse to accompany the lamb and the body to go with the cheese that would follow. He had a fine bottle of Monbazillac from Clos l'Envège as a dessert wine. He'd have to think which wine to offer with the first course.

Jack Crimson was spending his retirement

helping his daughter, Miranda, by doing much of the office work involved in the riding school and *gîtes* she ran with Pamela. Bruno sometimes joined him on the one day a week he reserved for his visits to the vineyards of the Bergerac, which he now knew as well as Bruno, if not better. Bruno recalled their visit to an English winemaker in his sixties who had been one of the pioneers of organic wines in the Saussignac region. He was now president of Vins Bios in France and had campaigned for years against the fertilizers and chemicals that were still pumped into so many of the wines of France and elsewhere. His modest vineyard was named Château Richard, after himself, and Bruno and Jack had been very impressed by a Cuvée Osée he had produced without any of the usual sulfur dioxide that was used to clarify wine.

Bruno smiled as he recalled Richard saying that he'd called it *osée,* which means "daring" in French, because so many experts had assured him he'd never be able to make a wine without sulfites. Richard had dared to prove them wrong. Bruno had bought half-a-dozen bottles and still had four in his cellar. That would go perfectly with the onion tart, and he'd enjoy telling the story of the organic English winemaker.

He called each of his friends to invite them to dinner the following evening. A Friday, it was supposed to be his day off so that he could be on duty for the Saturday morning market in St. Denis. Somehow he expected that his day off would fall victim to the inquiry into Claudia's death and J-J would probably insist that Bruno join him in seeing Bourdeille. He picked up his cap and with Balzac at his heels trotted down the old stone spiral staircase of the *mairie* and out to his van to head for the station and pick up Amélie.

The station was about a kilometer from the old town of St. Denis. The sprawl toward it now included a medical laboratory, a postal sorting office, a bus garage, a large builders' yard, a vet's office with kennels and a rash of new and nearly new housing. Built cheaply for the retirees from northern France who were steadily increasing the population — and the average age — of the region, the houses were built in modern, almost-prefabricated form rather than the traditional Périgord style of stone walls and red roofs. Still, they were well insulated, the shutters usually painted in gay colors, and each had its terrace with plastic chairs and tables and a barbecue. The new inhabitants were determined to celebrate their life in sunnier climes, and a growing number even had swimming pools. Bruno preferred to swim in the local rivers.

On the platform he found the local priest, Father Sentout, in his black soutane, a small wheeled suitcase at his side, heading for a church meeting in Agen. Old friends, although Bruno only attended church for weddings, baptisms and funerals, they touched cheeks as they embraced, and then the portly little cleric bent down to greet Balzac.

"A sad business about the American girl," the priest said. "From the photo of her in the paper she was obviously a lovely young woman. Are they planning a funeral here, do you know? And was she a Catholic?"

Bruno said he expected the family would want her remains returned to America, and he didn't know Claudia's religion, but he'd find out from her mother. Then he saw the barrier of the crossing coming down to block the country lane that crossed the track and heard the train approach.

"Waiting for a friend?" the priest asked.

"Yes, that singer from Guadeloupe with the lovely voice who sang at Clothilde's wedding. She's coming back this summer to perform at one of our concerts and doing a special Josephine Baker concert at Château des Milandes. It's going to be televised."

The priest nodded and lifted his suitcase as the train drew to a halt and the doors slid open. Wearing a white turban, jeans, a red shirt under a leather jacket and a brilliant smile, Amélie leaped down from the train into Bruno's arms. Expecting this, he had braced himself, since even her best friends would never have described her as slim. He gave her a warm hug and then she knelt to receive Balzac's fervent greeting.

"God bless you, Bruno, and you, too, my child," the priest said as the train door closed behind him. Four other passengers descended from the second carriage, one elderly couple and one much younger, and looked around in vain for whoever was supposed to meet them. Then a large SUV screeched around the bend and into the station forecourt. It braked hard, and Philippe Delaron stepped out.

"Him again," said Amélie dryly. On her last visit, she had not taken to the young reporter and photographer for *Sud Ouest.* Philippe had long seen himself as God's gift to the female sex and used his camera and press card to worm his way into conversation, and whatever else he could manage, with every young woman of the region.

"He's changed a bit," said Bruno in a low

voice. "A love affair that ended badly for him has helped him grow up. I think for the first time in his life he had his heart broken. Be polite, because I want him to give us lots of publicity for your concerts."

"Hi, Bruno," said Philippe, hand outstretched. "And welcome back to you, Amélie. I remember you singing at Horst and Clothilde's wedding. You were terrific."

"The mayor and I agree with you," said Bruno, smiling. "So she'll be singing at our summer concert."

"That's great. I'd love to take a picture when it's convenient. But right now, we have a family weekend, and I'm here to pick up some cousins." He waved at the four people on the platform, who picked up their bags and began to head their way. "How long are you here this time, Amélie?"

"The whole weekend," she said, politely if not warmly. "Call Bruno and we'll fix a time for a photo. And we may have some news for you after tomorrow about a special concert."

"Great, thanks. Anything you can add to my story this morning, Bruno? You probably heard that the radio followed up, and now the Paris papers are calling."

"Not a word, Philippe. It will all have to

come from the official spokesman in Périgueux."

"Understood." Philippe gave a cocky wave and went to embrace his cousins. Bruno installed Amélie and Balzac in his van and set off for Ivan's bistro.

"Philippe's less bouncy than I remember," she said. "It's an improvement."

"When are you seeing the people at Château des Milandes?" he asked.

"Later this afternoon, but I'll need to rent a car."

"Use my old Land Rover," he said. "You can take it from my place after lunch. And you'll be the star guest at the dinner I've planned for tomorrow evening. Pamela, the baron, the mayor and Jacqueline, Florence, Laurent and two American fans of Josephine Baker." He explained the presence of Hodge and Claudia's mother. "I thought it might cheer her up, or at least take her mind off her daughter's death."

"Have you solved that yet?"

He shook his head, parked and led the way into Ivan's bistro.

CHAPTER 23

Although it was getting late for lunch in France, Ivan's was still half full, mostly of people who recalled Amélie from singing at Clothilde's wedding. They included Horst and Clothilde, who were the first to come up and embrace her.

"What a welcome," Amélie said with a happy smile when she and Bruno could finally sit down. Ivan brought a tureen of thick vegetable soup and then came back with bread and a small glass dish filled with a thick green sauce flecked with red. Amélie laughed out loud when she saw it, a rich and generous sound that Bruno remembered with affection. It made everyone in earshot want to laugh too.

"So you're still stealing my mother's recipe for Haitian *épice,* you naughty man." She rose and gave Ivan a hug. "I'm so flattered you're still making it."

"Bruno wouldn't have my cooking any

other way," said Ivan. "Today's menu is venison terrine, then Wiener schnitzel with potato salad and apple cake with ice cream to follow. Red wine or white?"

"Just mineral water for me, I'm driving," she told him. Bruno asked for just a single glass of white.

"How's life as a magistrate?" he asked. When the socialists had lost power, Amélie's job in the justice ministry had ended, and she was now a very junior magistrate in Paris.

"Depressing," she said. "I'm working in the juvenile system, based in Belleville, trying to keep kids out of detention centers."

"I thought Belleville was the trendy new district," said Bruno.

"Parts of it are, around the parks and Ménilmontant. But a lot of it is still working class, immigrants, unemployed, grim schools with drugs on the playground, the seamy side of big-city life. What about you? Enjoying your promotion?"

"I'll tell you as and when my paycheck comes." He grinned. "It's a lot more travel, up and down the valley, a lot more paperwork. I've one very promising young colleague, Juliette, in Les Eyzies, and one stubborn old-timer in Montignac who thinks he should have had the promotion instead of me. Still, Louis knows his area, and that's very useful. What about your other life? Are you still singing in Paris?"

"Two evenings a week, jazz clubs mostly. The kids I work with call me the singing magistrate, which is cool, makes me recognizable. It means they know me from something other than the law, and that helps. Some of the schoolteachers I have to deal with also like it."

"And politics?"

Amélie sighed. "It was a bad defeat, so morale is low, and we'll need a long time to rebuild the party. On top of that we need to define our priorities and what we stand for. It's not enough anymore to rely on the trade unions, since their members are disappearing even faster than our votes. But I don't think we have any choice. If we can't engage with the working class to battle the extreme right, nobody else will even try. I see your Périgord voters still support the left."

"Even though we don't have much of a working class down here and hardly any factories," Bruno replied. "Maybe your party needs to work out why that should be. But you're not down here to talk politics. You spoke with Mademoiselle Neyrac over the phone. Was that just to arrange today's meeting, or is everything settled on the contract?"

"Mostly settled. She's saying the audio and visual should not count as two separate recording fees, but I think we'll reach a compromise. And after going through a Paris winter, I think I needed this break down here. It's good to know I have quite a few friends in St. Denis. That reminds me, I saw Isabelle yesterday, and she sends you her love. She's planning to come down here the week I'm doing my concerts."

"Do you see much of her?" he asked, thinking that Isabelle never missed an opportunity to keep contact, to reach out to Bruno's friends in Paris and to those in the Périgord like J-J and ask to be remembered to Bruno, to pass on her love. Then there were the enigmatic postcards she sent him from wherever her coordination work might take her: London, Berlin, Brussels, even Washington. They usually contained exaggerated words of affection for Balzac and a token kiss for Bruno. He knew it was her way of staying in touch and in his bitter moments thought of it as a way to keep her hooks in him. But he knew the hooks were of his own making, that he neither could nor would resist her.

"We have lunch from time to time,"

315

Amélie said. "And she's brought me into a women's group of cops, security-service people, the law — we meet every month for dinner. It's a great way to widen my acquaintances. Sometimes she comes to my concerts. Isabelle's good at staying in touch, or should we say networking."

She paused and then looked at him intently. "You haven't asked about Yacov. You know we broke up."

Bruno nodded, keeping his eyes on his plate. "He told me. He sounded regretful about it."

She put out a hand to his chin and pushed it up until he was looking into her eyes. Then she spoke, keeping his head still so he couldn't move away.

"It was a lovely affair while it lasted, which wasn't very long, but I have no regrets because he's a good man and we both had fun. You don't need to tiptoe around the subject, Bruno. I'm a big girl, and he wasn't my first lover and he certainly won't be the last. You can talk to me about Isabelle as much as you want. I know you're crazy about her, and she feels the same way about you, but it's never going to work. She wants her career and Paris, and you want the Périgord. So find someone new who wants what you want. You know I'm right, no?"

He nodded. "You're right. But then we meet again and bang. We can't stay away from each other."

"I know, she says the same. But at least she talks about it, which means she'll eventually talk herself out of it. I understand it's tough for you guys with your macho posturing who've never learned to admit your vulnerabilities. But you're going to have to learn to talk about your feelings, too. We all have them. There, lecture over."

Before the dessert, Amélie slipped out to the ladies' room, which gave Bruno a chance to push her words to the back of his mind and check his phone for messages. There was one from J-J, saying he'd see Bourdeille at nine the next morning, and another from Madame de Breille, saying simply, "Call me."

"My appointment is at three," Amélie said, returning and attacking the apple cake. "Should we skip coffee?"

Bruno nodded and called for the bill. Ivan shook his head and shrugged.

"It's on me, I already paid. This is instead of an agent's commission," Amélie said. "Besides, you're giving me supper tomorrow."

He drove Amélie to his home, handed over her suitcase and the keys to the Land Rover and a map and said, "If you see a very old man in a wheelchair with the falcons, say hello to him from me, and say hello to the falconer, Laurent."

She opened the door, climbed in, unfolded the map.

"Just stay on the main road to Le Buisson, Siorac toward St. Cyprien, then turn off to Allas-les-Mines and follow the signs to Château des Milandes," he said, and then paused.

"And thanks for the lecture," he added. "I think I needed it."

"In that case, there's hope for you yet. Is it okay if I take your car back to Pamela's place?"

He told her to keep it for driving around the next day; she could bring it back in the evening when she came to dinner. He might see her again at Pamela's that evening when he came to exercise the horses and wished her good luck with her meeting. After he'd waved her off, he sat awhile with Balzac in his garden, trying to rekindle that thought he'd had about Claudia and the drugs.

What if the second drug, the *yaba,* was not hers? Could somebody else have climbed the balcony into her room and hidden that straw full of the pills in her rucksack frame? The same person could then somehow have slipped her one. They would have to know that in combination with the opioids she was taking it would be dangerous. It sounded far-fetched even to him, but it was possible. Maybe it was in her fruit punch before the lecture. He tried to remember what Florence had said about the prelecture drinks. And wasn't it Félicité who had been serving the punch?

He still couldn't see a motive for killing Claudia. Bourdeille might have had one, but he seemed relaxed about her claims that he'd falsified some attributions. The woman at the Louvre had dismissed them, and even Professor Porter had poured cold water on her suspicions. Her ex-boyfriend Jack seemed to be ruled out, as was Marcel.

At his feet, Balzac lay slumped, eyes closed, with his head resting on the ground between his outstretched front paws and his ears flowing out to each side like a set of heavy curtains. His tail wagged automatically when he felt rather than saw Bruno's attention shifting to him. Bruno felt a wave of affection for his dog and bent down to scratch just behind his ears. Balzac rewarded him with a sound Bruno had heard from no other dog: a long, soft, satisfied rumbling that was more than a breath, less than a growl. Had Balzac been a cat, he'd have called it a purr.

Bruno leaned back, telling himself to start from first principles. Motive, means and opportunity — these were the three elements of a crime that had been drummed into him at the police academy. Even the means were less than clear; had it been the well alone or the well plus drugs? Not only did he have no motive, he had yet to establish that anyone had the opportunity to thrust her into the well. Everyone at the lecture had been accounted for. Florence had been sitting by the door and was certain that nobody else had left early. He knew from his own climb that someone could have come into the gardens unseen by the others.

Who else did she know in the region? Could Claudia have arranged a discreet meeting with someone in the gardens and only pretended to be ill to have an excuse to slip out? And maybe it had not been a murder. He tried to concoct a plausible scenario. She had heard the kitten meow, got the mystery man to boost her onto the rim of the well and then lost her balance, perhaps when the cat scratched her, and had fallen in.

Who might she have been meeting and why? Could it have something to do with her suspicions about Bourdeille, or perhaps with her plan to buy his house and collection? But why go to such lengths to keep the meeting secret? Bruno's thoughts went back to his talk with Dominic. He'd said he darted out to pee as soon as the lecture finished, so who might have beaten him to the single toilet? Might it have been Claudia? He hadn't thought of that. Had Félicité checked the toilet before locking up? He'd have to ask her.

He frowned, thinking about the timing. Dominic had said when he'd finished there were only Pamela, Florence and Clothilde still chatting by the gate. How long would a pee take? A minute, maybe two at the most, since Félicité had recalled that Dominic was still doing up his fly when he emerged from the bushes.

How long would it take a lecture hall of thirty people to empty? They had to get their coats on and say their good-nights. That would take more than two minutes. So maybe Dominic was out there longer. Would there have been time for him to find Claudia somewhere in the gardens, thrust her into the well and get back to the main gate? Probably not, unless he had an accomplice who had already found Claudia. But what motive might Dominic and his accomplice have to kill her? It didn't add up. He was getting nowhere.

Then his phone vibrated. It was a local number from a fixed line, not a mobile phone.

"You're not very polite, Monsieur le Chef de Police," came a crisp Parisian voice. "When a lady asks you to call her, you're supposed to reply."

"Madame de Breille," he said, his own tone as flat as he could make it. And he was damned if he was going to apologize to her. "Bonjour. How can I help you? I assume your own phone is out of order. Or are you simply trying to keep your number to yourself?"

"You can start by calling me Monique. My phone is fine, but I'm in a café, and since I'm not alone, I didn't want to call from my table. I presume you've read today's *Sud Ouest*? Now that this story has gotten into the papers, the pressure is going to build. And I have some information for you. Are you in St. Denis?"

"I can be there in ten or fifteen minutes. And yes, I read today's newspaper with the remarks by Claudia's mother."

"I'll see you in that convenient café behind the *mairie*. Ten minutes."

Chapter 24

Madame de Breille was wearing another expensive-looking suit, and she was not alone. A burly man in his fifties sat beside her, wearing an out-of-fashion dark suit, heavy black shoes and a blue silk tie around his bull neck. Bruno thought he looked vaguely familiar, or perhaps it was just that he looked like a cop.

"Meet Gustave Pellier, private detective, based in Périgueux, and something of an expert on Bourdeille."

"Madame de Breille, Monsieur Pellier, this is my dog, Balzac," said Bruno, shaking hands. "Would you care for a coffee?"

"They're on the way," said Madame de Breille. She ignored the dog. Pellier leaned down to stroke him.

"That's a fine dog. Is he fast enough to hunt?" Pellier asked.

"Yes. He can't sprint, but he can follow a scent and keep trotting all day. Deer, wild boar, he just wears them out, but mainly we hunt *bécasses.* He's brilliant at that. And I'm training him to find truffles."

Pellier continued to stroke Balzac and smiled up at Bruno, as if some masculine bond had been established.

"I was working with J-J in the detective squad when you first came to St. Denis. We met once on a bank robbery case, that gang from Toulouse," Pellier said, sitting back up. "Took my retirement, got bored with the garden and went private. I was hired by the real de Bourdeille family when this art historian decided to change his name and declare himself a member of the clan. He hired a fancy lawyer from Bordeaux and came up with a document supposedly from the abbot of Brantôme and written in the sixteenth century, which provided for some land and a sum of money for a woman to pay for the education of her son. He also had a family tree in an old Bible, which he said supported his claim that his mother was a direct descendant of the abbot."

"This isn't new. It was in that report on Bourdeille that you did for Claudia," Bruno said to Madame de Breille. "You said that his connection with the forger Paul Juin meant he could fake old documents almost at will."

"Together with the other instances that Claudia unearthed, it suggests a pattern of forgeries that Bourdeille used for personal gain," she said as a waitress brought three cups of coffee and a metal bowl of water for Balzac. "But this story isn't finished. I told the family about the link to Juin, and they decided they were prepared to go to court, call Juin as a witness and refute Bourdeille's claim. That was when he backed down."

She went on to explain that the de Bourdeilles' lawyer had met with the lawyer for the art historian and proposed a compromise, a settlement out of court in which the family would withdraw their objection to his use of the name and Bourdeille would sign a formal undertaking that he would not seek any claim on the family's estate. Rather than face the cost of a court case that could go on for years, the family agreed to it.

"The point is that he backed down," said the ex-cop.

"Perhaps," Bruno said. "Or maybe he didn't want his friend Paul Juin to go through a grilling in court, during which he'd have to prove a negative, that he hadn't forged the document. And that kind of mud tends to stick."

Pellier shrugged, took a sip of his coffee and said, "That's true."

"Did you have the document examined by an expert?" asked Bruno.

"Bourdeille suggested that we submit it to the Louvre or the Bibliothèque Nationale, but since he was a big shot there, we weren't too keen on that. That was when the idea of a settlement came up."

"It's striking that ancient documents seem to emerge conveniently just when Bourdeille needs them," interjected Madame de Breille.

"Do you have anything else?" Bruno asked. Pellier shook his head.

"Would you wait a moment, please, while I see Monsieur Pellier out," Madame de Breille said, rising. Bruno noticed that at the door she slipped the ex-cop an envelope.

"I hope you think that was worth it," Bruno said when she returned.

"At least it brought you to the table," she said. "I like your theory that Claudia might not have known she was taking those Burmese pills. Her father will like it even more than I do. He's excited that you and your doctor have established that his daughter wasn't alone when she went into that well."

"You have access to our case file?" he asked sharply. The computerized case files were supposed to be secure.

"I don't, not directly. But Hodge does and

he's under orders from his ambassador and from the FBI to share information with me as the representative of Claudia's father. And since you're the one who seems to be coming up with ideas on this case, I thought I'd ask what ideas you haven't put into the file."

"None."

She gave him a sardonic glance. "Okay. But let me see if I can help. I have access to resources and methods that might be beyond you. I can hire private eyes, researchers, bribe filing clerks, get into bank accounts and tap phones. If you need that kind of help, just ask for it. Her father has given me an open budget."

Bruno pushed back his chair. "I'll let you know, madame."

"I told you, my name is Monique. And I'm hoping that we might be colleagues. I had you checked out, Bruno, so I know about the army, Sarajevo, the Croix de Guerre and your connections with the security services. I even recognize that phone you carry. It's one of the few I can't get into, and General Lannes doesn't give out many of those."

Bruno assumed that Yacov Kaufman must have told her about his connection to the man he knew as the brigadier, a senior figure in the French security service. Whichever political party was in power, General Lannes always worked on the personal staff of the minister of the interior.

"By the way, Isabelle sends her love," she added, with a tight smile as she saw the surprise on his face.

Bruno had never been very good at hiding his emotions, just as he could never stop himself from blushing. The best he could do was the old soldier's trick of a wooden expression, his eyes focused on the officer's cap badge and repeated barks of "Yessir!" That wouldn't work in this situation.

"I know you called Yacov to ask about me, and now I presume you'll call Isabelle, too," she said. "Go ahead. Give Isabelle a call. If you want privacy, I'll go outside and have a cigarette while you phone her. You can even give her my regards. We're old friends."

"What is it you want from me that you can't get from Hodge and reading the case files?" he asked.

"I told you before. I want to recruit you for Hexagon. I know you make seventeen hundred euros a month. We'll pay you five times as much, with a signing bonus of twenty thousand. That's more than your life savings, not counting those shares you have in the town vineyard."

"So you can read my bank account. I'm not sure I'd like to work for people who can do that and tap phones without getting a warrant," he said. "I really don't think I'd fit in with the way your company seems to work. And I don't think I'd be much use outside of my home ground of St. Denis and the Périgord, where I've known people for years and they trust me enough to tell me things. I'd be lost in a big city."

"That's not what your military record says," she countered. "Bosnia, Chad, Ivory Coast, you did well in some very different situations. And I've heard from Isabelle something of your work down here."

"Hexagon deals mainly in financial inquiries, an area where I wouldn't know where to start," he said.

"Financial experts are easily found. That's not how we'd use you, Bruno. You have contacts in French security, with the British and the Americans, and people in a position to know such things tell me that you're an all-around useful man. You can fight." She paused and then gave what seemed like the first genuine smile he'd seen from her. "Isabelle tells me you can even cook."

"I'd have to move to Paris," he said, wondering if this was why Isabelle had talked to this woman about him. Isabelle had always said that getting Bruno to move to Paris was the only way they could be together, that she couldn't compete with the Périgord.

"We don't care where you live as long as you can get quickly to where we need you. That could be anywhere. I hear your English is only just serviceable, so we'd put you through an intensive course, probably in London. You could visit your friend Inspector Moore from their Special Branch."

Again she gave that tight, unconvincing smile, taking pleasure in the way she doled out these details she knew about him and his contacts, like a cat toying with a mouse. He wondered if that was how she saw herself. As something feline, as a manipulator, a woman who had learned how to work in a predominantly masculine world. She would not be an easy colleague, Bruno thought. And he would never be able to trust her, never certain there was not some hidden motive.

Perhaps he was being foolish in that characteristic masculine way, making an excuse for the male difficulty in understanding women by claiming they were too subtle, too devious. He remembered Fabiola once saying over dinner that women were more intuitive and better at reading character because for them it was an essential survival skill. As the physically weaker sex, women had developed over the millennia the innate ability to assess the mood and atmosphere of any given situation before they found themselves at risk. Bruno didn't know if there was any science behind it, but the theory made sense to him.

"Don't give me an answer right away. Think about it," Madame de Breille said, rising. Bruno refused to think of her as Monique. "And if there's any research or inquiries we can make to help you on Claudia's case, just call me."

"How far did you check Pellier's story about the de Bourdeille family?" he asked. "Did your colleague talk to the family, to the two lawyers?"

"Offhand, I don't know. I doubt it, but if you think it's useful, we can get it done. Anything else?"

"There were some family photos in Claudia's room, one of her as a child with her parents and another taken when she was grown up. It showed her with her father, but the person standing beside him had been cut out, so the photo looked strange, much narrower than a normal print. I know her father divorced Claudia's mother and married again. The truncated photo suggests some family tension there."

"That's the client's business," she replied. "I really don't think we want to go there."

"Why not? Think like a policeman. Claudia is the daughter of a very rich man, so we can assume that she stands to inherit the bulk of his wealth. The new wife looks to me like the only person with an obvious motive to kill her. Do you know if the new wife has children?"

"Forget it, Bruno."

"You see the difference between us, madame? You work for the client who pays the bills. I work for justice."

"*Touché,*" she said. "That's a good line. I'll remember it. My offer to help still stands, and the job remains open. Think about it."

Bruno watched her leave, wondering if there was a Monsieur de Breille and, if so, whether they were still married and what kind of man he might be. Whoever he was, he had Bruno's sympathies. Then he went up the steps to his office to put a note into the case file about Muller's second wife. Hodge would see it, which meant so would Madame de Breille. Bruno knew that he was being petty, but it would be interesting to see if it led anywhere. Prunier and J-J had promised to pursue all leads. That implied asking Hodge if the FBI could look into it.

Had such a request come to the French police from the FBI, they would at least interview the second wife.

Not that Bruno thought it likely that Claudia's stepmother was involved. If it was murder, her killing required too much local knowledge — about the Sunday evening lecture, the gardens, the work on the well and the way it had been left unguarded. It was either a murder of opportunity or more likely an accident in which the man who lifted her had panicked and fled the scene. And if there had been a man who fled the scene, the place to ask questions about that would be in Limeuil. Bruno phoned David to be sure Félicité was working that day.

CHAPTER 25

It was turning into a beautiful springtime day as Bruno and Balzac took the familiar road to the hilltop of Limeuil. He slowed his van outside the town vineyard to see the first buds just starting to peek from the vines, and on the other side of the road he saw the rich pink of cherry blossoms. Balzac, sitting on the passenger seat, looked at his master expectantly, probably hoping for a walk in the fields. Bruno fondled his dog's ears, telling him he'd have the whole hilltop garden to explore.

They found Félicité in the avenue of chestnut trees, using a pitchfork to turn the thick piles of last autumn's rotting leaves in the long wooden compost frames. She took off a work glove to shake his hand, then bent to greet Balzac, looking mildly curious about Bruno's visit.

"I just wanted to clear up one or two loose ends," Bruno said. "Dominic told me that he only went out to pee in the garden because the toilet was occupied. Any idea who might have been using the bathroom?"

She shook her head as she rose from Balzac's attentions. "I was clearing away the punch glasses and tidying up, so I don't know. Sorry."

"Did you check that the toilet was empty before you locked up?"

"I think so, we always do. It's routine. But I can't say I have a specific memory of doing it on Sunday. When I turn the central lights off, they go off in the bathroom, so somebody would have shouted."

"Not if they were unconscious or ill. Or drugged."

She shrugged. "Yeah, I guess you're right."

"How close were you to Claudia?" he asked, knowing they shared a bathroom and a toilet at Madame Darrail's.

"We were friendly but not especially close. I mean, she's mega rich, and I'm broke. It's not easy to connect to someone with a wardrobe full of designer dresses. Even her jeans were Armani."

"It sounds as if you were a little bit jealous of her." Bruno said it lightly, with a grin, trying to make it sound like banter rather than accusation.

"I wasn't jealous of her, I mean, she was

nice. But the general situation got to me, that she's born rich and I have a full-time job but I still have to work Saturdays in the *bio* shop just to get by. And I don't even have a car."

Bruno nodded. "It doesn't seem fair," he said, the sympathy in his voice made genuine by the memory of Madame de Breille offering him untold riches if he started to work for people who were far richer still.

"And she was beautiful, that perfect skin and her figure," Félicité went on as if she hadn't heard him, her eyes looking away over the valley. "Men just looked at her and gaped. I can't say I blame them." She sighed. "And I'm not even pretty, with fat thighs and hair I can do nothing with. *Merde,* what am I saying? Hell, Bruno, I liked her and I miss her and I'm really sorry for her mother. Claudia had everything, and it was all taken away, just like that."

"And you're alive and young," he said. "You say you aren't pretty, but you're wrong. You have lovely eyes, good cheekbones, and you've got one of the healthiest jobs in the world with a view people pay money to see. Madame Darrail's next lodger will probably be envying you."

She laughed. "Thank you. And you're right: I'm alive and I have a job I love, even if it pays less than the minimum wage until I get my *brevet*."

"When do you take the test?"

"At the end of June, so I won't know if I'm a fully qualified gardener until sometime in September, which means another summer vacation of camping *sauvage* and sleeping on the beach."

"And living off pizza." He laughed. "I've been there. You're young enough to love it. Where do you go, Provence?"

"No, Gruissan, near Perpignan, in the national park with its beaches. It's beautiful there, do you know it?"

He shook his head but felt that he'd established enough of a rapport to start probing. "How much time did you spend with Claudia? I would think you had breakfast together most days."

"Yes, usually upstairs in the kitchen, one of Madame Darrail's supermarket croissants and weak coffee. Last week, when the weather was good, we'd eat on the balcony. One of us usually had some orange juice, which we'd share. A couple of evenings she took me out, once to the hilltop restaurant here and another time to the pizza place at the bottom of the hill."

"Did she talk about her work, her thesis?"

"A bit, not much. She talked about some

mec she'd been seeing for years and how she was going to break it off and go out with different guys while she was still young. And she complained about guys hitting on her, trying to pick her up. I told her to send some of them my way, and we laughed about it."

"Did Madame Darrail ever join in this girl talk?"

"*Mince,* no, we didn't like her, a real old *facho* who loves Le Pen and talks about how she hated de Gaulle. What do you expect? She's a *pied-noir,* came from Algeria as a baby when all the whites fled from independence. She can't stand Arabs. Funny that the whites are called *pieds-noirs.* Do you know why that is?"

"It's because when the French troops first invaded, they all wore black military boots, so the Arabs called them *pieds-noirs,* black feet."

"Makes sense. You learn something every day."

"Was there any particular guy who used to pester her here?"

"David, a bit, but he's harmless. And Dominic kept at it, trying to get her to take a canoe trip with him. Claudia thought he was creepy."

"Dominic was hinting to me this morning

that you and he had a thing going at one time. Is that right?"

She stared at him levelly, eyes narrowing. "Is that any of your business?"

"Yes, I'm a cop investigating what may be a suspicious death. It's not just my business — it's my duty."

Félicité's eyes widened. "But everybody said it was an accident." She looked horrified.

"We aren't sure about that," Bruno replied. "That's why we have to keep on asking questions until we are. Let's start again. You and Dominic had a fling. How did it end?"

"I suppose you could say by mutual agreement. It only lasted a couple of weeks, and I was on the rebound from a *mec* in Sarlat who I'd really liked. Dominic asked me out, took me to dinner a couple of times, bought some nice wine, and I was, like, why not. But we had nothing in common. I'm a Green and he kept making jokes about tree huggers. And about feminists. He had one joke that really ended it for me. He asked, 'What do you call a boatload of Arab migrants at the bottom of the sea?' And his answer was 'A good start.' That one sickened me. Politically he's just like his mother. If there was any other place in Limeuil as

339

cheap for me to live, I'd take it."

"Did Dominic then make a play for Claudia?" Bruno asked.

She nodded. "Like he couldn't see she was way out of his league. But he kept trying. He only went along to the lecture Sunday evening because she was there. He'd never been to a lecture at the castle before. He didn't even pay much attention, kept looking at his phone. You could tell when the lights went out for the slide show, there was this glow from his phone lighting up his face."

"He probably wasn't the only one. People seem to spend half their lives on their phones these days."

Even as he said the words, Bruno felt the familiar vibration at his waist, excused himself and turned away to answer, nodding in agreement when Félicité asked if she could continue with her work.

"Are you trying to get me fired?" came Hodge's angry voice. "What's this *merde* you put into the file about Claudia's stepmother?"

Bruno was startled by Hodge's tone. He knew the FBI agent was usually relaxed. He had an image of Hodge that came from Western movies: a man who made a point of staying calm, a laid-back sheriff who could be tough if he chose to be but was not easily rattled. The bad guys might come, but Hodge would take care of them. Bruno understood that Hodge was under pressure from his chiefs. Bruno caught himself. It was one thing to be pressed by his bosses in the FBI who knew something of the complications of law enforcement. It was something else entirely to be pressured by a diplomat or, worse still, a political appointee who served and enjoyed the pleasures of being the American ambassador in Paris at the pleasure of the wayward man in the White House.

"Most murders are committed by people who know the victim," Bruno said, stepping away for some privacy and keeping his voice calm and his tone reasonable as he explained that every cop in France was taught that. "And family members without direct blood ties are statistically more likely to commit murder than others.

"It's just common sense to check whether there could be inheritance issues involved between Claudia and her stepmother," Bruno added. "You were the one who first mentioned it."

"I didn't think you'd be fool enough to pursue it!" came the angry retort.

"Looking into potential beneficiaries of a

death is basic policing, and people would start asking questions if we failed to do it. That's all I was pointing out. I'd like to know that the stepmother was in New York when Claudia died, whether her relations with Claudia were good or bad. You remember that family photo with one person cut out?"

"I know what you're saying, Bruno, but these people are personal friends of the ambassador. They get invited to the White House, for Christ's sake. And now it's all over the media."

"You can't blame me for that," Bruno said. "You're the one who is supposed to be babysitting Madame Muller, and she was the one who chose to speak to a reporter."

"I know, but we've already got American newsmen in Paris asking the ambassador why he hasn't intervened to get the body released. Now you want me to have the stepmother interviewed. The ambassador will go ballistic."

"Why don't you explain that what you are doing is following up on a routine query from the French police to exclude your ambassador's friends from suspicion. I don't see the problem."

"I sure as hell do. The media is on the

case already, asking if this was just an accident."

"In that case, suggest the ambassador recommend that his friends issue a short statement of grief and how they are content to leave matters in French hands. And since you're with Madame Muller, couldn't you ask her how Claudia got on with her father's second wife? When you think about that photo, it's a reasonable question. By the way, you haven't told me how things went with Professor Porter."

"Who? Oh, the Yale guy. I told him what I could, and he said Claudia's father was an important donor to the university, so as a courtesy the professor has agreed to take a second look at Claudia's allegations against Bourdeille. He's gone off to some Bordeaux museum. At least it keeps him out of the way. I don't suppose you know how *Sud Ouest* got that story. I seem to remember you being friendly with the reporter."

"I think you'll find he got a tip from someone working at the hotel."

Hodge grunted. "Just do me a favor, Bruno. Tell me before you drop any more grenades into the case file."

CHAPTER 26

Bruno thanked Félicité for her time and whistled for Balzac as he headed back to his van, wondering how many more times he'd visit these gardens. On the way, he turned off to check that the well was still sealed. It was not, but men were working on it, one standing on the rim with his back to Bruno and holding a rope and calling down to a man below.

"Have you got permission from the *procureur*'s office to resume work?" he asked the man he could see.

The man turned angrily, a burly man in his thirties with a broken nose and a shaven head. Tufts of black hair thrust out from his collar and the turned-back cuffs of his work shirt. There was something familiar about his face, Bruno thought. His stance was instinctively aggressive, jaw jutting forward and eyes narrowed. It remained that way even when he first saw Bruno's uniform, but then he seemed to relax a little.

"Oh, it's you. Yes, they faxed the permission through this morning after I sent them a photo of it being sealed last night, and we'll seal it again tonight. David has the fax in the office, okay?"

"Just checking," said Bruno in a friendly way as Balzac emerged from the bushes to stand at his side. "Were you the ones working here before the accident?"

"Yes, me and my partner, Grégoire, though he likes to think of himself as the boss. Aren't you the bastard who dropped us right into the shit for leaving it unsealed?"

"No," said Bruno, not taking offense. "I'm the bastard who had to go down the well on Monday morning to see if a missing woman might be down there. I wouldn't want to do that again."

"So why did you look down the well, then?"

"My dog was following her scent from her room at Madame Darrail's place, and he led me right here."

The man grunted and said, "That's a good-looking hound. I know who you are, Bruno from St. Denis."

"That's right, and who're you?"

"I'm Luc Bonnet. I think you know my mother."

"If she's the Madame Bonnet who looks after Monsieur Bourdeille, then, yes, I do."

"I'd shake hands, but my partner's down there," Luc said, gesturing at the well.

"Grégoire would be the one on the town council, I suppose." Bruno was wondering if he knew Luc from somewhere. He could be a rugby player or a member of another hunting club. Maybe he sometimes worked on a market stall when building work was slow.

"That's right. In a little place like Limeuil it's hard not to get put on the council. I'll probably have to do it one day, but they'll have to catch me first."

"Don't I know you from rugby?" Bruno asked.

"Could be. I used to play for Limeuil for a few years. Anyhow, we're busy. Got to get this well finished."

"So I see. Take care, and don't forget to seal it again when you go."

"We won't, and maybe you might think of hauling in that ex-convict for some questioning. You know who I mean, Laurent, the one who did ten years for killing those Boy Scouts when he was drunk."

"What makes you think he was involved?" Bruno replied, startled. "I thought the American girl just fell down the well."

"Maybe, maybe not, but I hear he was hanging around her, taking her to see the sights. Ten years inside, no women, he must have been pretty desperate when he got out."

"We talked to him, and he's got an alibi."

"Just make sure you double-check it, then."

Bruno was struck by the venom in the way Luc spoke. He decided to probe a little. "Do you know him?"

"I was at school with the bastard. He was stuck-up, always had ideas above himself, going off to that agricultural college. It served him right, going to jail."

"That's kind of harsh," said Bruno. "He got a tough sentence, and he's served his time. He deserves the right to rebuild his life."

"That's the problem with this country these days," came Luc's retort. "Even the cops are going soft. Arab immigrants everywhere, calling themselves refugees. The Muslims are taking the country over, terrorists half of them, and you guys are doing nothing to stop 'em. It makes me sick."

"There were times when a lot of our own people had to flee France and were glad to find refuge elsewhere," said Bruno.

"Yeah? Well, good riddance is what I say.

If you don't love this country, you can damn well leave it."

"Funny that you never put your money where your mouth is," said Bruno.

"What do you mean?"

"I spent ten years in the army before I took this job," Bruno said crisply. "And I served with a lot of good men — Arabs, Africans, you name it. Some of them got killed; others got crippled wearing a French uniform. I doubt you ever loved this country enough to fight for it."

Luc turned away with a sneer. Bruno shook his head and went back to his van, thinking that there was an ugly mood building in the country. It wasn't the first time he'd heard such sentiments, although not often expressed so crudely. He sighed and headed up past the hilltop church, through the stone archway, and took the road to the upland plateau where Sylvestre, a member of his hunting club, raised the best sheep in the district.

Bruno's mood eased as he turned into the familiar lane and saw the clumps of ewes with their snow-white lambs nuzzling at the teats or gamboling in the fresh green grass. He found Sylvestre's wife, Marie-Hélène, sitting on a bench outside the stone farmhouse, enjoying the sunshine and feeding a small lamb with a baby's bottle. He told her not to move as he kissed her on both cheeks and asked how the lamb was doing.

"She'll be all right, but she was one of three in the litter, and the mother seemed to think she had enough on her plate with the first two. So we're starting this one off ourselves," she said. "You want some lamb for your dinner?"

"I've got some friends coming tomorrow, we'll be ten, and I thought of doing a *navarin*," Bruno said. "I remember one you made here last year. It was delicious."

"That will please Sylvestre. Most people want a leg or a shoulder even though the tastiest meat is in the neck. It's always the hardest to sell. Anyway, you'll find him in the barn."

Sylvestre was busy with a very pregnant and sick ewe, so he told Bruno to help himself from the top shelf of the big refrigerator, where he'd put the neck chops from two one-year-old lambs that had been butchered that morning. Bruno pulled out a plastic bag marked COLLETS and put them on the scales. They weighed two and a half kilos. He asked Sylvestre what he owed him.

"You never charged me for that half of the boar you shot last month," he replied. "So I won't take your money."

"That's different," Bruno replied. "You helped me carry it in."

"You've done the same for me often enough," came the reply. Bruno had half expected this, so he nodded, thanked Sylvestre and took the lamb back to his van. From under the seat he grabbed a bottle of not-quite-legal eau-de-vie made by a friend and took it back to the barn, putting it on a shelf out of reach of the livestock.

"Have this one on me," he said as Sylvestre grinned at him from the stall where he was squatting beside the sick ewe. "And thanks."

Knowing that a *navarin* always tasted better on the day after it was cooked, Bruno drove home, turned his oven to a hundred and eighty degrees centigrade and washed his hands. He rinsed the lamb chops and put them in a bowl in which he'd mixed a heaped teaspoon of salt and another of ground black pepper, three teaspoons of *herbes de Provence* and three tablespoons of flour. He tossed the chops until they were thoroughly covered. Then he peeled and halved the half kilo of shallots from his garden along with six garlic cloves. He turned on the gas under his biggest casserole, turned it down to a low heat, put in a tablespoon of duck fat and tossed in some *lardons*. He went out to the garden and picked three sprigs of fresh rosemary.

Once the *lardons* had turned golden he removed them onto kitchen paper with a slotted spoon and began browning the lamb chops, three at a time, and turning them to be sure they were done on all sides before removing them and adding new ones. When they were all browned and removed from the casserole, he lowered the heat and put in the shallots and garlic. After five minutes he added the lamb and *lardons,* a half bottle of dry white wine and half a liter of duck stock. He bruised the rosemary sprigs with the side of his chopper to release the flavor and added them and waited until the stew started to simmer. He put the lid on the casserole, placed it in the oven and then cleaned up the kitchen.

As so often when he cooked, questions that had been quietly doing their own stewing at the back of his mind began to fall into place. On impulse he called the hotel in Trémolat and asked if Madame Muller was available. He was put through to her room.

"Hello?" she said with a catch in her voice that made Bruno think she'd been weeping. At once he felt a touch of guilt. He identified himself and apologized for disturbing her. While her voice was hesitant and muffled, he could tell that she was making an effort to pull herself together.

"Ah, you're the policeman who has kindly invited us to dinner tomorrow evening," she said. "I met Jacqueline yesterday and she told me a lot about you. How can I help?"

"Do you have a few minutes for some questions, madame?"

"I'll be grateful for the company," she answered. "Professor Porter has gone to Bordeaux, and Hodge always works in his own hotel around this time of day so he can be in contact with Washington."

Twenty minutes later, they were sitting at a table in the garden of her hotel, admiring the precision of the topiary that marched down the lawn in an orderly pattern of spheres and obelisks. A glass of wine stood before each of them. With red-rimmed eyes, she had greeted him with a handshake still damp from the handkerchief she'd been clutching. She had seemed grateful for the presence of Balzac, whom she had petted and admired before he trotted off to explore the large garden. She smiled as she watched the dog tackle with determination the challenge of lifting his leg at each of the many pieces of topiary.

"I'm sorry to intrude upon you, Madame Muller, but I wanted to ask you how Claudia got on with her father's second wife," he asked.

"She didn't," she said with disdain, something fierce flashing in her eyes. "Claudia simply chose to ignore her existence. When she had to greet that woman at some social occasion, she did it as a stranger. She was very upset by the divorce."

"Why was that?"

"The breakup of our family came as a shock to her and to me. His request for the divorce was very sudden." Her mouth worked as if she was trying to turn a grimace into a smile, but she didn't succeed.

"I'm sorry if this is intrusive," he said.

"Of course it's intrusive — it has to be," she said with spirit. Bruno was struck by the way the topic of divorce had turned her grief into anger. It gave her energy.

"But I'm glad that somebody is starting to ask the obvious questions. The woman he left me for was one of his work colleagues. They had a fling, and she got pregnant. My husband was desperate to have a son, which I couldn't give him. I had a very difficult birth with Claudia, and I couldn't have any more children."

"Claudia has a half brother?" Bruno asked.

"No, his new wife had a miscarriage after their honeymoon and has not become pregnant since. I hear she's having fertility treatment." This time she managed a smile, albeit a rueful one. "I try not to gloat."

"Was Claudia still on reasonable terms with her father?"

" 'Reasonable' is a good word. She was polite, would occasionally have lunch with him on his or her birthday, but only in restaurants, never at his new home. And since the trust is a family firm, she was on his board of directors, so she went to those meetings."

"Does that mean Claudia was his only heir?"

"And now he has none, except for his second wife," she said, sipping at her drink. "The woman has a haunted look these days, I'm told, as if fearing that he'll dump her for a newer, fertile model. Or maybe he'll use his money to hire carefully chosen women from around the globe to bear his children and spread his precious genes."

"You don't like him anymore?"

"I still love the man he used to be when we were young and starting out and Claudia was little," she replied, choosing her words with care. "But I don't like what he's become in recent years. The money did it, the outrageous, monstrous amounts of money along with the fawning praise from his investors that went to his head and made him feel like a superman, as though his skill and luck in making money translated into some special moral virtue. You have no idea of the obscene displays of flattery and adulation that the superrich can attract. I imagine few human beings could withstand it."

"Claudia seemed to me and to my friends here to be a very levelheaded woman," Bruno replied. "She was discreet about her private life and her family and never talked about her money, although one or two women seemed to have noted the quality of her clothes. Do you think she could have withstood the impact of wealth?"

"I had my hopes, and she seemed to be doing fine, determined to get her doctorate and have a career in an area she loved. I was proud of her. But now we'll never know, God rest her soul."

She picked up her glass and drank, but her hand trembled as she replaced it on the table. Bruno told himself he was dealing with a formidable woman, a professor who was accustomed to a certain deference. She was wealthy in her own right and at the top of her profession, helping to set policy for the central bank of the world's largest economy. But she was also a mother who had just lost her only child. It was a daunting combination for a country policeman trying to get to the bottom of what remained a suspicious death.

"Let me ask you a question," she said. "In the United States, if someone seems to be winning an argument, the other person is likely to say, very aggressively, 'If you're so goddamn smart, how come you aren't rich?' Have you ever heard that in France?"

"Not quite like that, although we do have sentiments that aren't very different."

"Maybe it's just us Americans," she said with a tight smile. "I'm comforted to learn that she had friends here. And please, do call me Jennifer."

"With pleasure. In France we're familiar with the syndrome of too much wealth or power or deference. Louis Quatorze comes to mind, along with some other kings, and then there is Robespierre, Louis-Napoléon, Maréchal Pétain. Too much of it can drive men mad. I remember reading that owners of powerful newspapers are particularly vulnerable to fits of insanity."

Jennifer laughed out loud. "That's reassuring," she said. "It's such a relief to be able to laugh again, despite . . . Hell, Bruno, you know what I mean. I need taking out of myself. Would you be my guest for dinner here this evening?"

"Thank you. I'd like that," he said, realizing that he meant it.

In the hotel restaurant, the arrival of the menus interrupted her reminiscences of living in Paris nearly thirty years earlier. They chose foie gras poached in white wine with an apple-and-walnut compote. This was followed by *coquilles St. Jacques* and then pigeon, its breast roasted, a thigh prepared in confit.

They asked Yves, the maître d'hôtel, to choose some suitable Bergerac wines and, like more and more restaurants these days, they had installed a storage system for opened bottles that meant they could offer excellent wines by the glass. Bruno was delighted to be served some of his own favorites, a glass of Tirecul la Gravière, a Monbazillac with the foie, some Château Feely with the shellfish and then a glass of Montravel from Château Puy Servain with the pigeon. They stayed with the Montravel as they toyed with the cheese board until they ended with a soufflé flavored with an eau-de-vie of plums.

"You remember I said that people had commented on Claudia's clothes," he said over the dessert. "I was thinking of that young woman in the gardens, Félicité. She shared lodgings with Claudia, they had breakfast together, chatted a lot, went out for meals. They were friends, and she's very poor. Unless you have any other plans for Claudia's clothes and stuff, it would be an act of kindness to let her have them, even if they might not fit. And perhaps you'd like to talk to her, get a sense of Claudia's life here. I think she enjoyed it."

"That's an excellent idea, Bruno. I was dreading the thought of packing up her things, and I was wondering if there was a local charity that might take them. It's good to know they'll be used and appreciated. And she did mention in an e-mail being friendly with a girl in the same house."

"You can find Félicité at the gardens in Limeuil. And there's someone else you might like to talk to, a man she met the first day she arrived here."

"She wrote to me about him, Laurent, with whom she went to Lascaux."

"That's the one I was going to mention," Bruno said. "It wasn't romantic, I think, but they just warmed to one another. And she was interested in his job."

"Hawking. She told me about that and some lecture on medieval hawking she attended with you. I'd love to meet him because she mentioned him two or three times in her e-mails to me, and always very fondly."

"You'd better hear this from me, since someone else is likely to tell you in a cruder way." Bruno explained the accident that had sent Laurent to jail for ten years.

"Ten years!" she exclaimed. "You don't get that for murder. And he wasn't even drunk, you say?"

"He was just a hair over the limit. Had there been no accident, no dead Boy Scouts, he'd have been waved on by most cops after a Breathalyzer test. If they had proceeded, he'd have lost his permit for a few months, and that's all. But with the dead boys and the new law going through the National Assembly and the lobbying groups, he didn't stand a chance. It's amazing that he's not more bitter."

"Did Claudia know about all of that? She never mentioned anything of it in her e-mails to me."

"I don't know."

"I'd still like to see him and talk to him. Claudia thought of him as a friend, a good man."

"Maybe we could arrange something for tomorrow afternoon. He works with the hawks at Château des Milandes, where a jazz singer friend of mine is going to do the Josephine Baker concert. She may be there too, but in any event you'll meet her at dinner tomorrow night."

They decided against coffee, and she waved at Yves to get the bill.

"I'd like to share this," said Bruno, reaching for his wallet.

"Absolutely not," she declared firmly. "Not only have I enjoyed an interesting evening, but for the first time since I heard of Claudia's death I've been able to think and talk of something else. I invited you and you're having me to dinner tomorrow evening, which I'm looking forward to. Hodge tells me you're a fine cook," Jennifer said as they rose, replete, from the table. "Thank you for joining me, Bruno."

CHAPTER 27

Bruno rose just before dawn to jog through the woods with Balzac at his heels. For the first few minutes everything was still and crisp with just the sound of his dog's panting and his own breath and footsteps, until the life of the forest began to stir. Then the hound was distracted by some tantalizing scent just as the sun peeked above the horizon to send slanting rays through the woods. It woke the birds, and they began to greet the new day with song, filling Bruno's heart with pleasure until he thought back on the previous evening with Jennifer Muller. She had impressed him as a woman of courage and dignity as she battled to cope with the most grievous loss that can befall a mother.

And she had been kind and courteous to him, one of the policemen who was supposed to bring some order to the chaos that had invaded her life. So far, the police had not even been able to ascertain whether Claudia had died by tragic accident or by malice. And now their work was being dogged by this grim woman from Hexagon Trust who seemed hardly to care whether the head she delivered to her client was that of a killer or of a cop. Bruno tried to think if there was anything he had left undone, any avenue unexplored. Perhaps this morning's session with Bourdeille might spark some new idea.

Back at his house Bruno fed his ducks and chickens, refilled their water bowls and collected their eggs. He checked the lamb he had cooked the previous day and spooned off the surface fat that had set overnight. He showered, shaved and dressed in his old uniform, and with Balzac on the passenger seat drove to Pamela's riding school to saddle Hector and join his friends for the morning exercise of the horses. Shortly before eight, he had made his first patrol of the town, more like a pleasant stroll through the town, shaking hands with the men and kissing the women on each cheek.

Then he went to enjoy his coffee and croissant at Fauquet's counter while checking *Sud Ouest* to see what new embarrassment Philippe Delaron had concocted for him. It was on an inside page under the headline "Limeuil Death — U.S. Steps In." This was based on a bland statement from the American embassy's press spokesman saying that they counted on the French authorities to complete their investigation "with all due dispatch." No problems there, Bruno said to himself.

"What did you make of the radio news?" asked Fauquet, using the excuse of a cursory wipe of the counter to lower his mouth to Bruno's ear. "Is it true?"

"Is what true?"

"About this dead girl being about to expose some big art forgery before she was silenced. It turns out she was a star researcher attached to the Louvre. The radio said that came from some American newspaper."

Bruno opened his phone and searched Google to find the France Inter website quoting the *Washington Post* on Claudia. She was described as "a brilliant young art historian attached to the Louvre" making shocking allegations of forgery against famed French art scholar and Resistance hero Pierre de Bourdeille. The police were to interview him today.

Merde, he thought, instantly suspecting that the source was Madame de Breille, who would know from the case files that J-J would be seeing the old man. But as he read on, scanning quotes from Madame Massenet at the Louvre on Claudia's scholarly talents, Bruno saw the only other quotes came from "veteran French police detective Gustave Pellier." Either the private eye was getting himself some free publicity or Madame de Breille was using him as a conduit for her own purposes. Bruno recalled Hodge's warning that if Hexagon couldn't solve the case themselves they'd do what they could to discredit the French police.

"Well?" asked Fauquet, intent on adding another nugget to the store of gossip that was as much his stock-in-trade as the peerless croissants he made and the excellent coffee he served.

"Amazing, these journalists," Bruno replied vaguely as he put down a two-euro piece and some copper coins and headed for the door, half-eaten croissant in hand. "What will they think of next?"

The efficiency of his exit was spoiled by Balzac, who had not yet been given his morning treat of a corner of Bruno's croissant and who therefore stayed stubbornly by the counter, eyes switching from Bruno at the door to Fauquet looming overhead. Bruno sighed, bent down and made the

364

necessary offering. Balzac then trotted contentedly at his heels on Bruno's second stroll through town by a different route, which ended in front of the gendarmerie, where he'd parked his van.

A few minutes before nine, Bruno pulled up outside Bourdeille's *chartreuse*. The balcony above the main doorway, where Bourdeille so often sat, was empty. There was no sign of J-J's car, but Philippe Delaron's SUV was parked in the driveway, and Philippe was standing at the door, ringing the bell in vain.

"You can't force them to answer the door, Philippe," Bruno said. "If I were you I'd see if Amélie would find this a good time to pose for your camera. I don't think you'll get anything out of Bourdeille."

"Why are you here, Bruno? Are you going to interview him?"

"No, I'm here to defend a citizen, a taxpayer and a Resistance veteran from being pestered by the intrusive media when he doesn't want to be. He's ninety years old, for heaven's sake. Where's your sense of respect?"

"I can't leave here with nothing. My editor will give me hell, scooped by the damn radio."

"Have you read the full *Washington Post* story?"

Philippe shook his head.

"The real story is the guy they quote, the ex-copper, now a notably unsuccessful private eye in Périgueux. He's behind this. You didn't hear this from me, but he's been hired by a woman called Monique de Breille, staying at the Vieux Logis. She runs the Paris branch of a shadowy firm of ex-spies and top accountants called Hexagon Trust, which seems to make most of its money investigating tax havens for fat-cat clients — including the dead girl's father. That's the real story. If you leave now, you might just catch de Breille at breakfast."

Philippe's car was disappearing out of sight to the east as J-J's big Citroën appeared from the west. He parked beside Bruno's van and lumbered his bulk from the passenger seat. His assistant, Josette, turned off the ignition, opened the rear door and heaved a bulging shoulder bag onto her back before offering her cheeks for Bruno's *bise*.

"You heard the radio news?" J-J asked. "Pellier was never more than just barely competent when he worked for me."

"Madame de Breille is behind Pellier," Bruno said. "She hired him and brought him to St. Denis yesterday to try and sell me the same story."

J-J grunted. "This whole case is a can of worms."

"Don't say I didn't warn you," said Josette, looking crossly at her boss. "I still think we should have handed this to the art squad."

"They'd take forever to respond and I'm already getting flak for spending too long on it."

Bruno offered to take Josette's heavy bag, but she tossed him a scornful look, marched up to Bourdeille's door and hammered hard on the wood with the side of her fist. Bruno glanced at J-J and raised his eyebrows in question. J-J shrugged and looked baffled. Josette was usually as cheerful and friendly as she was efficient in managing J-J's life.

"Police, we're expected," Josette barked and marched in as soon as Madame Bonnet opened the door. "Commissaire Jalipeau to interview Monsieur Bourdeille."

Madame Bonnet led the way upstairs to a large library where Bourdeille in his wheelchair awaited them behind a large table, presumably the place where Claudia had worked. A tray with a coffeepot, cream, sugar and three cups and saucers lay on the table with a plate of cookies. In front of

Bourdeille was a slim folder, an ashtray and a pack of cigarettes.

"*Messieurs-dames,* welcome to my home. Madame Bonnet, we will need an extra cup if you please," said Bourdeille, glancing at Josette, who placed her bag on a chair and followed Madame Bonnet back downstairs. That was routine. J-J always liked Josette to take a good look around any new location and to keep an eye on others in the building.

"Bruno, I want to thank you for that introduction to Laurent and that marvelous day I spent with him and his hawks. And that young Caribbean friend of yours is delightful. She gave us a couple of songs in the main hall of the château. She said she needed to assess the acoustics, but I got the impression she was singing for her own pleasure. It certainly added to mine."

He turned to J-J and asked with an attempt at old-fashioned courtesy, "And how may I help you, Monsieur le Commissaire?"

J-J opened Josette's shoulder bag, pulled out a bulging box file and said, "The late Claudia Muller has made some serious written accusations against you of fraud and forgery to her academic adviser in the United States. I'm curious as to whether those charges might have been linked in some way to her death."

"You imply that I may have ended her life to shut her up?" Bourdeille said lightly. "How do you think I managed it, at my age and in this contraption?" He tapped the arms of his wheelchair.

"I'm aware that you told Chief of Police Courrèges that you didn't think her death was an accident."

"That's true. I don't," Bourdeille said. "Claudia was an intelligent and capable young woman with everything to live for, not someone who'd make a fool of herself at a dangerous well."

"She accuses you of forgery in her e-mails to her professor at Yale. I have the details here. She mentions the works of Antoine Caron, Josse Lefrinc, Ambroise Dubois — did she mention these to you?"

"Have you ever heard of those names before?" Bourdeille asked with a smile. "Do you know if they are painters, engravers, sculptors?"

"I'm not an art historian, monsieur. And I'm the one asking questions."

"Let's be precise. Claudia did not question the paintings," Bourdeille said, explaining that it was nearly impossible in modern times to forge a medieval painting. The forger would have to fake the wood, the canvas or linen, the way the surface was prepared, the paint, the aging and so on. Modern scientific techniques could detect such fakes.

"The three paintings exist, and scientists agree that they and their canvas and frames date from the right period," he went on. "The question is, Who painted them? Many, perhaps most, scholars would agree with my attributions because of the subject matter, the style, the individual methods and brushstrokes of the painter."

If there was no other evidence, such subjective attributions by known experts were often sufficient, Bourdeille explained. In the cases Claudia had raised, his archival research had unearthed some documentary evidence that reinforced his finding. She had not questioned whether the letters and archive entries he had found were genuine. Her complaint was simply that she had not found parallel records in other archives.

"She picked three cases out of hundreds of attributions I have made in my long career," Bourdeille said. "In the vast majority of cases where I have unearthed hitherto unknown documents, they were later corroborated by documents in other archives. Claudia's three cases may be easily resolved simply by asking the experts at the Louvre to examine them to see if they are genuine documents or if they were forged. I suggested to her that this should be done, and indeed I myself wrote to the Louvre proposing this step. Here is a copy of my letter."

He opened the folder before him, pulled out a photocopy and slid it across the table to J-J.

"And you should know," Bourdeille continued, "that Claudia never used the word 'forgery' in this context in my presence nor when she raised the matter with Madame Massenet, her supervisor at the Louvre. I'd be surprised if she did because she'd have been aware that the same modern forensic techniques that make it almost impossible to forge a Renaissance painting also apply to documents."

"Antique paper may be bought, monsieur," said J-J. "I believe there is a lively trade in historic books of blank paper."

"There used to be," Bourdeille replied. "But mass spectroscopy analysis and peptide mass fingerprinting have made the traditional paper from hemp and linen rags much easier to date. We can now tell whether the paper was dried with pressed felt or after the 1790s by a pneumatic press. By that time, of course, cotton was coming into the rag mix. Even if one can obtain paper of the right period and the right region, the almost universal use of iron-and-oak-gall ink contains organic elements which these days can be analyzed and dated with great precision. Any attempts to age the ink artificially with chemicals such as hydrogen peroxide and ammonium hydroxide, as in the Hofmann case, can be detected with ultraviolet light. You may recall his forgery of early Mormon documents."

Bruno bit his lip, sure that J-J beside him was feeling the same sense of inadequacy, even of humiliation, as Bourdeille casually displayed his mastery of the subject to toy with the two lumbering policemen.

"You are claiming that it is impossible to forge the documents you found to make your attributions?" J-J said.

"No, not that it is impossible to forge them. People try. But it is impossible to do so without a modern forensic laboratory being able to detect it."

J-J tried another tack. "You were a close friend and associate of Paul Juin, the master forger."

Bourdeille leaned back, shaking his head and chuckling. "Paul was a great forger in the days before mass spectroscopy and X-ray luminescence. He'd have been caught if he tried it now, when every little airport has a handheld spectrometer. They even use them here in garbage dumps to identify scrap metals."

Bourdeille leaned forward to fix J-J with his gaze. "I get the impression that you have not been in touch with your expert colleagues in the art squad of the Police Nationale, whose forensic facilities are among the best in Europe. Might I suggest that before you come here with such ridiculous and ignorant accusations, you contact the deputy head of the squad, Marc d'Alentour. He is a world-renowned expert. I trained him myself."

"Are you saying, monsieur, that these new technologies are infallible?" Bruno asked, more to ease the tension between J-J and Bourdeille than because he thought the question pertinent. Bourdeille's expertise was evident.

"Infallible? I'm not sure anything is infallible. Let me give you an example, the case of the Vinland map, which was claimed to be the first chart showing the Norse settlements of North America some decades before the voyage of Christopher Columbus. It was hailed as genuine when it was found in 1957 and sold for three hundred thousand dollars. But later analysis found traces of titanium dioxide, which under the commercial name of anatase had been used in some pigments only since the 1920s. Did that destroy the map's credibility? Not entirely, because such traces of anatase could have come from the sand used to dry ink in medieval times. Then researchers at the Smithsonian Institution in Washington found that anatase could be produced in the early stage of manufacturing oak-gall iron ink. The problem is that the ink on the Vinland map was not made from oak gall but appears to come from soot.

"One interesting footnote is that the first researchers to express doubts came from the British Museum, who noted that while the parchment clearly dated from the early fifteenth century, it contained a substance they could not at that stage identify. We now know that these were traces of radiation, nuclear fallout from the atom-bomb and hydrogen-bomb tests of the 1940s and 1950s. We now find such traces of fallout in every archive in the world. But none of that fallout has yet been found on top of the ink, which suggests to me and I think to many scholars that the map is probably a fake. But is that judgment infallible? No."

Bourdeille beamed at them as if ready to take a bow. Bruno was tempted to applaud. It had been a bravura performance. He glanced at J-J, who was nodding thoughtfully. J-J then pointed at Bourdeille's cigarettes with a brief "May I?" The old man pushed the pack across, and J-J extracted and lit one before sitting back in his chair.

"If there's no fallout on the ink, that suggests it was written after the fallout," J-J said. "But those nuclear tests went on into the 1960s. Maybe the ink didn't absorb the fallout. Have they looked under the ink to see if there is any fallout on the parchment below?"

"An excellent question," Bourdeille replied, lighting a cigarette for himself. "I suggested it myself at a symposium some years ago. Or at least making tests to see if that ink is truly resistant to radiation."

"What do you think happened to Claudia?" J-J continued.

"I wish I knew. I suppose she may have been murdered, although heaven knows by whom or why. Maybe she was drunk, ill, disoriented or possibly somebody made her that way." Bourdeille shrugged and blew out a long stream of smoke. "That brings us back to murder."

"Why do you want to give your home and your paintings to St. Denis?" J-J asked, his tone affable. "Why not to the Louvre, which has been your academic home?"

"The Louvre has far more paintings than it can display," came the reply. "It has satellite museums in Lens and Abu Dhabi and is building a new storage facility at Liévin. It is overwhelmed, and my little offering would not get a great deal of attention. In St. Denis it would be a great and valued addition."

"Very well, monsieur," said J-J, rising and stubbing out his cigarette. "Thank you for your time. I don't think we need detain you further."

He shook hands and led the way down the stairs in silence. Josette was waiting for them in the hall. As they walked out to the cars, she pulled out her phone, pressed a button and began to play a recording of someone speaking.

"You'll want to hear this, J-J," she said. As she held up the phone, Bruno realized he was listening to Bourdeille talking about the Vinland map. "I was in the kitchen with Madame Bonnet, and when she went to the loo I saw a small loudspeaker, fiddled with the knob and began hearing this."

"He's an invalid. It's probably the equivalent of a baby alarm or a way he can say he wants his supper. It's just a useful bit of technology," J-J said.

"Or it could be a way for her to overhear

him," said Bruno. "How long had you been waiting for us at the bottom of the stairs?"

"Since I heard you coming out of his room."

"Did Madame Bonnet hear J-J's final question?" Bruno asked her.

"I doubt it, because I turned the volume back down when you said you were leaving and went out to the hall to wait. She hadn't returned by then."

"Unless she has another loudspeaker somewhere."

"Where are you going with this, Bruno?" J-J sounded and looked impatient.

"Bourdeille has been keeping to himself this plan to give everything to St. Denis. Madame Bonnet thinks she's his heir and will inherit it all. If she finds out he's planned it differently, things could get complicated."

"They already are." J-J grunted and heaved himself into his car. He gestured to Josette to drive off. Bruno remained standing by his own car, wondering how much Madame Bonnet had heard of Bourdeille's plans, or of Claudia's offer to buy his estate.

CHAPTER 28

This was supposed to be Bruno's day off so he considered changing out of uniform, but since Amélie had his Land Rover, he was stuck with his police van, so the uniform stayed. When he parked in Le Buisson, where it was market day, he took off his police jacket and slipped on a windbreaker to look at least partly civilian as he shopped for dinner. He needed cheese, a kilo of red onions, some *lardons,* puff pastry, cream for whipping, lemons, some young turnips about the size of a baby's fist and a round *tourte* of bread from the bakery. The rest he had already in his garden or his pantry.

He stopped first at Stéphane's stall for the cheese, buying some aged Comté from the Haute-Savoie, a quarter of Brie and a generous slice of Bleu d'Auvergne. With the cream he also bought a half kilo of the butter Stéphane made himself. Finally, loaded down with his purchases, at Léopold's stall he bought some of the Burundi coffee he'd come to like.

Back at home, Bruno quickly cleaned the sitting room, brought in wood for the stove, put the white wines and Monbazillac in the fridge and set the table. He scribbled down the timing he'd have to follow. The lamb would need reheating before he added the vegetables, so that would need less than an hour. The guests were coming at eight so they'd have the first course at eight-thirty and the main course at nine. He'd have to be back well before seven to decant the red wine. The *tarte Tatin* would take thirty minutes to cook, so he'd put that in just before the guests arrived. The lemon syllabub would take ten minutes, and then he'd put it in the fridge. The peas, new potatoes, baby carrots and salad could stay in the garden until needed. He washed his hands, prepared the tools and dishes he would need that evening and checked the table. Then he laid out the cheese board and covered it with a dish towel.

He drove to Pamela's riding school to pick up Balzac from the stables where he'd left him after the morning ride and took the road past Audrix to Le Coux and Siorac to head along the Dordogne Valley to Château des Milandes. He parked, kept Balzac on his leash because of the birds and found Amélie, Hodge and Jennifer Muller being shown through the mews by Laurent. Balzac nearly tugged Bruno's arm off in his determination to see Amélie, one of his favorite people. She dropped to her heels at the sight of him, spread her arms wide and braced herself for Balzac's leap onto her chest and his affectionate licking of her neck.

"I wish I got a welcome like that," said Hodge, grinning at the scene. Amélie disentangled herself from Balzac's embraces and came up to hug Bruno.

"Have you eaten?" Laurent asked. "We just had a quick lunch at the brasserie here, only a *croque-monsieur,* since we're all looking forward to your dinner tonight. I was just about to fly my hawk, and then Amélie will show our visitors around."

"I'm fine, thanks," said Bruno. "Let's see your redtail." And Laurent headed inside the mews.

"I went to see Félicité in Limeuil this morning, Bruno," said Jennifer. "Thank you for the tip. She could not have been nicer. She got the key to Claudia's room from Madame Darrail to show me around, and she was overwhelmed when I told her to take the dresses and whatever else she could use. She showed me some lovely selfies she'd taken of herself and Claudia together and forwarded several of them to my phone. Now Amélie is arranging for me to have lunch with her and Claudia's friend Chantal at the Louvre when I get back to Paris. Everyone is being so kind."

Then she broke off and gave an exclamation of surprise as Laurent emerged with his hawk on his gloved hand. Its hood was on and its jesses attached to the gauntlet.

"My Lord, I never thought the hawk would be that big," said Jennifer, clearly awed.

Balzac lowered himself to the ground and gave a low growl until Bruno bent down to stroke and reassure him, keeping a tight grip on the leash.

"Will your hawk be happy with my dog here?" he asked Laurent, who said there should be no problem and led the way to steps that opened onto the wide garden. He removed the hood, bending again to use his teeth while his right hand loosened the strap, and once its head was free the hawk looked around and gave a low cluck. Already Balzac's attention was being diverted by some movement in the lower meadow and Bruno said softly, "Rabbit at four o'clock."

"I see him," said Laurent and loosed his hawk.

He flew straight for perhaps five meters and then soared high over the trees, circling and climbing until he hovered, as if searching the ground. The rabbit had been still when the hawk was released, and it should have stayed that way. But it seemed aware of the menace high above and suddenly darted to one side as if heading for the cover of some undergrowth around a copse of trees.

The movement betrayed it, and the hawk appeared to pause and then seemed to tuck its wings tightly against its body and then dived almost too fast for the eye to follow. Bruno was sure it had missed, aiming for a point where the rabbit had been rather than where it was heading. But just before it slammed into the ground the hawk flattened its dive and at less than twenty centimeters above the ground flew straight and low after its prey. It seemed to anticipate the rabbit's last, despairing veer to one side and then pounced, its talons striking, and with two punches of its beak the rabbit lay still, just its legs twitching.

Then the hawk lifted, the rabbit hanging from its talons, the great wings spreading as it gained height, circling back to Laurent. He gave a long, clear whistle, took some meat from his falconer's bag and held it high in the gauntleted hand. The hawk swooped gracefully down, dropped the rabbit at Laurent's feet and landed on his glove to take the beef as Laurent retied the jesses to secure it and then bent down to take the rabbit and stuff it into his bag.

"Mon Dieu," said Bruno. "That was beautiful — terrifying but so efficient, amazing to watch."

"Does he only eat the meat you give him?" Hodge asked.

"No, hawks eat mice or voles or small birds because they need the roughage they get from the fur of small animals or feathers from birds. But he associates this beef with me." Laurent replaced the hood on the hawk, again bending to use his teeth to help tighten the strap.

"How long did it take to train him?" Jennifer wanted to know.

"A long time because I was learning," said Laurent. "The longest part is what we call the manning, getting the bird accustomed to me and to the gauntlet and the hood. That takes months. But an experienced falconer can train a hawk to take a lure, which is how we start them hunting, in two or three weeks. It took me two months, but he was very patient with me."

"What's a lure?" Amélie asked.

"It's a dummy," Laurent said. "I have one that is like a small bird, two sets of wings sewn onto a small sack, and then I attach a piece of meat to it and start training him to take it. When he understands that, I'll start twirling the lure around my head very fast, swooping it up and down on the end of a rope, so he learns to take a bird in full flight. My other lure is a model rabbit with two big ears, and again a piece of meat tied on with string. Then I start pulling the lure, jerking it this way and that so he learns how rabbits can move over the ground. They catch on fast."

"But how do you get them to drop their catch and settle for a small piece of meat on your gauntlet?" Amélie asked.

"That's not so much training, more the trust that develops between a hawk and a human. He knows that every time I hold up my gloved hand and whistle for him to come, there will be a treat for him."

"That sounds like training a dog or a horse," said Bruno. "It's based on the trust even more than the reward."

"It's amazing when you think how important this has been to us humans, learning to train hawks and dogs, horses, even dolphins," said Laurent. "I'm not sure we could have developed civilization without the relations we developed with our fellow creatures."

"That's quite a thought," said Jennifer. "Did Claudia come out hawking with you?"

"Yes, just a couple of times, but very close to the château like we're doing now. She asked if one day we might try it on horseback, but I told her the hawk would need some training for that."

"But you can ride?" Bruno asked him.

"I learned. They say you never forget."

"Hawking used to be very common, yes?" Hodge asked. When Laurent nodded his agreement, Hodge had a further question. "So why did it stop? Did it just fall out of fashion, or did some problem emerge?"

"No, it was late seventeenth, eighteenth century, when guns became sufficiently accurate for hunting. But even now, few hunters can hit a flying bird with a rifle. Most hunters for birds use shotguns, firing out a small cloud of shot. That's a problem for falconers. You never want to feed your hawk any meat or any game that might have some lead shot inside it. It can kill the hawk."

"What will you do with the rabbit?" Amélie asked.

"I was going to offer it to Bruno, but otherwise I'll give it to Arnaud and Myrtille, my boss and his wife, for their supper."

"I'll be glad to have it," said Bruno, and Laurent pulled it from the bag by the ears and handed it over. "Thank you."

He went to open the back of his van, pulled out a plastic bag, placed the rabbit inside it and turned to see Balzac almost drooling as he watched. Bruno smiled to himself. Balzac had never caught a rabbit, although not for want of trying. He could run all day but never nearly as fast as a rabbit, and while Balzac's powerful paws could start to dig their way into a rabbit hole, the warrens went farther and deeper than any single basset hound could hope to reach. Terriers were the dogs for rabbits, able to squirm their way inside the warrens and scare the rabbits out, where other terriers stood in wait at the opening. That was not the kind of hunting that Bruno enjoyed. It seemed too mechanical, almost industrial, with none of the excitement and whiff of danger of the hunt, none of that extraordinary and thrilling touch of wildness that he had felt when Laurent's hawk had swooped to strike its prey.

"Can you show them around the château, Amélie?" Laurent asked. "I have to clean the mews and tend the hawks before I leave for dinner tonight."

Bruno tagged along, more in the hope of hearing Amélie sing than from interest in the exhibits he had seen before. Jennifer and Hodge were clearly fascinated by the history of Josephine Baker, born into poverty in St. Louis in 1906, who went on to be the first black international superstar. Known as the Black Pearl, she became the world's highest-paid entertainer after taking Paris by storm in the Jazz Age with her show at the Folies Bergère, dressed only in a tiny skirt that appeared to be made of bananas.

The original skirt, made of cloth bananas, had over the years aged from yellow to brown, as if it were real fruit. Hodge examined it minutely while Jennifer spent most of her time in the hall with many of Baker's other, more decorous costumes. Bruno liked the way her years in the Resistance and the multinational family of children that she raised got just as much coverage as the nightclub years. He was still moved by the photo of her, old and broke and humiliated, as she sat on the steps of her château after she had been evicted for not being able to pay her debts.

"This is where I'll be singing if the weather lets us down," said Amélie, leading them into the great hall. "But if it's a fine evening, we may put the chairs on the terrace, and I can sing on the balcony, with a backdrop of the château for the TV cameras. That means we can probably get more people watching from the gardens. Outdoor acoustics can be tough. In here, the sound is great."

She stepped up onto a small bench, and her body suddenly seemed to contain an enormous force that projected her voice as she launched into "Sous les Ponts de Paris" — "Under the Bridges of Paris."

As she continued the song, Bruno suddenly realized he'd never properly listened to the words before. What he'd always assumed was just another romantic tune of Paris was in reality an attack on poverty. She sang of the homeless mother with her children sleeping there, of a lover who could only afford to give his love some flowers plucked from a park, of a couple only able to make love in the shadows of the quay as the river flowed past. And the last lines were blunt — "If we could help just a little all the truly wretched, no more suicides or crime, under the bridges of Paris."

And then she launched straight into the romantic "En Avril à Paris," her voice changing from the somber to the playful as she sang of the city reawakening with springtime and the sun's return from exile, the stolen kisses in the Jardin du Luxembourg, of the whole of France rushing to Paris, all blown away by love.

"She's wonderful," said Jennifer, standing beside Bruno, applauding as Amélie stepped down. Bruno glanced at Jennifer and saw her brush away tears with her hand. Amélie gave a mock curtsy as she grinned at them like a teenager, waved briefly and disappeared behind a door.

"Did you know she was this good?" Jennifer demanded of Hodge.

"Why do you think I told you we had to see her, listen to that voice?" he replied. "She's got an amazing vocal range. I closed my eyes and I could be hearing Ella Fitzgerald, but then it's another song and she could be Sarah Vaughan or Judy Garland. There are moments I'm tempted to throw in this job and become her full-time manager and conquer the world."

"You'd have to compete with politics," Bruno said. "That's what she wants to do, and I think she'll be pretty good at that, too. Having worked with her, I can tell you she'd also make a brilliant detective."

Amélie came back, transformed. She was wearing a clinging robe of white silk, a white fur cape around her neck and big white earrings. Her hair had been plastered down with kiss curls on each cheek. Bruno heard

Jennifer and Hodge beside him gasp at the sudden image before them of the woman who had bewitched a continent.

She closed the door behind her, and the voice that had been deep and sad and then light and seductive suddenly broke out in a much higher register, a soft and entrancing soprano in the exact same tone that Josephine Baker had sung her most famous song, "J'ai Deux Amours" — I have two loves, my homeland and Paris.

I close my eyes and it's her, it's La Baker, Bruno said to himself. It's uncanny. This is the living image of a woman whose own mother was raised by former slaves; who fled her hometown after race riots in 1917; who gave up her American passport to become French; who hid Resistance documents in her underwear to get past Nazi checkpoints and wrote notes on Nazi troop movements in invisible ink on her sheet music; who refused to sing before segregated audiences in the United States; who marched beside Martin Luther King Jr.; who bankrupted herself for the dream of a multiracial family beyond racism.

Overcome, Bruno brushed away the sudden tears that gathered in his eyes, aware that Jennifer beside him was weeping openly now.

"It could be a ghost," she murmured. "It's her. She's Baker. I have never seen anything like this."

Suddenly he was aware of someone else at his side, Mademoiselle Neyrac, who had negotiated with him with such cold efficiency, taking off her own glasses to dry her eyes.

"Whatever we pay her, she's worth it," she said. "Bruno, thank you for bringing her to us."

CHAPTER 29

Bruno drove back with only Balzac beside him on the passenger seat. Hodge and Jennifer were going back to their respective hotels and would see him at eight. Amélie would bring Laurent in Bruno's Land Rover. The others would come separately. He stopped in Le Buisson to buy some bottles of Badoit, thinking his guests might prefer mineral water to wine. There was time to take Balzac on a trot through the woods and put the lamb in the oven before he showered and changed.

Now for the *tarte Tatin.* He scattered some flour over the small marble slab he used for his pastry, rolled it out to a size that would fit his baking dish, made the pastry and put it into his fridge to cool.

He changed into his tracksuit and took Laurent's rabbit from the back of his van, skinning and gutting it before washing it in the sink and putting it in his pantry. Balzac watched him hopefully, but Bruno knew small rabbit bones could be dangerous for dogs, so he sealed the guts and paws in a bag and distracted Balzac with a quick jog. On his return, he picked two heads of lettuce and dug up some new potatoes, young carrots, and then chose the plumpest of his spring peas. He lit the wood-burning stove, peeled his red onions, took a quick shower and dressed in khaki slacks and a favorite old woolen shirt. It had once been dark green, but over the years and after many washings and drying out on the line in the sun, the color had faded to something almost autumnal.

He looked around the room and at the dining table to be sure all was ready for his guests, the wineglasses shining, the napkins in place. Then he thought that with ten diners, he should put out place cards so people would know where to sit rather than dithering around. He used his business cards, bent double, and wrote down each name, putting Jennifer and Amélie beside him in the middle of the table, where he could serve more easily. Pamela and Jacqueline were on either side of Hodge, Florence and the mayor at the head and tail of the table and Laurent between Florence and Jacqueline.

The baron was between Florence and Amélie.

In the kitchen, Bruno washed and shredded the green salad. He'd leave making the vinaigrette until it was needed, but he shelled the peas and washed the carrots and new potatoes. Then he set the oven to a hundred and seventy degrees centigrade, sliced his red onions in half, melted about a hundred grams of duck fat in a heavy-bottomed but shallow pan and stirred in two teaspoons of sugar when it began to sizzle. He laid the onions, cut side down, closely together and chopped the last half onion into quarters to fill the gaps between them.

He covered the pan and let the onion brown gently for fifteen minutes before lifting the cover and sprinkling over the pan a tablespoon of balsamic vinegar, salt and pepper and the leaves from six sprigs of fresh thyme. He used the time to make the syllabub, whipping a hundred grams of fine sugar into the half liter of cream until it stiffened and rose in soft peaks. Then he stirred in a generous glass of white wine and the juice and half the zest of a lemon. He spooned the mixture into glasses, topped them with the remains of the zest and put the glasses into his fridge to cool.

The onions were browned, so he replaced the cover and put the pan in the oven for forty-five minutes until the onions softened. Then he turned to the *navarin,* putting the dish on the stove to reheat. When it started to simmer, he added the small carrots and potatoes and put it in the oven on a low shelf with the heat turned up to two hundred. He set the timer for fifteen minutes, after which he would add the small turnips, and after ten more minutes stir in the peas and leave it for ten minutes more.

It was time to bring out the onions and test them for softness, which he did with the point of a knife. It slid in easily, so they were done. There was still a little juice at the bottom of the pan, so he put it over medium heat and reduced the juice until only a little thick syrup remained. He rolled out the pastry on a board dusted with flour until it was about five centimeters wider than the circumference of his pans.

Carefully, he placed the pastry on top of the onions, folding the edge back under itself and pressing it down lightly. He pierced it here and there with a fork so the steam could escape and then put it on the high shelf in his oven. It would take about forty minutes to become crisp and golden, and he'd have to remove it from the oven and set it aside to cool for about fifteen minutes before serving. Finally, he washed the used pans, set them to dry, sliced the *tourte* into two halves, sliced them in turn and prepared two baskets, one for each end of the table.

With everything done and ready, he took Balzac out to watch the slow setting of the sun toward Bordeaux and the Atlantic Ocean beyond. It sank through layer after drifting layer of thin clouds, their edges turning pink and then gold and then a deeper pink as the shadows from the trees steadily lengthened and the birds fell silent.

Pamela, Florence and the baron were the first to arrive in his stately old Citroën DS, the baron bringing a bottle of chilled champagne. Barely had Bruno welcomed them when the mayor and Jacqueline turned into his driveway, bearing more champagne, followed by Hodge and Jennifer with yet another bottle in the Peugeot Hodge had rented. Now Bruno heard the familiar sound of his Land Rover coming up the lane from the main road with Amélie at the wheel and Laurent beside her. By now Balzac was almost beside himself with excitement at seeing so many old friends and meeting new ones.

Bruno led them all indoors, suggesting

those with coats should leave them in his bedroom. He started to open and pour champagne as he made the necessary introductions. Formal condolences were offered to Jennifer by the mayor, swiftly followed by compliments on her French. Pamela told Jennifer how well Claudia had ridden the horses, and Florence followed that with an awed description of the T-bone steak dinner Claudia had prepared. The baron began reminiscing with Hodge about the time the FBI had called him "a deputy," just like someone in the Western movies the baron adored.

Bruno felt a discreet pressure on his arm. It was the mayor, who steered him to one side to murmur that the meeting of Bourdeille with the group he called "the wise men" to establish that he was fit to arrange his own legacy was set for the next morning at ten in a lawyer's office in Périgueux. The mayor had arranged for the use of the disability vehicle from the retirement home. Would Bruno kindly drive them? Bourdeille wanted to invite them for lunch in Brantôme afterward. Bruno quickly agreed, and the mayor rejoined the party. Bruno paused to text Juliette, his colleague in Les Eyzies, asking if she could take over the market patrol the next morning and offering to buy her breakfast at Fauquet's at eight.

Laurent was kneeling by the fire, caressing Balzac and looking around with a slightly dazed smile. Bruno realized that this might be the first such occasion he'd known for more than a decade, but then he noticed that Laurent's eyes kept coming back to Florence, who was looking very fine in a beautifully cut dress of heavy cream silk that showed off her slim figure. Regular Pilates classes and riding and tennis games were making his female friends glow with health, Bruno thought. He wondered whether Laurent had been the fortunate man with Florence the night he had babysat her children.

Aware of his duties as host, Bruno went across and steered Laurent into a conversation with Jacqueline and Jennifer about hawking. Amélie circulated in the amiable, relaxed way that is the mark of a born politician until the mayor recognized a fellow spirit and they began talking politics. Bruno slipped into the kitchen to check on the *tarte* and the lamb, opened another bottle of champagne and went around the room refilling glasses.

"That's enough for me," said Laurent. Bruno, recalling Luc's comments at the well the previous day, asked if he'd known Luc well at school. They'd been together all through primary school in Limeuil and then at the *collège* in St. Denis, Laurent told him.

"We weren't friends, rather the reverse. Luc was always with Dominic and we called them the cousins, since they were apparently cousins by marriage. They were both thugs and bullies. Bernard and I had one stand-up fight with them, half the school standing around and cheering us on. I finished up with a black eye, Bernard got a split lip, and one of us somehow managed to bloody Luc's nose, so naturally we were the ones who got punished. But it was worth it."

"What started the fight?"

"Because it was them, because it was us. We just didn't like each other from the first day. But do you remember that anti-racist campaign with the slogan *Touche pas à mon pote* — 'Don't mess with my buddy'?"

At this point Florence, Jacqueline and the mayor had started to listen. Laurent glanced around as if embarrassed, but Bruno told him to continue.

"There were buttons, bumper stickers, posters — you remember? The cousins used to jeer at Bernard, who wore one, I think he got it from his big brother. And then Luc and Dominic started picking on an Arab kid called Karim, who turned out to be the son of the guy who later taught us math in the *collège*."

"You mean Momu?" Florence asked eagerly. "He's still here, and so's Karim. He's the star forward of the St. Denis rugby team."

"He runs the Café des Sports with his wife, Rashida, and they have a couple of kids," the mayor broke in. "I'll take you to see them. I'm sure he'll remember you. But tell us how the fight started."

"He was the only Arab kid in school at that time, and they began calling him names, you can imagine. I think one of them was from a *pied-noir* family, and they hated Arabs. At election times they'd stomp around chanting 'Front National' and 'Arabs go home,' and one day, it must have been the election in '92, they tried to kick Karim out of school, literally. That's when the fight began."

"Did this animosity continue when you got to the *collège*?" Florence asked. "I ask because I teach there, and Momu's a good friend."

"Yes, but those two were pretty dim or maybe just lazy, so we were in different classes. And on the rugby team we didn't interact much."

"I remember those two," said the baron,

who had for many years helped to train the youth teams. "A nasty pair, lots of dirty play of the kind you don't often see in kids' rugby. We had to suspend them at one point."

"Did you have any more fights with them?" Pamela asked.

"Not really, there'd be nasty looks, insults, some jostling in the corridors. But they knew that if they attacked one of us they'd have the other to deal with, and most of the rest of the kids disliked them anyway."

"So they were cousins, and pretty close," Bruno said, thinking aloud.

"Inseparable," Laurent replied.

From the kitchen, Bruno heard the discreet ring of the timer, excused himself to take the *tartes* out of the oven, ran a knife around the insides of the pans and turned the dishes upside down so the contents landed on the plate with the red onions uppermost and a lovely scent of thyme. He crumbled a *crottin* of dry goat's cheese onto the top of each *tarte.* He checked the *navarin,* added the baby turnips and returned to the party with a new bottle of champagne while the *tartes* rested. When the timer went again, he added the peas to the *navarin* and brought the *tartes* to the dining room, invited everyone to take their place at the table and to bring their champagne glasses. He left them briefly, saw that Juliette had replied to his text saying she'd take care of the market and see him the next morning, and then rejoined his friends carrying two bottles of Cuvée Osée.

"Here is an interesting local white wine from Château Richard, wholly organic and no sulfites," he said. "The winemaker calls it Osée because the experts said he could never do it, and he dared to prove them wrong."

"The *tarte* smells wonderful, I love the scent of thyme," said Jacqueline as Bruno began serving. "My mother would make me thyme tea when I was little and had a cold or a sore throat. It reminds me of those days, but of course the thyme is so strong a flavor that it can mask other scents."

Bruno felt some faint bell of memory tinkle at the back of his mind, but the conversation turned to herbal teas and herbal remedies until Bruno had finished serving, and then the mayor tapped his knife against his glass and said, "I suggest we make a toast before dinner to Claudia and her memory."

Glasses were raised, everyone spoke her name, the champagne was sipped, and then a brief silence fell, and Bruno as host became a little uneasy, as he could think of no topic that would restart the conversation without seeming disrespectful. But Jennifer spoke a brief and graceful word of thanks to the mayor and to Bruno.

"Claudia would have loved to be here with us this evening. She enjoyed good food and friendship and I know from her e-mails that you all helped to make her very happy here," she said. "You've all been so kind to me; I can understand exactly what she meant."

That was kindly and gracefully done, thought Bruno. Now everyone was asking Amélie which songs she would perform until the baron — inevitably — asked if she intended to wear La Baker's famous banana skirt.

"You're a naughty man, Baron," she said, grinning at him and wagging a finger. "Next I suppose you'll be asking me for a private viewing. But Bruno says I should never wear it because it would ruin my political career. Do you think he's right?"

"I think you'd win every male vote in France," the baron said, laughing and raising his glass to her. "You'd be the only left-wing vote I ever cast."

The talk turned to politics as Bruno took the plates into the kitchen, and Pamela followed him with the empty serving plates that had held the two *tartes.* Bruno went to the patch of mint outside his door to pick some sprigs, which he chopped and sprinkled over the *navarin.* He took the casserole to the table and asked the mayor and the baron to pour the red wine.

Once he'd served them all, a brief silence fell, a moment that Bruno savored, and it was broken only by murmurs of appreciation until Laurent asked what Bruno planned to do with the rabbit.

"It's in the pantry, but I'm planning to cook it the old-fashioned way with *verjus,*" he said. "You'll have to come again for that, Laurent."

"Thanks to our foreign guests we've become very adventurous with our food here. I've even learned to enjoy lamb with Pamela's mint sauce," said the baron. "And I will take Amélie's *épice* from Haiti with almost anything. You know Ivan is still serving your *épice* in our local bistro, Amélie? It's very popular. I like it best with a venison terrine or a *pâté de campagne.*"

The decanter of Château de Tiregand went around the table again, plates were emptied and second helpings taken.

"It's delicious, and I love it with the sprinkling of mint, but I'm not sure I have much room for any more, Bruno, since I know you always like to give us a dessert. What's it going to be?" asked Florence.

"It's a secret until the lamb is gone, followed by a little salad from the garden, with the cheese. Then you'll find out."

There were a few shreds of meat left when Bruno finally took the dish into the kitchen and gave the scraps to Balzac. Pamela followed him in with the plates and said softly in his ear, "I'd like to stay tonight, but since I'm going back with Florence, I don't want there to be talk. Maybe tomorrow night, I'll call you."

She kissed his cheek and took the waiting pile of salad plates back to the table. Bruno made his vinaigrette, hazelnut oil and truffle vinegar from Tête Noire, a small local firm, poured it over the salad and tossed it. The decanter of wine was empty, which meant that the party was starting to become boisterous, with the baron already asking Amélie when she was going to sing. Bruno opened another bottle of Tiregand and called for a toast to his friend Stéphane, who had supplied the cheese.

Once the cheese board was empty, Bruno went back to the kitchen, where he took the syllabubs from the fridge along with a half bottle of Saussignac dessert wine that he'd left chilling.

"Et voilà," he announced. "Syllabub of lemon, a dish that I learned from Pamela to be washed down by this lovely sweet wine of Saussignac. And then we'll have coffee and maybe a song?"

"Just one," said Amélie. "I can barely move, I've eaten so well."

The mayor tapped his glass with his knife and said, "I have a very pleasant announcement to make. I'm sure you'll all join me in congratulating Florence. I'm always delighted when someone from St. Denis wins an election, and I heard today that she was this week elected to the executive committee of the teachers' union for the *département.*"

"I almost wasn't there for the speeches and the vote in Périgueux," Florence said after glasses were raised to her. "None of my usual babysitters was free, and if Bruno hadn't stepped into the breach it wouldn't have happened."

Ah, Bruno thought, with a curious sense of satisfaction. It wasn't a man who had lured Florence away. And so the evening ended, with the coffee from Burundi, a glass of Armagnac for the baron and the mayor and Amélie's slow, languorous performance of a Cole Porter classic: "Just One of Those Things."

CHAPTER 30

The following morning, after Bruno's usual jog with his dog through the woods and a brisk thirty-minute canter with Hector and the other horses, Pamela edged her own mare, Primrose, close to him as they descended from the sunlit ridge into the thinning belts of mist that clung to the river valley.

"What about tonight?" she asked quietly. "Do you have plans?"

"No, would you like to come to my place or go out to dinner?"

"The thing is," she said, "if you come here, Miranda is likely to know. But she'll also know if I come to you and my car is out all night. And if she knows, Jack will know and Gilles and Fabiola and Florence and the baron. We might as well put an ad in *Sud Ouest.*"

"And word will flash around from any local restaurant we visit," said Bruno, smiling, a little surprised by Pamela's caution but only too aware of the interest his own love life seemed to attract in the neighborhood.

"Now I begin to understand the logistical challenges that adulterers have to face," she said, smiling back at him. But there was something stiff, almost uncomfortable, about her posture, she who usually rode a horse so easily that he envied her.

"But what the hell," she went on. "I'll come to you and arrive back in the morning with fresh croissants. That's my alibi."

Bruno wanted to ask why she was nervous about Miranda knowing that they were sleeping together but thought he'd better save that for the evening. He knew Pamela to be a woman who guarded her privacy.

"The mayor will have me tied up for most of the day," he said. "I should be back by six or so, and there's enough in the garden and in my cupboard for dinner. I'll look forward to seeing you."

"Nothing too heavy on the stomach," she said, with a roguish lift of an eyebrow, and touched her heels to the sides of her horse to take it ahead of Bruno into the stable yard.

Twenty minutes later, Bruno had greeted the stallholders in Fauquet's café and was about to look through the café's copy of *Sud*

Ouest when Juliette arrived looking smart with her hair tucked up into her képi. The uniform suited her now that she'd had it tailored to fit her. She greeted Bruno with the customary kiss and asked, "What's up?"

"I have to attend a meeting in Périgueux with the mayor," he said, ordering two coffees and croissants and steering her to a corner table. "Thanks for stepping in."

"You've done the same for me often enough," she replied. "Is this still about the dead American girl? Have you seen the story in today's paper?"

"No, the Périgueux meeting is about something else." He unfolded the copy of *Sud Ouest,* passed his hand tiredly over his eyes and muttered, *"Merde."*

The main story on the front page was about the new fast train from Paris to Bordeaux taking only two hours. But there was a second story, a single column headed "Drugs and an Ex-Con — the Secret Life of the Dead American Girl of Limeuil."

He turned to the inside page and found two full pages, each carrying a byline from Philippe Delaron. One featured a photo of Claudia that looked like it might have come from her passport and a headline that read "Drugged When She Died." The other page carried a mug shot of Laurent and a head-

410

line that read "Ten Years in Jail — White House Girl's Secret Boyfriend Was Ex-Convict."

"From the look on your face, I'm guessing that you're not the source, even though it quotes the official toxicology report," said Juliette.

"No, I'm not. But I'm pretty sure I know who is. Have you come across a Madame de Breille, an expensive private investigator who wears designer suits?"

"Never heard of her. Who's she working for?"

"Claudia's father." Bruno skimmed through the stories and saw that Philippe had been only partially briefed on the drugs. He wrote about the opioids, which he stressed were prescribed by an American doctor but not legal in France. But there was no reference to the *yaba* pills. The story on Laurent was heavily inflated, calling him Hawk-man and noting that he and Claudia had been on several dates, including romantic picnics and trips to Périgueux and Lascaux. Above all, and heavy with insinuation, the article stressed that he'd been present at the lecture in Limeuil on the night Claudia had died.

The attribution was "police sources." If Madame de Breille had been feeding Philippe extracts from the case file, that was true enough, however infuriating. But she'd been careful to exclude her own name — and her agenda — from the story. Nor did it say that Laurent's alibi had been checked and confirmed.

Bruno tossed the newspaper back onto the counter and began eating his croissant. Between bites he explained the background to Juliette.

"So you're pretty sure she was murdered, but you don't yet have a suspect," Juliette said. "The real killer will read today's story and think he's off the hook. It almost says Laurent was the murderer. Look on the bright side — this might lead the real killer into a false sense of security, assuming that Laurent is innocent. Do you have any serious suspects?"

Bruno looked at her thoughtfully. "Laurent's innocence hangs on the word of two friends of his, his boss at Château des Milandes and his wife. They have given sworn statements that they were with him all evening and then drove him home."

"Could they have a motive?"

"Not that I can see. There are several people with motives, possibly to inherit from Claudia, possibly to stop Claudia from buying Bourdeille's art collection. But there's nothing we can nail down yet. I've tried running various scenarios involving each one through my head, but I'm not making progress. The problem is that nobody knew that Claudia would feel ill and leave the lecture early."

"What if somebody did know that she'd be taken ill?" Juliette asked. This question jolted him. Why hadn't he thought of that?

"She was on these opioids that were legal as far as she was concerned because they'd been prescribed by her American doctor," Juliette went on. "But what if she was slipped something else? Could anybody have done that?"

"Only in the punch served at the lecture, but she had hardly any of it, and others were drinking it with no problems," Bruno replied. "And more of those *yaba* pills she took were found stashed in her room, though I've always struggled to see Claudia taking them. It just doesn't fit with what I know of her personality."

"Where was Claudia before she got to the lecture?"

"At Bourdeille's place, but she left early to go shopping, then back to her room, where she declined any food," Bruno said, and then stopped himself. "She had some herb tea, prepared by her landlady."

"And does the landlady have a motive?"

"Not that I know." Suddenly he recalled that Madame Darrail had said she'd given Claudia herb tea made from thyme, and then the word seemed to echo in his head. He'd heard it the previous evening over the *tarte Tatin* when Jacqueline had said that thyme covered so many other tastes.

"Have you ever had thyme tea?" he asked Juliette, who at once opened the web browser on her phone and began typing something in the search box.

"My mother used to give it to me for headaches and when I had a sore throat," she said. "But listen to this."

She began reading aloud from the web page: " 'Thyme contains a compound called carvacrol which is an excellent natural tranquilizer and has a tonic effect on the entire nervous system.

" 'Thyme is a good source of pyridoxine,' " she continued to read, " 'which is known to play an important role in manufacturing gamma aminobutyric acid, or GABA, levels in the brain which aid in regulating sleep patterns, and benefit neurotransmitter function in the brain.' "

"A natural tranquilizer on top of opioids," said Bruno, thoughtfully.

" 'Thyme tea in too strong an infusion can

414

have side effects of nausea and dizziness,' " Juliette read on and then looked up. "I don't know how much reliance we can put on these health sites on the Internet, but I remember my mother saying that the taste would be much stronger if it was infused overnight rather than just before drinking. And she would always add honey when she gave it to me and sometimes ginger."

"That could mask other tastes," said Bruno. "I think you're onto something. But, look, I have to go and you need to start patrolling the market. Let's discuss this later when we've thought more about it."

Bruno picked up the bill and, as he paid Fauquet, a sudden thought came to him, something that might teach Philippe Delaron a lesson. It could also reassure the real killer into thinking the police had been successfully duped.

"You seemed upset when you saw the paper," said Fauquet, leaning forward over the bar, his way of inviting the confidences and pieces of gossip that he loved.

"It's that damn Philippe and his story this morning. I wish I knew where he gets these stories from. It's starting to get in the way of proper policing."

"You mean that story about the ex-convict and the dead girl?"

Bruno nodded. "He's not supposed to know about that, so some irresponsible cop is leaking stuff to him, and that's a real problem. The last thing we want is for the suspect to read the paper and take flight."

Fauquet nodded sympathetically, and Bruno was convinced that within the hour Philippe would have heard that he was on the right track with his story about Laurent. Thinking he'd look forward to the next day's paper with particular interest, Bruno walked to the retirement home where the mayor had arranged for their special vehicle, equipped for wheelchairs, to be available. Before he went in to pick up the keys, he called Laurent.

"I thought I'd better warn you there's an unpleasant story in *Sud Ouest* this morning," he said.

"I know, I've seen it," Laurent replied angrily, almost spitting the words. "I've been called in later today to see Neyrac, the boss, just as I'm about to get through my probation period. And now it looks as though I'm going to be fired. Who are these police sources the paper cites?"

"Don't worry," Bruno reassured him. "Take it from me that you're not a suspect, and I'll call your boss if you have any trouble. But it might be useful for me for the real killer to think he's off the hook and that we're focused on you. So grin and bear it for a little while. Can you do that for me?"

There was a pause before Laurent replied, "If you say so, Bruno. And thanks for calling. By the way, Bernard is driving me over to the Café des Sports later to see Karim, so I have something to look forward to."

"I'm glad to hear it, and you can tell Karim from me in confidence that the story in today's paper is a bunch of *merde*," Bruno replied, ending the call.

Bruno picked up the keys and headed for Bourdeille's *chartreuse,* wondering if Madame Darrail might conceivably have had a sinister motive in giving Claudia the tea. Her real interest, he'd assumed, was to get Claudia together with Dominic, her son, who had been at the lecture but had never left the room until it was over.

But wait, he told himself. Who had said that Dominic had been using his phone during the lecture, that they recalled his face being lit by the phone's glow? He cast his thoughts back and was sure it had been Félicité. Could Dominic have been using it to send or receive a text? Maybe he'd been telling someone else that Claudia had left the lecture, someone who could then have climbed into the gardens. That could make sense, but where would be the motive? He almost banged the steering wheel in frustration as he pulled up outside Bourdeille's home.

The door opened before he could ring the bell, and Bourdeille was waiting in the hall in his wheelchair, dressed in a suit and tie, a thick file in his hand. He explained that Madame Bonnet had decided to spend the day in Bergerac, since he had business away from home.

"Do you have a phone number for her son's friend Dominic?" Bruno asked.

Bourdeille looked mystified and shook his head. "But Madame Bonnet keeps a list of numbers by the phone in the kitchen. Go and take a look if you like."

A landline phone hung on the kitchen wall. On a small shelf alongside it was a notepad and pencil and a small list of names and numbers: for her son, Luc, for Véronique, whom Bruno recalled was Madame Darrail, and for Véronique's son, Dominic, and for Claudia. There were other numbers listed for people called Émilie, Mireille and Marie-France, and more for the *mairie,* the doctor, the bank, the pharmacy and a pizza place. Bruno scribbled them down and leafed back through the notepad, finding doodles, jotted numbers without names and not much more.

Once Bourdeille was installed inside the vehicle, Bruno set off for St. Denis to pick up the mayor. On the road to Périgueux, the mayor explained that they were heading for a lawyer's office where Bourdeille would be questioned by an eminent group. It included a former mayor and senator, the recently retired senior judge on the appeals court in Périgueux and the female professor of psychiatry at the central hospital.

"I'd like to see any lawyer daring to challenge their findings," the mayor said, turning around in his passenger seat to face Bourdeille. "Bruno and I will wait outside, since I might be said to have an interest in this matter, but you won't be alone. Maître Lucier, the lawyer our town often works with and whose offices we are using, has agreed to advise you if required."

"Thank you for making these arrangements. I have with me a formal written statement from my own doctor testifying to my mental health and fitness," Bourdeille said. "I'm wholly confident of my abilities, and once this formality is complete I look forward to taking you both to lunch. I've booked us a table at Le Moulin de l'Abbaye, which has just been awarded a Michelin rosette."

"That's very generous of you," said the mayor. "We'll look forward to that, won't we, Bruno?"

Once he'd parked outside the lawyer's office, Bruno wheeled Bourdeille into the elevator and into Maître Lucier's chambers. The mayor waited in an anteroom, and Bruno went to park the van before rejoining the mayor.

"You saw *Sud Ouest?*" the mayor asked when they were alone.

"Yes, and I'm pretty sure I know who was behind it — that Madame de Breille, muddying the waters and showing Claudia's father how hard she's working. But I've had an idea."

He called the special security number for France Télécom, identified himself with his own official code, and asked for a list of the phone connections made to and from Dominic's phone on the Sunday of the lecture. He was promised the list would be e-mailed to his official computer address at the *mairie* in St. Denis.

"What about text messages?" he asked the security official. "Can you read them?"

"Yes, but you'll need a warrant," he was told.

Next Bruno called J-J, explained his new theory about the thyme tea and Dominic's use of his phone during the lecture and asked if J-J could arrange for a warrant to view Dominic's messages.

"You don't need me," J-J said. "Call your magistrate friend, Annette. She's handling the criminal negligence case against the builders, and there could be a connection. She can issue the warrant herself. Let me know if this leads anywhere."

"Thanks, J-J, I should have thought of that." Police had to request a warrant through a *procureur*'s office or through a *juge d'instruction* handling a criminal case. Annette could issue her own warrant. He called her at home, explained what he wanted and why, and she promised to fax the warrant to France Télécom. Bruno sat back with a sigh of relief.

"Making progress?" asked the mayor.

"I don't know," Bruno replied. "Maybe. At the very least it will prove a negative."

Just over an hour after Bourdeille had gone into the chambers, Maître Lucier emerged, smiling, to report that the meeting was over and that the informal tribunal had declared Bourdeille to be in full possession of his faculties. Bourdeille then wheeled himself out, waving a formal-looking document at Bruno and the mayor, and announced, "Messieurs, we have a celebratory lunch to attend. Maître Lucier, I'd be delighted if you would care to join us. I'm sure you know the Moulin de l'Abbaye in Brantôme?"

Bourdeille asked Bruno to drive through as many of the narrow streets of Brantôme as the one-way system permitted, saying he wanted to remind himself of the town, this Venice of the Périgord that his putative ancestor had saved from the Protestant army of Admiral Coligny during the religious wars. He instructed Bruno to set him down at the Pont Coudé, the famous dogleg bridge that led to the abbot's lodging, the abbey stretching away magnificently to their right. Bourdeille and the mayor waited until Bruno had parked and rejoined them and then he wheeled the old man across the bridge and along the riverbank to the restaurant, where Maître Lucier was already seated.

The lawyer rose and asked them all to call him Jim, a nickname he'd acquired at school when an English teacher had informed the class that the name Jacques in English was James, usually shortened to Jim.

Bourdeille had ordered the meal in advance: smoked salmon with a gravlax of beet, followed by duck breast with roasted apricot. Then came a deceptively simple and delicious dessert, an apple that had been cooked for ten hours and served with a cider sorbet. They each began with a glass of champagne, followed by a bottle among the four of them of a magnificent Hospices de Beaune, a 2006 Clos des Avaux.

"Forgive me if I offend your local loyalties in wine, but I think a great Burgundy goes well with duck," Bourdeille said. "I asked them to decant it when I ordered the meal earlier this morning."

"It's wonderful, and it's a pity Claudia can't be here with us to enjoy it," Bruno said. "I know how much she appreciated the wines you shared with her. And that reminds me that you may not know that Claudia's mother is here in the Périgord. I know she'd very much like to thank you for your kindness to her daughter and to see the art collection Claudia told her about."

"And I would like very much to offer her my own condolences," said Bourdeille. "How long is she here?"

"Until the police investigation is complete and the body is released by the *procureur.*"

"Perhaps you might like to bring her tomorrow before lunch, at about eleven. I'm in no position to offer her lunch, but I can certainly provide a glass of excellent wine."

"That sounds good," said Bruno. "I'll try

to arrange it and let you know."

"My thanks for this splendid lunch," said the mayor. "Perhaps this is a good moment to explain how we plan to administer your generous bequest to our town and see if you approve. As a town council, we're not equipped to run an art gallery, so I thought we might establish an independent foundation, with trustees from the Louvre and the museum in Périgueux as well as the mayor and the *collège* headmaster from St. Denis. We'd also like to include a special exhibit on the work of your friend Paul Juin in the new Resistance museum we're building."

Bourdeille nodded slowly without speaking, but Bruno's attention had been caught by what looked like a flash of surprise in Maître Lucier's eyes when the mayor had spoken of the bequest to St. Denis. It had been swiftly followed by the customary expressionless mask of a veteran lawyer. Lucier had been in the room when Bruno and the mayor had waited outside. What did the lawyer know that they did not? And whose side was he on?

CHAPTER 31

After the lunch, Lucier made his farewells, and Bruno and the mayor could hardly refuse Bourdeille's request that they return by way of the town and château whose name he carried, just a few kilometers from their direct route back to Périgueux and St. Denis.

"I'd like to see it one more time, for who knows how many more opportunities I may have," the old man said as Bruno wheeled him through the double towers of the medieval entrance into the courtyard. Ahead of them soared the fourteenth-century octagonal stone keep, and all around them were the fortress walls. To the right was the jewel within this stone setting, a sixteenth-century Renaissance palace.

"I'm sure you two have both been here before, but the name and place mean a great deal to me, even though the link with the family has gone. The widow of the last de

Bourdeille donated the castle to the *département* more than fifty years ago. I've loved this place since I was a boy and my mother told me of our ancestry. It was private in those days, of course, and we could look at it only from the town and the bridge. She told me that it had been taken twice by the English and recaptured each time. In my years in prison during the war, the thought of another foreign occupier being finally ejected from this place gave me confidence, a sense of historical perspective, perhaps a kind of strength. And now I will trespass no more on your goodwill, and we can return to St. Denis."

The old man dozed in his wheelchair on the way back, and Bruno and the mayor remained silent rather than disturb him, although Bruno was almost bursting with questions about the lawyer Lucier and his role. But he had other questions about Madame Bonnet and what she knew of Bourdeille's plans, and one almost flippant question that had interested him since their visit to the château.

When they reached Bourdeille's home and Bruno began to extract him and his wheelchair from the van, he asked the question: "Why is your name Bourdeille without an *s*, but the château is Bourdeilles

426

with an *s*?"

"I have no idea, except perhaps that the château was for the whole Bourdeille family and so it took the plural, or perhaps because the outer wall contains two châteaux in one. It's an interesting question."

"I have another," Bruno said, wheeling him into the *chartreuse* with the mayor following. "You recall when I came with the chief detective and you told us in your library about the Vinland map?"

"Of course, an interesting conversation."

"You may know that the young woman with us, the detective's assistant, was able to hear your remarks from a loudspeaker in the kitchen."

"I have a small speaker in each of my rooms so I can summon Madame Bonnet if necessary, and I sometimes forget to switch them off."

Bruno asked if he could double-check the speaker system. The old man waved a hand as if giving his blessing, which Bruno interpreted as granting permission. Bruno asked the mayor to listen at the speaker in the kitchen. Then he went upstairs and began counting to ten in each room until with the mayor's help he found the location of each microphone. He found the bedroom, bathroom, library, a small sitting room with a television and a large study. There was also one balcony above the main door, and he found another microphone there.

"I could hear you in every room you went into, including the balcony," said the mayor when Bruno went downstairs again.

"Let me try again when I turn off the mikes." Bruno went back upstairs, found a switch on each mike, turned it off while still counting and identifying each room. Then he went back downstairs.

"I heard a click when you turned each one off, but I could still hear you," the mayor said, by now intrigued. "I'll look for more speakers while you go and check the wiring on the switches. And keep talking — that will help me find other speakers."

Bruno did as he was told, taking a small metal nail file from the bathroom to unscrew the back of the microphone in the library. It was wired direct, avoiding the switch. He checked the others, and they were all the same. Bourdeille might think he could not be overheard, but Madame Bonnet could hear everything he said. Back downstairs, he found the two men in a small sitting room behind the kitchen, evidently Madame Bonnet's private lair, in which were an easy chair, family photos, a tray with some glasses and a bottle of *vin de noix.*

"All the mikes upstairs are permanently on, even when the switch is off," Bruno said, addressing Bourdeille. "The system has been rigged so that Madame Bonnet could hear every word you said. She would have known from your conversations on the balcony that Claudia was trying to buy your *chartreuse* and its contents."

"So what?" demanded Bourdeille. "I never said I'd sell and there's not a damn thing Bonnet could do about it, anyway. And I can't say I'm greatly surprised to learn that she's been spying on me."

"It's not you I'm concerned about," said Bruno. "It's what happened to Claudia."

Bruno was looking around the small sitting room. Among the photos was one of a young Madame Bonnet in a wedding dress alongside a tall, skinny man who looked to be a good ten years older, maybe more. They were standing in a garden in front of the *mairie* of Limeuil. There was a photo of the same couple in what looked like a hospital, and she was beaming as she lay in bed holding a newborn baby. Then there was a final photo of the same two adults with a little boy in shorts. He was not much more than a toddler, maybe three or four. There were no photos of Bourdeille or anyone else.

"It's been a long day," said Bourdeille. "Would you be so kind as to follow me upstairs and help me onto the couch in my study? And perhaps the mayor would like to look at my art collection. Here is the key." He took from a waistcoat pocket a small but very modern-looking key, with tiny indentations rather than the usual blade and cuts of a conventional house key.

The mayor took the key and Bruno wheeled the old man into his elevator. There wasn't room for him, so he took the stairs. He helped the old man to take off his jacket and then settled him on a handsome chaise longue.

"Anything I can get you?" he asked. "A drink, a book?"

"I have books here that I can reach," Bourdeille said. "And I have some thinking to do about what you just said. Assuming Madame Bonnet overheard Claudia's attempt to buy this place, do you really suspect she may have had a motive for Claudia's murder?"

"I don't know, nor do I know what she might have done if she did suspect it. But it's food for thought. Did you have any other private conversations upstairs, or phone calls, that you would rather she hadn't heard? I recall that you made a point of coming to the *mairie* to tell us of your bequest."

"I've been trying to remember. When I made the appointment to see you and the mayor, I may have used the word 'bequest.' Mostly I used e-mails from my computer and sometimes through my cell phone."

"Could she get into those?"

"I have a password for the computer that should be private and a simple four-figure access code to my phone, but I think she knows that. She said she might need it in an emergency, so she may have read some of my exchanges with my lawyer or my accountant. She may know what I told you in the *mairie,* that the house is in an SCI, a company which would allow me to sell the shares."

"And thus to disinherit her," said Bruno.

"If she knew enough about inheritance law and the implications of the SCI structure, then I suppose it's possible she might have deduced that. I doubt it. But I see your point about Claudia. And now I'd like to rest, please."

"One last question before I go. When you spoke to the tribunal today, did you show them the text of the will you signed in their presence?"

The old man glared at him. "What the devil do you mean?"

"I'm wondering what the will actually says, whether St. Denis is really the beneficiary or if you had some devious plot in mind that leaves your fortune elsewhere."

"Why should you think that?"

"Because we haven't actually seen your will, and I think we should, the one with the signatures of the witnesses at today's tribunal."

"You're insulting me. Please get out and let me rest."

The old man's eyes were darting about the room as if searching for something. Bruno suddenly knew what it must be, so he smiled and said goodbye. He trotted down the stairs and out to the van, where he found the file Bourdeille had carried into the meeting that morning. The question about the spelling of his name must have distracted him so Bourdeille had forgotten to take it with him. Bruno opened it and began scanning the documents inside. The top one was a written statement, signed by the four witnesses and by Maître Lucier, attesting that Monsieur de Bourdeille had satisfied each of them that he was of sound mind and under no duress when he read aloud and signed the will in their presence and demonstrated to their satisfaction that he knew its contents and understood them.

Beneath it was the will, signed and witnessed that day. Bourdeille had left the shares in the SCI that owned his house and land, his art foundation, which owned his collection, his personal library and his shares in something called Entreprises Juin Société Anonyme to an entity named Fondation Juin-Bourdeille. In a separate legacy, Madame Bonnet was bequeathed the house she lived in, as was his gardener, each to be given an annuity that would guarantee them a pension of a thousand euros a month.

"We've been screwed," Bruno murmured to himself.

Bruno skimmed through the rest of the file, looking in vain for some indication of what the Fondation Juin-Bourdeille might be. He found an accountant's report of the various shares being held in the Société Anonyme, a range of oil and insurance companies, banks and a multinational printing corporation. The total current market value was listed at more than four million euros.

Bruno went back into the *chartreuse* and found the mayor standing at the doorway to the sixth and last room, the one Bruno had never seen.

"It's a double shrine," the mayor said, not turning his head. "Half of it is dedicated to his supposed ancestor Pierre de Bourdeille, with first editions of his books, framed letters he wrote and letters to him, including one by Mary, Queen of Scots, portrait engravings and so on. The other half is dedicated to the life and deeds of Paul Juin, including the original parchment signed by de Gaulle naming him as a Compagnon de la Résistance."

"And none of it is going to St. Denis," said Bruno, handing the mayor the file. "The little ceremony we were not allowed to attend witnessed Bourdeille's real will, which leaves everything to something called Fondation Juin-Bourdeille, and I can't find out from the file what it might be."

He opened the web browser on his phone and tapped in "Fondation Juin-Bourdeille." There was no dedicated website, but he found a formal registration document of its origin the previous year, stating that it had been established under a law of 1987 that defined a *fondation* as "an institution designated by the act by one or several persons, physical or moral, deciding upon the irrevocable grant of goods, rights or resources, to the realization of a nonprofit work of public interest."

"I see no indication that this *fondation* intends to devote its resources to something to be run by St. Denis," said Bruno.

"Let's not be hasty," the mayor replied. "Don't forget what I told him over lunch, that I don't want this to be run by St. Denis. A *fondation* of this type is exactly what I had in mind — a nonprofit organization in the public interest. But I confess that I had assumed that we would be setting it up rather than him. And since we're here, let's go and ask Bourdeille exactly what he has in mind."

The old man was dozing on the chaise longue when they entered his study. Then one eye opened and looked at them vaguely before the second eye opened with a snap and they were being examined with a piercing gaze.

"You forgot this in the van, monsieur," said the mayor, putting the file on the desk.

"Am I to presume you have studied the contents?" he asked.

"First, let me say how impressed I am by your art collection and by the remarkable room dedicated to your ancestor and to Paul Juin," said the mayor politely. "Thank you for letting me see it, and the other artworks in your collection. It reflects a life of great scholarship and remarkable taste."

"So you've read it." Bourdeille's voice was an accusation.

"Of course we've read it, we have a direct interest in the contents," the mayor said agreeably. "Your *fondation* seems very much like the structure I was proposing to you over lunch."

"What did you do with my jacket when you helped me take it off?" Bourdeille asked Bruno.

"I put it on the coat hanger on the hook behind the door," Bruno said. "It seemed the logical place."

"You'll find another document in the inside breast pocket. Take it out."

Bruno complied. There were perhaps four or five folded sheets of good-quality paper, folded in three to fit the pocket. Bruno handed them to Bourdeille unopened.

"Give them to the mayor. Let him read it."

Bruno did so, and the mayor began skimming through to the end, and then started again at the beginning, and read aloud: " 'The Fondation Juin-Bourdeille seeks to preserve in perpetuity the *chartreuse,* contents, lands and art collection, assembled through the labors of Paul Juin and Pierre de Bourdeille, for public access, edification and education in partnership with the mayor and council of St. Denis. The *fonda-tion*'s funds are to be devoted exclusively to this purpose. The *fondation* will be administered by trustees to be appointed jointly by the mayor, council and education authorities of St. Denis, and by the current trustees of the *fondation,* Pierre de Bourdeille and the grand master of the Confrérie du Pâté de Périgueux.'

"That seems to be the most important part, and this document is defined as a codicil of your will and is signed by the members of this morning's tribunal, including Maître Lucier," the mayor said. "In the name of St. Denis I am most grateful."

"You seemed a little suspicious, Bruno," Bourdeille said.

Bruno nodded. "It's my job to be suspicious. I'm also curious. Why the grand master?"

"I understand your suspicions." Bourdeille waved a hand in what might have been a gesture of forgiveness. "The grand master is an old friend and the custodian of something that is precious to this region and to me. Paul Juin loved the pâté and provided the funds to rebuild the ancient *confrérie.*"

"Why did you take the *fondation* document from the file and put it in your pocket?" Bruno asked, his voice expressing honest curiosity rather than accusation.

"Because of something the mayor said over lunch about Paul Juin and your museum of the Resistance. I wanted to get the codicil redrafted to take account of that. But I suppose it's good enough as it stands, so why don't you take it? I can always get them to send me a copy."

"Does Madame Bonnet not bring your mail to you?" Bruno asked.

"Yes, but I can tell if she opens it first. She never does."

"But you couldn't tell if she simply failed to hand it to you. And now you know that she has arranged your audio system so that she can hear everything that's said up here."

"I realize that," said Bourdeille. "I'll have an electrician here on Monday to change it."

"I understand your thinking, but I'm not sure you should do that," Bruno said. "I think we can all imagine circumstances where it might be useful to mislead Madame Bonnet."

As he spoke the words, Bruno wondered if he could also use the case file to mislead the tiresome Madame de Breille. Perhaps she in turn could mislead Philippe Delaron.

"Interesting," said Bourdeille, interrupting Bruno's thoughts and studying him thoughtfully from beneath those bushy white eyebrows before nodding agreement.

"Does that mean you have some kind of plan, Bruno?" the mayor asked.

"Not yet, but I'm working on it."

CHAPTER 32

It was shortly after four in the afternoon when they left Bourdeille's *chartreuse.* "What do you plan to do now?" the mayor asked on their way back to St. Denis.

"Go to my office, open the computer and start looking at genealogy," Bruno replied. "Those family photos in Madame Bonnet's sitting room triggered my interest. I want to identify the man and child."

"You mean she's not the only one who may have a direct interest in Bourdeille's inheritance?"

"Exactly, so we need to know who else might be interested."

Bruno dropped the mayor at his home and returned the van and its keys to the retirement home. Once in his office, he logged on to the police computer and found the e-mail from France Télécom listing the phone activities he had requested, giving the caller and recipient numbers for each phone, texts as well as calls. Each contact was timed and located by the nearest cell-phone tower. He checked the numbers against his lists, and his suspicions began to harden.

Then he began searching for the wedding in Limeuil of a man named Bonnet. There was a Jean-Luc Bonnet who married a Nathalie Descaux in September 1987. Descaux had been Bourdeille's family name before he changed it. Presumably that had been done after the issue of Nathalie's birth certificate. She was eighteen at the time of her marriage, and her profession was listed as student nurse. Her husband was thirty-six, a farmer. Bruno then looked for births and found a Luc Bonnet born on March 1, 1984. He smiled to himself as he added up the months from wedding to birth.

Bruno looked for other families in Limeuil named Descaux and found none. He widened the search to the whole *département* and found scores of them, mainly born around Mussidan in the west and Brantôme in the north. Rather than wade through, he looked for Juin and found a note that the records had only been digitized as far back as 1980. Earlier searches would have to be done by hand. Searching for the name Bourdeille took him to a family living in the small town of that name, presumably the legitimate descendants of the sixteenth-century courtier. Finally he found the section for formal changes of name and came across the art historian, formerly Pierre Descaux and now officially known as de Bourdeille. As far as Nathalie was concerned, she was the man's legitimate grand-daughter.

He e-mailed a request to the *département* registry, using his return address on the police computer, asking for an urgent manual search for copies of birth, death and marriage certificates relating to Paul and Rebekkah Juin of Périgueux, to Rebekkah Descaux and to Rebekkah Bourdeille. Then he searched the police and gendarmerie databases for Jean-Luc and Luc Bonnet, giving their dates of birth. Jean-Luc, the father, was clean. Luc Bonnet had one conviction for stealing a car when he was sixteen and another for assault two years later. He was charged alongside Dominic Darrail for beating up two other youths outside a bar in Bergerac; the owner had called the police. Neither offense carried a jail term, but the connection with Dominic was interesting. Each man's birth had been registered in Limeuil in the same year, which suggested they had grown up and been to school together.

The birth certificate said that Dominic's mother, Véronique Darrail, had been born to the family Cassini in Bab el-Oued in Algeria in 1959. That was the district of the white working class, the biggest concentration of settlers in the country. It was also the heartland and bastion of the movement to keep Algeria French. Bruno recalled Félicité saying that her landlady was a *pied-noir* who despised Arabs. She also hated de Gaulle for negotiating Algeria's independence, which the *pieds-noirs* claimed condemned them to a choice between *la valise ou le cercueil* — the suitcase or the coffin. Véronique Cassini had married Jacques Darrail in Bergerac in 1982. Her profession was shop assistant, and his was self-employed waterman. Bruno presumed that meant canoe rentals.

Bruno called the baron, a veteran of the Algerian War, to ask if he'd ever heard of a *pied-noir* family from Bab el-Oued called Cassini. They had supposedly fled Algeria and moved to the region.

"Not off the top of my head," he replied. "Do you want me to ask around among the Anciens Combattants? Some of the veterans stayed in touch with the *pieds-noirs*, mostly the right-wing ones. Not that I have anything to do with them, or rather they don't want to have anything to do with me, since they're in the Front National and I'm known as a Gaullist."

The baron gave a short laugh. "The difference between me and them was that I had a transistor radio, and they didn't. When the generals launched the putsch of '61, most of the officers wanted to join it, but we conscripts all had our little radios. Usually we listened to pop music, but we all heard de Gaulle's speech denouncing the coup and demanding the army remain loyal to France. That's why we stayed in our barracks and the coup d'état failed."

Bruno said he'd be grateful for any help the baron could give and ended the call. Then he contacted Juliette in Les Eyzies and began by thanking her for patrolling the St. Denis market that morning.

"I remember you saying that your dad was in the First Gulf War in '91," he said.

"That's right, in the signal corps. It was his last tour of duty before he got out. I was just a kid when he came back and I was really excited. We were living in Châlons then, where he'd been based, and then we moved down here when he got a job with France Télécom. Why do you ask?"

"I wanted to ask if he was in the Anciens

Combattants?"

"Yes, when he was running for the council seat he thought it would be useful, and then Grandpa really wanted him to join."

"Why was that?"

"Grandpa was in the Algerian War, so the Anciens Combattants always meant a lot to him. It still does. He goes to all the meetings and parades."

"How's your grandfather's health?"

"Excellent. He's eighty years old and sharp as a knife."

"Could you ask if he knows of a *pied-noir* family who moved here around the time of independence called Cassini?" he asked. "Some of them are in Bergerac, some around here. One of the daughters, Véronique, born in 1959, married a guy in Limeuil."

"No problem. I'm seeing him at a family lunch tomorrow. I'll call you back, or do you want his number to ask him yourself?"

"I'll leave it to you. Thanks."

Then Bruno sat back, thinking and sketching doodles on a pad, a *B* for Bourdeille in a circle with an arrow pointing to *R* for Rebekkah Juin. He added another arrow to *MC,* for Michel Cagnac, the Vichy cop who had arrested and tortured Bourdeille and raped Rebekkah Juin. Then he drew another circle with a *C* for Cassini with a question mark above it. He picked up his desk phone again and called the Centre Jean Moulin in Bordeaux, one of the largest of all French archives on the Resistance with a unique collection of taped interviews with old *résistants.* Alain Tournoux, the research director, had become a friend after Bruno had treated him and his wife to a lavish lunch to thank him for his help in previous cases.

"What can I do for you, Bruno?" Tournoux asked.

"I'm interested in a member of the *milice* in Périgueux, Michel Cagnac. He was imprisoned after the Liberation, later joined the French army to fight in Indochina and finished up in Algeria where he joined the OAS. Do you have anything on him?"

"That's interesting. You're the second inquiry I've had about Cagnac this week. A man from Périgueux came in yesterday. That's why I have Cagnac's file right here on my desk."

"Was he a man in his sixties, an ex-cop named Pellier?"

"That's right. I presume this is police business?"

"Very much so. I'm trying to track down Cagnac's family history and whatever you have on him. I'm especially interested in

446

what happened after he was freed from prison after World War Two and again after he joined the OAS."

"Cagnac was a nasty piece of work," Tournoux replied. "Not just a Vichy loyalist but a real Nazi."

He went on to explain that Cagnac in 1941, aged eighteen, joined the SOL, the Service d'Ordre Légionnaire, which began as a militant political group supporting the Vichy regime. Viciously anti-Semitic and anti-Communist, they saw themselves as the French version of the Nazi Party. He transferred from that into the *milice* as soon as they were formed in January 1943. By September of that year he was attached to the office of Michael Hambrecht, the Gestapo chief in Périgueux and an *Untersturmführer,* or lieutenant, in the SS.

"Wait a minute," Bruno said. "When he tried to arrest Bourdeille and Paul Juin in 1942, you mean Cagnac wasn't a cop?"

"No, at the time he was in the elite section of the SOL known as the Avant-Garde, living in barracks and acting as police auxiliaries. They went armed on what were called antiterrorist missions."

"What was his background?"

"He came from a working-class family in Périgueux. His father died of wounds suffered in the Great War not long after his son's birth. His mother married again and Cagnac hated his stepfather. He was a Communist and trade unionist in the railway works in Périgueux who used to get drunk and beat up his wife and stepson. So Cagnac went the other way and became a Nazi."

After the Liberation in August 1944, Tournoux told him, Cagnac joined the retreating German troops, and like a lot of *milice* members was conscripted into the Charlemagne Division, the Waffen SS unit of French volunteers that fought on the eastern front. By February 1945, only about eight thousand of them remained, and they were thrown into the battle to defend East Prussia, where they suffered heavy casualties. Only about a third of them reached the coast where the German navy evacuated them to Denmark. They were refitted there and then thrown into the Battle of Berlin, fighting on around Hitler's bunker against overwhelming odds.

"One of them," Tournoux concluded, "Hauptsturmführer Henri Fenet, another ex-*milice* man, was awarded one of the last Knight's Cross medals Hitler presented."

"And Cagnac?" asked Bruno.

"He served under Fenet, whose squad

destroyed fourteen Soviet tanks in the ruins of Berlin. He got out of Berlin with Fenet. They managed to reach the British troops at Wismar, where they were taken prisoner and eventually handed over to the French. Fenet was sentenced to twenty years' hard labor, and Cagnac got ten. He was allowed to join the French Foreign Legion in 1950 after the Korean War broke out and Ho Chi Minh's troops launched an offensive that destroyed the French forts along the Chinese border."

Bruno was hastily taking notes while Tournoux continued speaking.

"Paris was in a panic. The government didn't want to risk conscripts in that wretched war, but the army was desperate to find volunteers. They trawled through the prisons offering freedom in return for military service in the Foreign Legion. And Cagnac, whatever else we may think of him, was a brave and highly experienced soldier."

"I thought I knew a bit about history, but all this is new to me," said Bruno. "I mean, I'd heard of the Charlemagne Division, but not about their fighting in Berlin."

"Oddly enough, we know more about Cagnac before 1950 than after it. The Legion is very secretive about its troops. We know that Cagnac was wounded at Dien

Bien Phu in Vietnam and was one of the last casualties to be evacuated by air before the fort was overrun. By 1955 he was in Algeria with the new REP, the Regiment of Foreign Legion Parachutists under Colonel Paul Jeanpierre. Many of those troops were Germans, Wehrmacht and Waffen SS veterans, which is ironic because Colonel Jeanpierre was in the Resistance, captured by the Gestapo and survived fifteen months in Mauthausen."

"Was Cagnac in the Battle of Algiers and in the putsch of 1961?" Bruno asked, scribbling in his notebook again.

"Yes, he was identified in that famous newsreel film of the paratroops returning to their barracks in trucks after the putsch failed, all singing the Edith Piaf song 'Je Ne Regrette Rien.' That's all we know from the available records, except that he was an adjutant in a company led by Lieutenant Roger Degueldre, a hero of the Indochina War. After the failed coup, Degueldre left the army to form the Delta commandos of the OAS, and Cagnac went with him and took part in at least one attempt to assassinate de Gaulle. Cagnac was killed in a shoot-out in Madrid at the end of 1962."

"Army records wouldn't tell you any more about him, whether he listed any marriages or dependents?" Bruno asked.

"No, the Foreign Legion records are kept sealed in a special section. What's your interest in him?"

Bruno recounted the story of the arrest and rape of Paul Juin's sister, Rebekkah, and the birth of her daughter.

"Because Bourdeille believes Cagnac was the girl's father, he's determined that her descendants won't inherit his wealth, even though by marrying Rebekkah he became the girl's legal father," Bruno explained. "And that question of inheritance may be involved in our murder investigation."

"A police inquiry might get more out of the Legion records than we can, so good luck. But because of de Gaulle and the Charlemagne Division, anything involving Cagnac will be highly sensitive."

"Thanks, Alain. I owe you another lunch next time I'm in Bordeaux."

"I'll look forward to it."

Bruno ended the call, read through his notes and shook his head at the extraordinary saga of Cagnac's life. Would it have turned out differently if his father had not died of wounds or if his stepfather had not been a brute? Or a Communist? And what if he hadn't served under the charismatic Lieutenant Degueldre?

There was a man who could command intense loyalty. Anyone who served in the French army knew of Degueldre's sordid death at Fort d'Ivry after he was captured and sentenced to be executed. Three French officers refused to command the firing squad for a man they considered a hero of France. Most of the squad aimed deliberately high. Only one bullet hit him. The young junior officer who had been ordered to command the squad was required to deliver the coup de grâce. Close to hysterics he made a mess of it, emptying one magazine into Degueldre's wounded body and needing a second to finish the job.

Bruno pulled from his desk drawer a burner phone that he sometimes used when he didn't want his calls to be traced. He'd bought it for cash in one of the shady shops around Barbès-Rochechouart in Paris, where the staff wasn't particular about logging the names and addresses of buyers. He called the private number of an elderly man in army records who'd been helpful before, and when he answered, Bruno said, "I hope you recognize my voice."

"I believe I do, and good to hear from you. Why the precautions?"

"I'm trying to find out about an ex-paratroop *légionnaire*," Bruno said, explaining Cagnac's tangled and politically sensitive history.

"The Foreign Legion records are kept separately. They take very seriously their promise to let a recruit forget his past and start again under a new name. You could go through channels, but in this case because of the OAS connection you'd probably get nowhere. Is there any special aspect of his life that interests you?"

"His time in Algeria. Did he get married? Did he list any dependents for pension rights? Did he have comrades who might still be alive? Does the family name Cassini appear anywhere?"

"Call me back tomorrow and I'll see what I can do."

Bruno put away the burner phone and pulled out the special phone that he'd been given by the brigadier. A duty officer answered the phone. Bruno knew there would be no need to identify himself; the phone itself would do that. He asked to speak to the brigadier in person.

"Concerning what?"

"It's a sensitive matter for his ears alone."

"I'll pass on your request."

Bruno's phone rang a few minutes later with the flashing green light that signaled someone on the brigadier's secure network.

"Ah, Bruno, I was wondering if I might hear from you. I was interested to see your name coming up a couple of times this week on the death of that girl whose father has friends in the White House."

"It has turned into a murder investigation and I need to get into the records of Michel Cagnac, a former member of the Foreign Legion who then joined the OAS. I need to see if he listed any dependents for pension rights," Bruno said, explaining Cagnac's background.

"*Putain,* Bruno — Charlemagne Division, Foreign Legion *paras,* OAS, Delta commando with Degueldre, de Gaulle. You don't want much. Those records are very tightly sealed."

"That's why I called you, sir."

"And that's all you want? His listed dependents?"

"Yes, sir." Bruno usually found himself reverting to old soldier habits when dealing with the brigadier.

"Are you close to an arrest?"

"I'll let you know when I'm sure, sir."

The brigadier ended the call.

The baron returned his call to report that the Cassini family had moved from Algiers to Bergerac, where there were jobs available in the big tobacco factory and in the munitions plant. A large family with three brothers and four sisters, they had prospered and spread across France. The only Cassini who lived near St. Denis was Véronique, in Limeuil, who had arrived in France as an infant. One of her brothers had been a Front National candidate in Bergerac during the last parliamentary elections and had failed to be elected.

Bruno made one more call, to Hodge, to say that Bourdeille wanted to present his condolences to Madame Muller and had invited her and Amélie to his home, where they could see the art collection that had so intrigued Claudia. If Jennifer was at Café Fauquet around ten the next morning, Bruno would lead her there, along with Amélie.

"And there's something you might be able to help me with," Bruno added. "During the last case you and I worked on, the FBI was able to get into Facebook pages. Could you do that again for me, for two French citizens? I need to know if they traveled overseas."

"Give me their names, and it would be helpful to have addresses and their dates of birth."

CHAPTER 33

Bruno arrived at the riding school shortly after the others had left with the string of horses for their evening exercise, but Hector was still waiting for him in the stables. Balzac, who had spent the day with his giant equine friend, recognized the sound of Bruno's Land Rover and was waiting at the stable door to greet him. On the double wooden door was tacked a note saying "Ridge trail, St. Chamassy — P."

Bruno took a carrot from the bag he kept in the cargo net above the front seats of his vehicle and gave Hector his treat before saddling him and slipping on the bridle. He donned his riding boots and cap, then set out in a threesome that felt as old as history: a man, his horse and his dog.

Hector enjoyed riding alone without other horses to slow him down and set out up the slope at a brisk pace that had Balzac panting to keep up. Bruno slowed his horse when they reached the ridge and reined in, thinking they had maybe another hour of daylight. Balzac was close, but his sensitive nose was entranced by the scent still leaking from the long-disused rabbit warren that he had investigated dozens of times before. And Hector was edging back and forth and from side to side and then pawing at the ground as he saw the great expanse of the ridge opening before him, just made for the run that he craved. Bruno whistled to catch Balzac's attention, pulled down his cap, bent down in the saddle and flicked the reins to unleash his horse.

Hector sprang forward, leaping with two strides into a canter and then with the third he was springing into a gallop and the wind was in Bruno's face, forcing him to narrow his eyes and bend lower in the saddle so that his entire world was focused on the gap between his horse's ears and the open ridge ahead. All he could hear was the drumming of hooves and all he could feel was the surging pace of his horse.

As the ridge narrowed and the belt of woodland neared, Bruno relaxed back into the saddle, and even though he had not touched the reins, Hector began to ease his pace, slowing into a canter and then into a trot and finally a walk as the trees approached. Hector half turned and stopped, still quivering with excitement, his head cocked as if watching for Balzac pounding gallantly along far behind, the long basset ears flapping, his tongue hanging from the side of his mouth. Bruno was panting even harder than Hector. He leaned forward, patting Hector's great neck and murmuring, *"Merci, mon brave."*

From this vantage point he could see to his right the village of Limeuil clambering up the hill from its grassy beach and the junction of the two rivers. Behind the gray walls of the Moorish castle lay the gardens and the well where Claudia had died six days ago. Bruno felt almost sure of his suspicions. He knew the means, the opportunity, the motive; but he did not have the proof. All his evidence was circumstantial. Could he set some kind of trap to tease out the truth? What might he use as bait?

Hector suddenly tossed his head, eager to be off again, and Bruno looked to his left searching for the short spire of the church of St. Chamassy and, slightly lower, the conical roof of the manor house. Walktrotting their way up the hill toward these buildings was a chain of mounted horses, some of them familiar by their gait and by the way that Pamela, Gilles and Fabiola rode. At the tail was the figure of Félix. From the pricking of Hector's ears, it was clear that he'd seen them too. With Bruno's slight forward urging of his seat, Hector bounded forward to cut them off at the cemetery beyond the village. The horse knew this route at least as well as Bruno, probably better, but Bruno slowed him to a canter so that Balzac could keep up.

"Glad you were able to join us," said Pamela, waving. "We're about to head back. Fabiola and Gilles are taking Félix to the cinema at Le Buisson. They're doing a series of classics and tonight is *Jules et Jim*."

"Too bad I'm tied up with the mayor tonight," said Bruno loudly, for the benefit of the others, falling into step beside Félix. "It's one of those films I'd like to watch again."

"And I have a tower of paperwork awaiting me in the office," echoed Pamela. "*Gîte* bookings for the new season, cookery-school accounts, new sign-ups for the riding school. And that's just the start."

Bruno smiled to himself, thinking their alibis were now in place.

The three of them dashed off to the movies while Bruno and Pamela grinned at each other. They rubbed down and bedded the horses, refreshed their feed and water and

459

put away the saddles and bridles.

"I'm off to shower and change and I'll see you in half an hour or so," she said, opening her arms wide. "But come here a moment and hug me. I love the horsey smell of a man who's just been riding fast."

She had always been a wonderful woman to kiss, thought Bruno, taking her in his arms, her lips full and soft, lovely purring sounds in her throat. And she was right about that smell of horses.

"That's enough," she said, pulling away. "Otherwise we might end up making love here in the stables, and I really don't want a rump full of straw. I'll see you soon."

Bruno raced home with Balzac, pausing only to buy bread and feed his ducks and chickens, collect his fresh eggs and pick some herbs. He quickly showered and shaved and changed his sheets. He brought in wood and lit the fire, decanted a bottle of red from Château Lestevenie and set the table for two.

Am I keeping so busy, he asked himself, because I'm uncertain whether I really want to resume this affair with Pamela? He remembered the faint sense of relief he had felt when Pamela had ended their liaison the previous year. She had kept it so light, so casual, while it lasted, but expected him to be available at her whim. Did he want to fall into that pattern again? Or was it because he didn't know how it might progress, how it might end? But love affairs are always like that, he told himself, voyages to unknown and unknowable destinations. Aware of his own rising excitement and expectation as he heard the familiar sound of Pamela's car turning into his driveway, he knew whatever the spirit might say, in his case the flesh was weak.

"You look wonderful," he said, taking her hands and standing back to admire her. Beneath the open trench coat, she was wearing a new, slinky black dress that he hadn't seen before, clinging to the curves of a body made taut by her endless riding. It fell to just below her knees, and beneath she was wearing light gray stockings that matched her shoulder bag. Her auburn hair was piled atop her head to reveal that long, white neck he loved to kiss. She wore just the merest trace of lipstick, and he caught that scent he remembered, Guerlain's Vol de Nuit.

"How do you do it?" he asked, smiling with deep affection. He lifted their joined hands so he could twirl her around. "Just moments ago you were a passionate stable girl, and now you arrive like a model in an exclusive nightclub."

She came into his arms.

"This welcome is very flattering," she said after a long and delightful moment. "But do you think I might slip off my raincoat and put my bag down?" She gave him a final peck on the lips. "I have another bag in the car with jeans and a sweater, since I don't think anyone would believe tomorrow morning that I'd just slipped out to buy some croissants dressed like this."

"Why the secrecy?" he asked. "All our friends know we were lovers."

"I don't know. Maybe I'm a little shy, or perhaps I just want to keep this to ourselves. I'm not sure. Maybe the secrecy adds a little whiff of spice to our encounter. But I'm very glad to be here, and to see the fire lit, the wine decanted. This may not sound very romantic, Bruno, but I could eat a horse. Well, not exactly, but you know what I mean. Oh, and I brought some cheese. It's in the bag in the car."

"I'll get that," he said. "You hang up your coat, make yourself comfortable by the fire, decide what you want to drink, put on some music if you like, and I'll be right back."

He returned to hear the sound of a CD he did not own. She must have brought it specially. They were the original versions of songs of Jean Sablon in the late thirties and forties, some of which he knew almost by heart, since he'd heard them sung so often by other artists.

"Sablon's were the first French words I ever heard," she said, standing by his CD player and swaying in time to the music. "He was singing 'C'est Si Bon' on the radio when I was very young, so young I couldn't quite understand why anybody would want to speak a different language."

He came up behind her and ran his fingers down her arms, to her waist, her hips, her thighs, and suddenly felt the tiny button that meant she was wearing a garter belt, an item of lingerie he'd always found powerfully erotic. She turned into his arms.

"You found it," she said, kissing him on the chin and putting her arms around his neck to fondle his hair. She was suddenly shorter, having kicked off her shoes, and she was swaying in time to the music. He picked up the hint and began to sway with her and very slowly to dance.

"I was hoping to surprise you," she murmured.

"*Mon Dieu,* you already have."

One of her hands had trailed to the back of his neck, under his collar, and he felt a fingertip tracing a lazy circle at the top of his spine. Her other hand was unbuttoning

463

his shirt and sliding in to caress his chest. He heard himself groan aloud.

"And you've shaved for me," she said, brushing her lips along the side of his jaw.

Her eyes were closed and he kissed her eyelids. He wanted to pull her to him, to press himself against the length of her, but told himself to let Pamela set the pace. In the back of his mind a thought came that she had planned this lovemaking step-by-step, caress by caress. He could almost imagine her thinking of it, considering each move, his reaction, her response. But that could hardly be right, for there was nothing cool or clinical about this. From the purring sounds in Pamela's throat she was enjoying this as much as he was.

"I was wrong. I really don't want any food yet, not for quite a while," she said softly, almost into his ear. Then she let her lips drift back to his, and he felt the tip of her tongue tease gently at his lips.

"I think I'll do this for hours," she said. "How does that sound?"

"It's wonderful, but I'm not sure I can stand it." His hands were clasping her just above the waist. He could feel her heart beating through her ribs.

"Oh, I think you can. I think you'll have to. I'm enjoying this." Her tongue teased his lips again, and she began to remove his shirt.

"And so am I, but surprised."

"Why? Because I wasn't always so . . . forward?" She began to roll the nipple above his heart between two soft fingers.

"*Ma belle,* you were always forward but also eager." Bruno was breathing hard. "You've developed a most delicious patience."

"I had many months to think about this." Her other hand crept around his back, and she raked one fingernail gently down his spine. He gasped, feeling the soft sensation of her breath in his mouth.

"But we made love the other night."

"That was eagerness," she said, a gentle chuckle in her throat. "This is still desire, but also something else."

She dropped her hand to the waistband of his trousers, turned and pulled him along behind her to his bedroom.

Some time later, the candle burning low, Pamela was lying on top of him propped up on her elbows. She was gazing down at him with a smile that he'd never seen before. It seemed to be full of secrets. Somehow her hair, earlier coiled atop her head, was hanging loose and tickling his shoulders. Her lipstick had all been kissed away.

He raised his head to kiss her again and

asked, "Are you hungry?"

"Now that you mention it, I could eat two horses."

"Do you want to eat here in bed, in front of the fire or at table?"

"The fire."

"This is for you," he said, rising to take a large terry-cloth bathrobe from the cupboard and draping it over the end of the bed. He went into the bathroom and then rummaged in the kitchen. He came back in a light cotton bathrobe bearing a glass of wine that he put on the bedside table beside a pile of books.

"Five minutes," he said and returned to the kitchen, where he began to sauté gently in duck fat the small green buds from the *pissenlit* plants he'd picked earlier. In the sitting room he added some kindling and a well-seasoned log to the fire and brought in plates, cutlery and the decanter from the dining table. Back in the kitchen, he opened a can of the venison pâté he had made that winter, put it on a plate along with a small bowl of gherkins and the cheese she'd brought. Then he began cracking eggs, whipping them lightly, adding salt and pepper and a splash of cream and putting a small slice of butter into his omelette pan along with more duck fat. He cut some generous slices of bread from the round *tourte,* saw the fat was just on the point of browning and added the eggs, moving them around with a fork for even cooking and tipping the pan this way and that. Just before he folded the omelette, he added the *boutons* of *pissenlit,* savoring the nutty scent they gave off.

"Dinner is served," he called, and she emerged from the bathroom with her hair brushed and wineglass in hand, her face shining and a tantalizingly faint hint of scent around her. She pulled a couple of cushions from his sofa, tucked her feet beneath her, put the plate on her lap and began using a hunk of bread to push bite-sized portions of omelette onto her fork.

"Just what I needed," she said when her plate was empty, the pâté finished and just a glass each left in the carafe.

"Coffee?" he asked.

Pamela shook her head, put her plate aside, slid off the cushions and came to lie against him, her back to his chest, and said, "I do like watching a good fire, and resting against you like this means my back doesn't get cold. My mother used to tell me when I was young that you could see faces in the fire, and girls at school said you could see the face of your future husband. Did you have legends like that?"

"I remember one about staring into a well on the first full moon after Easter to see in the still water the face of your own true love."

"We had something about the still water of wells, but I forget, and it's made me think of Limeuil. Have you found out yet what happened with Claudia?"

"I may be getting close. That reminds me, would you like to come see Bourdeille's art collection before lunch tomorrow? He's asked me to bring Claudia's mother and also Amélie before she goes back to Paris."

"I'd like that, Bruno, but that's tomorrow. Now what I'd really like is for you to take me back to bed."

CHAPTER 34

Bourdeille could not have been more gracious, welcoming Claudia's mother on his doorstep, holding her hand and telling her that Claudia had been the most interesting and promising student he'd ever had and that he deeply mourned her passing. He was warm to Amélie, complimenting her singing at Château des Milandes and saying that he hoped he'd be able to attend her Josephine Baker concert. He had caught something in the tone of Bruno's introduction of Pamela to realize that she was more than just a friend. He kissed her hand and asked if she was the horsewoman that Madame Bonnet still referred to as "the Mad Englishwoman," the nickname the locals had coined before getting to know her.

Bruno had been busy already that morning, seeing with satisfaction that *Sud Ouest* had a story saying the police feared that their chief suspect, Laurent, might try to leave the area. Philippe would have some explaining to do. Bruno's suspicions were hardening after calls from Juliette and the baron about the Cassini family and their continued devotion to the lost cause of Algérie Française. And a call from Professor Porter had been even more useful. Bruno had accordingly made several phone calls to prepare the ground for the operation he'd planned for later in the day. J-J, hoping to spend the morning on the golf course, had wanted to know whether Bruno was sure of his theory. Sure enough, Bruno had replied, on the basis of what he'd learned from Annette's warrant.

But Bruno was still feeling nervous as Bourdeille wheeled himself from room to room of his art collection. The old man wore his scholarship lightly and was making an effort to be entertaining as he explained the history of each painting and how he'd acquired it. In the last room, Bourdeille recounted something of the life of his illustrious ancestor in the sixteenth century and then of the friendship he had shared with Paul Juin. Once the tour was complete he invited his guests up to his study, where they found two bottles of Château Haut-Brion 2009 already standing open.

As he filled their glasses, Madame Bonnet

arrived with a tray of canapés: small squares of toast covered in foie gras; others topped with smoked breast of duck or halves of deviled eggs; a plate of charcuterie and small cubes of cheese and fruit impaled with cocktail sticks.

"I'd like to offer a toast to Claudia's memory and record my own deep grief at the premature ending of such a promising and vibrant young life," Bourdeille said. "You too, Madame Bonnet, you knew and liked this young American woman." Over her protest, Bourdeille half filled a glass for her and then raised his own.

"To the lovely, intelligent and much missed Claudia, may she rest in peace," he declared, raising his glass and then sipping as everyone in the room echoed his toast and followed his example.

"And now, Madame Muller, might I presume to ask you to say a few words about your wonderful daughter?" Bourdeille added.

Jennifer took a long sip at her wine, took a deep breath and then looked at each of them in turn before speaking.

"I know from what she wrote to me that Claudia was happy here among you all. And I know that my daughter was interested, intrigued, fulfilled by her work here and that

471

she made friends who will remember her and the brightness she brought into our lives. Thank you for welcoming her into your homes and making her last weeks of life a happy time. And thank you all for being here with me today, sharing the hospitality of Monsieur de Bourdeille among these works of art of his that she loved so much. I shall never forget the welcome you all showed her here in the Périgord."

"Thank you, madame. We were honored to have her here among us," Bourdeille said and then looked around the room.

"Mademoiselle Amélie, I hesitate to ask, but I do love your voice. Might you sing something for us to commemorate Claudia's passing?"

"Happily," Amélie said, and paused a moment, her hands clasped loosely at her waist, and then she started to tap her foot slowly, raised her head and began that lovely gospel song from the cotton plantations of the Deep South that had for centuries given the comfort of faith to the living and solace at the time of death.

I looked over Jordan and what did I see,
Comin' for to carry me home?
A band of angels comin' after me,
Comin' for to carry me home.

Swing low, sweet chariot,
Comin' for to carry me home.

When she finished, Jennifer came forward with tears in her eyes to hug Amélie before leaning down to plant a kiss on Bourdeille's forehead. Bruno noted that Madame Bonnet took advantage of the moment to take the tray away and slip out of the room. Jennifer stood up, and there was a short silence before Bourdeille spoke.

"How close are you to resolving this mystery, Bruno?" Bourdeille asked, his eyes darting quickly to the microphone on the desk beside him.

"Close," said Bruno, picking his words with care. "Just before I came here, I heard that our forensic experts have been working on the samples they took from the well and from the stone walls where they think someone may have climbed in. They have isolated some new DNA traces of Claudia and whoever was with her at the well. What the scientists can do these days is amazing. But they say they don't have enough, so they're on their way back to the well to gather more. They think they'll be able to identify who was with her, and as soon as I leave here I'm going to Limeuil to stand guard until reinforcements come from Périgueux this afternoon."

"Why do you need to stand guard?" Bourdeille asked. "Wouldn't the DNA evidence remain?"

"Not if the suspects were able to drench the key areas with bleach or gasoline," Bruno said. "A lot of criminals know about that these days. In fact, I'd better go. Thank you for this very moving moment, Jennifer, Amélie, Monsieur de Bourdeille."

"Oh dear," said Jennifer. "I was hoping to invite you all to lunch at my hotel, but of course I understand, Bruno. Perhaps the others will join me? I reserved a table and the special taxi for your wheelchair, monsieur."

Bruno ran down the stairs and out to his Land Rover and drove like the wind to the Limeuil hilltop, parking beneath the outer wall. The place looked deserted, but he could hear the Sunday sound of hymns being sung in the hilltop church. Quietly, he opened the rear door of his vehicle to take out the rope and spike he'd borrowed earlier that morning from the public works depot. He removed his SIG Sauer handgun from its holster to check the action and the magazine. The restaurant beside the entrance was closed and silent, and the entrance to the gardens was locked as he had requested, a hand-lettered sign on the barred gate saying CLOSED FOR REPAIRS.

Bruno went down the pathway to the left of the gate, threw the spike over the wall and scrambled up the rope. He took the rope and spike with him and trotted up the path, past the medieval garden and the giant sequoia and past the beehives to position himself on the high ground, screened by bushes.

To one side he could see the well, now sealed, and to the other he could watch the section of the wall that he had climbed earlier in the week. Looking directly ahead, he knew why this was called the panoramic gardens. The view was spectacular over the two rivers and their valleys and then over the wide water meadow to the west, which the swollen River Dordogne used to flood each winter.

He turned his phone to Vibrate and settled down to wait. He checked the screen. There were two text messages, one from J-J saying he was in place. The other was from Hodge. It read: "Facebook shows your suspects took package tour, Phuket, Thailand, November 15–29 last year." Bruno smiled to himself, thinking another link in the chain of evidence was now in place. He checked his weapon and wondered whether his suspects would show up. He would look like a fool if they didn't.

Time passed. A low wind rustled the young leaves. The occasional young bee, flying as if drunk and still learning its geography, blundered past him. Bruno had been there long enough and stood so still that the wildlife would be growing accustomed to his presence. As soon as Bruno formulated the thought, something very small rustled near his feet: a vole, perhaps, or a field mouse. Laurent's hawk would have good hunting here.

If Bruno's quarry came as expected, he asked himself, what would they use, bleach or gasoline? On a Sunday morning gasoline might be easier to obtain, but fire would raise an alarm and make it harder to slip away unobserved. The big supermarkets were open until midday, and they sold bleach in ten-liter *bidons,* the kind the cleaners used at the *mairie.* That would not be easy to carry if his suspect planned to climb the wall, so he should expect someone wearing a rucksack, which would mean reduced mobility. It would also make it harder to climb the wall unobserved, which probably meant using the same access point that Bruno had scaled. However, if a key had been obtained to the outer gate, which

476

was what Bruno anticipated if his theory was correct, he should hear footsteps coming up the gravel path. But he must not spring the trap too soon. He needed real proof of guilt.

Stop fretting, Bruno, he told himself. You have waited in more dangerous moments, more dangerous places, than this, stood in the shadows with the lives of other men under your orders and depending on your judgment. If you're wrong and nobody comes, the only price you pay this time will be a little humiliation. It might even be good for you.

He felt his phone vibrate in the pouch at his waist, coming in short bursts, which meant a text message rather than a call, and the green light was on so it had come from somebody on the brigadier's network. He slid it from the pouch and read what he realized were almost the final pieces in the jigsaw:

"Cagnac — one dependent listed, a daughter, Véronique Cassini, born 30 March 1959."

Interesting, thought Bruno, a daughter but nothing about a wife. And Véronique's birth date came just nine months after the army coup in Algiers of May 1958, which had toppled the Fourth Republic, brought de

Gaulle to power and launched frenzied celebrations among the French army and the *pieds-noirs* who believed this was their guarantee that Algeria would remain French. Véronique's mother would not have been the only *pied-noir* to welcome a *légionnaire* with open arms in those heady days. How wrong they had been, he thought. And how subtly de Gaulle had played his game, saving a democracy in France by becoming a kind of dictator. And then he had stepped down of his own accord.

The history of France, he thought, we can never escape it. And here am I, standing in the precincts of a Stone Age settlement that became a fortress of the Gauls, and then of the Romans, of the Franks and the English. And in living memory German troops had shot French partisans against the wall at the bottom of this hill while Charles de Gaulle was rallying France from England and grumbling at his dependence on Anglo-American support.

Bruno heard voices before he heard footsteps and then the clang of the iron gate being closed. Of course, they used the key issued to the workmen. He heard voices of two men, speaking in grunts and panting as they climbed the path, as if burdened. As they came into view, he felt a small glow of satisfaction. Dominic and Luc, just as he had thought, loaded down under rucksacks, two descendants of Michel Cagnac, a Frenchman who hunted down other Frenchmen, fought for Hitler and then fought Vietnamese and Algerians in the name of France. Two descendants, one from his affair in Algiers and the other from his rape of Rebekkah in 1942, each one prepared to commit murder to protect their fabled inheritance.

They eased the rucksacks from their shoulders, opened them and pulled out two *bidons* labeled EAU DE JAVEL, named for the district of Paris where commercial bleach was first made. Bruno waited until each man had opened a *bidon* and had his hands full before he stepped out from the bushes, his gun still in his holster and his arms spread wide.

"Luc Bonnet, Dominic Darrail, you are under arrest on suspicion of conspiracy to murder," he declared.

Before he finished speaking, a fat *bidon* was being slung at him by Luc, bleach spilling as it spun through the air, and Luc was charging after it toward Bruno.

Bruno had expected this. He waited until Luc was almost on him and then side-stepped before pivoting to slam the side of his boot into Luc's knee. As the man went down, Bruno caught one flailing arm and twisted it hard and high behind Luc's back as the man landed on the ground, bleach bubbling from the *bidon* beside him.

Bruno looked up to see Dominic standing aghast and immobile, his *bidon* still in one hand, the cap in the other, uncertain what to do.

"Be careful, Dominic," said Bruno, pulling out his weapon. "I'm armed."

Slowly Dominic bent to put down the bleach and then stood with his hands in the air. Behind him, J-J and Josette and four armed gendarmes led by Yveline were spilling out of the main door to the Moorish castle and carrying handcuffs.

"Bring some water to wash the bleach off this man," Bruno shouted, putting the *bidon* upright and rolling a whimpering Luc away from the spreading pool of bleach. Josette darted back into the castle. Gendarmes handcuffed the two men.

"Take your trousers off," Yveline told Bruno. "You've got bleach all over them and it will burn through to your legs."

"Him first," said Bruno, pointing at Luc as Josette reappeared with a bucket of water. "He's got bleach soaked all down his side."

Bruno took his boots off and then his

trousers, took them into the toilets inside the castle, doused them in cold water at a sink and then rinsed his legs.

"Nice operation," said J-J, coming in and leaning against the door.

"Those *yaba* pills — Dominic and Luc took a package tour to Thailand in November," Bruno said. "Do you need me for the interrogation?"

"Not really. Thanks to Annette's warrant we've got the phone texts between Dominic in the lecture hall and Luc waiting outside. It makes it clear how they planned to kill Claudia. Josette will take charge of searching their homes, and I'm prepared to bet we'll find more of those *yaba* pills they fed her in the herb tea. Yveline's next job is to arrest Dominic's mother. We've got her phone records, and then we'll pick up Madame Bonnet."

"Would you like to leave that to me?" Bruno asked. "Or will you join me? You don't need to start the interrogation right away. I remember you telling me it usually helped to let suspects sweat a little in their cell before starting to question them. In fact, it might be helpful if you came along, because I don't think this is over yet."

CHAPTER 35

Bruno donned a pair of tracksuit pants from the back of his Land Rover and with J-J beside him drove to the Vieux Logis at Trémolat. J-J was reporting success back to Prunier in Périgueux, and Bruno stopped to make two phone calls of his own before thinking through his theory and his plan on the way. He hoped he was right.

"We have to pick someone up here," said Bruno once they arrived at the hotel. "He should be getting back anytime now."

"Do you mean Hodge?" J-J asked.

"No, Claudia's American professor, his name is Porter. I spoke to him earlier this morning, and I want to stop him before he goes into the hotel. That could upset everything."

J-J glanced at him, mystified. Then J-J's phone rang. It was Josette, reporting that a stash of *yaba* pills had been found at Luc's home, inside a suitcase underneath his unmade bed.

"Well, that's good news," said J-J, closing his phone. "Now what? Do we sit here and twiddle our thumbs?"

"No, we sit here and you try to pick holes in my plan."

"What holes? We have the two killers, the proof of their premeditated murder in their phone texts, their motive and opportunity. And we caught them in the act of trying to wash away that supposed DNA you fooled them into believing was still there. Now we have the pills. And I want to arrest Madame Bonnet, who tipped them off when you set your trap this morning."

"It might be a little more complicated than that," said Bruno, stepping out of his vehicle to wave down a car that had just pulled alongside the hotel.

Porter was at the wheel, and J-J waited as the two men spoke, nodded agreement and then Porter drove down to leave his rental car in the parking area and climbed into the back of Bruno's Land Rover. Bruno made the introductions and drove to the bottom of the hill below Limeuil and turned into the rough lane beside the Chapelle St. Martin and parked. J-J and Porter paused to read the small plaque erected for tourists.

"I always wondered about this place," said

J-J while Porter strolled into the graveyard to admire the church. "So it's twelfth century. A handsome structure, Bruno. What do you know about it?"

"It was built by England's King Henry the Second on the instructions of the pope as penance for the murder of Thomas Becket, archbishop of Canterbury," Bruno said. "Henry was the local duke at the time, having married Eleanor of Aquitaine, which led to some three centuries of war between England and France. The chapel has some fading medieval frescoes inside and wonderful acoustics. We sometimes have chamber-music concerts here in summer."

J-J followed Porter into the churchyard, picked his way through the tombs and into the deserted church, down some shallow steps and into the nave. Above them was a barrel roof and a hole through which a long rope dangled. Bruno explained that it was used to ring the bells during the occasional burial in one of the family tombs outside.

"Why are we here?" J-J asked.

"We're waiting for Madame de Breille."

"I can't stand the woman, but I suppose she, or rather Claudia's father, is entitled to be brought into the picture," said Porter. He advanced to look at the frescoes and let out a low whistle. "Wow, these are wonderful — thirteenth century, I presume?"

"I believe so," said Bruno. "The church was consecrated in 1194, but it's built on the foundations of a Roman temple."

J-J ignored him. "I want to know why Bourdeille wanted to keep Madame Bonnet from inheriting if she's his heir? And what has St. Denis ever done for him that he makes this generous bequest to your town?"

"That is the question," Bruno replied. "Or at least one of them."

"I remember you telling me that Claudia was trying to buy Bourdeille's paintings," J-J went on. "I hope they're in better shape than these frescoes. The damp has got to them."

"I'm sure he'd be happy to show you his collection," said Bruno. "It's supposed to be worth four or five million."

Porter was peering at the frescoes. "I see an entry into Jerusalem, and that's either an Annunciation or the nativity, I can't be sure because of the fading. Then there's a crucifixion and a descent from the cross. They're wonderful. And who are these two?" he asked, turning to the frescoes of two men standing together on a side wall.

"Some say they depict King Henry and Thomas Becket when they were still friends," Bruno said, turning at the sound of high heels on the gravel outside. He went to the door to greet Madame de Breille, wearing yet another elegant suit, but this time flaunting a large bright red silk scarf at her neck that matched her lipstick.

"You might want to let your client Monsieur Muller know that this morning we arrested the two men who murdered his daughter. They are local men but with an interesting heritage," Bruno said. "Excuse me, I'm forgetting my manners, you know Professor Porter and you have heard of J-J, Commissaire Jalipeau."

"Messieurs," she said coldly, acknowledging their existence but nothing more. "That is interesting news, but who are the murderers and why are we meeting here?"

"Each of the men we arrested is a descendant of Michel Cagnac, the *milice* cop whom your private detective Pellier was researching in Bordeaux last week," Bruno said. "One of them, Luc, is the son of Madame Bonnet, who is Bourdeille's official heir. The other is the grandson of Cagnac, the result of a romantic liaison Cagnac enjoyed in Algeria. The two men are friends as well as cousins, and I think they and their mothers have worked out an agreement to share Bourdeille's inheritance. Cagnac's daughter from Algeria, who is

Dominic's mother, slipped Claudia the *yaba* pill inside a strongly flavored herb tea. She has also been arrested."

"So it's all wrapped up? Congratulations," she said dryly. "You could have told me that over the phone."

"I thought you might want to join us for the next phase of our operation. I invited you here because I believe Monsieur Muller needs to know about this. Excuse me while I make a call."

Bruno tapped in Pamela's number, learned that everyone had just finished lunch and that Bourdeille was being taken home in the special cab. Then he called the mayor and said simply, "It's time. We're heading there now."

"Right, now we can go," Bruno said, closing his phone. "We're going to Bourdeille's place so that J-J can arrest Madame Bonnet, and the rest of us can join Monsieur Bourdeille in listening to Professor Porter's findings and then see how justice might be done."

Bourdeille was already in his study when Bruno entered. Porter, the mayor and Madame de Breille followed behind him.

"You missed an excellent lunch, Bruno," said the old man. "Bonjour, Monsieur le Maire, an unexpected pleasure. And who is this charming woman and the gentleman with you?"

"Madame de Breille represents Claudia's father, and Professor Porter of Yale was Claudia's thesis adviser. He wants to say a few words."

Porter glanced nervously at Bruno as if uncertain of his role. Bruno smiled reassuringly and Porter ran his fingers through his hair, turned to Bourdeille and began.

"I believe you know that Claudia was a very gifted young scholar, and despite your reputation, Monsieur de Bourdeille, I thought I should take seriously her concerns about some of your attributions. I spent the last couple of days in the lab at the museum in Bordeaux. At the same time your former colleagues at the Louvre, including your former pupil Mademoiselle Massenet, have also been busy with their own research. To be blunt, monsieur, we are now convinced that the two questionable attributions we have examined so far are based upon forgeries of eighteenth-century documents. Claudia was right all along."

"You are correct, Monsieur le Professeur," Bourdeille said politely, "Claudia was indeed a very gifted scholar. I am desolate at her loss, and at the news of these forgeries. But I trust there is no suggestion that I might have had access to modern forensic tools at the time I made my attribution. Science has advanced far and fast since those days. Naturally I would be glad, in the light of new knowledge, to correct any error that I may have made in the past."

"Indeed the science has advanced, monsieur," Porter replied, sounding more confident. "Gas chromatography and mass spectroscopy combined are wonderful things. The documents we have examined, from different countries and different centuries, turn out to have used the same ink. And what is even more remarkable, the same ink was used by your friend Paul Juin when he signed the affidavit of his oral interview at the Centre Jean Moulin, the Resistance museum in Bordeaux. You'll recall that you also gave an oral interview that day, and you signed yours in the same ink."

Bourdeille stared at him without speaking for a good ten seconds until the silence in the room became almost deafening. Bruno was holding his breath. Finally, Bourdeille said, "I seem to recall that I may have borrowed Paul's pen."

"That is a pathetic excuse and you know it," snapped Porter. "You're a fraud, monsieur."

"I think we can go further than that," said

Bruno. "I'm trying to decide whether you'll be charged as an accessory to Claudia's murder or as a coconspirator.

"You knew she was onto you, that she was the kind of scholar who would not let it go," Bruno went on. "You had a motive to have Claudia silenced but in a way that would never point to you. And you knew perfectly well that all the microphones upstairs here had been fixed so they were permanently on, so that if you fell or had a seizure, Madame Bonnet would come to your aid. You deliberately schemed to exclude her from her inheritance, but you also used those microphones to warn Madame Bonnet that the real threat to her and her son's legacy was Claudia. And we know the rest."

"Are you mad, Bruno?" Bourdeille asked. "Prove it."

"I'm not sure I need to," said Bruno. "We'll see what Madame Bonnet has to say. She's just been arrested downstairs, and her son and Véronique Darrail and her son Dominic were arrested this morning in Limeuil. I'm sure they'll be interested to learn of your backup plan to exclude them from the inheritance by donating your estate to St. Denis. Or is that another of your frauds?"

"St. Denis won't get a penny out of me,"

Bourdeille said, sneering at Bruno and then at Porter. "And what's this damn woman doing here?"

"I'm the one who will be advising Monsieur Muller to bring a private prosecution against you, even if the police can't make their case stick," Madame de Breille said coldly. "He'll ruin your reputation and he'll sue you and your estate for every last centime you have."

The door opened and Madame Bonnet entered, J-J behind her.

"Of course he knew the microphones were always on," she said, fixing Bourdeille with a fierce glare. "We have the electrician's contract on file downstairs and it specified they should always be on. You said it was for your own security that I should be able to hear everything, and you had extra microphones installed in every room in my own house so I could always be at your beck and call. You got my son and Dominic into this mess, you pompous old cripple. No wonder my grandmother threw herself under a train rather than be married to you. I spit on you."

She turned to face J-J and put out her hands as if expecting handcuffs. "Take me away. I can't stand the sight of the swine."

"Monsieur de Bourdeille, I must ask you

to accompany me to the *commissariat de police* in Périgueux for questioning," said J-J. "And I'm sure my colleagues from the art squad will have their own questions for you in due course."

The Château des Milandes looked wonderful in the magical light of an early summer's evening at one of the loveliest spots in the Dordogne Valley. Bruno was feeling uncomfortable in his rented dinner jacket. But beside him Pamela was looking magnificent in a floor-length evening gown of woven white brocade, her slender shoulders rising above the fabric and her throat displaying the emerald necklace she had inherited from her mother. The glorious green stones matched her eyes, he thought, and perfectly set off her hair, half auburn and half bronze.

They were standing on the balcony, watching Laurent fly his hawk to entertain the throng of guests, all similarly dressed in formal evening clothes. The baron and Gilles were paying more attention to the falconry than to the women they escorted, and so Bruno turned to include them.

Fabiola, wearing a high-waisted *directoire*

dress, was listening to Florence explain how she had found at a local *brocante* the length of heavy burgundy silk that she had made into her own dress. She had learned to sew, she told Fabiola, when she'd had to make clothes for her own children and found that she enjoyed it. Curious, Bruno asked if he could feel the material, and Florence allowed him to touch the scoop neck where it went over her shoulder. It was thicker than he'd expected, not what he usually thought of as silk, and draped beautifully.

"It really suits you," he said. "And you all look wonderful — the Three Graces." He turned to Pamela. "Who was the man you mentioned to me once, the one who said his idea of socialism was a society in which every young woman could go to a ball wearing an evening gown?"

"George Bernard Shaw, but if he tried saying that today his reputation would never recover," she replied. "Do you think we should rescue Jennifer?"

Jennifer Muller was looking distracted as she stood silently beside the American ambassador, who was giving an interview to a TV camera. But before Bruno could react, Hodge appeared, his wife at his side, to sweep up Jennifer and join them while skillfully holding three filled flutes of champagne in each hand.

"Handling multiple champagne glasses is something you learn on the diplomatic circuit," he said, offering a flute each to Bruno, Pamela and the others. Bruno extracted each glass with care to hand them on.

"Have you seen Amélie?" Hodge asked.

"Not since we had breakfast together," Bruno replied. "She's been rehearsing and doing interviews all day. But you know Amélie, it takes more than a grand concert and a TV spectacular to faze her." He turned to Jennifer. "Did you just arrive?"

"We all came down this afternoon in the ambassador's plane, the cultural attaché and his wife. Cheers." She raised her glass.

"It's a great way to travel," said Hodge. "The downside is that we have to go back with him tomorrow."

"You'll have to bring Eleanor back here for a holiday and get to know the Périgord," Pamela said, smiling at Hodge's wife.

"Did you get to Bourdeille's funeral?" Hodge asked Bruno. The old man had died in his sleep, in the hospital, just ten days after J-J's questioning. He had never been formally charged nor arrested.

"Yes, I went with the mayor and some of the remaining old veterans. Whatever crimes

Bourdeille committed, what he did in the war deserved an honorable send-off. Yacov Kaufman came down for it. Apparently Bourdeille spent twenty years helping Yacov's law firm recover artworks the Nazis stole from Jewish families and refused to take a centime for it."

"Ironic that the paintings he identified all turned out to be genuine," Hodge added. "It was only the documents of provenance that were faked."

"I wonder if Bourdeille knew they were faked or if he simply trusted his friend Paul Juin," Jennifer mused.

"We'll never know," said Hodge. "The ambassador wants me to come down for the trial of the others. Is there a date yet?"

"Not before the autumn," Bruno said. "Probably October, but the word from the magistrates is that Luc and Dominic will plead guilty. I'm not sure about Madame Bonnet or Madame Darrail."

A gong sounded, and people began to drift in from the balcony to the rows of seats in the hall. Amélie had arranged special places for Bruno and Pamela, so they let others go ahead.

"You look wonderful," he murmured, his mouth close to her ear.

She smiled at him and squeezed his arm.

"I'm so glad they've made it a formal occasion," she said. "Why aren't you wearing your medals? Several of the men here seem to be wearing theirs."

"It's not that formal. And my medals are pretty modest. Besides, if I'm escorting you, people must already know I'm the luckiest man in the château."

"You realize that none of this would be happening without you, that Amélie would not have been discovered, that the American ambassador would never have made such an event of it."

"Amélie was born to be a star, and it was Hodge who got the ambassador to come," he said. "I had nothing to do with it."

Suddenly Pamela stopped, and her grip on his arm tightened as a familiar slim figure emerged, slipping gracefully through the crowd toward them. Isabelle was looking characteristically striking. Her hair was in a short bob plastered tightly to her head in the style of the 1920s, and she was wearing a long halter-neck black dress with a sash of red silk around her waist that fell to the floor. Earrings of some red stone that matched her sash provided her only jewelry, along with the black plastic Swatch that was always attached to her left wrist.

A rush of memory brought Bruno back to

those times they had spent together when it had been the only thing she wore. One night, wondering if he should buy her a grander timepiece for her birthday, he had teased her about it, and she had replied, "The bare minimum of efficiency is always the purest style."

"Bonjour, Pamela, you are looking splendid," Isabelle said coolly and then pecked Bruno on each cheek. "*Ça va*, Bruno? It was so kind of Amélie to invite me down. I wouldn't have missed this concert for the world. The brigadier is my escort, and I know he's looking forward to having a word with you after the concert."

Still stunned at the sight of Isabelle, Bruno stammered some words of greeting while wondering why Amélie had arranged this encounter. The memory came to him of the lunch at Ivan's when Amélie had gripped him by the chin to hold his gaze and told him to be grown up and accept that he and Isabelle had no future. So why had she invited her? Was it as simple as Amélie inviting Isabelle as her friend too?

All this swept through Bruno's head as his eyes drank her in: that stance he knew so well; the look of self-assurance that so convincingly shrouded the vulnerabilities within; the half-concealed shapes of the

498

body he knew as well as his own, perhaps better; the curve of her ear; the set of her chin and the way she could put an entire speech into the raising of a single eyebrow; that flash of challenge in her eyes; the half smile on those soft, half-pouting lips that he longed once more to kiss.

And some other remnant of his senses was aware of the stiffness in Pamela's pose beside him, the urgent grip of her hand on his arm.

Isabelle gave the merest nod of her head to Pamela and turned away to find her place among the rows of seats.

"Did you know she was coming?" Pamela asked, in a voice like frozen chips of ice.

Haplessly, Bruno shook his head and tore his eyes away from Isabelle's departing figure to ask himself what on earth he might say to reassure Pamela. He was saved by Jennifer, who arrived, the ambassador and his wife on each arm, to introduce Bruno to them as the man who had solved the case. He wrung Bruno's hand heartily, said something about Hodge having briefed him on the case and said it was time to take their seats.

They were among the last to sit, and to Bruno's surprise and Pamela's evident pleasure, Amélie had placed them alongside

Jennifer and the ambassador. The murmur of the audience diminished into silence, and then they broke into applause as the members of the small orchestra picked up their instruments and began tuning up. The conductor emerged to bow, and the applause redoubled before dying down as the curtains slowly began to draw back, and they heard the opening bars of "J'ai Deux Amours."

I also have two loves, thought Bruno, trying not to think what the brigadier might want from him this time. But I wish I felt half as happy about them as Amélie does while singing Josephine Baker's iconic song.

ACKNOWLEDGMENTS

I have long wanted to write about Limeuil, which is rightly proud of its title as one of the loveliest villages in France. The hilltop town that clambers up from the point where the River Vézère flows into the Dordogne is much as I have described it: the prehistoric art school; the Iron Age hill fort; the Roman oppidum; the medieval castle with its well and the neo-Moroccan addition. The castle grounds today constitute a very fine garden, well worth the visit with its giant sequoia tree and its specialist corners of apothecary and herbal plants.

It was while showing some American friends from the island of Boca Grande in Florida around this garden that I saw the deep — and safely sealed — well. It was at that moment that the idea for this book was born. Some of it was written on that island on the Gulf of Mexico, in the hugely welcoming and literary home of Jane and Bob

Geniesse. The medieval walls of Limeuil's fortress can indeed be climbed as Bruno did, and its hilltop restaurant, with the imaginative name Garden Party, is highly recommended.

But all the characters in this novel are figments of my imagination. The stalwart river folk who run the popular canoe-rental business are of unblemished character. There are no such people as the Darrail and Bonnet families, and the last mayor, Guy Thomasset, is a fine and imaginative man who, with his wife, Terez, has been responsible for widening our district's cultural horizons by bringing us broadcasts of operas from the New York Metropolitan Opera. Monsieur de Bourdeille is also an invention, although his putative ancestor, Pierre de Bourdeille, was indeed the indiscreet chronicler of the court of Queen Catherine de Médicis and the soldier who escorted Mary, Queen of Scots, back to her homeland.

Claudia and her family are also wholly fictional, although if they were real they would certainly stay at the Vieux Logis in Trémolat, where my friend, Chef Vincent Arnould, cooks so sublimely, where Yves runs a majestic and imaginative cellar and Estelle manages the place with a discreet and charming efficiency that is close to genius. I am honored to count as a friend the legendary owner Bernard Giraudel. He is still going strong at the age of ninety-two, and his grandmother founded the inn in the old priory where the family had lived for five hundred years. A great raconteur, gourmet and literary man, Bernard remembers as a boy greeting the unanticipated arrival by canoe of the American writer Henry Miller: "Barefoot, dressed only in shorts and bald as a newborn babe, he asked for a bed for a night and stayed for a month."

The Vichy loyalist Michel Cagnac is invented, but his subsequent career in the French army in Vietnam and Algeria, and the details of the last fight of the French volunteers in the SS Charlemagne Division around Hitler's bunker in the ruins of Berlin, are all based on historical reality. It was indeed a French soldier, Henri Fenet, who was awarded the last Knight's Cross of World War II, and the botched execution by firing squad of the legendary Lieutenant Degueldre took place as recounted here. In Algeria as in Indochina the old French empire died hard.

History produces dramas that no novelist would dare to make up, and the history of France is more dramatic than most. It remains for me an enduring fascination and

503

also an inspiration as I write in this valley of the River Vézère, which contains more of the sagas and memorials of humankind than any other single place on earth. Within strolling distance from our house is a château that was the secret Resistance command post in 1944; a cave with Cro-Magnon engravings of various beasts, interspersed with the claw marks of real cave bears; a nunnery that was looted and despoiled by Protestants in the Wars of Religion and closed by the French Revolution; medieval castles; Renaissance châteaux and a Neanderthal cemetery, seventy thousand years old, which embodies the first evidence we have of our remote ancestors burying their dead with ritual and respect.

Along with all of this are vineyards, woodlands that provide the truffles, venison, boar and mushrooms, and farms that produce the ducks and geese, the lamb and veal and acorn-fed pork, that have made the Périgord the gastronomic heartland of France. The account of the annual tasting of the *pâté de Périgueux* is based on personal experience, and I am privileged to be a member of the *confrérie*. And now that we have salmon and sturgeon back in the rivers, thanks in part to the European Union's admirable rules on restoring water purity, they are a source of great bounty, as they were twenty-five thousand years ago when the meter-long engraving of a salmon was carved into the rock of the Abri du Poisson in the Gorge d'Enfer near Les Eyzies. And each year on the waterfront at Limeuil at summer's end is a massive fish-fry, open to the public, to remind us of the food the rivers have so long produced.

After twenty years of having a house here, and nearly forty years of regular visits, my passion for the Périgord is undimmed. It has been enriched by the many friendships our family and basset hounds have made here, the tales and legends we have heard around the tables where we feasted and drank the wines we have come to revere and enjoy. Without these stories and friendships, the food and the history, there could be no Bruno novels.

A special debt is owed to my beloved wife of forty years, Julia Watson, always the first to read my drafts and to compose my recipes and improve Bruno's cooking, and to our daughters Kate (for the website) and Fanny, for the algorithm that keeps track of people, places and meals in the novels. Caroline Wood, a friend as well as a wonderful literary agent, is a constant support. I am blessed with great editors: Jane Wood in

London, Anna von Planta in Zurich and Jonathan Segal in New York.

One of the lesser-known pleasures of being an author is the opportunity to meet and befriend so many booksellers, who along with winemakers and cooks are responsible for much more than their share of human gratification. They are invariably kindly and welcoming folk and many around the world have become friends. People who keep and work in bookshops seldom become rich in terms of money, but the rest of us would be incomparably poorer without them. It has been a great pleasure to introduce so many of them, and so many readers, to the unique and timeless charms of the Périgord.

Martin Walker, Périgord, 2018

ABOUT THE AUTHOR

Martin Walker served as a foreign correspondent for *The Guardian* in Africa, the Soviet Union, the United States and Europe and was also the editor of United Press International. He was also a senior scholar of the Woodrow Wilson Center and senior director of the Global Business Policy Council, both in Washington, D.C. He now shares his time among the United States, Britain and the Périgord region of France, where he writes, chairs the jury of the Prix Ragueneau cookery prize and is proud to be a grand consul of the wines of Bergerac. He enjoys writing a monthly column on wine for the local English-language paper, *The Bugle,* and with winemaking friends produces an agreeable and unpretentious red wine, Cuvée Bruno.

The employees of Thorndike Press hope you have enjoyed this Large Print book. All our Thorndike, Wheeler, and Kennebec Large Print titles are designed for easy reading, and all our books are made to last. Other Thorndike Press Large Print books are available at your library, through selected bookstores, or directly from us.

For information about titles, please call:
(800) 223-1244

or visit our website at:
gale.com/thorndike

To share your comments, please write:
Publisher
Thorndike Press
10 Water St., Suite 310
Waterville, ME 04901